JUDAS TREE

Also by Simon Clark

Nailed by the Heart

Blood Crazy

Darker

King Blood

Vampyrrhic

The Fall

JUDAS TREE

Simon Clark

Hodder & Stoughton

British Library Cataloguing in Publication Data

ISBN 0 340 73913 4

Typeset by Palimpsest Book Production Limited,
Polmont, Stirlingshire
Printed and bound in Great Britain by
Mackays of Chatham PLC, Chatham, Kent

Hodder and Stoughton
A division of Hodder Headline PLC
338 Euston Road
London NW1 3BH

For Janet

There is a pleasure sure
In being mad, which none but madmen know.

John Dryden (1631–1700): *The Spanish Friar*, II.i.

Fate

———❧•◦•❧———

Oracles are the e-mail of the gods. They relay divine messages to men and women on Earth. For thousands of years the oracle of Voros has offered only three prophecies.

The first promises: 'The reward for ignorance is bliss.'

The second has been lost to history.

The third warns: 'If you remain on Voros long enough you will never, ever leave.'

People came to the island for different reasons.

But the reason each individual made the journey to this remote part of the Aegean, where Voros thrust its great stone head out of the sea, was a single trigger event. Without that trigger event their lives would have run along on altogether different courses. Some call this Fate.

The chain of events that brought Julius King to the island began one Hallowe'en night more years ago than he cared to remember.

The drive from the Las Vegas cabaret theatre to his desert home took thirty minutes. Or, if the audience had been on particularly good form and he felt the adrenalin singing in his veins, it might take as little as twenty minutes. That Hallowe'en night the audience had been nothing less than magical and his silver sports car spirited him home in a shade under nineteen.

He opened the living-room door to find that Ricky had

hanged himself. There was the usual paraphernalia of the suicide. Photographs of happier times scattered on the coffee table. Cigarettes. Pills spilling from bacofoil wrappers. A vodka bottle that was more empty than full. And there, weighed down by Ricky's heavy gold rings, the suicide note.

Julius.

I'm sorry it's come to this. But the truth is I've been taking your money for years. Thousands and thousands.

This was followed by a page and a half of illegible hand-writing. In different-coloured ink was a word that might have said *mother*. Then again, it could have been *murder*. Julius couldn't make out the scrawl. The note, however, terminated with a neatly printed sentence:

I'm sorry I deceived you — I'm sorry I was stealing your money behind your back.

'Oh, I knew you were, you silly boy,' Julius whispered up at the hanged man. 'I knew all along and I didn't mind at all . . . silly, silly boy.' Then he put his face in his hands.

For Catherine Thomas it began ten years before she even set eyes on the island. On her seventeenth birthday she had walked out of her home without telling anyone where she was going. It had always been drummed into her that she was the black sheep of the family.

She had tried hard to live up to those expectations. She dated boys who stole cars. She went to clubs where the music was loudest and where she danced the longest, and where she was on first-name terms with the most vicious-looking doormen. When she left home, however, it seemed she left the wild child behind.

She'd no money, so rather than sleep on the streets she went with the first man she met.

He owned a house with high walls that surrounded a secret garden.

The man had three brothers who shared the house with him. Straightaway Catherine became a live-in housekeeper. Most of her days were spent ironing shirts, washing great baskets full of sheets, cooking pies the size of kitchen sinks and making jam from fruits provided by the gardener.

The gardener must have been eighty if he was a day; he was very thin, very wrinkled, had a yellowish complexion and a bald head that forever shed skin like bad sunburn.

He's at death's door, she told herself. But he was amazingly strong. And so full of energy that he could dig great tracts of soil in the secret garden for hours without pause.

Catherine Thomas found herself enjoying the life so much she never left the house. She grew her hair long and dressed in long skirts. Of course she slept with the man who'd found her and soon became a wife to him even though there was never any ceremony.

Then one night she awoke to find someone in her bed who wasn't her husband. The man's skin was as wrinkled as that of a walnut. In the gloom his huge eyes glinted with spectral fire. And when he held her close she felt something like a monkey's paw pressed against her stomach.

She wondered what her husband would say when he discovered that the gardener had taken his place in bed.

But she soon realized that her husband and his brothers were watching from the open doorway.

The following day Catherine Thomas opened the door in the garden wall and walked to the railway station where she bought a one-way ticket. Then she stepped onto the train and never looked back.

Rachel Stone would never have dreamt of going to the island. It wasn't part of her plans. And since she'd planned her life in such meticulous detail there'd never be time even for the journey, never mind sitting in the sun all day. Holidays, if she took them, were short, sharp trips to the coast. Even then, she'd keep in touch with the office on her mobile.

Each working day began with orange juice and dry toast (one slice); she drove the children to school; then she hit the city-centre traffic like an armour-piercing shell; within twenty minutes of leaving home she'd be marching into the office where she ruled her empire of thirty-eight men and women with a steel rod. Lunch was something organic from a vacuum pack. At five o'clock she grudgingly allowed her staff to go home. Then she'd work another couple of hours before going home herself to relieve the babysitter.

On the day before her youngest son's birthday it all went pear-shaped. Rachel Stone made an even earlier start. After kissing the children goodbye she drove briskly into town to buy Ivan a present. All the time she scanned the timetable she'd inscribed upon her memory:

8.30: Hardy's for computer game.

8.45: Collect suit from cleaners.

8.55: Hit the phone. Pearson to confirm tender prices. Ensure Ivan's cake will be delivered by six. Chase up contracts in legal.

9.20: Meeting with section heads regarding Turner Bridge deal; imperative: must close by lunchtime.

At 8.50 she stood at the crossroads, watching rush-hour traffic flood into town. In her left hand was a carrier bag containing a computer game; in her right, a smart Chanel suit in a polythene cover that bore the name of a dry-cleaner's.

Rachel knew she had something important to do. Only, for the life of her, she couldn't remember what.

The car was parked somewhere nearby, but even if someone had held a gun to her head she couldn't have told them what colour the vehicle was.

She shook her head as a buzzing sound lodged itself in the back of her skull.

A drop of rain fell on her hand. Above her the sky had grown dark, almost black, as angry thunder clouds scudded over the office blocks.

She couldn't stand here for ever, she told herself. She'd best go home. After a couple of hours in bed she'd be right as rain.

Mustering her old steely authority, she hailed a cab.

'Where to?' asked the cab driver.

She looked at him as if he'd just said the stupidest thing in the world.

'Where to?' he repeated.

'I don't know.'

'What do you mean, you don't know?'

'Home.'

'That's a start, sweetheart. Now – where's home?'

For a moment she stared into his eyes. Right then she wondered why on earth she was carrying a computer game in one hand and a smart business suit in the other.

'Look, sweetheart, I've got hungry children to feed and my meter isn't running. So do you want this cab or don't you?'

Rachel gave a sudden twitchy shake of her head and stood back from the kerb.

The cab driver shook his head more knowingly, muttered something under his breath, then drove away.

Rush-hour traffic thundered past. Pedestrians brushed by Rachel Stone. Elbows knocked against her, moving her first one way, then the other.

Skyscrapers towered around her, the gravestones of giants. Shrieking through the giants' crumbling bones beneath was the never-ending rush of underground trains.

She backed away from the edge of the street until her back met the wall of a building. At that moment, a little laugh escaped from her mouth. A cracked bell of a sound. She'd have a funny story to tell tonight over dinner. 'You know, the strangest thing happened to me today. I parked the car and forgot where I'd left it. Then I couldn't even remember where I lived. Can you believe that? It was only when I looked at my driving licence that it all came flooding—'

She reached for her purse. Once she saw her home address in cold print she knew memory would come merrily dancing back.

Only her purse was gone. She frowned. She must have put it down somewhere. But where? She pressed her lips together in a thoughtful, worried expression.

She'd been amused a moment ago about the prospect of telling her husband the funny anecdote. Forgetting her home address? What a scream! Her husband would . . .

But what was her husband's name? Strange. It had slipped her mind entirely.

And why was she carrying this suit and the computer game?

And why did the traffic sound so loud?

And why was she surrounded by the tombstones of giants?

As Rachel Stone turned and walked into the crowds it began to rain at last. A real drenching downpour that ruined her hair. But she never even noticed. Another question preoccupied her now.

And that was:

Who am I?

Lucy Morell needed an island retreat to repair a broken heart. She was a cheerful and bubbly young woman (normally, anyway) to whom strangers warmed instantly. She was also psychic. At least, she believed she was.

From a very early age she'd taken pains to hide what her Irish grandmother mysteriously called her 'gift'. It was so very hard to have a normal childhood when she could see what she thought she could see. Friends either ran screaming when they got wind of her 'gift' or they mocked her, calling her 'Spooky Lucy'.

At sixteen she found work in a supermarket and tried hard to be normal. By twenty-one she'd given in to the power of her 'gift'. She became a consulting psychometrist. Basically, this mouthful of syllables meant that people went to her and handed her a personal possession that she'd hold in her hands, her eyes closed. Then she'd tell people all about themselves. Sceptics might ask why go to all the trouble (and expense) of finding out about yourself when you should know already?

But people still came to her, paid their consultancy fees – and Lucy Morell made a far better living than she could ever have done in a supermarket.

She could afford a house and car that stood out from those of her neighbours. But she was never lucky in love. Martin lasted eighteen months. He was amused by her novel profession at first. Soon, however, he sensed there was far more money to be made from Lucy's gift than she herself realized.

Martin worked hard to exploit it, writing to television

companies, suggesting that Lucy should be given her own show. Nothing much came of it. And within a few months Lucy's gift appeared to conspire against him. Most nights he was awakened by the sound of the toilet flushing (when Lucy still lay sleeping at his side and with no one else in the house). The microwave constantly blew its fuse. His mobile phone wouldn't work anywhere in the home. The answer machine switched itself on in the middle of his telephone conversations, filling the earpiece with the ghostly whine of feedback. Cans of beer left in the house for more than a day or so would taste stale – at least, to Martin's tongue they did. Alone indoors, he would hear footsteps running up and down the stairs. Then light bulbs would blow, one by one.

His hairdryer bursting into flames in his hand was the last straw.

And so, suddenly one frosty Thursday morning, Lucy was alone once more. For a couple of months she soldiered bravely on. She always wore a bright smile for her clients. Only, when she looked in the mirror, she saw that her reflection was neither cheerful nor bubbly. The characteristic sparkle had gone from her eyes. That was when she told herself enough was enough. She immediately contacted her nearest travel agent, badgering them to find her somewhere that was hot, sunny – and as far off the beaten track as possible.

And that place, for Lucy and maybe a dozen others, was Voros.

Greece has three thousand islands. Voros is one of the smallest. It lies off the shipping lanes in disputed waters between Turkey and the Greek mainland. Little more than the top of a once-great mountain that sank beneath the sea, it is of no strategic importance to the national economy nor to the military.

With an area of less than eight hundred acres it is too small to accommodate even the most modest of tourist complexes. There are, however, a dozen villas with brave names such as Firefly, The Rocket House, Poseidon and Persephone (side by side), Sirocco, The Palms, The Sundial, Valentine, and The Eighty-Eight. The villa names are so intensely personal that often only their owners know the story behind each one.

Apart from the villas there are no other buildings of note. However, long ago there was a tiny harbour here (another of Caligula's attempts to cock a snook at Neptune). But the devastating earthquake of 1779 sent it plunging to the bottom of the sea.

Despite an outwardly rocky appearance the island is rich in plant life. Cooks' herbs grow in abundance – oregano, thyme, sage, rosemary, garlic – so Voros's home cooking is distinguished by memorable flavours. Standing like sentinels across the landscape are the thin, dark shapes of the funeral cypress; while mastic trees infuse the air with the scent of their aromatic resin.

In spring something magical happens. The whole island is transformed from its customary rocky grey to bright pink. This is when the island's thousands of Judas trees blossom. For all the world the rock itself looks as if it is blushing.

The island has been thoroughly mapped (what little there is of it); its rocky surface and substrata are well known to geologists. All the plants from the Judas tree down to the tiniest yellow crown daisies have been identified. The few species of wild animals that live on the island – such as the tamarisk shrew, the pipistrelle bat, and the four indigenous varieties of lizard – have been catalogued, and were painted in delicate watercolours by the famous zoologist Hans Primptz when he was a German artillery officer stationed on Voros during the war.

What is intangible, not to say completely unquantifiable, is the *feeling* that the island possesses something else – some other ingredient – that hasn't been identified, mapped or catalogued.

Any visitor who is at all susceptible to this kind of thing would claim Voros is haunted. That it is a place full of ghosts.

The ghosts of who – or what – no one can ever say. There's only a pervasive feeling that there's a presence here. That there's *a something* about the island that makes people want to look over their shoulder. Or that compels the more sensitive to sleep with the lights on. Or that leads others to hang crosses on doors and windows.

There are even a fearful few who nail portraits of the island's patron saint in each corner of the house; an echo of pagan practices from ancient times.

This patron saint, St Demetrius, is a fiercely bearded, wall-eyed man who looks more psychopath than cleric. No one can say for sure why he was canonized. Certainly the Vatican never recognized him. Even the patriarchs of the Greek Orthodox church long ago left him on the ecclesiastical equivalent of the substitutes' bench.

Despite this, St Demetrius still holds sway on this rock that lies firmly, and unshakeably, in the heart of nowhere.

All in all, people agree on one fact: that there's an aura about Voros that makes it seem unreal, even other-worldly. Most credit it to the Judas trees. The way their pink blossom makes the island look spectral. As if some eerie world in the depths of space has shed a fragment of itself. And that fragment has plunged from the sky into the Aegean Sea and taken root there.

Of the three thousand Greek islands that there were to choose from, a handful of people picked this one: Voros.

And thousands of miles away one more person was making plans to come here, too.

Chapter One

The letter from mother to daughter was short and to the point.

Dear Amelia,
Yes, yes, of course. Come here if you must. A change of air might do you some good. But I have to warn you that Voros is about as lively as a grave.

Amelia Thomas read the letter again. It was the first letter she'd received from her mother that could be taken as an unequivocal invitation to visit her.

Quickly, she pinched the corner of her bedroom carpet between a finger and thumb, then pulled it up from the pointed grip track. Beneath the carpet, spread out as flat as she could possibly make it, were bank notes, a bank card (folded inside a tissue) and a cheque book. The cheque book had posed a problem. Its thickness would have betrayed its presence to anyone standing on it; in the end she'd had to tear out all but five cheques and flush them down the toilet.

As she laid the letter alongside the cash that formed a papery underlay she heard the voices of her cousins outside her bedroom door.

They were twin girls, eleven years old, and they had all the spite of a dozen witches. 'Is Humpty Dumpty in her room?' she heard one ask the other.

'Open the door and have a look,' suggested the second.

'No. She might be doing that thing again . . . you know, when her eyes go funny and she breathes hard.'

'Knock, then.'

'What for?'

'So we'll know she's in.'

'She'll be in; she's always in. You know full well they don't let her out of the house.'

Amelia froze. The last thing she needed was for the girls to see her secret hiding place. Quickly she let the carpet drop. No! She'd been too clumsy. Some of the bank notes wafted up from under the carpet. They now stuck out from the edge against the skirting board in plain view.

Clenching her teeth, heart thumping, she snatched the notes out of the carpet, ripping one on the points of the grip track as she did so.

Damn those girls, she thought hotly. Couldn't they think of anything better to do than hang around outside her door talking about her as if she was deaf or something?

'Oh, leave it, Trish,' said one in a loud whisper. 'Humpty's in there. I can hear her moving about.'

'Do you think she's doing that thing again?'

'Probably. You can just see the expression on her face, can't you?'

'Her eyes going like this . . .'

It didn't take a great leap of Amelia's imagination to guess that the girls were pulling absurd faces as if they were true impressions of her.

A moment later the door of the girls' room closed. The voices became so muffled she couldn't hear what they were saying, although one briefly began to sing. It didn't matter that she couldn't make out individual words. The song was identifiable enough:

> *Humpty Dumpty sat on a wall,*
> *Humpty Dumpty had a great fall,*
> *And all the king's horses and all the king's men*

Couldn't put Humpty together again

Oh, yes, very funny, Amelia thought, her face flaring hotly. *That's it: make a joke of it. But it wouldn't be so funny if it happened to you.*

More than anything in the world right now Amelia wanted to be stepping onto the beach on Voros. She imagined the heat of the sun on her skin, could conjure up the scent of the herbs that, so her mother had told her, covered the islands in one vast aromatic rug. She wanted to embrace the whole experience of the island. The sounds: waves on rocks; cicada insects chirping. The sights: how the whole island was magically transformed into a pink, living thing by the Judas trees when they blossomed in spring. Which must be any day now.

Yet here, in this filthy northern town, the March weather was anything but springlike. Freezing slush that was as filthy as the buildings thickened every pavement. Gales whistled round the eaves. People moved around so hunched inside their coats that the entire local population appeared headless. And all the time dark, scowling clouds formed an oppressive lid on the world.

There was nothing Amelia wouldn't give to escape from this dreary prison. There was no price too high.

Amelia Thomas was twenty-five years old. Right at that moment, as she sat on the bed in the grey house in that grey town that squatted on a grey, melancholy landscape, she felt as if she was the victim of a cruel practical joke.

It wasn't supposed to be like this. She was young; she was attractive (or so she had once thought); she was physically healthy; she had a career.

Brought up by a cheerful maiden aunt, she'd been something of a tomboy. Right up until her early teens she'd scrambled through trees with the boys of the neighbourhood. She'd played football with them; whupped them stupid at tennis. She'd made friends with ease. No one in their right mind would have described her as shy or timid.

In class she was always the one scolded for being a chatter-box, but she was popular with the teachers. Her infectious grin and sheer energy carried her effortlessly through school. Later, she breezed through exams and equally easily breezed into a public-relations job that was the envy of her friends.

It's said that you should try to get the things that make you happy. But if you can't do that, you should be happy with what you've got. Amelia Thomas managed both. She acquired an apartment, a car, clothes that were good without being overly flashy. She rarely bothered with make-up because of her good complexion and high cheekbones. And what she couldn't change in her life she managed to live with quite happily.

Maybe, she'd gloomily tell herself later, it was all too good to last.

Now everything had changed. Here she was in the grey house in the grey town.

With the maiden aunt who'd raised her now dead, Amelia was forced to live with another aunt and her family. She hated them so passionately that she'd lie awake at night and grind at the crowns of her teeth.

Once she had been fearless. Now she was fearful. She wanted to go out by herself; equally, she knew she'd be afraid of the noisy, crowded streets. The truth of the matter was that she'd been knocked out of synch with the world. Now it seemed a loud place where people marched to and fro to their own secret agendas. If she could only get away from here. She was certain a month or two on a sun-kissed island would repair the damage that had been inflicted in one savage incident fifteen months ago.

She looked up. The girls were singing the Humpty Dumpty song again.

Oh, blow them, she thought sharply. She was going to escape this dreary hole if it was the last thing she did.

First things first. She decided to spend half an hour or so making a list of things she'd need. She looked for the pen with the MTV logo. A boyfriend had brought it back from a trip to the studios years ago. It wasn't much, but in the absence of large pleasures in her life it formed part of a mosaic of things that at least offered her a few comforts.

She looked in the chimpanzee cup where she kept her pens, then checked the shelf, the bedroom floor and behind the bed. Then she realized, with a sigh, that the pen had gone, too.

By the time Amelia had hidden her holiday list beneath the carpet (this time taking extra care to lower the carpet gently onto the money) the pain had begun above her left eye again. It was a sharp pain, as if someone was forcing a skewer through the bone above her eyebrow. The specialist said the pain would reoccur. Especially when it was cold and damp. And it was both of those things now.

She held a handkerchief against her eyebrow. If she pressed hard it dulled the pain. Not much, but a little, anyway. By now she also knew that the pain tended to start when she was facing a difficult situation. And she knew she'd face one in a few moments when she told her uncle and aunt that she wanted to go into town alone.

'Just to do a little window shopping,' she'd say casually.

Still pressing the handkerchief to her eyebrow, she left her bedroom and closed the door quietly behind her, while wishing she could fix a lock to it; a dirty great big one that those two little witches couldn't shift even with dynamite.

A door opened on the landing.

'Hey, Amelia . . . what's cooking?'

Her heart sank at the sound of her cousin's voice. John, at the age of eighteen, was locked into an intense and deeply unusual relationship with the Internet. His eyes were always sore-looking, as if he'd stared so long and so hard at the screen that his eyeballs had begun to dry out – which, she suspected, was about the size of it anyway.

'Nothing's cooking,' she said carefully, trying to keep her voice neutral. 'I'm just going down to have a word with Mae and Brian.'

'Might not be a good time.'

'The shop's usually quiet this time of day.'

'It's coming to the quarter-end. They'll be stocktaking.' He spoke in a disinterested way, but she sensed he was building up to something. In fact, it would be a cold day in hell if he didn't grab any opportunity to make it clear he hated her.

He looked at her from beneath his red-edged eyelids. 'What have you been doing this morning?'

'Nothing much.'

'Don't you get bored?'

'I've been reading.'

'Reading.' He echoed dully. Then he gave her a look. 'Hey, Amelia, why don't you come and see what I've found on the Internet?'

'No, thank you.' Amelia tried not to sound prim but she'd fallen for that one before. When it came to finding bizarre websites her cousin was second to none.

'C'mon. I bet you've seen nothing like this before.'

'I believe you.'

'C'mon. Lighten up.'

'I need to speak to Mae.'

'Suit yourself. Is your eye hurting again?' John assumed a sympathetic expression.

'A bit. Not much.'

'It must take some getting over.'

'What does?'

'Breaking your noodle the way you did.'

'Well, I'm better now.' She started to walk along the landing but he'd moved to stand in her way. He was playing it cool. He could have just been moving forward to look at her and play the concerned cousin bit. It would be churlish to interpret it as deliberately obstructing her.

She pushed the handkerchief inside her sleeve and made herself smile.

'You don't look that rosy,' he told her. 'Can I get you a glass of water?'

'No, thanks. I'm fine, honest.'

'Seen any more zombies lately?'

16

She kept the smile on her face, pretending he was simply being playful. 'John, they weren't zombies.'

'Ghosts, then.'

'I didn't see any ghosts either.'

'It's not what you said, you—'

'John—'

'You scared the twins half to death that time you told them you could see ghosts coming up the stairs.'

'That was just after I came out of the hospital.'

'But you still see things?'

'No . . . not for ages.'

'But you sometimes look over people's shoulders when you're talking to them as if you can see—'

'John. Really, I've got to talk to Mae: it's important.'

'OK,' he said blandly. 'I just wanted to make sure you were feeling all right.'

'Thanks for your concern, John.'

'I'm having some friends up later for a takeaway. Want to join in?'

'Thanks, but no. I'll probably have an early night.'

'We might get noisy. Those websites I've found are red-hot, you know?'

'I'll sleep, don't worry.'

He stepped back into the doorway of his room and waved her through with a theatrical gesture. 'Watch how you go, cuz.'

Amelia tried to keep the exchange with John light-hearted but she knew he was about to slip in a provocative comment.

'Thank you,' she said.

'Careful on the stairs. Specially halfway up.'

'What do you mean, John?'

'I don't want you to fall, Amelia.'

'Don't worry, I'll be careful.'

'I know, but it just goes to show, doesn't it?'

'Shows what?'

'One minute everything's right as rain, then it only takes one little fall.' He slapped his forehead.

'John.' She spoke through gritted teeth. 'I didn't fall.'

'Oh, yeah. My mistake.' He shot her a phony smile. 'You were *pushed*. Right?'

Anger fluttered inside her like a bird trapped in her stomach. She glared at John.

His smile widened. Then he gave her a little Oliver Hardy wave with his fingertips. 'Bye-bye, cuz.'

As he closed the door, still wearing that slippery smile, she realized he'd completely derailed her. Every so often she'd feel a ghost of—

Ghost? Why did she use the word 'ghost'? She felt herself floundering; quickly she took a deep breath to steady her.

Every so often she felt an *echo* (*Yes, 'echo', that's a better word*) . . . every so often she'd feel an echo of her old self-confidence. But even that short exchange with her cousin had been enough to kill it. Where once she could express herself accurately and succinctly, now she sensed herself fishing haphazardly for words; even when doing nothing more taxing than talking mentally to herself.

When she'd left the bedroom moments before she knew exactly what she was going to ask . . . no, *tell* her uncle and aunt. Now she felt like an ugly old beetle that had been flipped onto its back, its legs scurrying stupidly in the air as it tried to right itself.

No, Amelia. Today is the seventh of March. This time next week you're going to be sitting in the sunshine, by a pool, while gazing out over a perfect sea.

Now come on: you've a little white lie to tell.

Chapter Two

'No,' Amelia's aunt told her. 'No. I don't think that would be a good idea. Do you, Brian?'

'Not advisable,' her uncle agreed. 'Not until we're sure you're up to it.'

'And that might be some time yet. The specialist said not to rush things.'

'You never know,' Brian said. 'That old trouble might start all over again.' He didn't so much say the word 'trouble' as slowly and lovingly extrude it from his lips. And he adorned it with so much emphasis that Mae mouthed the word 'trouble' after him like a member of a Baptist congregation.

'And that's the last thing we want again,' Mae said with feeling. 'If it was only yourself we had to worry about, dear, it wouldn't be so bad. We'd do our best to help you more. But we have to think about our children.'

'Our children.' Brian had picked up Mae's habit of echoing key phrases.

Mae looked at Amelia with an expression of sympathy. 'You see, after your last bit of trouble we couldn't do a thing with the twins. They had nightmares, their school work suffered, Kirsty started doing that thing with her fingers again. Brian here had to go and have a word with their teacher. It really was a terrible time for all of us, wasn't it, Brian?'

'Terrible,' he echoed.

Amelia gave a little disbelieving shake of her head. 'But I only want to go into town by myself.'

'No, dear. I'm sorry.'

'Just to go window-shopping. I won't even take any money with me.'

'If you want anything John or I'll go for it while Brian minds the shop.' Mae pressed her lips firmly together.

'But if it's clothes . . .' Amelia struggled to express herself clearly and calmly. 'I need to choose them—'

'Describe what you want, dear. We'll buy them for you.'

'—And try them on. I need to know that they fit.'

The attempt to persuade her uncle and aunt to let her out on her own had all gone wrong. Of course, the window-shopping trip had been the white lie she'd had to tell but even being denied that had made her flustered and exasperated. Now the pain had started above her eye again. That pain, as fiercely sharp as a dentist's drill, screamed against her skull.

The three of them – Amelia, her aunt and uncle – sat in something like a living room-cum-storeroom to the hardware shop. Her aunt and uncle were getting on in years now and could no longer stand for hours behind the counter. So they sat back here in a pair of armchairs, waiting for the door chime to sound. Then they'd take it in turns to serve the customers. Their biggest line now was dog food (even though the sign outside did still insist it was a hardware shop and that there were seven different types of hammer to choose from and close on twenty thousand nails).

Boxes of dog treats stood on shelves in the storeroom; a kind of fatty smell pervaded the air. When Amelia had first come in here after being discharged from hospital she'd thought she was still hallucinating. Everywhere she saw pig faces. Not toy masks but real skin peeled in one piece from the heads of real pigs – complete with eyeholes, pigs' ears and snouts. This artefact, as Amelia mentally referred to it, had a baked-dry appearance, yet was disgustingly greasy to the touch and bristled with pig hair.

She'd blinked and swallowed more pills. But the pig faces

had stayed. It took her some time to grasp that these monstrosities were, in fact, real.

The pig faces still proudly dominated the room as she
endured this circular conversation with her aunt and uncle.
The two of them sat placid and comfortable in their armchairs,
their hands resting on their rounded stomachs.

This frustration at not being able to get the old couple to
see it was a sensible move in her . . . in her rehabilitation (*Good
word, Amelia*) introduced a note of anger into her voice.

'I should be allowed out of the house by myself,' she insisted
at their bland faces. 'After all it's over a year since I—'

'Since your fall.'

She didn't split hairs but pushed on. 'I think it would be
good for me to have my cash cards back; then I—'

'Your cash cards.' Mae tut-tutted. 'Not yet. I blame myself
for that.'

'She does, you know,' Brian added. 'I tell her not to, but
Mae insists it's her fault, the way you went through all that
money so quickly.'

'I was ill, Uncle. I think it was the . . . the medication as
much as anything.'

'But I should have realized you couldn't remember anything.' Mae's eyes became shiny. 'I feel such a fool now.
Anyone could see that your memory had gone. And − and
there you were just going off and seeing things that weren't
there − awful things, you said − and you were spending money
right, left and centre on nonsense. And going out at night . . .
wandering round and the police finding you with . . . well,
all dirty.'

'Mae . . . now, now,' said her husband soothingly. 'Don't
go upsetting yourself.'

Amelia's carefully structured argument was in ruins. The
pain above her eye was now nothing less than biting. She
found her eyes drawn to her uncle's checked shirt. Suddenly the
straight lines began to misbehave: she found herself staring as the
pattern became a spaghetti tangle that knotted and unknotted
itself dizzyingly.

Oh, God. No . . . please, not now.

The thick bone above her head felt as if it was suffering the assault of a high-speed drill bit. She wanted to press the handkerchief there, but to do so would draw attention to the fact that she wasn't as well as she pretended.

That comes with breaking your noodle, her cousin had cheerfully announced.

'I'd like to go out by myself,' she insisted; her voice sounded small. 'Just for a little while.'

Still kindly, Mae said, 'No, dear, we promised your mother.'

'But—'

'Are you sure you're feeling all right, dear? You look sallow. Doesn't she, Brian? Looks sallow.'

'Sallow,' he agreed.

The drill-point of pain had made its way through her skull; it plunged over the top of her eyeball, stabbed through her brain, then bit deep into the back of her head. She tried to avoid looking at the pattern on her uncle's shirt and the writhing spaghetti-like strands that knotted, unknotted and knotted again with a sickening speed.

They're not real, she told herself. *They're not real.*

'I'll get the twins to make us all a nice cup of tea,' Mae said. 'Why don't you go back to your books for a little while, dear?'

'And don't worry.' Brian smiled. 'You'll be able to go out by yourself before you know it.'

In that mood Amelia felt her reticence beginning to slip. She wanted to ask why she never saw her bank statements any more. She'd built up some pretty healthy savings before her fall.

(That wasn't a fall at all, she corrected herself.)

Now they hid her bank books from her, and the statements and the credit cards. And how come her cousins had suddenly acquired new computers just weeks after her arrival here?

And little things like the MTV pen. Right at this moment she wanted to burst out with: 'Those two little witches you call your daughters have been stealing from my bedroom. First it was perfume, then chocolate, now pens.'

She allowed her eyes to drop to the table beside Mae's armchair. On it was a wordsearch puzzle book. Next to that was a pen. Clearly visible, the MTV logo.

'Have a nice lie-down this afternoon,' her uncle said as the squirming spaghetti patterns moved up from his chest to flow across his face. 'The weather's not fit to go out, anyway.'

Mae gave a generous smile. 'And if it's dry tomorrow I'll ask John to drive you down to the lake. You'll enjoy that, won't you?'

Amelia didn't have a lie-down. Instead, she returned to her bedroom where she sat hunched on the floor, arms folded, glaring at the wall.

So Plan A had failed. They wouldn't allow her out of the house by herself. And *they* weren't going to return control of her money to her. If there was any left.

In her bedroom she counted her cash. Then she found her life-insurance policy in the back of a file of old household documents. Her head still throbbed so she pressed the handkerchief just a little above her eyebrow where she'd suffered the depression fracture. Actually, it *was* tempting to lie down for an hour or so. The bed looked inviting. But enough of her old will-power had returned for her to see this through, come hell or high water.

Now for Plan B.

This was more seat-of-your-pants stuff and would require timing and a good deal of luck.

She unfolded the life-insurance policy and scanned it. It was a with-profits scheme that matured on her twenty-eighth birthday. Of course, the company would pay out before then should she not be so lucky the next time she fell off a bridge . . . *was pushed off a bridge*, she corrected.

Now, Plan B was simple. She'd already surrendered the policy for its cash value as it stood (which meant she'd lost a heck of a lot of money, but that didn't matter). There was enough surrender value in the thing to buy her a one-way plane ticket to Athens and from there she could get the daily ferry to the island of Limnos. The next leg of the journey was something of a mystery. But once on Limnos she'd telephone her mother to find out how she could reach Voros.

Of course, there would be a big fuss about running out on her uncle and aunt like that without telling them where she was going. But she didn't care. And no doubt there would be more than one person to shake their head knowingly at her stupidity. And then tell her that she'd lose a whole hatful of money by surrendering her life-insurance policy prematurely.

But life insurance? Hell's teeth. She didn't care about that, either.

Chapter Three

Amelia Thomas's great escape began at five o'clock in the morning. It wasn't without its setbacks. She couldn't have believed that simply getting out of bed, packing a holdall and walking out of the house would be fraught with so much difficulty.

Firstly, her ability to concentrate evaded her. She began to experience that same sense of dislocation she'd felt on leaving hospital. Then, if offered two different types of cake, she'd found it nigh impossible to choose which one to eat. Even if one had been coffee: she hated coffee-flavoured cake. She'd stare at the two cakes, swallowing rapidly, her eyes watering, palms sweating, breathing becoming shallower and shallower until she felt she'd run screaming from the room.

And sometimes, to her later shame, she did.

But no, she was over that now. Breathing deeply, she began pulling clothes from the drawers and wardrobe, folding them despite her trembling hands. For the ninth time she checked that she had her passport in the zip compartment at the end of the bag.

The clock told her it was five-thirty.

Time to go.

What, in your pyjamas, Amelia Thomas?

Shakily, very shakily, she stripped off her nightclothes and got dressed.

A few minutes later she was all ready to leave, only to

realize she'd forgotten her money beneath the carpet. It was all so laborious. She tried to steady her hands as she lifted the carpet from the grip track and picked up each banknote in turn. But, the harder she tried to move with the delicacy of a surgeon, the more ham-fisted she became: her elbow clanged against the radiator, her head banged against the cupboard door (instantly triggering the searing pain above her left eyebrow).

All she needed now was to wake her uncle, aunt or cousins with her clattering and they'd stop her from leaving. She remembered the trouble when she went on that mad spending spree (buying baby clothes, for Godsakes!); how they'd simply telephoned the hospital. And back she'd gone for a fortnight.

After a further ten minutes of furtive packing, checking, combing her hair, she was ready.

The next stage was the bathroom. She hadn't wanted to go a moment ago but now she knew she couldn't wait even until the public lavatory in the station. It was nerves, she told herself; she was trembling like a jelly. Without switching on any lights she crossed the landing by touch alone.

'Hello,' the man said. She sensed that he was standing by the shower. She paused halfway across the bathroom, her heart beating painfully.

Frozen in mid-step, she stared back at his shadowy outline.

'Go on,' he told her. 'Don't mind me.'

'You're one of John's friends.' She remembered how John had told her about the Internet party. This one must have stopped over. Now he stood there: somehow she just knew that he was grinning at her in the dark.

The shadow nodded toward the toilet. 'Go on,' he said again. 'Nothing I haven't seen before.'

Still she froze and stared. Even if she left now he'd wake John and tell him that his cousin – the loopy one – was leaving home with a holdall over her shoulder.

Back to hospital for you, my girl. Her uncle's words were already ringing in her ears.

'Don't be shy.' The man's teeth gleamed in the dark like neon. 'Go if you have to.'

She shook her head.

'Can't pee if watched?'

'Sorry.'

'For what?'

She sighed. 'Never mind.' Hell, the game was up. What now? Go back to bed? Wait for the questions in the morning?

Why do it, Amelia? they'd ask. *Why run away?*

The man said, 'Aren't you the one who saw zombies?'

'Ghosts, actually – not that it's any of your business.'

Her head ached.

'Bad ghosts?'

'They were hallucinations. They weren't real . . . just . . .' The pain sharpened. 'Just like you . . .'

The man had gone. She looked round for a moment, holding her breath. Then, slowly, she understood he'd never been there at all. She took a moment to stand there, breathing deeply while pressing a handkerchief to her eyebrow once more. The pain began to recede. *It's the tension,* she told herself. *It's making me see things that aren't there again. Never mind, once I'm on the island I'll recover properly. There are no roads there – no bridges, come to that. I can relax.* A few hours sunshine would be worth a hundred pills.

By this time she could allow herself a smile.

Five minutes later Amelia slipped out through the back door. It was dark and it was cold, a bone-juddering cold: there was frozen slush covering the pavements. She didn't care. She'd begun the first leg of her journey to freedom.

The night-time streets were deserted. Her uncle's and aunt's hardware shop lay in a sprawl of Victorian streets on the edge of town. Once the area had been a prosperous suburb, its big houses tended by servants; now it was simply described as bedsit land. Most of the shops had become takeaways or videotape rental outlets, with a smattering of second-hand stores. The rest were boarded up.

Amelia walked fast. Her breath billowed white. The sound

of her feet on frozen slush crunched loudly enough to echo from the drab brickwork.

Her plan now dictated that she should catch an early train. It didn't matter so much where she went as long as it was far enough away from here so that her uncle and aunt couldn't catch up with her. That, and somewhere where there would be a travel agent.

In theory, she could be at the station in ten minutes. But that would mean using a lonely footbridge. At this time of night there was no telling who might be lurking there. No one would hear her if she had to shout for help.

Not that anyone would hear her on this street, probably. Or, if they did, most likely they wouldn't bother to look out of the window to see who was being murdered on the road below.

A cold breeze moved across the rooftops, droning mournfully among the chimney pots. It was the saddest sound in the world.

Dear God, the sooner I'm away from here the better . . .

With this thought burning inside her head Amelia walked still faster.

Already she could imagine her cousin John's running feet as he chased after her. 'Amelia, what on earth are you doing? You come back home with me . . .' And she could imagine herself being led uncomplaining back to the house where her uncle and aunt would look pityingly down on her.

Maybe she should risk the footbridge after all?

She imagined herself rushing across it in the space of a few seconds. Then she'd be in the station, safe and sound.

But that old memory came rolling back to her. That old, dreadful memory.

Fifteen months ago she'd crossed a railway footbridge not unlike the one that now spanned the tracks to her left.

It had been the night of a New Year party. Tipsy and giggly, she'd left the celebrations. Taking only seconds to sober up in the cold night air, she'd headed home.

Then came the event that grabbed hold of Amelia's life and threw it in a completely different direction. (*Nice choice of word*, she thought grimly: *threw*.) She'd been halfway across the deserted footbridge, the stars bright above her.

Quite simply, someone had appeared behind her. Grabbed her tightly. They'd said nothing but she'd heard the sound of his breathing.

(Oh, that phrase haunted her later: 'The sound of his breathing.' For reasons she couldn't explain, she'd lie in bed, awake, repeating mentally, 'The sound of his breathing. The sound of his breathing. The sound of his breathing . . .')

Then it was all over so quickly.

He'd simply manhandled her over the railing, held her for a moment beneath her arms, perhaps allowing her to admire the steel tracks shining in the starlight below — a long, *long* way below her swinging feet.

'Please,' she'd managed to say.

His breathing had grown louder in her ear; then, without a word, he'd dropped her.

The sound of his breathing . . .

A man walking his dog late at night had come across her. After that . . . well . . . she got to know the taste of hospital food very well indeed. If she ever *saw* another hard-boiled egg she'd throw up violently enough to crack the china.

No. There was no way on God's Earth that she'd use the footbridge.

Calves aching — she just wasn't used to walking any further than the kitchen — she pressed on. The houses lining the street glowered like fortresses. Windows gleamed bleakly, like the eyes of blind men. Street lights cast a dull glow that was closer to brown than to orange. There wasn't another soul to be seen. And the wind still played that mournful dirge around the chimney pots. This wasn't so much a town as a place for the dead.

At last Amelia reached the dual carriageway that ringed the town.

Here a delivery van or two rumbled by. The town, thank the Lord, was beginning to wake.

Across the road the lights of the station blazed.

Trying not to allow her pace to slacken, she followed the ramp down into the underpass, taking care not to slip on the patches of frozen slush.

The underpass was a bare concrete conduit with the obligatory graffiti. She walked through it alone.

Constantly she strained to hear the running feet of her cousin. Surely her uncle and aunt would have realized she was gone by now, wouldn't they? She could imagine her twin cousins' delight at the drama of her escaping.

Humpty Dumpty sat on a wall.
Humpty Dumpty had a great fall.
And all the king's horses and all the king's men . . .

She saw the two little witches singing delightedly as their brother set off after her. 'This is what happens when you break your noodle,' he'd tell her with deep satisfaction. 'Your skull heals up OK, it's your brain that gets all broken up inside. Mark my words, cuz, it'll be a cold day in hell before you're right in the head again.'

Amelia shuddered. The underpass air was cold and tomb-like. It smelt like every inner-city underpass she'd been in. Cardboard boxes littered the place. There was a discarded sleeping bag; some kind of juice stained it. Just ahead of her a mound of blankets looked like the carcass of some decaying animal.

Welcome to hell's waiting room, Amelia told herself.

Then, just as she knew they'd come, she heard them. Running feet. Drumming hard against the concrete floor.

Dear God, I'll fight them if they make me go back this time. I'm never going back. Never!

The footsteps grew louder. She tried to run but the holdall was too heavy. She was exhausted already; a mighty itch had begun between her shoulder blades where she'd begun to sweat.

She tried not to look back as the footsteps approached.

But within seconds it sounded as if a herd of cattle was stampeding through the tunnel.

She couldn't bear it any longer.

With a sharp breath she turned.

Approaching at a breakneck sprint came two men. Their eyes blazed like lamps; exertion turned their mouths into snarling slashes across their faces.

One carried a VCR, the other a long-handled hammer. Both wore baseball caps.

If she didn't shift out of their way they'd knock her down and trample her as if she was nothing more than a dandelion in the grass.

Amelia lunged sideways to the wall.

What she'd taken to be a pile of soft blankets was rock-solid and she tripped, dropping down hard onto her knees.

Seconds later, the running men were gone.

As she tried to shoulder the heavy holdall again and climb to her feet, the blankets erupted under her.

A pair of hands shot out and caught the front of her coat. Fingers hooked around the material, pulling her forward.

Now a face set with wide grey eyes was emerging from beneath the blanket with all the swift savagery of a conger eel's head lunging from its undersea cavity.

There was an uncanny fire in that cold stare. It held Amelia's own gaze, and for a dozen heartbeats she remained frozen, her own eyes locked onto his, the tips of their noses almost touching.

At last, the spell broke. 'Let go of me,' she panted and tried to pull herself free. *'Let go.'*

'What y'doin to me! What y'doin?' came a man's voice. 'I an't 'urt yer, 'ave I? Look what ya done to my face! Look what ya done!'

She stopped tugging. Blood formed a great red patch on his cheek. 'What ya gone and kicked me for?' he begged. 'What ya do that for?'

Amelia looked down at the man in shock. She'd done that to him? She must have when she fell on him, unless it was one of the running men who had accidentally kicked the homeless man as he raced by.

The cut looked nasty. But it was the homeless man begging for mercy, perhaps thinking Amelia had attacked him just for the hell of it, that shocked her to the core.

'A'm sorry Ah look like this, Miss. Things 'aven't been easy. A'm sorry; don't kick me again. I'll keep out of yer way in future, but don't 'urt me again, please . . .'

'No,' Amelia said quickly. 'I'm sorry. I didn't mean to hurt you.' She looked at his bleeding face and felt faint. 'I – I fell over you. I didn't realize you were under the . . .' She looked round, bewildered. They were still alone in the underpass.

He said, 'A'm sorry I frightened you. Ah didn't mean to grab at you like that. But Ah thought they'd come back for me again. A'm sorry . . .'

Amelia glanced at her watch. Six-thirty. Already early-morning trains would be running. She had to be on one. And fast. If she wasn't going to be caught by John, that was.

Immediately, she felt guilty at simply shouldering her bag and walking on as if nothing had happened. Here on the floor was a man she'd injured. It didn't seem right just to shrug her shoulders and leave as if he was nothing more than a crushed woodlouse.

'Here,' she said fumbling a ten-pound note into his hand.

He looked at it, blood still trickling down his cheek.

'I'm sorry,' she repeated. 'I hope your face . . . I hope you feel better soon.'

Amelia backed away.

'Wait,' he said. 'No. Wait.' From beneath the blankets he pulled a handful of magazines. 'Here. Thank you, miss.' He handed her a copy of the *Big Issue*. It felt damp.

'Thank you.' She pushed the magazine into her coat pocket.

'Wait . . . I'll get your change. 'S here somewhere.' On his hands and knees he began searching through the blankets.

'No . . . no, really, it doesn't matter . . .'

'But I—'

'No, please, keep the change: it's the least I can do.'

He looked up at her in near-shock. 'I can't . . . it's too much!'

'Of course you can.' She heard anger force the words from her mouth. *'Take it.'* Instantly a surge of guilt rose within her. *God, why am I angry at the poor man? I've just gashed open his face and now I want to swear at him.*

Because, along with the pity she felt for him, she also felt distaste at the sight of a grown man sounding like a pathetic child.

Frighteningly, her disgust for him was so strong that she had a near-overwhelming urge to push his face into the wall. And to make his left cheek as bloody as the right.

Amelia took a deep calming breath. 'Please . . . no, listen to me . . . please take the money. I want you to. OK?'

He looked at her, working through the implications in his mind. At last he nodded. 'Thank you,' he said, taking one of her hands in both of his and looking searchingly into her eyes. 'Thank you. Jesus loves you. He loves you harder than the rest.'

'OK.' She tried to ease her hand from his grasp. 'OK. I need to go now . . . I'm late for my train.'

'I'm sorry . . . I didn't mean . . .'

'That's all right . . . I just need to . . . there. Look after yourself.' With that, she managed to extricate herself from the man's grip. Swiftly she walked away, with the man kneeling there in his rags and gazing adoringly after her.

'Jesus loves you!' He called after her, his voice echoing from the hard, tomb-like walls. 'He loves you. He's got a place in his heart for you. He won't forget you for this! He's going to take you to Him and hold you in His arms for ever and ever . . .' The voice rose in pitch. *'His arms are like iron! His grip's eternal! He'll never let you go. Remember that: He'll never let you go!'*

She didn't look back.

As she left the underpass she thought she heard laughter. It was hard. Cruel. Mocking. Amelia didn't know where it came from.

Chapter Four

The journey.

It was a mosaic of events, images, petty difficulties, easy transitions, waiting, moving forward, obstructions. Things that should have presented no problem were suddenly complicated. Right from the start, when Amelia walked up to the timetable boards in the station, she thought she'd encountered a fundamental problem.

Suddenly the timetables meant nothing to her. They were lines of equations that were pure gibberish. Fifteen months ago: no problem. Now, after her head had cracked like a dinner plate: big, BIG problem. For ten minutes she'd stared at them. Her shoulder ached from the weight of the bag; the itch between her shoulder blades worsened; she longed for coffee – and those damn' timetables might have been calculations of rocket trajectories, for all she knew.

She stared at columns of figures that were accompanied by letters, symbols and pictures of buses.

Buses in a train station?

It took a while for the penny to drop and for Amelia to realize that the train journey would be broken and that part of it would have to be made by means of a bus link.

More pondering over a symbol that looked something like a pair of scissors standing on its handles. Eventually she translated it as meaning that there would be a refreshments-trolley service on the train.

The pain above her left eye nagged. She paused to take her handkerchief from her coat pocket and press it to her eyebrow.

She stared at the timetable through one eye.

So what do I do now?

Public-address announcements about trains and a lost brief-case echoed through the station. Passengers flowed onto plat-forms. Whistles sounded. Trains came and went.

Still Amelia didn't know what to do. *Great*, she thought miserably, *I'll stand here all day with my handkerchief pressed to my eyebrow.*

Then it came to her. She opted for a solution so simple it seemed almost as if a wise man had whispered it into her ear. She crossed to the ticket office and said to the counter clerk, 'A single to Harbrough, please.' As the man printed the ticket she casually asked, 'What's the time of the next train there, please?'

'Five minutes. Platform two.'

It was as simple as that.

This must be like being born, she thought as she waited for the train. A whole sequence of stopping and starting down the narrow channel between the pelvic bones. Similarly, there was so much to impede the baby's passage – the size of its head, the cord, its shoulders. *It's a wonder we ever manage to get born at all*, she mused.

The peculiar line of thought continued.

Amelia found herself thinking: *If anything, I'm being reborn now*. After a fifteen-month gestation in those gloomy rooms above a hardware store, she was at last struggling to escape into the light.

Again the vision of the Greek island formed inside her head. There'd be sunlight, laughter, new friends, exercise in the pool, walks through olive groves and – who knew? – perhaps even love.

The train pulled into the station at last. Grateful, she quit the cold and windy platform for the warmth of the carriage.

At seven on the dot the motors hummed and the station platform slid away from her. This was it.

The parts of the journey Amelia thought would be difficult, such as booking a flight for Athens that left that same day, were remarkably straightforward. True, she had to change flights in Amsterdam, but that was no hardship, really.

Trying to find the right departure lounge at Amsterdam airport was more problematic. As she walked along one of the interminable thoroughfares she suddenly felt faint.

The pain above her eye returned with a vengeance. Only at that moment did she really wonder if the flight was too much after all. Perhaps she had been wrong about her state of health. Maybe she wasn't up to the journey.

'That's what happens when you crack your noodle,' her cousin told her.

'You're not real,' she told the apparition sharply.

And it wasn't.

Her cousin vanished as quickly as he had come. She was left only with the suspicious stares of other passengers.

You're in control of this now, Amelia told herself. She hated the word 'hallucination'; it had all the melodrama and stigma of stark, staring lunacy. And she wasn't a lunatic, not by any stretch of the imagination. The specialist had told her that everyone hallucinates – after all, wasn't that exactly what a dream was? Only, for everyone else, those hallucinations occurred when they slept.

'For you, Amelia,' the neurologist had told her, 'imagine that the on/off button that controls the dreams has been damaged by the fall . . .'

That 'F' word again. Fall. She didn't fall.

'So, Amelia, sometimes you dream when you're awake. The trick is to learn to differentiate these dream images from reality. Then tell yourself they're not real. That will be enough to make them simply evaporate in front of your very eyes.'

And in most cases it was. So her magic spell was simply to tell any phantom images that might pop up in front of her:

'No. You're not real. You're not real.' And that was enough. They vanished.

Over the PA she heard the Athens flight being called.

Don't you worry, she reassured herself, *you're nearly there.* Nearly there.

Chapter Five

The flight from Amsterdam's international airport to Athens takes four hours.

The sun was setting at the tip of the starboard wing. In the window seat Amelia Thomas drowsily watched the solar disc turn from gold to red.

The sounds of the jet engines were whispery enough to be soothing. Already the coast of Greece was slipping beneath the metallic belly of the jet. From the ground the big airliner would be almost invisible, a tiny spark of silver moving across the sky and nothing more.

For the first time in months Amelia felt truly safe. The rest of the flight's hundred and eighty passengers seemed relaxed too, their mood aided, no doubt, by a good supper and more than a few drinks.

A stewardess glided up the aisle, carrying cartons of duty-free cigarettes. Another of her colleagues collected empty meal trays.

Amelia settled back luxuriously into her seat. Beyond the plexiglass window the wing gleamed a warm orange in the sunset as ailerons responded to the flight computer's instructions; everywhere snowy pillows of cloud hung in the calm sky.

We're a big fish swimming through a deep blue sea, she told herself, yawning. The notion amused her. *We're fast, we're silvery, we're swimming where no fish has swum before.*

A soft electronic 'Ping' came from somewhere far away.

She yawned again. The couple in the seat next to her were sleeping. The man's glasses had slipped down his nose, almost to its tip.

How odd it is to sleep in the company of strangers, she mused. She wouldn't normally dream of such a thing. But here a good quarter of the passengers had dozed off.

She turned her head back to the window.

What's that man doing out there? she asked herself, puzzled.

Before she could even begin to wonder how the man could stand upright on the wing against the five-hundred-mile-an-hour slipstream, he'd wrenched open the window, pulled her from her seat – and was dangling her thirty thousand feet above the mountains now slipping beneath her.

And all she could hear was the sound of his breathing.

Louder, louder. *Louder* . . .

Amelia opened her eyes to see the woman in the seat in front of her staring back suspiciously. She looked to her left; the couple were looking at her, too. The man gave a smile, but he eyed her warily. 'Are you sure you're all right?'

He must have asked the question already and she must have answered, though she didn't recollect doing so. She nodded.

The man's companion said to Amelia, 'I could call the stewardess?'

Amelia shook her head. 'I'm fine . . . I must have dozed off,' she added, trusting that would be some kind of cover-all answer.

The man and woman looked at each other and nodded. Both then stared in front of them; their eyes, however, were a trifle glassy: the way people look when a stranger's behaved in an embarrassing way, and yet they continue to pretend nothing socially awkward has happened.

But what did happen? Amelia asked herself.

She'd dozed off and begun to dream, she knew that. Then she'd woken up with a start.

Had she been crying out in her sleep? And thrashing her arms about for everyone on the plane to hear?

She shot a surreptitious glance towards the people sitting

across the aisle. No. No-one was looking this way, so perhaps she'd done nothing more than mutter in her sleep. Even so, she felt awkward now. She even wondered if she should try and explain to the couple. But what could she say? 'I fell and broke my noodle.' (No, Amelia, say 'skull' – no more of cousin John's quaint words now.) 'So now I see things that aren't there . . . oh, and I rave in my sleep sometimes . . . oh, yes, and I used to wander away from home and the police had to bring me back in their nice police car, and they didn't mind in the slightest that I made their upholstery damp . . . the police have seen worse things than that, you know.'

That was all a long time ago, of course. She wasn't like that at all now. Perhaps the long journey had been trying. All she needed was a shower followed by a good night's rest. The couple had seemed to dismiss the incident, so should she.

She settled back to look out as the plane made its descent into Athens' airport. There was no more sign of the wing-walker, and Amelia didn't fall asleep again.

In Athens Amelia spent the night in a hostel. There wasn't much of her life-insurance money left, but there was enough for the ferry ticket and a good breakfast: this consisted of bread, still warm from the baker's oven, Greek yogurt with a mighty dollop of honey, coffee and a cinnamon spiced bun to follow.

The car ferry left at nine in the morning. For the five-hour crossing she spent most of her time standing in the prow, delighting in the gentle breeze that blew her hair back in rippling waves. The March sunshine – warm, not searing – was a magic potion that chased the winter chills away. All around her, the sea was turquoise and calm. Flying fish skittered across the surface of the water ahead of the ferry's bow wave, while every so often a dolphin would appear from nowhere to ride it before vanishing again.

Early-bird tourists sunned themselves on the decks. The atmosphere was happy: there was a communal sense of anticipation and everyone was looking forward to what the coming days would bring.

Amelia kept her eyes on the horizon. She would only look forward now, not back. Never ever back.

After a while she saw the island of Limnos appear. Almost flat, with the exception of a few low hills, it emerged from the sea haze like a faery land. More people clustered in the prow of the boat to watch the island grow larger and more distinct. Someone pointed out the castle on a rocky promontory. Behind her a woman read to her husband from a guide book: 'Charles, listen to this. It says, "Be sure to visit the fine town beach; incidentally, it was there that the Amazons of Limnos slit their husbands' throats and threw their bodies into the sea".'

The man chuckled. 'Didn't I tell you there was nothing new about girl power?' He laughed again. Then he rubbed his Adam's apple as he watched the island approach.

Amelia found herself sitting on the harbour wall with a couple of hours to kill. She'd telephoned her mother and learnt that the ferry to Voros would leave in the late afternoon.

Not that she minded. There were far worse places in the world to kill time. To be marooned on a Greek island sounded far more like heaven to her than hell. It was pleasant to just sit and watch the little bustling port town with its whitewashed houses, red roofs, and a backdrop of hills that varied between blue and violet as the shadows moved across them. After a while she took the time to enjoy a long lunch in a pavement café where a football match was being shown on the television above the bar. Greeks clustered round the screen, concentrating so hard on the game that, as they leaned forward, their cigarettes smouldered right down to the webs of skin between their fingers before the sting of the burns reminded them that they were even smoking. There was a lot of gesturing. Passionate exchanges of views. Only when there was a let-up in the action on the field did the men return to tiny cups of coffee that looked as thick and as dark as engine oil. These they'd wash down with glass after glass of cold water.

Amelia enjoyed sitting near them; it was like a breath of fresh air. Even down to the sound of their language (of which she couldn't understand so much as a word). There was a music to it all.

For one reckless moment she nearly went for the deep-fried octopus but, realizing there was another ferry crossing, this one on a smaller boat that might be prone to a little more rock and roll on the swell, she opted for aubergine stuffed with ground beef and herbs. The vegetable's skin had turned a sunny yellow in the oven and the exotic flavours of the dish positively made her heart sing. *This is the life*, she told herself happily as she spread the napkin on her lap.

Accompanying the main course came a side salad of tomatoes, cucumber, cubes of creamy white feta cheese, all topped with a dash of golden olive oil.

Already the last fifteen months spent in her uncle's and aunt's house that was as grim as a hobgoblin's castle seemed less real than a dream. While memories of those stupid ghosts that had once plagued her imagination were rapidly evaporating in the light of the Greek sun.

As Amelia sipped her glass of beer she felt composed, calm and in control of herself.

Twenty minutes before the ferry to Voros departed she picked up her holdall, paid her bill and returned to the harbour.

The big ferries had gone now. She walked along a line of fishing boats where men with nut-brown skins mended nets or worked on engines. The vessels were little more than dinghies, yet each one had been lovingly painted in bright pastel greens and yellows.

Across on the beach she could just make out a group of tourists playing volleyball. Their excited shouts sounded far away.

Amelia scanned the boats again, looking for something that could be the ferry to Voros. Her mother had warned her it would be small, but had reassured her that the ferryman would look out for her. After all, she'd stand out a mile from the locals with her ghost-white complexion and her holdall.

There were perhaps twenty fishing boats moored against the

harbour wall, so she picked up her bag and walked along the line, glancing at each boat in turn. Most of the men were preoccupied with their work but a couple shot her grinning glances.

At the end of the line she heard a shout.

'Hey!'

She looked down to see a man of around fifty waving to her. He wore a denim cap, its peak pulled down to his eyes.

'Hey!' he shouted again and beckoned.

She paused and squinted down at him against the sun. 'Voros?' she asked.

The man scrambled forward over the seats in the boat, jumped onto the wooden engine housing, then out onto the harbour wall.

'Here,' he said in a surprisingly fierce voice. 'Come here. Give me the bag.'

'I'm waiting for the ferry to Voros,' she said uncertainly. 'I was told to wait at this side of the harbour where—'

'Give me the bag! Hurry up!'

'But I'm not sure that—'

'My son is waiting for you. He thought you'd gone back home without a word.'

'Pardon? I'm sorry, I think there's—'

'Give me the bag.'

'No, I think you've—'

'My son paid for the clothes in the bag. They're his.'

'Look, there's been a mistake.' Amelia felt her head swim dizzyingly. 'I don't know your—'

'Don't try that with me. I've seen girls like you come to the island. I know the games foreigners play. I lived in New York for three years. I know you like that!' He gave a savage snap of his fingers.

The men on the other boats were taking an interest now. One called in Greek to the angry man, who was now trying to take her bag as she backed away. The man answered ferociously – clearly he was saying something derogatory about Amelia. The other men shook their heads in sympathy with the fisherman's wronged son. One or two spat out the odd word in

44

Amelia's direction; they spoke in Greek except for one English word: 'Slut.'

'Now.' The fisherman advanced on Amelia, holding out his hand. 'Get into the boat. I'll take you back to my son.'

'No, you don't understand; I—'

'So you're going to run out on him, hey? You're not going to have the decency to explain, hey? You get in my boat. I take you home. Even if you're not going to share his bed again you can tell him to his face that you're through – yes?'

'No. Listen to me, I've never even been here before; I'm waiting for—'

'Foreigners. It's all just a holiday to you, isn't it? Come here, take all the beaches, waste all the water, spend your money. Take who you want, then throw them away like filthy rubbish.'

She was close enough now to see into his rage-filled eyes, while his gold-capped teeth glinted in the sun like razors. He jabbed a cigarette at her face. 'You going to get into my boat? Or am I going to throw you in?'

Amelia looked at him, horrified. This section of harbour wall was deserted, apart from the fishermen. There was no one to help her. Right then the choice seemed to be either between jumping into the sea and swimming towards where the tourists played volleyball or being manhandled into the boat and taken to God knew where. Clearly she couldn't get this man to listen to her.

He grabbed her arm. The grip was crushing. 'You come with me now. You face responsibility. Yes?'

'No. Let go of me!'

He pulled the holdall from her shoulder. 'My son bought everything for you. All this is his!'

'No.'

'I knew you made out with other men on the beach but I never told my son because he was happy. Now you've made me a bad father. I should beat you with a stick. Beat you till you yell!'

'Leave me alone.'

Once more she'd lost control of her life. She looked helplessly at the other fishermen; they grinned and nodded approvingly at their friend.

'We're going home,' the fisherman snarled. 'Then I'm going to find a stick; a stick as thick as this—' he held up his thumb '—then I'm going to watch my son beat you with it.'

The sun suddenly dimmed. Amelia rocked back on her heels, light-headed. The pain returned above her left eyebrow.

It was almost as if her uncle and aunt had formed a nightmarish pact with the mad fisherman. It was as if she couldn't escape them, whatever she did. Right at that moment she could believe that the fisherman would take her in his boat to some faraway house on a beach. And there, on the doorstep, would be her aunt, uncle, cousin John and the two witch twins.

'Why did you run away, Amelia?' Mae would ask, all smiles and sympathy. 'Why did you do it? Now come home with us.'

Amelia rocked dizzily on her heels.

'Let go of her.'

The voice was that of a younger man. It was followed by a rapid spattering of Greek words.

She suddenly realized that another man, had come between her and the Greek fisherman who was now backing away, clenching his fists angrily. The young man put up his hand in a gesture that said to Amelia clearly enough, 'Just wait a moment.' Then he turned back to the fisherman and there followed a fast exchange of words with extravagant gestures aplenty.

At last the older fisherman gave a huge shrug and returned to his boat.

The young man turned and smiled at Amelia. 'Sorry about that. Case of mistaken identity.'

'He said I'd run out on his son.'

'I know.' The man grinned broadly. 'He says all you foreigners look alike to him.'

But Amelia was still too rattled to let the matter drop. 'He nearly kidnapped me. He was going to take me somewhere and have me beaten.'

The outraged father had returned to his nets. For the benefit of the other fishermen Amelia said loudly, 'He should be locked up.'

'Don't worry. Forget it.' The young man smiled disarmingly. 'It's a strange world, strange things happen.'

Amelia wasn't convinced. And, in any case, she'd begun to shake so much her legs felt weak. With an effort, she picked up her holdall. 'No, let me,' said the young man. He held out his hand as if indicating she should walk with him.

'No, I don't think so,' she told him, the penny dropping. 'I'm waiting for someone.'

'I know. You've found him.'

God, I don't need this, she thought. *Why is it that the whole world wants to take control of my life?* 'Thank you for what you did. But I'm waiting for the ferry to Voros.'

'I know that, too.' He smiled, then thrust out his hand. 'My name's Bill. Your name is Amelia Thomas.'

Hesitantly, she shook his hand; her mind was taking its time catching up with the clues.

In any event Bill supplied the answer. 'I'm here to take you to Voros. Welcome to Greece, Amelia.'

This time she allowed him to lead her to a boat that looked no different to the fishing craft that floated on the turquoise waters.

In a moment the man had untied the lines and cast off. Then, sitting there alone with him, Amelia watched the harbour recede as the boat nosed its way out to sea.

Chapter Six

Voros was a good deal different from Limnos. As well as being far smaller, it was blocky in shape with vertical cliffs. If anything, it resembled a high-rise building towering from the sea.

Amelia's gaze roved over it; she found the appearance of the island surprising, if not downright startling. Just when she'd begun to think that it was a featureless block she at last glimpsed a deep ravine or two that revealed hillsides from which funeral cypresses grew as straight as telegraph poles.

The island's colour was startling, too. Grey. A hard, unyielding concrete grey.

'Voros,' the young man announced from the tiller.

'I expected it to be pink.'

'Pink? Ah,' the man said understanding. 'The Judas tree.'

'When does it blossom?'

'Next week. Always the first of April.'

'Always on that same date?'

'Always.'

'Why do they call it the Judas tree?'

He smiled back at her and she flushed. He guessed she was asking questions just for the sake of it.

He thinks I'm like a child, excited to be going on holiday. Next he'll be expecting me to ask, 'Are we there yet? Are we there yet?'

Amelia composed herself, straightening her back a little, and watched the island approach.

The sea here was no longer the turquoise of Limnos but a

deep, deep blue that even now slipped imperceptibly into black. If anything, the water itself looked thicker. Almost like cooking oil in a black pan.

The young man – Bill, she reminded herself, fixing his name in her mind – had a healthy tanned skin, dark hair and nut-brown eyes overarched by an impressive pair of black eyebrows. He had the wiry body of a fisherman. And, although clearly Greek in appearance, he had no real trace of accent. His face was wide-eyed and open-looking, somehow. 'Honest as the day is long' was a description her old Aunt Joan might have used approvingly. Come to think of it, if Aunt Joan was here right now she'd give Bill an appraising look, then shoot Amelia a glance that said, 'Yes, this one's OK; you'll be all right with him.'

Bill's gaze had been scanning the island as if searching for some sign that it was safe to approach. After a moment he seemed to see something. Just what, Amelia didn't know. His eyes locked on to some point high on the island for a moment, then he looked back at her, flashing a toothy grin.

'Is it how you imagined it, Amelia?'

'The island? How do you know I haven't been here before?'

'Because I'd have known if you had. All my life I've seen everyone who sets foot on Voros.' She realized he didn't want to seem like a cocky know-it-all when he gave a self-deprecating shrug and added, 'It's a small island; there aren't many visitors.'

She waited for a moment, listening to the beat of the engine. It sounded like someone slowly striking the bottom of a pan with a wooden spoon. The boat glided forward across the water, seeming to skim over its surface rather than cut through it.

She wanted Bill to ask her more questions.

Why are you here?

How long will you stay?

Where are you from?

What do you do?

She even found herself mentally supplying Bill with the

questions, but he'd returned his gaze to the island that now towered above them like an office block. She didn't think he was being stand–offish; if anything, there was more of a shy reserve. Perhaps people who live on small islands were like that.

'Bill. Is that a shark?'

Amelia pointed at an area of water near the boat.

'Where?'

'It's gone now.'

'You thought you saw a shark?'

'I think I saw a fin. A big black one . . . a dorsal fin.'

He laughed softly. 'A shark . . . not likely. We only have little sharks here. Like babies.' He held up his hands, about two feet apart. 'And they don't eat us.' He grinned. 'We eat them.'

'I saw something.'

'Dolphin, maybe. Now I don't eat dolphin. They're the ghosts of drowned sailors.'

She looked at him and couldn't tell whether he was teasing her or not.

'We'll land soon. I'll hold the boat against your mother's landing stage and you climb out.'

'You know my mother?'

He laughed again, amused. 'Of course. I have her shopping here. Some other people's, too.' He nodded down at a number of wooden boxes stacked in the centre of the boat. 'But I have frozen fish in the bottom crate. I have to get them to my father's ice house otherwise they'll spoil. So when you see your mother say I'll be back with her groceries in the morning.'

She nodded. Then added quickly. 'Beats pushing a trolley round the supermarket.'

He appreciated the joke and laughed, showing his teeth.

'Now . . . be careful,' he said as he brought the boat forward between two rocks that stood out like two halves of a wishbone on either side of them. 'The sea's temperamental today.'

Amelia didn't see how. The sea was flat; again, they could have been sliding over a lake of cooking oil.

Just a few yards ahead she saw a concrete landing stage. It formed little more than a large step about two or three feet above the surface of the water, and had been set into the side of a cliff. A little further back stood a small boathouse built of cinder block. From there a flight of steps that had been cut into the rock ran upwards, then twisted out of sight. She had expected beaches with people lounging on the sand and swimmers at the water's edge; this was secluded, to say the least.

Even when she scanned higher up, all she could see were a series of slab-like rock faces. There was no sign of villas, tavernas or any other sort of life. Only that impassive cliff face that wouldn't care if she lived or died.

'Careful, careful,' Bill abruptly sang out from the tiller. 'She doesn't want us to land.'

'She', Amelia hazarded, was the sea. Bill twisted the throttle; the rhythm of the pistons quickened. But at that moment the boat suddenly stopped, as if some force had gripped it; seconds later it began to slide back.

Whether this was dangerous or not Amelia didn't have a clue. Instead she shot a look at Bill, trying to gauge if his expression would reveal how serious this was.

Half standing, he looked forward and down to one side. The boat slipped further back to the wishbone-like columns of rock that they'd effortlessly sailed through just seconds ago. If anything, they now looked more like a pair of scissor blades, waiting for them to pass partly through before snapping together to cut them in two.

Bill opened the throttle more. The beat of the engine became a roar as blue smoke venting from the exhaust swirled around them.

Then, suddenly, the boat, far from being pulled back, abruptly shot forward.

It was as if there'd been a tug-of-war between the island and the sea. The island had pulled them towards it; the sea back.

The island had won.

With a rush, the boat now surged ahead. Bill had to throw

the propeller into reverse to prevent the prow smashing into the landing stage.

Then, just as quickly, the engine settled down into its usual measured rhythm. Amelia immediately sensed the silence pressing down on them: it was as if it slipped between the beats of the pistons like a physical presence.

Bill nodded at the cliff face. 'Voros was eager to have a new visitor. Did you feel its pull? Like a good strong ox.' He leaned against the tiller. 'I've never felt it as strong before.' He grinned. 'Voros wants you.'

'What was it?' Amelia still didn't know if she'd just gone through a life-threatening experience or what.

'Maybe your shark.' He spoke cheerfully and she guessed he was teasing her. 'Here . . .' He eased the boat alongside the landing stage. 'Put your bag off the boat first. Then you can step out. Don't worry, I'm holding the boat steady now.'

She did as he asked; within seconds the solid concrete was beneath her feet.

With a salute and a broad smile Bill called, 'Tell your mother I'll be back in the morning. And that I'm sorry there was none of her usual tea.'

Amelia nodded and waved back. With that he opened up the throttle; the boat sped out of the rocky inlet, between the two halves of the Wishbone Rock (as she'd already christened it), and took a curving path away to her right. Twenty seconds later the vessel, and Bill, were out of sight.

I'm right about the silence, she thought. With the boat gone, the stillness came rushing back, as if to fill a vacuum. It was a complete silence. *One I'm not used to*, she told herself. For the last fifteen months she'd heard the constant rumble of traffic on streets, the weird sounds coming from John's room as he cruised the Internet, or the twin witches' antics.

This silence was different. It seemed concentrated by the shape of the cliffs that rose on three sides of her. Yes, that kind of hush would take some getting used to. But she was going to be here for a while – a long, long while. She'd acclimatize, no doubt about it.

She shouldered her holdall and looked up at the daunting steps rising in front of her, up across the cliff face.

Under her breath she muttered, 'What? No welcome party, mother?'

Then she began to climb the steps, wondering what waited for her above.

Chapter Seven

Voros is an island full of vertical rock faces. Hardly any part of it is level. Cliffs lead to crags and crags lead to pinnacles of stone. In between are slopes that are either steep or *very* steep. Even so, a remarkable amount of vegetation erupts from crevices and soil-filled hollows.

From every crack in the rock a Judas tree grows. While here and there across the rockscape are mats of wild thyme, rosemary and prickly pear.

The steps went on, it seemed, for ever. Amelia Thomas climbed hard, her knees quivering with the exertion. The itch between her shoulder blades had begun again. Her holdall weighed her down so much that it could have been crammed from bottom to zip with solid lead.

Every so often she'd glance up ahead of her. The steps ascended between a crevice in the grey rock. Behind her, the sea lay a long way below. And already the landing stage where she'd first set foot on Voros was lost in shadow.

The sun was setting fast. Now it had become a red dome resting on the horizon.

She thought: *If I don't get a move on I'll be climbing these steps in the dark.*

Nearly there.

But she wasn't nearly there. What she'd taken to be level ground at the top of the steps was merely a patio-sized

plateau from which more steps rose before twisting again out of sight.

My kingdom for an escalator, Amelia thought grimly, moving the holdall to the other shoulder. She climbed again, panting hard; for the last fifteen months she'd walked no further than from her bedroom to the kitchen. Now, good grief, she was scaling a mountain.

Just when she'd begun to fancy she'd somehow entered an afterlife where she'd be doomed to climb these damned steps for an eternity she was suddenly free of them.

Her relief at being able to see more than a few paces in front of her was so great as to border on the absurd. But now there were no more of the damnable steps, and the weary grind of the climb was replaced by a surge of giddy euphoria.

A swathe of Voros stretched out to her left. Oddly, rather than the random bumps and mounds of a normal landscape, she saw severe geometric patterns. Hundreds of rock slabs mimicked the roofs of buildings. Even the funeral cypress trees stood in rows, as if someone had laid them out in lines like telegraph poles.

This was Mother Nature at her most mischievous: she'd created the image of an enchanted citadel.

To Amelia's right was her mother's villa. She recognized it instantly from the photographs she'd been sent. Now, instead of steps, a pathway ran up to the front of it.

Feeling pleased that she'd overcome the tug of gravity to make it so far, Amelia readjusted the strap of her bag and walked quickly now, her step lighter, her heart beating quickly. Right then, she felt a kinship with explorers who'd hacked a path through jungles and crested mountain ranges to discover lost cities. It had been a Herculean journey, fraught with difficulty, but at last she was here. The island and the villa were her rightful prize. She wasn't going to let go of either in a hurry.

The villa itself looked a bluey-grey in the twilight. It backed onto yet another cliff face so the effect wasn't so much of a building sitting on its foundation but of something that had been hollowed out of living rock. You simply couldn't tell where the villa ended and the rock face began.

In fact, the whole island was littered with yet more huge blocks of bluey-grey stone that could be part-formed villas in the making. She could easily imagine builders arriving on the island and looking over the blocks of rock before saying, 'This one.' Then, instead of building a villa from bricks, concrete beams, timber and stucco plaster, which they'd lather all over with limewash, they'd simply taken their tools, carved holes in the rock for windows and doors, then gradually worked their way into the boulder to hollow out the rooms.

As she neared the villa, Amelia saw there was nothing crude about the workmanship. The lines of the pillars that supported a projecting tiled canopy were absolutely straight. The windows of the building's two floors were large; the wooden shutters were neatly painted and looked to have been maintained with scrupulous care; no laths were missing or broken. Unlike most Greek island villas, which enjoyed an easy-come-easy-go ambience, this one seemed almost to have a military air: scrupulously tidy, fastidious, tolerating no sloppiness. If anything, Amelia told herself as she approached the front door, it would have benefited from climbing vines or a bougainvillea swirling around the windows to soften its hard lines.

Like an archaeologist–cum–explorer, hesitating at the entrance of a newly discovered tomb, Amelia paused. The villa's powerful façade held something of a challenge. It didn't invite people to drop by casually. She could imagine columns of people making their way up the hill to it in the same way as processions would approach a shrine. The building demanded a dignified approach.

Amelia tapped lightly on the door.

She listened for approaching feet, voices.

Nothing.

All she could hear was the chirp of cicadas in the trees followed by the thin-sounding cry of a bird.

She knocked again.

No reply.

Come on, Amelia, grab the knocker and play merry hell with it.

But no, she couldn't do that.

She tapped a little louder.

Listened.

Again, no sounds from inside the villa.

Surely her mother was expecting her? And there were the two women who shared the villa with her. Would they have gone out somewhere and left their new guest to her own devices?

Perhaps they were sitting out by the pool? Wherever that was.

She tapped again on the door.

This time it opened an inch or so; it couldn't have been closed properly.

Gingerly pushing open the door, as if she half expected a vicious guard dog to come barking out at her, Amelia leaned forward through the doorway.

Cool air formed an envelope around her.

Inside, the silence was deep.

With no lights, the interior was a shadowy place, its atmosphere more that of a cave than a house.

She hesitated again, not wishing to enter uninvited even though it was her mother's home.

'Hello.' Her voice sounded small.

Hello, came the whisper of an echo.

She couldn't have come all this way to turn back now. Could she?

No, don't be silly, she told herself. *Make yourself known. After all, nothing's going to jump out and bite you, is it, now?*

She took a deliberate step across the threshold.

Something rustled suddenly in the darkness ahead.

She paused, listening; the sound, however, wasn't repeated. After a while her eyes adapted a little to the gloom. She saw she was in a large entrance hall. Marble pillars supported the roof.

On plinths around the walls were statues. The effect was of a museum.

She walked across the floor. It was smooth marble, no carpets.

Ahead of her a broad staircase rose to an upper galleried floor. Someone had a great eye for detail. While the walls were flat, smooth and featureless, the corners were a profusion of detailed carvings – as if they'd somehow forced themselves through the crack where one wall met another. From what she could see, the carvings were of bunches of grapes and vines through which animal faces peered.

'Hello . . . I'm here.' The 'I'm here' part sounded lame but she wanted to fill that envelope of air that enclosed her.

Moving slowly, as if she was walking through a church, Amelia went from door to door, all of which led off from the hallway. One room was a book-lined library; another was a dining room with a table made of black wood that looked as if it could seat twenty people. In another room there were sofas and a large fireplace in which sat some mysterious iron device that looked like the workings of an ancient clock. The next doorway led to a kitchen. The place resembled a hotel kitchen rather than a domestic one, with long worktops and a catering-sized refrigerator; at least two dozen cast-iron pans hung from wall hooks. In front of her was a boxy-looking cooker with an oven that could easily have accommodated a full-grown man.

Feeling as if she was gliding now, rather than walking, Amelia moved upstairs. From a balustraded walkway, which gave a view of the entrance hall, yet more doors opened.

She slipped from one to another, feet whispering on the marble floor.

It only took a moment to discover that someone lay asleep in each of the three bedrooms she peeped into. With the shutters closed it was too dark to identify the sleepers. One, she guessed, was her mother; the other two were her mother's housemates.

For a full five minutes she wondered what she should do.

At last Amelia shouldered her holdall, returned to the entrance hall and sat down on a stone bench by the door. The statues gazed at her implacably. She stared into space. And waited.

Chapter Eight

<hr>

'Amelia. How long have you been waiting?'

'Not long,' she told her mother.

'But why on Earth have you been sitting here alone in the dark?'

'I didn't mind. All those steps . . . it was nice to sit for a while.'

Amelia's mother sailed down the stairs, sandals lightly clicking against the stone. She wore a long dark skirt of some satin-like material and a loose-fitting oriental-style top that was definitely silk. She had an aristocratic air and Amelia remembered her cousin John once referring to her mother insultingly as 'the Duchess'.

For a moment Amelia wondered if the hand her mother held out to her was to be shaken or kissed, but then her mother touched her shoulder and pecked her on the cheek.

'How lovely to see you, Amelia. How long is it now?'

'A couple of years,' she said diplomatically.

'More like five, dear.' Her mother breezed around the entrance hall, flicking hidden switches. Tiny spotlights sprang into life to highlight small details of the statues: a face here, a torso there. While a pair of cross-beams caught an enormous marble horse's head, its eyes bulging with such a thundering ferocity that Amelia found herself wondering what kind of person would display such a monster in their home.

'I suppose some might be shocked,' her mother was saying,

'that a mother and daughter don't see each other for years on end. But we're enlightened souls, aren't we?'

Amelia smiled in agreement.

Her mother continued, 'I expected you around now. Bill must have come back early. You should have woken me, Amelia. Now . . .' She turned to fix Amelia with her sharp eyes. 'How are you feeling these days?'

'Fine. I think I'm over it now.'

'Shocking business, though, wasn't it?'

Amelia nodded. 'I thought the change of air and some sunshine would do me good.'

'It might,' her mother allowed. 'How did Mae and Brian take the news that you were coming here?'

'They had no objections.' Amelia had planned to say that she'd simply slipped away, but suddenly, in the presence of her formidable mother, she shied away from the truth.

'Good flight and all that?'

'Yes. No problems.'

'What do you think to our poky little villa?'

'It's huge . . . more like a palace. I had no idea it was—'

'Cold as hell in winter. Which I suppose is a decidedly unchristian view of hell. But then, I always was a pagan at heart. Now. Hungry?'

'I am, now you come to mention it.'

'Thirsty, too, no doubt.' Her mother opened the twin doors of the villa and breathed the evening air. 'Wonderful. You know, we're so high up here that we're in an entirely different airstream to the rest of the islands. It positively hums with oxygen.'

'Yoo-hoo!' Amelia glanced up to see a small woman of around thirty clattering down the stairs. 'Yoo-hoo Catherine! So this is your Amelia? Goodness gracious! She's beautiful, absolutely beautiful; just look at that gorgeous hair!'

Amelia's mother said under her breath, 'Lucy is . . . *effervescent.*' Then she made a more formal introduction. 'Lucy, this is Amelia. Amelia, this human dynamo is Lucy Morell.'

'Pleased to meet you, Amelia. Gosh, you *are* beautiful!'

Grinning, Lucy shook Amelia's hand, pumping it up and down. 'And you look just like your mother.'

Catherine smiled. 'Heaven forbid.'

'Oooh!' Lucy Morell's exclamation echoed from the wall, then became an excited laugh. 'Oooh, I got such a feeling from you. Like electricity.'

Amelia's mother said matter-of-factly. 'Lucy's psychic. Now, where's Rachel? The final component of our ever-so-unholy trinity?'

'She's putting her face on,' Lucy said, looking Amelia over as if she was a rare find. 'Oooh, you must let me do a reading.'

'Later, Lucy. Later. Amelia's ready for a drink. And so am I.'

'Tea? Coffee?'

'Cocktails, Lucy; most definitely cocktails.'

'My! Is it that time already? I must have slept like they'd screwed the lid down.'

'Lead the way, my dear Lucy.'

'Poolside?'

'Too chilly. Lounge.'

'Come this way, then. I'll be mother.'

Catherine raised her eyebrows and, with a smile, murmured, 'Rather her than me.'

They crossed the entrance hall, with Lucy hurrying before them to hurl open the living-room door with a bang.

As they entered, Amelia's mother said briskly, 'Oh, Amelia. Before we go any further. You're now twenty-five and I'm . . . a trifle older. So no more "Mummy this" or "Mummy that". Call me Catherine.'

Amelia smiled weakly. 'OK. Catherine.' Her mother really did seem duchess-like. Amelia was in awe of her.

'Excellent. Now, Amelia . . . after you, dear . . . now, I did warn you that this island is about as lively as a tomb — a happening place it is not. You're more than welcome to stay as long as you like, but if you find it dull say so quickly because the day after tomorrow Bill is taking his boat to Limnos for a new engine and whatnot. That means we'll be without a ferry for at least ten days.'

Lucy's voice bubbled from the other end of the living room. 'We'll be marooned here, like the Swiss Family Robinson. Exciting, isn't it?'

Catherine arched a thin eyebrow again. 'Heart-stopping. So, Amelia, let me know if you want to decamp.'

'I'm sure I'll like it here,' Amelia replied, trying hard not to speak as if she was answering royalty.

Amelia found herself in a living room. Four comfortable-looking sofas covered in brown hide were arranged round a low coffee table. There were no carpets, only tiles in a greyish blue. She saw there were yet more statues of Greek gods and goddesses in white stone. Again, they were slightly larger than life and, as in the hallway, were arranged around the walls. One thing that did strike her was that none of the statues – not one of them – was complete: most had an arm or a leg missing; some consisted of muscled torsos alone or merely fragments of noble head. One warrior, sculpted in a creamy marble shot through with purple veins, was the most intact. Intact, that was, with the exception of his face – which had been roughly hacked out between eyebrows and mouth, leaving something like a crater that yawned unpleasantly at the spectator.

Again, Amelia wondered how someone could live with these great, looming stone figures.

'They came with the villa.' Catherine had noticed Amelia gazing at them. 'Spooky, aren't they? But short of taking a hammer to the things and chucking the bits over a cliff we're stuck with them.'

'Oh . . . they make the place look—'

'Like a museum, I know. Right, Amelia, what will you have? There's a choice of gin and tonic, brandy, ouzo or vodka. No sherry or alcopops; we enjoy only the company of spirits here.'

Lucy looked up from behind a table full of bottles. 'Well, there *are* soft drinks if you fancy one.'

Amelia smiled. 'Gin and tonic will be fine.'

'Same here, Lucy.'

As Lucy fixed the drinks she chatted happily, her eyes

twinkling. Amelia felt herself warming to the small woman. Her mother, however, went to stare out of the patio windows.

Lucy handed Amelia a tumbler. A disc of lemon hung suspended in the fizzing liquid like a brilliant miniature yellow moon. 'Let me know if you need more tonic. We get into the habit of making 'em strong here. How was the crossing to the island, dear?'

'Faster than I thought. It only took about forty-five minutes.'

'Gracious, I've never done it under an hour. Obviously the island wanted you here fast.'

'Pardon?'

'It's a local saying,' Catherine supplied, turning from the window. 'You know the sort? Quaint and quite meaningless.'

'I don't know,' Lucy said thoughtfully. 'Voros is unique. It exerts its own gravitational pull.'

'You mean like the moon?'

'Ships' compasses go haywire round here and pilots are forbidden to fly over the island.'

Catherine said dismissively, 'That's because the sea and airspace around here lie in an area of disputed territory, Lucy. Greece and Turkey have been falling out over it for years.' Amelia's mother wasn't exactly ridiculing what Lucy had said but there was a testiness in her voice.

'But Catherine, a scientific study was made of the island. It has its own tidal system; there are dozens of wrecks all around it.'

'And the scientist who conducted the investigations was thrown out because he was a drug addict. They discounted his tests, tore his papers to shreds, and very well you know it.'

Uncomfortable, Amelia sipped her gin and tonic. She was going to end up as a spectator to an argument and she hadn't been here more than an hour. Nevertheless, there followed a kind of lull after this prickly exchange between the two women.

Amelia sensed she should say something to take the conversation on a different track. 'There's one thing I've been wondering. How did the Judas tree get its name?'

'Ah, that one's easy,' Catherine said crisply. 'After betraying Jesus, Judas Iscariot hanged himself from a tree. And henceforth that type of tree was known as the Judas tree.'

'Oh? I guessed there had to be some connection.'

'But seeing as the trees on the island don't grow any higher than your elbow I don't see how the silly sod could have managed it.'

Lucy thought for a moment. 'Perhaps Judas was a very short man?'

'Really, Lucy.' Amelia thought Catherine would erupt angrily. Instead she merely allowed a small smile to turn up one corner of her mouth. 'Well, why not? What's more, it's not as if Judas Iscariot is a saint. So I think we can be as derogatory as we like about him, and with the bishops' blessing at that. Now, Lucy, you pour Amelia another G and T. I'll get supper.' She breezed toward the door. 'No one minds eating in here, do they?'

Amelia said she didn't mind at all.

'Good. Chicken salad. I made it earlier in the day so it won't take long. Ah . . . the final part of our trinity,' Catherine announced as a woman of around forty walked into the living room.

Dressed in black jeans and a black long-sleeved sweater, she was tall and very thin – very thin-faced, too, with a prominent nose that sharply divided a pair of eyes that made Amelia think of pointing, accusatory fingers. *She'd make a good prosecution lawyer*, thought Amelia; *she'd fix those eyes on their victim as he or she squirmed in the dock and dissect even the most elaborate testimony right down to the marrow of its bones.*

Lies wither and die before those eyes.

'Amelia, this is Rachel Stone.'

When Rachel Stone looked at Amelia it felt as if that gaze had pierced her right through to the very back of her skull.

Amelia nodded, said hello, and shook hands. Rachel had a firm, no-nonsense handshake.

'Welcome to the Palms. I hope your stay is a happy one.' The voice was cool, reserved.

You're not one to show your emotions, are you? Amelia thought. The phrase 'Ice Queen' slipped unbidden into her mind.

'Have you told your daughter all about our mysterious island yet?' Rachel Stone asked, her eyes narrowing.

'Not yet,' replied Catherine.

'You'd best warn her about the northern coast.'

'And about our neighbours. Oooh . . . now you *do* need to watch out for those.' Whereas Rachel had sounded serious, Lucy's eyes twinkled with mischief and good humour. 'They're a peculiar lot.'

Catherine drained her glass. 'There'll be plenty of time to tell Amelia everything over dinner. Right . . .' Standing, she smoothed her long skirt regally. 'I'll leave you three to chat among yourselves while I prepare supper. And, Lucy?'

'Yes, dear?'

'No ghost stories. We'll save those to have with the brandies at midnight. The witching hour.'

With that she breezed out of the room, leaving Amelia alone with the other two women.

Chapter Nine

Beyond the windows of the living room it is absolutely dark. There are no lights to reveal the positions of any other villas on the island. Certainly there are no street lamps for the simple reason that there are no streets on Voros. In the illumination from the window, bats flit to and fro outside. A nightbird cries. And in the breeze a Judas tree stirs.

Amelia had slid further back across the cushions of the sofa. The gin and tonic was comfortably stealing away the ache of the long journey down here. A million miles away, no doubt her uncle and aunt were playing merry hell over her disappearance. While rifling through what remained of those possessions she'd left behind.

Well, let them go to hell, she suddenly thought, dismissive rather than angry. She was sure they'd pilfered money from her bank accounts. *But they're history now: forget them.*

Lucy Morell was in a chatty mood: she buzzed about the room, refilling glasses in between pointing out features of the statues. 'I call him Mr Misery Guts.' She flicked a finger at a dour-faced god who glowered beneath a pair of huge, evil eyebrows. 'He stares at you disapprovingly, daring you to smile. So every time I come in here I go . . .' She stuck her tongue out at the massive statue. '"Sucks to you, Mr Misery Guts. Glare at me like that any longer and I'll put a paper bag over your head." The stone dolphins are quite pretty, though, aren't they? I know they're missing a fin or two, and this one has a chipped snout, but they could almost be alive. Can't you just imagine them leaping out of the water?' She dashed back across the marble floor and handed Amelia a replenished glass. 'Now, sing out if I'm making them too strong. As the night goes on the stronger they get . . . oooh, the blame I've had for some hangovers. How's yours, Rachel dear?'

'Fine, Lucy. Fine.' Rachel picked up a magazine and glared at the cover. If anything, the laser-eyed woman seemed too pre-occupied with some problem to participate in the conversation. Not that Amelia minded. Lucy had enough conversation for half a dozen people.

'Now, Amelia . . .' Lucy grinned brightly. 'Tell me what you think of Bill, our ferryman. Isn't he handsome? He's got the cutest smile in the *world!*' She somehow had the ability to put so much emphasis in the last word of every sentence that her voice soared with excitement. 'What did you *think?*'

'He *is* good-looking,' Amelia agreed, half wondering if she was letting herself in for some matchmaking. 'Does he live on the island?'

'Over the other side. The flat bit. Well, what passes for the flat bit. His family's got a farm—'

'The only farm on the island,' Rachel added in a tone-less voice.

Lucy gushed on excitedly. 'They supply eggs, milk, butter, fruit, fish, and even the electricity . . . in fact, they supply everything, one way or another. You might have noticed that Bill does our shopping, too.'

'Yes, he said he'd bring round the groceries in the morning. Oh, and he mentioned that he couldn't find Catherine's usual brand of tea.'

Lucy winked and smiled. 'Be here to say hello. He'd like that.'

'I imagine he's from a big family.' Amelia thought the comment seemed banal and added quickly, 'Greeks do have big families, don't they?'

'Well, generally, yes . . . Bill's got a father and mother . . .'

70

'He also has a brother.' Again, Rachel sounded if it was important that Lucy got her facts right, as if this was part of a testimony.

'Oh, yes.' Lucy's voice dropped to a secretive whisper. 'Gregoriou, but we don't mention him.'

Amelia half expected Lucy to add, 'Gregoriou chopped up our last guest and fed her to the pigs' or something equally lurid. But, lightly as a stone skipping across water, she was off on another subject entirely, eyes twinkling, a smile lighting up her face. 'Catherine tells me you might be here for a few weeks.'

'My mother thinks I'll soon be bored.'

'Bored? Gosh, nonsense! You'll love it here. You'll never want to leave. In fact you never ever will leave, *I guarantee it.*'

'How long have you been here?'

'Six years. *Six years?* I can't believe the time's gone so *quickly.*'

'Don't you ever think about going home?'

'Home? To that draughty, cold country? Not on your nelly. Just wait until you see our lovely sunsets, Amelia. And when you get the *feel* of the island. *Marvellous.* You know, I often think of this place as if it's a catchy tune. You follow? Once you get a catchy tune inside your head you can't get it out, not for love nor money.' Then, in a secrets-to-be-told whisper, Lucy added, 'You see, the island's full of spirits.' She laughed. 'I don't know if Catherine told you this but I used to have my own business. I was a consulting psychometrist.'

'A what?'

Lucy laughed amused. 'Consulting psychometrist. That means I practice psychometry.'

Amelia smiled and shook her head bemused. 'I still don't . . .'

'I know, I know, dear. Psychometry. Dreadful mouthful, isn't it? Well, basically, it means I'm a bit of a psychic, as your mother mentioned. I had an Irish grandmother who referred to it mysteriously as "my gift".'

'You mean you're *really* psychic?'

'Yes.' Lucy smiled warmly. 'Had it since . . . since – oh, I don't know; since I could talk, I suppose.'

Amelia didn't think she was a believer in ghosts, clairvoyance and such things, but as a guest in the villa she didn't want to appear impolite. 'Psychometry . . .' she rolled the unusual word across her tongue. 'How does it work?'

'Ah, that's easy, love. It means I'm what you could call *sensitive* to places and objects.' Lucy took a quick swig of her drink. 'Ooooh, that's lovely . . . *lovely lemon zest.*'

'You mean you can pick up psychic vibrations from things?'

'Psychic vibrations? That's a bit of an old-fashioned word; it makes you think of ectoplasm and spirit guides and nonsense like that.' She took another sip 'Well . . .' She considered for a moment. 'If I go into a room in an old house I can sometimes *read* the room. I can tell you what happened there hundreds of years ago. On a good day it's just like stepping back in time. I can see a family from years and years ago drinking their tea or playing cards, having a sing-song round the piano, or whatever they did.'

'Sounds unnerving. Seeing people who aren't really there. I mean, it's like seeing ghosts.'

'Not really, not when you're used to it.' Lucy gave that pleasant laugh again. 'It's no more ghostly than watching television. After all, psychometry's only images, or echoes of people, captured in the walls and furniture.'

'And people asked you to do this in their houses?'

'Oh no. That's just another string to my bow. People would come to me for readings. What they'd do would be to hand me a ring or a piece of clothing or even a lock of hair and I could tell them the history of the object, talk about the personalities of the man or woman who'd owned it – usually a close relative of the person who'd come for the reading, you know, someone who'd passed over.'

'Oh.'

'And I could tell the client something about themselves.'

Amelia wondered what the point was of a stranger telling you something about yourself. After all, you'd know all about yourself, wouldn't you? You don't keep secrets from yourself.

'I'm often asked what the purpose of it is,' Lucy said quickly, as if reading Amelia's mind. 'You see, every so often people – you, me, Rachel here; everyone – comes to a crossroads in their lives. They have important decisions to make about their future. And sometimes that person will want more information to help them make that decision.'

'So you can see the future?'

'Well, yes, in a way . . . but, more importantly, I can tell a person about themselves, and how they fit into the here and now, and the part they play in their families. Somehow, seeing themselves through a different perspective – through my eyes, after I've done a reading – helps them understand which route they need to take next in life.'

Rachel took a deep breath. 'Ten years ago I didn't know where to go . . .' Her sharp gaze was fixed on the floor. Amelia waited for her to continue, but Rachel merely shook her head and let her breath out through her nose as if some answer she'd been working on had suddenly eluded her again. She went back to reading her magazine.

'And you made the right decision and came here,' Lucy said, as if on Rachel's behalf. 'Blooming good choice, too.' Then an idea struck her. 'Why don't I do a reading for you, Amelia?'

'Now?'

'Yes.' Lucy smiled and wrinkled her nose as if to say *Let's have some fun*. 'Mum isn't here with the food yet; lots and lots of time.'

Amelia wasn't so sure. 'I don't know . . . I mean . . .'

'Don't worry, love, it's quite painless.'

'What do I have to do?'

'Just give me a personal object . . . something you've had for a long time is best. A ring or bracelet.'

'I'm wearing a gold chain.'

'Perfect.'

Amelia unfastened the gold chain from around her neck. 'I don't know how old it is. I was given it by—'

'Ah-ah!' Lucy held up her finger. 'Don't tell me anything about it. That's my job.'

As Amelia held out the gold chain, which was still warm

from being around her neck, Rachel looked up. She was taking an interest but there was something cool and dispassionate about her gaze.

For a moment Amelia experienced a reluctance to hand over the chain. Suddenly she felt vulnerable. As if she'd be exposing areas of her life that should remain private.

Lucy smiled. 'Now don't worry, love. It's just a bit of fun. People tell me they get really frightened before a reading. There's no need to be. I wouldn't embarrass anyone for the world.'

Amelia gave an uncertain smile. 'I . . . I've never done anything like this before.'

'Then there's a first time for everything, love. Pop the chain into my palm . . . there . . . now all I do is close my eyes, let my mind go blank before—*Ow!*'

Amelia gave a startled jump in her chair as Lucy suddenly clamped her hand over her eye. 'Ow . . . dear me! I'm not usually prone to headaches but . . . Oh.' She gave a watery smile. 'It feels just like an ice-cream headache.'

Alarmed, Amelia said, 'Where does it hurt?' The bone above her own left eyebrow began to tingle. Already she sensed the onset of one of her own headaches that would come like a drill bit screaming its way through the bone to the back of her head.

At that moment something thudded against a window-pane.

'What's that?' Amelia was shaken.

'Oh, what?' Face screwed up, Lucy sounded distracted as if she was trying to hear a faint voice coming from far away. 'Bat . . . just a bat, dear.'

'Bats don't fly into windows,' Rachel said coolly. 'They never do.'

Amelia turned her attention back to Lucy. She watched the woman's hand close up until she was holding the gold chain in her balled fist. 'Oooh . . . all gone.' She touched her eyebrow. 'There's a funny thing. As I say I'm not prone to . . . well, what have we here?' She closed her eyes again. 'Now I see a man . . .

quite an old man; he's working in a garden. Um, that's odd . . . he's very old but the way he's digging . . . digging fast with lots of energy . . . he's working like a young man. Oh, and all across the top of his head here.' Lucy ran her finger down the centre of her head. 'His skin is all—'

'You wouldn't believe the song and dance I've had.' Catherine's voice swept through the lounge like a gust of wind. 'I couldn't find the corkscrew anywhere. Looked high and low for it. And you'll never guess where I found it?' She walked in briskly carrying a tray full of food. 'In the cellar. What's more, someone had screwed it right into one of the ceiling beams, of all things. I mean – who in their right mind would do such a thing . . . what's going on in here? You're as white as a ghost, Amelia.' She paused part-way across the lounge and her eyes narrowed suspiciously. 'What are you doing, Lucy?'

Lucy blushed a little.

Rachel Stone, without glancing back up from the magazine, answered for her in that dry courtroom voice of hers. 'Another of her readings.'

'Mmm, plenty of time for that on another day. Amelia is tired after her journey.'

'Oh, of course; I am sorry. Here you go.' Lucy was about to hand the chain back to Amelia but then changed her mind. 'No, let me. The clasp will be fiddly.' Smiling brightly, she scampered round the back of the sofa and fastened the chain clasp for Amelia about her neck. 'Ooh, this lovely hair, Amelia. I wish I had hair like this. Mine's always been so fine it looks a perfect horror if it gets long. Now, Catherine, what's all this about the corkscrew?'

Looking composed, even regal, Catherine set the tray down on the coffee table between the sofas. 'Someone's been playing the devil. The corkscrew wasn't in the drawer. I found it screwed into one of the beams in the cellar.'

Amelia felt Lucy give a playful squeeze of her shoulders from behind.

'It'll be that Bill Simotas,' Lucy squealed. 'He was down in the cellar this morning when he brought in that wine.' She gave

Amelia's shoulders another squeeze and whispered breathily into her hair. 'You'll have to keep an eye on him, love. He can be a bit of a demon.'

'Rachel,' Catherine said. 'Would you pour the wine? Lucy, be a dear and pop and get the bread; it's on the worktop by the cooker. Now, Amelia, there's feta cheese mixed with the salad in that bowl there. And oil and vinegar if you want it. Now . . . help yourself. Don't be shy, get as much as you like.'

Dinner was more enjoyable than Amelia had anticipated. When her mother had entered the room to find Lucy holding the gold chain as she performed the 'reading', Amelia had sensed her mother was annoyed. But she didn't mention it again. And Amelia began to wonder if Lucy's 'psychic' ability was considered something of a harmless eccentricity by her other two housemates. An eccentricity to be humoured politely or glossed over when their patience with it wore thin.

The wine was good and the wandering corkscrew was pressed into service again to open two more bottles of white.

Catherine said in that brisk flowing way of hers, 'Foreigners will tell you that Greek wine is terrible. It used to be true of the wine the Greeks exported, because the simple truth of the matter was that they kept all the good wine for themselves. More chicken, dear?'

Lucy continued to be ebullient and cracked jokes easily. And even the ice maiden Rachel Stone thawed. She spoke of the views from the clifftops, and then about the swimming pool, mentioning that although it wasn't very warm now the temperature would soon climb with the arrival of April, which was only a few days away.

Perhaps the most disconcerting aspect of the room, Amelia told herself, were the statues. Although there were just four flesh-and-blood people in the lounge, there were a good dozen statues of men and women (not to mention the dolphins). So more than once Amelia found herself with the sense they were in a room full of people. Sometimes she even caught a slight movement from the corner of her eye, as if one of the naked goddesses had shifted her weight from her right foot to her left or had inclined a fractured head to one side to be able to hear more of the conversation.

Also a couple of the statues had been positioned so they gazed directly at the person looking at them – especially the one dubbed Mr Misery Guts by Lucy. He was a stern bearded patriarch. Father of the rest, Amelia guessed, who ruled his stone progeny with a fierce eye and a rod of iron.

Come on, Amelia, you'll get used to them, she told herself. And the room will look a different place in the morning with the Mediterranean sunlight streaming in. She leaned forward to help herself to another slice of bread; its texture was rough and strongly flavoured enough to reinforce the exotic atmosphere of the villa, and of the rocky island that lay beyond its walls.

'Does Amelia know anything of Voros?' Rachel asked Catherine.

'Oh, I think I've fed her a fair amount of information in my letters. Haven't I, dear?'

Amelia nodded and smiled as she sipped her wine. 'So much so that I feel as if I've been here before.'

'Have you been warned about the north coast?' Rachel returned to the subject she raised earlier.

'North coast? No . . .' She glanced at her mother, wondering just what was so sinister about that part of the island.

'Oh, nothing to worry about, dear.'

Lucy chipped in brightly, 'The north coast gets all the strong currents . . . ooh, pass me some of those olives, love . . . so if you're going for a swim stick to the south coast. Which is across that way.' She pointed vaguely with her fork. 'It's safe to swim down there.'

'What are the beaches like?'

'Oh, no beaches, love.'

'No beaches?'

'No,' Catherine told her. 'Voros is nothing more than the top of a submerged mountain.'

Lucy added, 'But there are swimming platforms cut from

the rock. You'll find most have ladders into the sea. Oh, and down by the 88 there's even a diving board.'

Catherine added coolly, 'But you'll need a good head for heights. There's a thirty-foot drop into the sea.'

'You'll break your neck,' Rachel said as she stabbed a tomato with her fork. Amelia didn't know whether the words were a warning or a promise.

Also, Amelia felt as if she were floundering. She struggled to catch up with the flow of conversation. 'The 88?' she asked, puzzled. 'What's the 88?'

'Oh, sorry, dear,' her mother said. 'It's all going to sound a little double Dutch for a while until you find your feet. The 88's a villa where the Oxfords live.'

Lucy smiled. 'It's called the 88 because during the war—'

'When Voros was occupied by the Germans,' Rachel added with precision.

'Yes, during the war the Germans quarried out a level stretch of ground and put one of their big guns there.'

'Which was an 88-millimetre artillery piece.' Rachel's laser eyes regarded the plate of chicken. 'We have the Germans to thank for making the island more comfortably habitable. They sank the borehole so we have fresh water. They also used dynamite to blast out several level platforms where they could install their guns and barracks. After the war these were removed and the villas were built.'

'Apparently,' Catherine said, 'a Hollywood movie director bought the island as a private retreat in the late forties. She had the villas built to her own architectural specifications, then moved all her family here where she made some surreal films.'

'She was a bit of an ogre.' Lucy rolled her eyes dramatically. 'Went by the name of Miss Zakarov. You can imagine the sort . . . walking around with a riding crop and barking orders at everyone.'

'And she made films here?' Amelia echoed. 'Have you seen any of them?'

'Oh, yes. Years ago. Julius King down at the Rocket House has got lots of them. In fact, he found the film cans in his attic.

None lasts more than around fifteen minutes and I'll guarantee you've never seen anything as peculiar in your life before.'

'Lots of nudity.' Lucy smiled cheekily. 'Lots of jiggery-pokery, too, if you get my meaning.'

'I'm sure she does, Lucy, dear. Your expression says it all. Now, who's for coffee? I've still got some of those Kenyan beans if anyone's got the energy to grind them.'

Amelia helped herself to more chicken. 'What happened to Miss Zakarov? Are any of her family still here?'

'Well, she ensconced each one of her four sons in a villa apiece and dominated them absolutely. It was all grimly Freudian, really. Anyway, they died off one by one and were buried on the island. Then one day around twenty years ago Miss Zakarov went for a swim and . . .' Catherine shrugged. 'Never seen again.'

'And that's why you should never swim on the northern coast: those currents are lethal. Right!' Lucy sprang energetically from the sofa. 'I'll go and grind the beans. Who's for coffee?'

It had to happen. Amelia felt as if a huge hand had suddenly pressed her into the sofa. She yawned. Exhaustion had caught up with her – that, the drink, and the meal made her so tired she could hardly hold her head up. 'I'm sorry,' she said. 'I don't think I can keep my eyes open much longer. Do you mind if I call it a day?'

'Oh, not at all,' Lucy cried. 'You get some shut-eye, then you can explore tomorrow.'

'I'll show you your room.' Catherine stood up and walked quickly from the lounge. Amelia followed in her wake, saying goodnight to the other two as she went.

Once more she climbed the broad stone stairs to the upper floor. Her mother paused impressively at the top of the stairs.

'Sometimes we sleep late. Help yourself to breakfast if you're up before us. Now: you've got your own bathroom. Don't worry if the lights flicker or dim – the electricity supply's a bit dicky round here. Best not drink the water; there're no nasty bugs swimming around in it but the mineral content can give you stomach upsets. I've left fresh towels on your bed.'

Drowsily now, as if she were already three-quarters asleep, Amelia entered her bedroom. It was spacious, with one wall that consisted almost entirely of windows. She noticed that a door led out onto a balcony, while the windows and door themselves were curtained with a creamy muslin fabric from ceiling to floor.

The bed was a double, and could be screened off from the rest of the room with yet more of the muslin curtain which she guessed served as mosquito nets.

Amelia looked round with drowsy eyes. 'This is nice.'

And no statues, she thought gratefully.

'Sleep well.' Her mother had moved back to the door. 'Good night, Catherine.'

Her mother left the room, closing the door behind her.

Well, I've made it, Amelia told herself happily. *I've made it. And I'm never going back. Wild horses couldn't make me.*

A moment later she made it into bed. There was no noise. Her witch cousins were thousands of miles away. She was safe and sound at last.

Chapter Ten

The voices came gently singing through the statues. Through the broken heads. Through the fractured arms. Voices leaked from cracked loins. They exhaled from eyes that were smooth, rounded marble.

Out from mouths that were as cool and pale as a dead lover's lips.

The voices swelled up the staircase. Ghostly soft, they slipped through the door where they found Amelia Thomas asleep in her bed.

> *Humpty Dumpty sat on a wall,*
> *Humpty Dumpty had a great fall,*
> *And all the king's horses and all the king's men*
> *Couldn't put Humpty together again . . .*

The voices leaked into the room as steadily as water leaks into a holed ship.

> *Humpty Dumpty sat on a wall*
> *Humpty Dumpty had a great fall . . .*

Amelia opened her eyes.

White forms moved towards her in undulating waves from out of the darkness.

She blinked.

The voices were gone. And the white forms were curtains being blown by the breeze admitted by the open windows.

Her witch cousins and that grim hardware shop in that grim northern town were a long, long way away. They were gone from her waking life, along with cousin John and her aunt and uncle, but it would take a little while yet to lose them from her dreams.

She swung herself out of bed and stood for a moment in the centre of the bedroom, drawing reassurance from the marble floor beneath her feet, which in turn rested on the living rock of Voros itself.

I'm here to stay, Amelia told herself. *I'm here to stay. There is no going back now.* She thought of how she'd cashed her life insurance, of how she'd spent what little money she'd had left, of that dream-like escape from her old home. She'd burned her bridges behind her.

No going back; only forward.

She glanced at the bedside clock. The time was a little after one in the morning.

And suddenly she felt awake and alive, more alive than she'd felt in the months since her fall.

(Fall or being thrown from the bridge, what did it matter now? It was history.)

And she could sense the blood running through its courses in her body.

Barefoot, she crossed the bedroom floor; the undulating curtains were like white-sleeved arms, reaching out to embrace her as she stepped through them to the door. Seconds later she was through it and standing on the balcony.

Although darkness hid the island, she could just make out the rocky outcrop rising in front of her, and beyond that the clifftop. Beyond the clifftop was the huge and empty void that stretched from here to the mainland.

To Amelia at that moment she could have been standing on the edge of outer space. Ahead lay emptiness everlasting. Filled with nothing but stardust and darkness.

Behind her the villa lay in darkness, too, its occupants, bar one, asleep in their beds.

From out of that near-cosmic void came a light breeze. In front of her the rocky outcrop moved slightly before it. A whispering reached her ears.

It's the Judas trees, she told herself happily, *they're moving in the breeze.* They were being caressed by the same zephyr she felt now.

She wondered if they could feel it, too. Were they conscious of that slight tickling of cool air across their bark as she felt it across her skin? A delicious feeling; like angel hair being drawn across her bare arms.

The breeze blew harder. Judas trees whispered more loudly. And suddenly the darkness in front of her didn't feel empty. It seemed as if it was being filled with a presence. She could not touch it, nor see it, nor hear it, but some perception told her it was there. Something that swelled massively above the trees.

Amelia wasn't afraid. If anything, a sense of wonder filled her. As if nature – or supernature – was revealing something normally kept hidden from everyone else.

The bone above her left eyebrow tingled; for once it was a pleasant sensation; there wasn't even a suggestion of pain or discomfort. *The island has a Midas touch*, she thought pleasurably. *It doesn't turn base metals to gold; no, it's far more miraculous than that. It turns loneliness into companionship. Misery into happiness. Pessimism to hope. Probably death into life, too.*

As quickly as she'd felt herself become wide awake, now she suddenly relaxed. A pleasant relaxation that spread out from her heart all the way through to her fingertips in a comforting glow. She yawned sleepily. She felt good. Secure. Warm.

Even just a few days ago Amelia had feared that her fall from the bridge had been more than gravity smashing her down to the ground. It had caused her to fall out of society. She'd lost her friends. She'd become isolated. Everyday conversations had become difficult, as if everyone else had suddenly begun to speak in an ever-so-slightly different language; one that she found she couldn't entirely understand. She had begun to be haunted by a spectre of her own future. She saw herself living alone, unable to find a rapport with people, and slowly, surely, irrevocably drawing away from the world until she realized she'd spend whatever time was left to her as a solitary recluse. An individual forced to endure the constant ache of loneliness.

As she lifted herself up on her tiptoes to inhale the fresh air she realized Voros had banished all that. Here on this island she would find a sense of belonging again. Someone would belong to her and she to them.

She tingled with anticipation.

For a long time she stood in the darkness. She sensed that presence poised before her; one that was vast and enduring and powerful.

The tingle above her eyebrow purred gently; there was something kitten-like about it; that screaming drill-bit sensation she was so familiar with was gone.

The breeze blew again; it made the Judas trees sing in whispers. Beneath her fingers the wrought-iron balcony railing was reassuringly solid. She leaned forward, allowing it to share some of her weight.

Her eyes became accustomed to the darkness. She could now see the trees, their shifting branches. Away to her right, steps ascended in a pale curve to the clifftop. To her left a chain swayed gently from a hook in the wall. Beneath that, on the balcony, there was a line of red plant pots.

She was sleepy, very sleepy, but it didn't occur to her to return to bed. The presence she sensed out there in the darkness captivated her. It was like a force of nature.

She remembered years ago watching waves explode against a sea wall. The power of those waves had captivated her, too. She'd watched the plumes of white water gush high into the air; she'd thrilled at the smack of a ton or more of water against stone. *Just one more wave*, she'd told herself, *then I'll go*. But when the wave had come and crashed against the wall, hurling spray and foam, she'd found herself waiting for yet another one. As if the one that was approaching might be even more powerful, even more awesome.

Her mother had been with her then, that day at the coast. Amelia must have been eight years old.

It was one of her mother's brief trips home. The next day Catherine would be flying back to join the cruise ship in the Caribbean where she worked as a dancer. In fact, Amelia's childhood had been punctuated by a succession of these short visits. This exotic stranger with the aristocratic air would fly in, stay a while and then, when Amelia had just begun to feel comfortable with her and call her 'Mummy', she'd fly back to her distant cruise ship.

'Where's your mother?' her friends would ask.

'In the Caribbean.'

'What does she do?'

'She's a dancer on a cruise ship.'

'Where's your father?'

'I don't know.'

'What does your father do?'

'I don't know. I don't even know who he is.'

But there was nothing unique about a single-parent family. One of her best friends used to boast she was the product of a one-night stand when her mother had seduced a Brazilian sailor.

Amelia didn't have such a yarn to spin. Except about her mother, of course. For some reason, she'd told everyone that her mother was a dancer on a cruise ship. It had just been a white lie but she'd repeated it so often that she'd found herself believing it was true. In reality she wasn't sure exactly where Catherine flew off to. By the time Amelia was twelve, however, she knew her mother had settled on Voros. Before that, for all she really knew, Catherine might have simply drifted on the trade winds of the Earth like some lost spirit.

Amelia stifled a yawn. The breeze stroking her face relaxed her. Drowsily, she looked out across the Judas trees. Branches rippled in the trees, their voices murmuring to her softly from out of the night. Seductive. Velvety. Sweeter than honey.

They were delicate things, those Judas trees; so how did Judas Iscariot hang himself from one? The branches would have broken before the rope had had time to draw tight. The thought came lazily to her, nearer to a dream than any waking notion.

Then it happened.

A change to the darkness took place. It occurred quite slowly . . . so slowly, in fact, she didn't even notice it at first.

But the darkness before her eyes was gradually becoming blotched with purple stains.

From the purple blotches lines spread like veins; they grew out towards her, touched her; entered her. Or so it seemed as she stood there more asleep than awake.

Penetration was painless. In her imagination she could see the veins growing out of Voros, then flowing smoothly up through the darkness and into her, making her one with the island, so that she, too, was sustained by the great heart that seemed to beat out there in the night.

It was a good feeling; she belonged now. There was a firm sense of connection. The sensation intensified as more veins of purple slipped out of the night air and into her. Through her skin to merge with the veins that ran through her own body.

It was a pleasant feeling . . . soothing . . . relaxing . . . good . . . a sensation sweeter than she'd ever experienced before.

With that connection made on the outside of her, something disconnected on the inside . . .

In her mind's eye she saw part of her slip away to dissolve out there among the trees. So minuscule traces of her merged with a branch there, a leaf here, or became absorbed by a root or stem. Other atoms of her *self* flowed downward to merge with soil, or the herbs, or they leaked down into the rock.

This felt good to her. The island itself was trying hard to reach out to her.

She reciprocated; she reached back with something inside herself.

At that instant she saw how she might live here. Growing golden-skinned in the sunlight, picking grapes from the vines, sipping wine on the terrace, getting to know her neighbours, spending time chatting with Julius King in his villa garden.

She heard him heard say to her: 'Careful, honey child, we'll suck you dry as bone. We so seldom have new blood here on the island. Now, we'll drink wine and chat and chat until we haven't another word left in our bodies.' And later she'd watch the goats graze on the hill, and the bees working the wild flowers. And she imagined herself riding the ferryman's boat across white-topped waves . . .

'We'll try here, Amelia.'

'Are you sure? Bill, I don't know. It looks deep.'

'Of course, that's the general idea, my bonny little pomegranate. Put on your mask.'

'I'll watch you first.'

'You'll do no such thing.'

'But—'

'Amelia, you promised.'

They sit so close on the tongue of rock their thighs touch. Sunlight glances on the water.

'Pull down your face mask, Amelia. Now put the weight line around your wrist.'

'Why can't we just swim? Why do we have to use these concrete weights?'

'We need them to sink faster.'

'Why?'

'Think of the exhilaration.'

Then his hand presses the middle of her back; she's falling forward. The water, when it hits her, is as cold as grave soil.

All around her the water is turquoise. Fish, tiny as teardrops, dart in front of her. The concrete block tied to the line around her wrist exerts a deadly force. Holding in the lungful of air, she rushes down vertically as if she's falling from a – from a . . .

—a bridge.

A bridge that's a thousand feet high.

Water streams past.

Her breath starts to escape from her lungs. They are burning because she needs to breathe so much. And above the noise of the bubbles she can hear laughter. Callous, mocking laughter.

Beneath her, water turns from green to dark green to black. Down she roars into it. The laughter grows louder. She wants more than anything to breathe. Fish spin past with a spectral flick of their tails. Beneath her are the ghostly wrecks of a hundred ships. They overflow with the bones of the dead.

She can't breathe. And the dead men in the ships below look up to watch the beautiful girl.

Hair cascading, bubbles streaming from her mouth, she descends upon them like a submarine angel. She's nearly at the bottom now.

She can't breathe.

And she can hear the dead men's thoughts rolling up from the depths with all the dark power of eternity itself: 'Didn't they tell you, Amelia? That if you stayed here long enough you'd never ever leave . . .'

The breeze was loud enough to rattle the branches of the Judas trees. It was the sound of skeletons dancing.

She squeezed the iron railings. They were cool and pleasingly solid – and dry.

I'm back on my balcony, she told herself as if waking from a dream. *My bed's waiting for me inside. I'll go back there, pull up the sheets and go to sleep now. Nothing can harm me.* She breathed deeply, filling her lungs with clean, cool air.

'Amelia . . . *Amelia.*'

She looked to her left. Fifteen feet away another balcony projected from the wall. Standing on it was Rachel Stone. She was staring hard at Amelia as if she'd done something unspeakably rude.

'Amelia.'

Amelia replied politely. 'Yes, Rachel?'

'Are you all right?'

'Yes, fine . . . why?'

'Who was that on the balcony with you?'

Amelia glanced left, then right. Apart from herself, the balcony was clearly deserted. Amelia looked back at Rachel, puzzled by the question.

Rachel spoke again as if something had startled her a moment ago. 'Amelia, I saw someone standing next to you on the balcony.'

'There's no one here, Rachel. I'm alone.' Then, as if she had to provide an explanation for being there, she added, 'I just wanted to breathe this fresh air. It's wonderful, isn't it?' She took another deep breath, then looked across at the thin stick of a woman. *She thinks I'm lying,* Amelia told herself. *She's telling herself I've sneaked some strange man up onto the balcony. I wonder what she'll say to my mother in the morning?*

Beware of your daughter, Catherine. Beware! She's taken up with a demon lover.

But what more could Amelia add? She'd told the truth (and nothing but the truth). Feeling uncomfortable now, she said, 'Good night, Rachel . . . sleep well.'

Seconds later she lay in bed, gazing at the ceiling. Shadows moved across it, cast by the muslin curtains still rippling as exotically as Arabian robes in the breeze.

She asked herself: *Why do we have to spend our lives explaining ourselves to others? Or having to explain situations or incidents that we're not responsible for?*

She remembered again telling her classmates that her mother used to be a dancer on a cruise ship. It wasn't a lie. It was merely a convenient explanation for a situation that was beyond her control.

No, it wasn't a lie. Like just now. When Rachel had asked her who else was standing on the balcony with her. And she'd replied that there was no one there. That she was all alone.

Even so, irrational as it might seem, she *had* sensed a presence there.

Chapter Eleven

'If you're thinking of going into the pool, I'd think again.'

Amelia looked across the swimming pool to where Rachel Stone, dressed in black jeans and a black sweater, stared at her. 'It'll be ice-cold,' added the woman.

Like you, Amelia thought. Then she smiled politely and said, 'I might go in later. It looks a lovely pool.'

'It warms up later in the day. But first thing it's always cold, this time of year.'

With that, Rachel turned and walked back into the villa, her duty done.

Amelia continued her exploration of the grounds. Now it was broad daylight, with the sun burning away the early-morning mist, she saw that the villa was perched on one of the highest parts of the island.

From where she stood at the poolside the island unravelled itself before her in a series of crags, plunging gulleys, rocks – and those curious cuboid boulders. Here and there, she glimpsed deep ravines that looked something like railway cuttings, although she knew full well there were no railway lines on the island. Perhaps, she surmised, they were the scars of ancient earthquakes.

Everywhere Judas trees grew from the fractured rockscape. In the still morning air they were unmoving clusters of black twigs, with no trunks to speak of. In fact, they were closer to bushes than trees, and they were still without leaves after the short, savage winter that had only just released its grip on the island. As Rachel Stone had coolly commented earlier, 'Voros is one of the few Greek islands to be covered in snow every winter. It gets very cold here.'

Well, that was changing now, Amelia told herself as she strolled around the pool. The sun felt warm on her bare arms. In three or four weeks the paving slabs would be too hot for her to go barefoot. She folded her arms so that she held an elbow in each hand.

She was going to grow to love the place, she just knew it.

Behind her the villa had turned a pinkish colour in the misty sunshine. Its windows had been opened to admit the air which was lightly scented with the pine odour of the funeral cypress. The balconies, she saw for the first time, were enclosed with ornate iron work that was as shinily black as licorice. And above each balcony was an iron canopy, again painted licorice black. The effect was as if each window possessed a heavy eyelid.

The villa's watching me. It's watching me through half-closed eyes. It's assessing me. Judging me.

Why, I'm only Amelia Thomas. Twenty-five years old. Recuperating from a nasty fall . . .

She folded her arms. That sudden bizarre train of thought made her uneasy . . . *Now, honestly, do houses* really *look at you?* Often her imagination ran away from her like that – just like an undisciplined dog slipping its lead and running off after other dogs in the park. Disconcertingly, it was often the early warning of the onset of one of her hallucinatory episodes. It was as if her imagination was testing how far it could go: first came funny thoughts – funny peculiar, that was. Then, when her imagination realized it had got away with that, it went further. Moments later she'd be seeing faces protruding from the villa walls and screaming eyes squeezing through the cracks in the paving slabs, all bulging and veined and . . .

No. She wouldn't let that happen. It was behind her now. It was caused by the fall from the railway bridge all those months ago. And as the bruises had faded from her face, so the *things* her errant imagination conjured up were fading, too.

Concentrate on what is real, Amelia told herself. The spar-
row sitting on the wall. The funeral cypress trees standing as
straight as telegraph poles. In the distance a white boat resting
on the sea.

Instantly she felt better. She smiled. *I've beaten it now*, she
reassured herself. *I won't hallucinate ever again.*

From the patio doors came the aroma of freshly brewed
coffee; somewhere Lucy was singing happily. Amelia imagined
the woman vigorously brushing her hair before rushing out to
embrace a new day in her typically enthusiastic fashion.

At the far side of the pool, steps rose up another rocky
outcrop, to where she did not know. But she added the steps
to her list of places to explore leisurely. Between the rising
rock and the walls of the villa was a gap big enough to give
her a breathtaking view of the sea. She was wondering whether
there was a way down to the sea at that side of the villa when
she heard the whisper of sandalled feet behind her.

She turned round. 'Oh, morning, mother.'

'Now, now, what did I say, Amelia? No more "mother".'

'Sorry . . . Catherine.' Amelia smiled. 'Let me help you with
the tray.'

'Thank you, and good morning to you, too. Have you had
breakfast?'

'Just some orange juice.'

'That's no good, we need to feed you up. There. If you can
just move the bowl from the table, although goodness knows
how that got there.'

Catherine set down a tray bearing a jug of coffee, bread rolls,
a large bowl full of creamy white yogurt and a jar of honey.

In white trousers and a tangerine blouse that seemed brand
new, Catherine looked as poised and as glamorous as ever. This
morning she wore silver-framed sunglasses that were positioned
part-way down the bridge of her nose. When she tilted her
head forward to peer over the top of them it was as if she was
appraising Amelia every time she looked at her.

'Tuck in,' she said, spooning yogurt into a smaller bowl
for herself.

Amelia helped herself to a bowlful of yogurt, too, then added a generous dollop of honey.

'The honey's out of this world,' Catherine said briskly. 'The Simotas family have their own beehives.'

'The Simotas sound indispensable.'

'Oh, they are, believe me. They act as housekeepers to everyone on the island. Of course, they're our ferrymen, too. Without them we'd be marooned.'

'And probably starve.'

'Yes.' Catherine suddenly gazed thoughtfully at the yogurt on her spoon. 'Yes, I expect we would.' She licked the spoon. 'And, as I mentioned last night, the boat is going in for a refit in the next few days, so we will be cut off here for a week or so at least. Coffee?'

'Please.'

'Be a dear and pour it for me, will you?' Catherine gazed again at the snowy mound of yogurt on her spoon. 'So, if you do want to leave the island, let me know by tomorrow morning so I can make arrangements.'

'I'm sure I'll be fine here. It looks so peaceful . . . "tranquil" is probably a better word. I could sit here and soak it in all day.'

'Well, "tranquil" is just a decorous word for "uneventful" – and uneventful can quickly become boring. Just tell me if you'd prefer somewhere livelier, then we can book you into a hotel on one of the other islands.'

She's inviting me to leave the island, Amelia told herself as she poured the coffee. *I don't think she hates me or anything like that, but it's as if she would be more comfortable if I weren't here.* But then, their relationship had always been one of polite distance, both physically and emotionally. All through Amelia's childhood, her mother would be out of the country for months on end. And when Catherine did spend time with her she always seemed a remote and distinctly aristocratic figure: more like a well-to-do cousin who occasionally made 'duty' visits to the poorer relations.

Was this just part of that cool remoteness?

Or had that ice maiden Rachel Stone nearly tripped over herself in her rush to tell Catherine about last night? About how she thought there'd been someone standing on Amelia's balcony with her.

Yes, of course there was. It was my demon lover.

Suddenly Amelia was tempted to say just that. For a moment she wanted to shock her mother, to try and provoke some emotional response from that coolly distant human being who, although she had given birth to her, had only played such a tiny part in her life. Always the glamorous stranger seen only once or twice a year.

Amelia watched her mother sip her coffee. Composed, regal–looking.

Does she ever find she has a drip of coffee on her chin? Or end up with crumbs in her lap, or catch her little toe on a chair leg and swear merry hell?

No, Amelia didn't suppose she ever did. Nothing could ever break that cool composure.

For one absurd moment, one savagely absurd moment, Amelia saw herself scooping a handful of yogurt from the bowl and smearing it in her mother's face. Her heart beat faster. She saw the fermented milk turning Catherine's neatly brushed hair into a mess of rats' tails, and her sunglasses knocked askew so they'd hang comically from the end of her nose. The look of astonishment on her mother's face would be priceless.

No sooner had the image raced mischievously across her mind than she pushed it away. She dropped her gaze back to the piece of bread she'd been eating. Why had she thought that? Why had she been so gleeful at the idea? Her mother had invited her here as a guest. A non-paying one at that. Amelia's sense of guilt intensified.

If anything, Amelia could be accused of sponging off Catherine. Could she just lounge by the pool all day expecting to live here for nothing?

Her mother glanced up from spreading jam on a piece of bread. Amelia felt as if she must look red and flustered, but her mother gave no indication of noticing anything out of the ordinary.

'Cherry jam,' Catherine announced. 'Not too sweet – delicious. Mmm . . . what do you intend doing with yourself today, Amelia?'

'I thought I'd explore the island.'

'Be sure to wear good shoes. Trainers if you have them; you'll need to do a lot of climbing.'

'Climbing?'

'There are no roads on Voros. And precious little in the way of footpaths, too.'

'How do you and the other two get around the island?'

'As a rule, we don't.' Catherine bit off a piece of bread. 'It is very beautiful, but also very rugged. If we're making social calls at the other villas we go by boat. Every villa has its own landing stage and dinghy. We have one in the little boathouse at the end of the landing stage.'

'You can't be able to get out much when the sea's rough.'

'No, we can't. As I said before, it can be very isolating here. Very lonely. Try the dark brown buns. They're spiced with cinnamon.'

'Thank you.'

'It *is* possible to make your way around on foot but you do have to climb at times. And be careful of the ravines. In places they're so narrow you can step from one side to the other, but some are a good fifty feet deep. If you fall down one of those you'll break your . . . well, needless to say, they're exceedingly dangerous. If you hear rustling from the bushes, don't think you're being stalked, it'll only be wild tortoises. Considering they're so small they actually make a terrific amount of noise when the undergrowth is dry. Oh, and if you make it as far as the other end of the island there's the remains of a watchtower. You'll have some incredible views from the clifftop there.'

The conversation continued pleasantly, if a trifle formally. Amelia was pleased now that her mother did seem more at ease with her and seemed to be enjoying her impromptu role of tour guide, pointing out interesting places to visit on the island.

'Oh, and be sure to see the caves: they're in a little bay just to the right of our landing stage as you go down the steps. Again, it's a bit of a climb over the rocks to get to them, but it's worth it, believe me. Uh-oh.' Catherine smiled. 'Here comes, Lucy. She's the only person I've ever met who is unfailingly bright every morning.'

'*Ooooh!*' Lucy's voice soared into the air like a rocket. 'Oooh, lovely day, isn't it? Morning, Catherine, morning, Amelia . . . Oh, look at this beautiful hair.' Grinning, Lucy made a beeline for Amelia, took a lock of hair in her hand and rubbed it between her fingers as if she was rubbing flour together. 'Oh, if only I had hair like this. When I see it I can't stop myself touching it.' Her eyes twinkled, catching the sun. 'You know something? That will be my new ritual every day. The first thing I'll do on a morning is grab a big handful of Amelia's hair.'

Catherine gave a little smile. 'I'm sure Amelia could be persuaded to part with a lock. Then you could keep it as a good-luck charm.'

'Like a rabbit's foot.' Lucy laughed, delighted at the idea. 'But no. Amelia's hair should stay exactly where it is. Never get it cut, love. Never. Ooh, yogurt and honey. You know, I always go mad with the honey. Of course, it's terribly good for you.'

Amelia smiled, warming to Lucy's irrepressible good humour. 'Coffee?'

'Oh, yes, please.'

'Only half a cup, Amelia.' Catherine said dryly. 'Otherwise the caffeine might make her excitable.'

A shriek of laughter escaped Lucy's mouth. 'Oh, Amelia, isn't your mother terrible to me? The things she says − and she's so dry . . . she says these things with such a straight face: you don't know whether to take her seriously or not.'

Lucy was a dizzying whirlwind of energy and laughter. When she spoke she gestured constantly or hugged herself, or she'd suddenly lean forward to touch Amelia or Catherine on the arm.

After a few moments Catherine glanced at her watch. 'Well, I have a few matters to attend to.' She looked at Amelia. 'I'll leave you in Lucy's capable hands. Remember my warning about the coffee.'

Lucy shrieked with laughter again. 'Stop it, you'll give Amelia the idea I'm a lunatic.'

'Barmy as the day is long,' Catherine said. 'Certifiable. Ciao.'

Breakfast was turning into a leisurely meal. Amelia drank more coffee and broke off a small piece of bread to nibble. Lucy talked on in her animated way.

'Oh, your mother's a devil, an absolute devil – oops, sorry, that should be Catherine – she hates to be called "mother", doesn't she?'

Amelia smiled. 'I expect she's not used to it.'

'We'll call her "mother" behind her back, shall we? Or leave little notes about the villa. "Dear Mumsie, we've run away with a pair of fierce Turkish sailors. Love, Amelia and Lucy."' Lucy giggled into her hand and managed to look all of eleven years old.

'Or buy her a cup with "Mum's Mug" written on it in big letters.'

'Gosh, aren't we wicked? If she hears us she'll chase us round the swimming pool with her broom.'

The image of her Duchess-like mother chasing Lucy furiously round the pool while waving a broom above her head seemed extravagantly funny and Amelia laughed until her stomach muscles ached.

'Aren't we a pair of monkeys?' Lucy wiped a tear from her eye and composed herself. Then she burst into a fit of giggles all over again. 'Mumsie will be cross. Now . . . deep breath, deep, deep breath. I'll be serious now . . .'

'But only for a moment.'

'Of course, love. I can't keep a straight face for long. Now, where were we? Ah, yes. Has your – no, Catherine . . . has *Catherine* told you all you need to know about the island?'

'Yes, she said that I need good walking shoes.'

'Absolutely. Although a pair of wings would be better.'

'So you do visit your neighbours by boat?'

'Oh yes! We have a little dinghy; it has an outboard motor you start by pulling a piece of cord. And it's dead easy once you get the hang of the steering; oh, and I do *love* zipping around in it . . . I always sing at the top of my voice.'

'What are the neighbours like?'

'Oh, weird as fudge.'

'Really?'

'You have to be a bit of a crackpot to live on this island. Well, it's so remote isn't it, love? No shops, no bars, nothing.'

'But there's Limnos nearby. That has a good-sized town with everything you need.'

'Yes, I suppose so.'

'Do you go there regularly – you know, to shop and have a night on the town?'

'Hardly ever these days. Come to think of it, must be two years since I was there last.'

Amelia thought she must be joking and laughed politely.

'In fact, it's a good eighteen months since I've been off the island at all.'

Amelia nearly laughed again. Then she stopped herself. Was Lucy joking? Or had she really not been away from this tiny rock in eighteen months?

Lucy helped herself to the last of the yogurt. 'Now, anything else I can help you with?'

'One thing did puzzle me.'

'Yes, love?'

'Why do they call the house The Palms? I've looked all round the place and haven't found a single palm tree.'

'Ah ha!' Lucy held up a finger as if Amelia had uncovered a secret. 'If you're in the mood for a walk I'll show you. Then the mystery will be revealed.' She leaned forward and, touching Amelia's forearm, whispered, 'Don't tell mumsie, but I might be able to give you a little surprise as well.'

Chapter Twelve

Lucy led the way. She even held her finger to her lips as if they were about to creep somewhere they shouldn't. Amelia followed her round the pool to the steps that ran up the side of the rocky outcrop.

By now the sun had climbed higher into the sky, its heat a potent force, tingling her skin.

They climbed the steps in silence for a while. Amelia wondered if they'd see the palms – after which, presumably, the villa was named – from the top.

Seconds later the steps took them out of sight of the villa below. Now Amelia had an uninterrupted view of the sea, which must have been a good two hundred feet below them. Although the steps were wide and there was a timber guard rail, she found herself walking more and more closely to the rock face that rose to her left.

'Nearly there,' Lucy called. She didn't appear out of breath and climbed easily.

'Where do the steps lead?' Amelia asked breathlessly.

'To the palms, of course.'

'There are palms up here?' She paused and looked up at the naked rock. Even the Judas trees hadn't rooted themselves this high.

'Yes, love.' Lucy shot Amelia that mischievous grin. 'My, you're out of breath for a young 'un.'

Amelia held her side as she caught her breath. 'I never used to be like this, believe me.'

'Oh, I'm sorry, silly me. Catherine said you'd been under the weather for a while. I should have thought . . . do you want to go back down?'

Amelia shook her head. 'No, I'll be all right. I'm just out of shape, that's all.'

Lucy looked genuinely concerned. 'Aren't I thoughtless? Are you sure you're OK?'

'Fine.' She smiled, then a thought struck her. 'Did my mother tell you that I'd been ill?'

'She said you'd not been at all well and that you'd been staying with relatives.'

'Did she tell you what was wrong with me?'

'No . . . only that you were ready for a holiday and a bit of sunshine, which for my money is good for all that ails anyone.'

Amelia had assumed that her mother's housemates would have known what had happened. Them not knowing made her suddenly more confident. She'd lived for so long in the role of invalid that it had become difficult to remember herself as being bright and outgoing and energetic. Now here was someone who knew nothing about the fall and who had no preconceived expectations of her. As far as Lucy was concerned, Amelia Thomas was a perfectly normal twenty-five-year-old.

Amelia took a deep breath, feeling something of her old zest returning. 'Right, you were going to show me those palms.'

'Okie-dokey, this way.'

Once again they climbed the steps. A few moments later they reached the top of the rock.

Amelia saw at once that it had been artificially levelled to form a platform that was perhaps the size of a tennis court. All she could see there was the slab of concrete she now stood on. There wasn't so much as a blade of grass, never mind a palm tree.

Amelia smiled at Lucy's impish expression.

'OK, Lucy. Where are the palms?'

'You mean you can't see them?'

'No.'

'You're standing on them.'

Amelia looked down. 'Oh, very funny.' She laughed. 'Is the villa really named after these?'

'I think the original owners were very whimsical; still, a strange sense of humour is better than none at all.'

Amelia stood to one side while still looking down at the concrete slab basking in the intense light of the sun.

There in the concrete were four sets of human palm prints. The fingers were splayed out and beneath each pair of palm prints was a name.

Josef . . . Erich . . . Albert . . . Gunther.

And then a year: *1944.*

'See?' Lucy smiled. 'We do have palms after all. As Catherine mentioned last night, when the Germans occupied the island in the war they levelled parts of it for their gun platforms. The men who laid the concrete for this one couldn't resist leaving something of themselves for posterity.'

'Joe, Eric, Albert and Gunther.' Arms folded, Amelia gazed down at the palm prints in the concrete. 'Four friends, I imagine. And a long way from home. I wonder what happened to them.'

Lucy considered. 'Well . . . shall I see if I've still got it?'

'You mean to do a reading?'

'Why not?'

'But here? Now?'

Amelia looked round at the concrete platform in the dazzling sunshine.

Lucy chuckled. 'Why not, love? Just because we're psychic we don't have to sit in parlours with the lights out.'

'*We*'re psychic?' Amelia smiled. 'No, *I*'m not psychic.'

'Oooh, you are. Can tell a mile off. Can tell a hundred miles off.'

'Believe me, Lucy, I'm not.'

She smiled. 'We'll see, dear. Now, to work . . .'

Amelia looked at Lucy, wondering if the woman would go

into a trance or something. Also, it was a bit odd to be standing here on top of this pinnacle of rock with someone who claimed to be psychic. She was tempted to make an excuse and return to the villa.

As it was, Lucy didn't indulge in any clairvoyant melodramatics. She simply crouched down, then ran her hand over the palm prints as if she was wiping a dirty mark off the concrete.

Then she straightened and lightly closed her eyes. 'Now.' She thought for a moment. 'Now . . . yes, there's someone standing there.' Eyes still closed, she pointed somewhere to Lucy's left. 'He's waiting for someone . . . or something . . . I can see he's waving his hand like this.' Lucy, her eyes still closed, waved her hand above her head.

Amelia watched with her arms folded. She realized the body language fairly yelled that she was sceptical, to say the least. Lucy was sounding pretty vague about the waving man. The description seemed a little on the woolly side, too.

'Now he's turning . . . he's turning like this.' Lucy pivoted until she faced the edge of the platform that looked over the sea. 'Yes, I'm getting something now.' Suddenly she sounded more confident. 'Oh, yes, I can see them. Three young men sitting on the edge of the platform across there. They must be the soldiers and . . . oh, just look at them.'

Amelia looked. She saw only the edge of the platform and a misty blue of sea and sky beyond.

All of a sudden Lucy found her rhythm and began speaking quickly. 'Oh! They're all dressed in shorts, grey shorts that come down to their knees, and they're sunbathing up here. There's the gun; a big black thing. And these men are so happy, they're laughing, joking; ooh, they're having the time of their lives. Can't you imagine them? Four young men, little more than boys, really, they're on this big adventure far away from home. The sun's shining; yes . . . I can see two of them are playing . . . oh, what do you call it? Checkers . . . draughts . . . only they haven't got a proper set, so they've drawn the game board on a piece of brown paper and shaded in the squares in pencil. And they're using boiled sweets as counters . . . oh, and one of them's popped one of the sweets into his mouth and they're laughing again. The third man is sitting on the concrete near them. He's having trouble with a pair of spectacles. He keeps taking them off his face; they're . . . yes, they have metal rims and he's saying there's something wrong with one of the lenses. Oh, and he won't stop fiddling with them. He keeps rubbing his eye like this.' She rubbed one eye with a fingertip. Then her forehead wrinkled. 'Ah. And . . . yes, I can see the fourth man. He's eating a water melon . . . a big pink slice . . . and he's spitting the seeds out over the edge of the cliff . . . and he's got juice all over his face here.' Lucy rubbed her chin. 'Sticky . . . really sticky, he's saying.'

'You can hear them as well as see them?'

'Oh, yes. I can also sense how they're feeling; they're all happy. The war's a long way from here.'

'You speak German?'

'No, but I sense the meaning of words. Like the blond one sitting over there. 'Sticky', he's thinking, 'sticky', and he's telling the other ones now that he's going for a swim to wash it off.'

'And you can see them across there? Even now?'

'Oh, yes.'

'Are they ghosts?'

'Oh no, love. In fact, they're probably still collecting their pensions in Germany as we speak. No, they're nothing but images. Like television pictures.'

'So you couldn't speak to them?'

'No more than you could have a conversation with a television.' She turned to look back at the edge of the concrete platform. 'Now the blond one's finished the slice of melon . . . there . . . there! He's just thrown the melon skin away like that . . .' She mimed an underarm throw. 'He's watching it fall into the sea.'

Lucy looked round the bare platform. It was featureless apart from the prints and a set of rust-stained holes where the gun itself had probably been bolted long ago. Of course that was gone now, along with Joe, Eric, Albert and Gunther.

All in all, Amelia didn't find herself impressed by Lucy's

talent. The woman appeared to genuinely believe in her 'gift,' and she was likeable. Amelia certainly had no intention of saying she didn't believe in her 'psychic reading'. But anyone with a little historical knowledge of Voros could have given the same performance.

Lucy walked towards Amelia smiling brightly. 'Oooh, I felt as if I was on good form today. Tell me what you think.'

'Well . . .'

At that moment, Lucy lightly touched Amelia's elbow.

'*Oh!*' Lucy clamped her hand over her left eye as if she'd been hit by a stone. She breathed deeply. 'Oh, there it goes again. Just like last night. Ouch, ouch, *ouch*. I never get headaches. I never ever . . . that does hurt.'

Shocked, Amelia took Lucy's arm. 'Do you want to sit down for a moment?'

'No, love. I'll be fine.' Lucy paused, blinking experimentally. 'There . . . it's going already. But something kicked me like a mule there . . .' She gave a watery smile. 'I must be coming down with a cold or something.'

Amelia looked at where Lucy was touching her forehead with her fingertips. The area where it had hurt her was just above the left eyebrow.

Amelia shivered. 'Did it feel like a sharp pain . . . as if something had gone right through your forehead?' Amelia found herself lightly touching the slight dent in her own forehead, just above the left eyebrow.

'Like a skewer; yes, it did. Right through to the back of my head; it was—' Lucy suddenly paused and looked at Amelia. 'Yes, it did. But how did you know?'

Amelia forced a thin smile. 'Maybe I am psychic, after all.'

'Yes. I believe you are.' Lucy took a breath and rubbed her eyebrow more vigorously. 'There. All gone.' She looked at Amelia again, this time more thoughtfully. 'When I started the reading last night I felt the same pain. And you asked me about it as if you were alarmed.'

'I was very tired. I was probably feeling edgy.'

Lucy looked up at her. Her face was open and sympathetic.

Before Amelia could stop herself she found she was telling Lucy everything. 'My mother was right about telling you I was under the weather. But the truth of the matter is I was quite badly hurt last year.'

'Oh, love. I *am* sorry.'

'I'm all right now. It was a good fifteen months ago.' She smiled. 'All the bumps and grazes have healed.'

'But you sometimes get the pain in your head?'

'Yes.' Amelia took a breath. 'I was going home late one night; it . . . was New Year's Eve; not that that's an important factor.' She realized she was beginning to stammer as the emotion gripped her. The memories were still raw and undigested. 'I was crossing a . . . a footbridge . . . over a railway. I was alone. And someone grabbed me and . . . and simply chucked me over the side.' She smiled but her knees were shaking.

'Oh, I'm sorry, love. It must have been terrible.' Lucy looked at Amelia sympathetically. 'I hope the police threw the book at the swine who did it.'

'No . . . no. They never caught him.'

'Oh, that's horrible. Horrible.'

'I can still hear the sound of his breathing. It was very loud in my ear. He gripped me under my arms and held me over the railway tracks. I remember seeing the rails shining and hearing the sound of his breathing in my ears. Then he . . .' She gave a trembling shrug. 'Well, I'm better now. But I still get this pain every now and again where my head hit a stone. It was what doctors call a depression fracture. It's what you or I would call a dent. Still, a dented head's better than a broken head.'

Lucy smiled and said gently. 'Why don't we go back down to the villa and I'll make us a cup of tea?'

'The physical injuries were bad enough. But what was difficult to get over was the damage to my *Self* – I suppose that's what you'd call it. It was the person on the inside of my body that was damaged the most. I don't suppose I'm explaining it very well, am I?'

'You're doing very well, Amelia.'

'After the accident I began seeing things that weren't there.'

'And the doctor told you they were hallucinations?'

'Yes.'

'And you were told to ignore them and they'd eventually go away?'

Amelia nodded.

Lucy said, 'Just because you can sometimes see things that others can't doesn't mean they're not there.'

'But these *were* just hallucinations.'

'Believe me dear, you're psychic.'

'Lucy, you don't understand, these things I was seeing weren't . . . nice. In fact they were awful things; bloody awful things; they haunted me; they all but frightened me to death.'

'Now, now . . .' Lucy's voice was soothing. 'I've seen things that shocked me, too. That's because I didn't understand them.'

'But they were ugly, evil-looking—'

'And I now know the things we psychics see are only images – they're patterns in the air; nothing more. They can't touch you; they can't hurt you. Now . . . tea – hot, strong and plenty of sugar. And I'll treat you to some of my home-made shortbread, too. There, I can't say fairer than that, can I?'

Amelia smiled. Just being in Lucy's company was a tonic in itself. And she was glad she'd told her about the accident. Well, 'bared her soul' about it would be more accurate.

'Now, what you must do is trust me.' Lucy linked arms with her and guided her towards the steps. 'I know the psychic ropes as well as anyone. So, if you do *see* any more of these things you've been told are hallucinations tell me about it. OK, Amelia?'

'OK, Lucy.'

'Good girl. Now, shall we count the steps together on the way down?' She laughed. 'You know, I never get the same figure twice.'

'*One, two, three, four, five, six . . .*'

Counting the steps, they descended. The sun shone brightly.

Swallows skated across the sky above them and a lone cicada had begun to chirp from a Judas tree below.

Chapter Thirteen

After returning from the platform on top of the rocky out-crop Amelia had drunk tea with Lucy. Catherine had joined them but no mention was made of what Lucy had said she'd seen.

Certainly, Lucy's 'gift' was no secret. But again Amelia wondered if Catherine and Rachel merely humoured what they considered to be their housemate's mild eccentricity.

The March sunshine was surprisingly powerful. Soon the three women retreated to the shade of a canopy that projected from a wall. Then, later, Rachel had joined them, slipping out from the shadowy interior of the villa like a ghost gliding from the depths of a tomb.

For a while they chatted about a meal they were planning for the evening. Lucy was all for being adventurous and barbecuing steaks on the patio. Rachel coolly reminded her that the temperature at this time of year would still drop sharply when the sun had set. The conversation moved on to Bill bringing a box of fresh aubergines up to the villa and how best they could be cooked.

'They must be salted,' Rachel announced. 'Slice them and salt them, then leave them for two hours, otherwise they will be bitter.'

'Oooh,' Lucy laughed. 'I've cooked aubergines before. I'll bake them in the oven with those tomatoes, and garlic and parsley.'

'Oh, Amelia.' Catherine looked over the top of her sunglasses at her. 'Bill was disappointed you weren't here when he delivered the groceries this morning. He wanted to ask you something.'

'Oh?' Amelia said carefully. 'What did he say?'

'He wouldn't tell me.'

'Ooh, very mysterious,' Lucy bubbled.

Catherine pushed her sunglasses back up the bridge of her nose. 'No doubt he'll catch up with you later.'

There was a pregnant pause. Amelia felt as if the women were expecting her to make some comment about Bill or perhaps even to gush breathlessly, 'Oh, isn't he handsome? Oh, I wonder what he wanted to ask me? Oh my . . .'

Instead, Amelia said quite casually, 'I thought I'd go for a swim this afternoon. In the sea.'

'The sea?' Lucy looked up. 'Ooh, now that *is* adventurous.'

'It'll be cold.' When Rachel spoke it was a statement rather than a comment. 'Very cold.'

'It's not *that* bad, Amelia,' Catherine said, smiling. 'A brisk swim in the sea would probably do you the world of good . . . wouldn't it, Lucy?'

'Oooh yes! The world of good.'

'But keep away from the north side of the island,' Rachel announced. 'The currents are treacherous,' she reminded Amelia.

'Oh, I don't know.' Catherine picked up a magazine and looked idly at the cover. 'I've swum from our landing stage many times before.'

'Really?' Lucy was wide-eyed. *'When?'*

'Last week. It really is quite refreshing at this time of year.'

'Oh, you can tell you're mother and daughter – you must have adventure in your blood. I'd never swim off the north side of the island. Never – *ever*.'

'That's because you don't swim at all well, Lucy. As I said, I think the strength of the current on the north side is greatly exaggerated.' Catherine gazed at the magazine again.

'But Constantine Simotas told us that—'

'All part of Greek bravado, Lucy dear. Sheer bravado. It's the way of the Greek male. They'll tell you how dangerous the ocean is. That you'll good as drown if you so much as dip a toe in it, then before you know it they're diving in to impress all us weak, tremulous women. Isn't that right, Rachel?'

'He told me about the snakes.' Rachel said with a sniff. 'Whenever I was out for a walk and I saw him he'd hold up his hand, then throw a rock into the grass; then he'd tell me a poisonous snake was lying in wait for me.'

'Snakes are more frightened of us than we are of them,' Catherine added. 'Like I say, Greek bravado.'

Amelia felt as if the conversation was excluding her. But all she could think of to say was, 'Constantine Simotas is Bill's father?'

'He is. A Greek of the old school. If you're generous you'd describe him as gallant; if you're a cynic he's as chauvinistic as the day is long.'

'Even so, love . . .' Lucy sounded almost nervous. 'I'd take your first swim from the south side of the island.' She smiled, pleased, as she plucked another reason for doing so out of the air. 'Besides, it's easier to reach. You just follow the path down between those two cypresses . . . over there, on the far side of the wall. Steps take you right down to a nice little bay.'

'There's no sand,' Rachel stated. 'No sand anywhere on the island. You must swim from rocks.'

Lucy appeared to work hard to soften Rachel's uncompromising statements. 'But there is a good level platform . . . and a ladder into the sea. There are no sharp rocks. It's an ideal place for a leisurely swim. Now . . . anyone for my shortbread?'

The cold made Amelia gasp. It was like leaping naked into snow when she leapt from the rock platform and into the sea.

My God, how reckless I am, she thought, surprised at her own bravado. *I might have cracked my head open.*

Even before the accident she'd have walked down the steps into the sea first. Then she might have dived or leapt in later, once she'd acclimatized herself to the temperature and had made sure that the water was deep enough. And that there were no sea urchins nearby, bristling with spines that would be as sharp as hypodermic needles.

But she'd simply walked down onto the landing stage, dropped her towel, kicked off her sandals and run forward, launching herself into the water.

She thought: *Maybe it does show I'm recovering. Maybe deep down I'm wanting to grab life by the scruff of the neck again and do what I damn well want.*

Amelia lay back in the sea, enjoying the swirl of water around her neck and the sides of her face. Looking up, she could see the cliff face soaring up to meet the sky. The sky itself had become a pale blue with a blazing sun in its centre.

Dear God, the sea was cold. But her mother was right: it was breathtakingly refreshing.

Now she was alone in her little island paradise. The height of the cliffs on three sides of her made the cove an intensely private place. She loved the solitude, while the feel of the water against her skin was nothing less than sexy.

Before she knew what she'd done she'd slipped off her one-piece bathing suit. With an overarm throw she hurled the sopping garment onto the landing stage.

Now the water raced icily over her skin as she swam.

She splashed the water with her hands and laughed.

If Uncle Brian and Aunt Mae and the witch twins – and strange, strange cousin John – could see her now.

There they'd be, huddled in the house in the cold northern town, where it never seemed to grow properly light in the mornings. There the frozen slush would still be clinging to the streets, as if desperate not to allow winter to leave and summer to enter that drab borough.

But here the whole place was drenched in light. The birds sang. Wild flowers were already breaking out in patches of brilliant lemon against the rocks.

Treading water, Amelia pressed her hand to her breast. Her

heart was beating strong and even. Her skin tingled. The salt water on her lips was nothing less than invigorating.

At that moment she wanted to yell at the top of her voice: 'I'm alive! I'm alive! I'm alive!' and hear the echoes crash back from the rock walls.

And what would the walls reply? What would they tell her? What secrets would they confide? A giddy rush of excitement ran through her.

She took a deep breath and jackknifed in the water. For a moment her legs were completely free of the surface and the weight pushed her down so she could touch the ocean bed with her fingertips.

She opened her eyes. The sea was a bright turquoise, while stretched out before her were the dark shapes of submerged boulders.

Light shone down through the water. Individual rays fanned out in a glorious sunburst.

The lungful of air she'd taken sustained her effortlessly; there was no burning need to rush to the surface to breathe again.

Moving her arms gently to maintain her position in the water, neither at the bottom nor at the surface but suspended in limbo between, she stayed there. Amelia listened to the beat of her heart; she watched the light play through the water. Silver speckles passed before her eyes. Fish or bubbles? Without a face mask her vision was too blurred to tell.

Seconds ticked away. Still she felt no urge to breathe. Filling her was a sense of comfort, well-being, and a deep, deep relaxation.

She closed her eyes.

I am a dust mote suspended in God's eye, she thought deliciously. *I am an atom lying between the stars . . . and I am filled with a cosmic serenity . . . floating . . . floating . . .*

As she drifted there underwater, eyes lightly closed, she allowed her arms to extend like wings, her fingers feeling their way through the water.

At that moment her fingertips brushed against a solid object.

Startled, her eyes snapped open. There, just a yard from her, floated the corpse of a drowned man. Wide-eyed, blackened, deformed, it must have drifted for weeks on end in the sea, its arms outstretched . . .

Even though she was still underwater Amelia cried out. The sound, mixed with a rush of bubbles, enveloped her head. Arms and legs flailing, she wrenched her way up through the water to the surface.

There she exploded out of the water and beat her arms as though, if she could only swim hard enough, she could lift her entire body out of the water and away from the dead thing that drifted there.

'I'm sorry. I didn't mean to startle you.'

Panting, she twisted round in the water; her heart thundered in her chest.

'Please . . . don't be alarmed . . .'

She turned to see a black face. From the face a pair of wide eyes looked at her. One eye was brown. The other was blue.

'Are you all right?'

She steadied herself with a deep breath.

Idiot, she told herself. *It's not a corpse; it's only another swimmer.* Her imagination must have slipped its leash again.

As she trod water she gave a cough to clear her throat, then she smiled. It was reserved, polite.

'I'm sorry,' she said. 'I didn't know there was anyone else swimming here.'

'No, I'm the one who should be apologizing, sneaking up on you like that.' He smiled; his teeth, she saw, were very white and perfectly even. 'I should have whistled or sung to let people know I was on my way.' Treading water, he broke into a song.

She laughed; a mixture of politeness and nervousness. The man's sudden appearance had been surprising enough. And yet, now she'd got over that, she noticed how striking his looks were. He was, she guessed, middle-aged, his skin a smooth, flawless black – a blue-black at that. What was more, there wasn't a hair on his head. Shaved, she guessed. But most striking were those eyes, with one brown iris and one that was a startling bright blue. He smiled pleasantly.

That was the moment Amelia remembered she was stark naked.

Treading water, she immediately allowed herself to drop lower into the sea, until the surface came just over her chin.

What if he's seen me? she thought. *He might have been watching me from a nearby rock. He might have seen I'm completely nude.* She thought how she'd jackknifed in the water, the way her bottom half would have lifted clear of the surface.

Oh, my God, he would have seen everything.

Suddenly she felt very naked, very vulnerable.

She glanced back at the platform. She was alone here with a strange man. If it came to it, could she outswim him to the platform? Then race back up the steps to the villa? She'd hear him running after her, feet pounding on the steps, closer and closer until she could hear the sound of his breathing.

– the sound of his breathing . . . the sound of his breathing . . .

His long arms were as muscular as a bodybuilder's.

Nervously, still treading water, she moved back a little.

He finished singing – a sentimental love song about part-ing being such sweet sorrow – then he smiled at her. 'You don't recognize it?' His voice sounded cultivated, yet curiously accentless.

She shook her head, trying to remain somehow emotionally inert so it wouldn't seem she was encouraging him.

'Pity,' he said shaking his head, feigning sadness. 'That was one of my best.'

'Oh.' Again she made sure she sounded neutral.

'I'd sing that every night during my cabaret. On a good night I could make the audience cry. Men and women both. Can you imagine that? Now that's a very eerie feeling, knowing you have the power to make people cry. But I suppose, when all's said and done, it was only another form of amusement. After all, you can't make people laugh all the time, can you?'

'No . . . no, I suppose not.' Amelia's voice had dropped to a near whisper. The man with one blue eye and one brown eye made her nervous. She was conscious of their isolation in this bay. If she shouted no one would hear.

Amelia was still intensely aware of her nudity. The way the cold water felt like probing fingers. Fish could have been swimming between her knees. She shivered, chilled to the bone.

The man smiled. 'There I go, down memory lane again. Now, you must be new to the island? I've never seen you before.'

'I'm stopping with my mother. Up at The Palms.' Quickly she added, 'She's due down here any minute with Mr Simotas.'

'Really?' He looked back up at the cliff steps. 'I don't see anyone yet.'

'I thought I'd come down for a swim first.'

'Which Simotas?'

'Bill.'

'I thought I saw him taking his boat across to Lesbos today.'

Hell's bells. She found herself floundering for something to say.

Instead the man said in a mild voice, 'Damn. Oh, 'scuse my French, but if I'd known he was coming here this afternoon I could have brought my shopping list and saved myself a trip to the Simotas place.' He peered up at the cliff steps again, then looked back at Amelia. 'I do beg your pardon, I haven't introduced myself. Julius King.'

He paused, tilted his head to one side. She realized he was waiting for her to respond. She gave a weak smile. 'Amelia Thomas.'

'Amm . . . melia. What a beautiful name. Amelia . . . almost rhymes with Arcadia . . . or Mona Lisa.' He grinned. 'Sorry. A songwriter's habits die hard. I always find myself finding rhymes to names. You know, Amelia, the sound of your name will be going round in my head all day now. I'll probably find myself sitting in front of the piano tonight saying your name over and over as I . . .' He shot her a smile as he played imaginary piano keys.

Is he trying to chat me up? Amelia felt even colder; a shiver juddered its way up the length of her bare back.

He continued conversationally, 'Of course, you do know Voros is the place where sanity goes to die?'

'Pardon?'

'We're all as mad as hatters here . . . you have to be. In fact, being mad is your passport to Voros.' He chuckled. 'And be careful of the locals; they'll suck you dry as bone. We so seldom have new blood here in the shape of visitors. They'll want to know everything about you.'

Is he just being whimsical? she thought; *or is he really insane?*

His long arms swirled the water around him as he floated there. 'Of course, you haven't met the other islanders yet, have you?'

'I only arrived here yesterday.'

'Ah ha, it won't have got to you yet. The mysterious zeitgeist of the island.'

She stared at him. She was utterly bewildered.

He pointed to his blue eye. 'Oh, I'm sorry. I keep forgetting what an oddball I must look. One brown. One blue. I imagine it takes some getting used to. The truth is, when I was a baby I went crawling through a patch of long grass and this bad old snake sprang out and bit me right in the eye. This eye turned blue overnight.' He smiled. 'At least, that's what my mother always told me.'

A swell had begun, pushing her up and down with each wave. And now the pain was starting above her left eyebrow. At the moment it was no more than a growl. But she didn't doubt it would soon increase in pitch to that sharp, howling pain she'd got to know so well over the past few months.

'I . . . I'm going to get out now . . . the water's colder than I thought.'

'Of course . . . I'm sorry, Amelia, that's my fault for keeping you talking. Now, why don't you call round for a drink at my place?'

'I'm not sure that . . .'

'Bring Catherine, too. She is your mother, isn't she?'

'Yes.'

'That would be wonderful. You know, I haven't seen her

in weeks. We could all have a good chinwag. Besides, I fix the best dry martini on Voros, she'll vouch for that.'

'I'll mention it to her. Thank you.'

'Excellent. I live at the Rocket House over yonder. Catherine knows the way. Tell her I'll give her a ring. Remember the name: Julius King.'

'Right.' Amelia felt herself relax and the smile came more readily. 'Julius King.'

Now came the tricky part. Getting out of the water. She'd thrown her swimsuit so far she couldn't reach it without climbing out in full view of the man.

As she started to dog-paddle towards the landing stage she heard him call out, 'See you around, Amelia. Take care, now.'

She thought he'd tread water there and watch until she climbed out. Instead, thankfully, he turned and swam away. His dark arms pulled him effortlessly through the water. It was then she saw his bottom half.

He's got no legs, she told herself in surprise. For a second she thought it was her imagination playing tricks again. But then she saw that his legs really did end in a pair of stumps just below his shorts.

She watched him go. He didn't pause or look back and continued swimming straight out to sea between the jaws of rock at the mouth of the cove. After that, he turned right and swam powerfully out of view.

Above her, clouds had slipped across the sky, and in turn their shadows slipped across the water. They reminded her of sharks swimming through the sea.

Shivering, she turned and swam for the landing stage.

Chapter Fourteen

'Yes, of course, I know Julius King.' Catherine breezed through the statue-lined entrance hall. 'Sweet man. Very well-mannered and witty with it. Used to be a songwriter . . . a cabaret singer as well, if I remember rightly.'

Amelia watched her mother switch on the tiny spotlights that illuminated the best – or the worst – features of the broken statues.

Catherine continued speaking briskly. 'What did you make of the one blue and the one brown eye?'

'Striking.'

'Very.'

'Was he well known?'

'Extremely well known about twenty years ago . . . if you like that kind of thing. In Las Vegas he was billed as the Jamaican Noel Coward.' She switched on more lights. 'Which is a bit of a misnomer, considering he actually came from Haiti – you know, the home of voodoo?'

'It's difficult to make out where he's from; he seems to have no accent.'

'Received English, dear. I expect he parroted what he heard on the BBC World Service.'

'Is he married?'

'What? Julius King?' Catherine laughed as if Amelia had just said something absurd. 'Oh, damn, one of our bulbs has gone. It's the awkward one as well, over Medusa's head; oh, never mind, we'll press-gang Bill Simotas next time he's here. Now, ready for a cocktail?' Without waiting for a reply she sailed away in the direction of the library, calling, 'Lucy? Lucy, dear . . . are you working this evening or are you joining us on the patio? Rachel says it will be too cool to eat al fresco, but she's compromised for taking a snifter or two out there.' Amelia listened to her mother's voice fading as she walked along the corridor, still talking. 'They say there's a new comet visible in the sky. Should be worth a peek. I know you'd say a comet's a harbinger of doom, but then . . .'

The voice faded at last to a kind of shimmering echo that Amelia found completely indecipherable. But then, even when she could hear every word her mother said she couldn't always understand her picturesque turns of phrase. The three women could be nothing less than inscrutable at times.

Shaking her head, she went up to change.

As Amelia regarded her meagre collection of clothes in the wardrobe and tried to decide what wouldn't look too dowdy against Catherine's flowing silks, she hummed to herself. Her second day was drawing to a close.

The island was peculiar, she'd decided. And perhaps not what she'd had in mind. She had envisaged something flatter . . . far, far flatter . . . possessing beaches of soft sand, with one or two tavernas to visit as the sun set. Its inhabitants, also, did seem a little on the eccentric side. Those that she'd met, anyway. In a nutshell, she guessed they needed to get out more. The old phrase was appropriate: it suggested that people who cloistered themselves away were apt to cultivate unusual interests and attitudes.

Probably the people of remote, isolated Voros had nurtured their own eccentricities here, so far away from the outside world. So much so that they never even noticed they behaved and thought a little differently from the rest of the great stream of humanity. Which was the way of the eccentric, wasn't it? You notice peculiarities in others, never yourself.

Oh well, she thought lightly. *Never mind*. It made the locals interesting, anyway.

She mused in front of the mirror. *Shall I wear the black dress, or trousers? Sandals or shoes? Silk scarf or no silk scarf?*

Outside a breeze stirred the Judas trees. They whispered: a sibilant hissing sound of many *esses*.

Amelia chose the black dress and went to shower.

The light falling on the patio was rose pink. The swimming pool had deepened into indigo. Above, swallows dipped and swooped in the sky. Someone had dug a trench in the shallow soil, perhaps to receive a line of bushes. Judas trees whispered busily to themselves in the shadows beyond the wall.

Lucy waved Amelia across to the table. 'Oooh, I do like the black dress.' Pixie-like, she hunched her shoulders and shot the girl a delighted smile. 'Ooh, little black dress and a naughty scarf. Love it.'

'Thank you.'

'Martini?'

'Let me get it,' Amelia said quickly. 'You mustn't wait on me hand and foot.'

'Be my guest. It's already mixed in the shaker; that's it, the silvery one. Ooh, would you be a dear and freshen my glass? Gosh, aren't we wicked? Leading lives of idle luxury like this?'

Amelia poured the drinks as Lucy sat back down to the table. Lucy wore loose-fitting trousers that were tight at her ankles and a waistcoat over a white blouse. 'I call this the Aladdin look, what do you think?'

'Very chic.'

'Come on over here, Amelia . . . take a seat. No . . . one at this side of the table and we can enjoy the lovely view and speculate what's happening on the cruise liner over there.'

'It looks more like a warship.'

'Let's *pretend* it's a cruise liner, then. Now. The captain will be sitting down to dinner with his guests.'

'All in formal evening dress.'

'Of course. And they'll eat lobster and drink white wine. There'll be a lemon sorbet for sweet; something zesty to refresh the palate.'

'And the men will retire to the smoking room for cigars, port and poker.'

'And the women will chase the poor sailors all over the blooming ship.'

Amelia sipped her drink. 'Where are Catherine and Rachel?'

'Rachel will be putting on her face. Catherine's looking for the corkscrew.'

'It's lost?'

'Again.' Lucy nodded. 'The thing's sprouted little tin legs.'

'We'll buy it a collar and chain.'

'Naughty things, corkscrews. Cigarette?'

'No, thanks.'

'I shouldn't, but I do.'

'I wonder if my mother's found that corkscrew?'

'It can't be far.'

'Maybe I should help her?'

'No. Stay here. Enjoy the sunset.'

'All right.'

'Amelia. Did I tell you I had a boyfriend whose hairdryer exploded in his hand?'

'No, really? Was he hurt?'

'No, but I think he took it as an omen to leave . . . *what?*'

Amelia looked round. 'The cicadas . . . I don't hear any cicadas tonight, do you?'

'No. They make the sound by rubbing their back legs together.'

'They're quiet tonight.'

'They've gone on strike.'

'I wonder where my mother is with that corkscrew?'

'Or Rachel.'

'Does Rachel smoke?'

'No . . . *yes.*'

'I wonder how long she'll be . . . *oh* . . . My mother's here now.'

'Yes.' Lucy sighed and relaxed back into the chair. 'Yes
. . . she's found it. We'll have to chain it up so it doesn't go
walkabout.'

Catherine walked across the patio, holding up the corkscrew. 'In the freezer. I'll throttle that Bill Simotas.' In her
other hand she carried a bowl of creamy dip. 'Tzatsiki,' she
said, 'it's yogurt and cucumber. Feel free to dip in. There's
baby sweetcorn and breadsticks on the plate.'

'Catherine, Amelia was just saying we need to get the
corkscrew a collar and chain.'

Catherine looked at Lucy over the top of her sunglasses.
'Are you feeling all right, Lucy dear? You look a little—' She
considered. 'Glittery.'

'Oh, fine, love. Do you need a hand in the kitchen?'

'Everything's under control. Amelia, dear, would you pass
me a cigarette? Thank you.' She held up the cigarette elegantly
as she lit it. 'You don't, dear, do you?'

Amelia shook her head.

'Just as well. Now, dinner will be ten minutes or so yet.
You were right about those aubergines, Lucy. Best I've seen
this year.'

'Imported, I expect; it's a little early in the season.'

'Mmm, probably Egyptian. Oh, I thought we'd try the
retsina. Keep an eye on that corkscrew, won't you.'

'We will, dear, we will.' Lucy beamed.

Regally holding the cigarette, Catherine strolled across to
the pool where she gazed into the water for a moment. After
that she strolled to the far side of the patio where the twin
funeral cypresses grew as straight as poles. There she gazed over
the jumble of rocks and crags of the island's interior.

Lucy said, 'Try the tzatsiki, Amelia. It really is delicious.'

'I don't think I'm hungry.'

'I'll get you another drink. A stiff one.'

'Thank you.'

As Lucy poured the drink she looked at Amelia. It was a
long, hard look. Then she glanced across at Catherine as if to
make sure she wasn't paying any heed to their conversation.

'Ice?'

'It doesn't matter.' Amelia took a deep drink of the cocktail. There was a pause. At last a lone cicada began to chirp in a Judas tree.

Softly, Lucy began, 'Amelia . . . when we were talking just then. Before your mother came of the villa. Did you see a figure come onto the patio?'

Amelia hesitated for a moment. 'Yes.'

'What did you make of it?'

'There was something wrong with its face, wasn't there?'

Chapter Fifteen

'Lucy? What was that figure? What was wrong with its face?'

Amelia Thomas hadn't actually spoken the words aloud but the questions echoed darkly inside her head.

She saw Lucy look sharply at her: her eyes had taken on that glittery quality once more. She opened her mouth to reply. Then:

'Lucy. Amelia.' Catherine's voice was as bright as a silver bell. She'd heard nothing of their conversation just then. 'Come across here and look at the moon. Doesn't it just look as if it's being swallowed by that cleft in the rock across there?'

After looking at Lucy again, Amelia picked up her drink and crossed the patio. Lucy didn't waste any time following close behind. The woman was scared. Amelia could sense it: a shivering fear that shuddered down to the very marrow of her bones.

Then, standing in a line, all three watched the blood-red moon descend into the earth

It was as if Voros had the power to swallow entire worlds.

Rachel stepped out onto the patio only far enough to tell the three others that it was too cold to stay out there any longer. Besides, the baked aubergine was ready.

They trooped into the kitchen where the table was set. Amelia, for one, felt grateful to be there. The heat from the oven was palpable, the lights bright, and a wonderful smell pervaded the air.

What's more, the solid walls gave her a sense of security.

No one will come after me in here, she thought, sitting to the great oak table. *Not when the four of us are together.*

Catherine took the bottle of wine from the fridge, then turned to look at Lucy and Amelia. 'Now . . . who forgot to bring in the corkscrew? You were supposed to be guarding it, remember?'

There was a pause.

'Could someone be a dear and pop and bring it back from the patio before it scampers off again?'

Amelia looked at Lucy. She knew neither of them wanted to venture back out onto the patio now it was getting dark.

And that figure . . .

Amelia clenched her fist. 'I'll get it.'

Expressions of relief followed by guilt raced across Lucy's face. 'I'll come with you.'

'Goodness, does it take two of you?' Catherine smiled. 'The pair of you won't have to wrestle it to the ground, you know.'

Rachel sniffed at a steaming pan. 'Heavy things, cork-screws.'

Amelia guessed it was the nearest thing the ice queen would ever make to a joke. She forced a smile. 'It's OK, Lucy. I'll get it . . .' She shot Lucy a look. 'But if you hear me yell, come running . . . it'll mean the corkscrew's getting away from me.'

This is like pulling plaster off, she thought. *Just do it fast; get it over with.*

She walked quickly out of the kitchen, through the lounge full of statues. The dour one with the beard glowered fiercely down on her. What dark thoughts did that stone head harbour?

Then she was through the patio doors and crossing the stone slabs. Ahead of her, the swimming pool was like a vat of ink. The moon had gone, devoured whole by the gluttonous island. Above her, stars burned with cold witch fires.

A bat twisted and turned through the air, its wings fluttering like scraps of veined leather. And somewhere Judas trees murmured in the breeze, as if to warn each other: *She's here, she's here . . .*

Not now, she thought, *not now*, as the bone above her left eyebrow began to throb.

She took a deep breath. Walked faster. The table lay in front of her; she could see the blue-handled corkscrew lying there in the centre.

Don't sprout legs. Don't run out on me. Deliberately she ran flippant thoughts through her head so there'd be no room for anything else.

Why is it so dark out here on the patio? Why didn't they leave the lights on? Or at least the pool lights?

The shadows were dark, graveyard things. As if they'd oozed from the rock beneath her feet

She walked faster. If anything, it was the table that had moved. Suddenly it seemed further away than the last time she looked.

Tables don't move by themselves, do they?

Why not? Tables do have legs.

And chairs, too.

Suddenly, thoughts that were supposed to be flippant enough to distract her from the darkness – and from what she had seen earlier – began their insidious tormenting.

Suddenly they had all the malice of her twin cousins, the little witches whose teasing had become a running sore.

Humpty Dumpty sat on a wall
Humpty Dumpty had a great fall . . .

That damn' table was moving, wasn't it?

Was it nearer to the funeral cypresses now? Near to where the figure had stood?

Was that corkscrew the bait now?

Luring her further and further from the safety of the villa.

A figure sprang from the darkness.

Heart lurching, she gasped as a claw of a hand flashed at her. It seized her arm and pulled.

'*Amelia.*'

'Lucy? *Lucy!*'

'There . . . you nearly walked straight into the pool.' Lucy composed herself, then flashed Amelia a smile. An uncertain, scared smile, but a smile nonetheless. 'We should have left the lights on. You couldn't see the pool in the dark.'

'No.' She laughed, but it sounded very feeble. 'I've still not got my bearings yet.'

Lucy let go of Amelia's elbow and patted her forearm. 'Silly me, I forgot my cigarettes. I must have left them on the wall across, there . . . no, oh, I can't see them.' She talked quickly, almost running one word into another. 'No, I must have taken them inside, after all.'

Amelia looked at Lucy gratefully. 'I think I saw them on the worktop.'

'Ooh, I'll forget my own head, won't I? Right, you grab the corkscrew, then we can get back to the villa. And get the door locked behind us.'

Within ten seconds they were back in the kitchen.

'Very, very heavy things, corkscrews,' Rachel remarked as she stirred the sauce in a pan.

'Oh, nearly forgot,' Catherine announced. 'Julius King phoned. He's invited us to one of his teatime barbecues.' She took the corkscrew from Amelia, shot it a stern glare, then began twisting it into the bottle of wine. 'Saturday at four. You know, we really must get another couple of corkscrews. If this vanishes we'll really be up the creek.'

Rachel glanced sideways at Lucy. 'Perhaps one of your spirits moved it?'

'Nonsense.' Catherine sounded brisk. 'Now, have I put enough garlic in those mushrooms?'

The conversation turned to the meal. Nevertheless, as they sat down to the table Amelia couldn't help but notice that Lucy glanced at her repeatedly. They would have to talk about what had happened, but now wasn't the time. She knew Rachel and Catherine would give short shrift to the subject.

Rachel began discussing commodities investments and the price of copper with Catherine as the two women worked on the meal. They made no attempt to involve Lucy in the conversation and Lucy made no attempt to contribute. At one point, when the two were busy with the oven at the other end of the kitchen, Lucy raised her eyebrows and whispered the words, 'Stock markets: it's all rocket science to me.'

'They invest?'

Lucy raised her eyebrows again and nodded. 'Successfully, too.' She glanced at the two women as they lifted a huge iron baking tray from the oven. Steam billowed. 'And don't worry about the . . . you know, *thing*. It can't hurt you.'

'But what was it? I saw . . . a figure just walk onto the patio. It was—'

'Now, sleep on it tonight; we'll talk tomorrow. Ladies, do you need a hand down there?'

'We're in control now,' Catherine replied.

Amelia heard Rachel murmur, 'Not nearly as heavy as a corkscrew . . .'

'I'll get the plates,' Amelia said, deliberately ignoring the aside. 'Do you need the spatula?'

'Yes, please. The metal one . . . not the plastic . . .'

'I'll get it.' Lucy moved athletically to the far end of the kitchen.

Amelia returned with four dinner plates from the cupboard – only to find that the corkscrew had managed to disappear from the table once more.

Chapter Sixteen

Amelia went to bed. The mattress looked broad and welcoming, the sheets were crisp, white and fresh-smelling. She slid into bed gratefully, feeling as snug as a letter being slipped into an envelope.

And if I was a letter where would I wish to be posted?

Here, she thought deliciously. *I still want to be on Voros. And on Voros I want to be in this villa and in this villa I want to be in this bed.* The sheets were like angel's kisses. Soft. Cool. Loving. Serene.

Amelia yawned. A nightcap of Metaxas brandy had made her drowsy.

She'd left the other women talking in the entrance hall after saying goodnight. Now, in turn, each would be sliding into bed.

Conscious of not wanting to appear as if she was simply there to laze the days away and be waited on hand and foot by the others, Amelia had insisted that Rachel, Lucy and Catherine should take their coffees into the lounge while she washed up the dinner things, taking particular care of the brassy cutlery, polishing the knives, forks and spoons until they shone like rose gold. The iron baking tray had been a monster. She couldn't fit the entire thing in the sink and could only shift the shreds of aubergine skin that had caramelized themselves to the tray by boiling umpteen kettles of water and repeatedly dousing them. Then they'd eventually yielded their grip beneath the blade of a knife.

Once she'd done with the pots and pans she'd mopped the floor tiles with an eye-watering cocktail of scalding water and bleach. By the time she'd finished, perspiration dripped from her nose like dew.

Now they wouldn't think she was sponging off them, would they?

Not even the chisel-faced Rachel Stone would think that of her, surely?

And why not reinforce the idea that she was there as a working guest, if not a paying one?

Lucy had a sweet tooth. Amelia would bake a cake or two tomorrow.

The night breeze blew the white muslin curtains. Their white shapes billowed gently. In the distance came a hissing sound. It was too far away to tell whether it was the sea against the cliffs or the breeze passing through the branches of the Judas trees.

What was the sea like now?

She thought of her swim earlier.

What if I creep down to the landing stage one night? Wouldn't it be thrilling to peel off my clothes and slip into the water when it's pitch dark?

Would I dare hold my breath and swim underwater, my hand stretched before me, feeling my way through the black ocean?

What would it be like, holding my breath and falling into the darkness; the same kind of soft darkness that lies between the stars?

One moment before midnight she knew she was a twenty-five-year-old woman lying in bed in a Greek villa known as The Palms. One moment after midnight the balance had shifted subtly from wakefulness to sleep. Then she was a little girl swimming through the sea, accompanied by dolphins that sang her name. And that kept away the sharks and the savage things that swam there, too . . .

Amelia woke knowing that the bed was too big for the room. She knew also that she must make it fit back into the bedroom, but the bed was swelling and growing painfully large.

She sat up, touching her forehead.

It felt as if the bed was in there. It was growing larger and larger by the second. *It shouldn't be in there; not a bed that grows. Anyone knows a bed can't fit inside your head.* It was all right when it was small but now it grew, bigger, bigger; her head couldn't contain it.

Heart pounding, she spun out of bed, dragging the sheets out behind her; she tried to drive her fingers into her skull and pull out that malignant bed . . .

She took a deep breath.

I'm awake . . . it's OK, she told herself quickly. *It was only a dream . . . it wasn't real.*

Uneasily, she looked at the bed as it stood there, headboard to the wall. The bed itself was enclosed by muslin curtains. There was something disturbing about it now in a way she couldn't put her finger on.

She ran her fingers through her mussed hair, flattening it to her head. Then she took a deep steadying breath.

Silly me, she thought firmly. *Frightened of dreams at my age.*

But, my God, I need a breath of air.

She looked at the door that led onto the patio. No, it would be utterly dark outside. She didn't relish going out there alone . . . even onto the balcony. It was raised a good dozen feet from the ground, but . . . no. Not out there. Not alone.

Thing, she thought inarticulately. That *thing* on the patio this evening . . .

The bump in the bone above her eyebrow began its low, growling ache. She touched it lightly.

Seeing that *thing* . . . or imagining she saw the *thing* with the ruined face on the patio had triggered the nightmare.

Come to think of it, had it really been there? It might have just been one of her hallucinatory episodes.

But then, why had Lucy said she could see it, too?

Didn't Lucy claim she was a . . . a what-d'you-call-it? A – a psychometrist? A kind of psychic who could see things that weren't there anyway? Perhaps Lucy was trying to bolster her own belief-system by pretending to see Amelia's hallucination as well?

That made sense, didn't it?

If one person sees an angel they're nuts. If a dozen people see it, then it's a miracle. Wasn't that how these things worked?

Amelia looked back at the bed. She didn't want to stand around barefoot on the marble floor all night – the stone was icy against the soles of her feet – but then again she didn't care to get back into bed right away.

She felt a little jumpy inside. The dream of the bed growing inside her head was still potent enough.

No, she'd help herself to a drink of water first. She headed for the bathroom. Once there she switched on the light and looked at her reflection in the mirror. It was one of those uneasy moments when the reflection didn't seem to be hers.

No, that wasn't quite right. She recognized the reflection as one Amelia Thomas, former publicist and damned good tennis player . . . *But I don't feel like me on the inside. I feel like a stranger looking at an individual called Amelia Thomas.*

It only lasted for a moment or so before that odd sensation of mental dislocation passed.

She ran the cold-water tap.

Damn.

I can't drink the water here, she remembered. Instead, she splashed water onto her face, dried herself with a towel, then went down to the kitchen to find a bottle of mineral water.

The hallway clock indicated it was a little before one a.m.

She went nimbly down the stairs without switching on the lights. The illumination from her bedroom showed her the stairway clearly enough. She'd switch on the light in the kitchen for sure.

I don't want to surprise the corkscrew romancing the wooden spoon. She smiled at her own flippant turn of mind. *That's better*, she thought. *Nearly back to normal.*

The presence of the statues halted her at the foot of the stairs. They fixed her with their stone eyes. There was something cold and knowing about them. They formed a clique and she was the outsider. She made a point of meeting their gaze as if she could actually outstare them. And force them to break eye contact.

Of course, those broken figures stared back. With their missing noses, shattered torsos, fractured heads, heads without ears, heads with snakes growing from them.

At that moment Amelia realized she was hearing voices.

They were coming from the lounge. There was soft laughter. A clink of a glass.

She moved noiselessly across the hallway. The door to the lounge was open by no more than six inches.

Barely any light came from the gap but the voices continued; a conversation was under way that deeply involved the participants.

Amelia walked up to the door. Through the gap she could see that candles had been lit. The statues inside the room cast giant shadows that flickered and swayed on the walls like phantoms dancing.

Moving her position a little more Amelia could just see in. Catherine sat with her back to her, Lucy to her left on a sofa and Rachel to her right on the other sofa that had been pulled closer to the table.

All three were peering down at objects on the coffee table.

It took a full moment for Amelia to realize they were playing cards. As they played they talked to each other. Clearly, all three were engrossed in the conversation. Although they spoke quietly their gestures were animated and there was a lot of nodding.

Amelia was surprised. She'd assumed the other three had gone to bed at the same time. Clearly that wasn't the case. They'd merely moved through into the lounge to play cards.

Why didn't they ask me?

Perhaps the emotion that came strongly to her then was childish, and yet she felt strongly as if she'd been left out. They'd excluded her from their late-night card party as adults exclude a child by sending it to bed early.

No, that wouldn't be true . . . *Amelia, you are being childish*, she scolded; *they haven't left you out deliberately*. It was probably a spur-of-the-moment impulse on their part. Only she, Amelia, had gone to bed by then and they were considerate enough not to disturb her.

Even so, the urge to sail through the door with a breezy 'Hi. You nightbirds still up?' evaporated as quickly as it came.

The sensation she'd experienced upstairs in the bathroom returned: Amelia felt dislocated not only from herself but also from the people in the lounge. She'd been set suddenly apart from them. And there was now too great a distance between herself and the three women to be bridged simply by opening the door and saying, 'Hi! Couldn't sleep. Anyone for a cup of tea?'

She paused there in the limbo of the entrance hall. In the company of those broken statues she too was unmoving.

It wasn't her intention to deliberately eavesdrop; in fact, she'd already taken a step back in the direction of the kitchen. She planned to slip inside, take a bottle of water from the fridge and return upstairs without disturbing anyone.

But as she stepped back she found herself tuning in to the conversation.

'. . . ace of clubs. Cigarette, Lucy?' It was Catherine's voice.

Lucy said something and Rachel Stone laughed. It was the first time Amelia had heard Rachel so genuinely amused.

So, the ice woman thaws . . .

Amelia took another step back into the shadows of the hallway; as she did so she heard her mother speaking again: 'Cut the cards, Rachel . . . so, you first . . .' The clink of a glass. 'As I was saying, I'd found the wasps' nest in the hedge by the front door.'

'So that's where the monsters were coming from,' Rachel said.

'A huge thing it was. I didn't know they had nests of that size. Like a ball of paper the size of a football, at least . . . well, it broke open as I pulled it out of the bushes.'

'Lucky you didn't get stung. Another brandy?'

'Thanks . . . oh, there were no wasps; at least, none that were going to do any damage . . . remarkable thing, the wasps' nest. They'd built really quite a complex structure out of what I suppose is papier mâché. Inside there was a hive effect of hundreds of little cells for the devils. What struck me most was that there were still some wasps inside.'

'Alive?'

'Only just. But they were funny part-formed things; as if they'd not made the transformation fully from wasp grub to grown wasp. They were all shrunken and the yellow stripes were dull.'

'Obviously they were in no shape to leave the nest.'

'No, I expect they just stayed there until they died. Never made the grade as a fully paid-up member of the wasp fraternity. Pitiful things. What struck me is they reminded me of her. Uh, I think you've won, Lucy.'

'You owe me fifty drachma, Catherine.'

'I won't flee the country, trust me.'

They chuckled.

Outside the lounge door Amelia suddenly stiffened. The conversation had suddenly turned from being a conversation about a wasps' nest to an assessment of someone's character. That someone was a *'her'*.

Amelia's stomach turned unpleasantly. *No, surely . . .*

'I wouldn't have thought she'd be like that,' Rachel was saying. 'But I have to say your comparison with the part-formed wasps is accurate: she's a part-formed human being.'

'Psychologically and emotionally.'

'There *is* something stunted about her,' Lucy agreed. 'And, in fact, I would say she is pitiful. Absolutely pitiful.'

'Another one?'

'Please . . . with a little soda this time, Catherine dear.'

Amelia found herself holding her stomach. She was absolutely horrified.

They're not talking about me . . . never in a month of Sundays are they talking about me.

But the ache in her stomach told her otherwise.

This time when one of them spoke Amelia heard Rachel Stone laugh. It was a cold and utterly scornful sound.

Amelia felt sick to her stomach. There was no other description for it.

What she'd heard wasn't merely derogatory: it was an out-and-out character assassination.

But you don't know they're talking about you, do you? After all, did you hear them mention your name?

No, she hadn't.

But then, *who* else could they be talking about?

For a while she stood there, straining to hear whether her name was mentioned or if they would drop a clue into their conversation that would point the finger at some other individual who was so pathetically ridiculous that they had provoked Rachel Stone's scornful laughter.

But the conversation had returned to the card game.

Try as Amelia might to convince herself that there was no shred of evidence to suggest they were speaking about her, she went to the kitchen in a daze, not really wanting the water now but not knowing what else to do.

Surely her mother wouldn't be cruel enough to denigrate her own daughter as devastatingly as that?

She took the bottle of water from the fridge, then all but fled upstairs to bed.

Chapter Seventeen

Amelia Thomas woke angry. After making her way back to bed the previous night she'd lain awake for a good hour or more, thinking about what she'd overheard. Had her mother, Lucy and Rachel really been talking about her in such a dismissive manner? Comparing her to stunted wasps that couldn't even manage to leave the nest?

Perhaps she was jumping to conclusions. After all, they might have been talking about someone else entirely.

But who?

At last she did fall into a fitful sleep. But it was a restless night. She awoke every time she turned over. Outside, the Judas trees were whispering in the breeze.

Wasps . . . wasps . . . wasps . . . Amelia Thomas is just the same as those wasps . . . emotionally retarded . . . stunted . . . incapable of being part of the human race . . . wasp hearts beating, tiny . . . feeble . . .

Oh, yes, her ever-ready imagination soon turned the sibilant hiss of the branches into words that would torment her. Finally she did sleep property but her dreams were disturbing: a mosaic of Judas trees that whispered in code; or of wasps that crawled across the mutilated faces of the statues downstairs; or of the moon sinking into the heart of the island; or sometimes some weird confabulation of all those images. Statues. Wasps. Moon. Judas trees reaching out bony branches to invade her bedroom . . . to curl around her throat . . .

At seven o'clock Amelia sat bolt upright in bed. The sun hurled shafts of light through the muslin curtains, filling the room with a hard brilliance.

Her mind was sharp. She was wide awake.

And she felt angry. That anger worked inside her; it was a source of energy; it made her too restless to stay any longer in bed.

Deciding the last thing she wanted was to sit down to breakfast with the other three women she scrubbed her face in the bathroom, attacked her teeth with the brush, spat fiercely into the sink, then dressed in shorts and a T-shirt.

After that she stuffed a canvas beach bag with her swimsuit, a towel, a paperback novel, sun lotion and a comb.

As she left her bedroom she realized that no one else was up. Quickly she grabbed a breakfast of fruit juice and bread. Then she added a bunch of grapes and a bottle of water to the beach bag.

She was ready to simply pull on her trainers and march away from the villa without letting anyone know where she'd gone. But, again, common sense nagged her hard enough to accept the possibility that the three women hadn't been laughing scornfully about her the night before as they played cards.

Grudgingly Amelia wrote a note saying she was going exploring; she looked at it for a while, then added a deliberately cheerful PS to the effect that she'd taken provisions with her – she wouldn't starve – and that she was going to make a day of it.

After putting the note under a lemon on the kitchen table so it would be easily found she left the villa by the back door.

The sun raked the patio with its light. The pool was perfectly still, the sky cloudless. And there on the patio table was the errant blue-handled corkscrew.

'So, you've been out for a night on the town with your friends,' she told it sharply. 'I can't say I blame you.'

With that she slipped on her sunglasses before taking the path that led between the two funeral cypresses into the heart of the island.

Summer had come early to Voros. Despite it being only March (and early in the morning, to boot) the sun packed a fierce punch. Grey rocks threw back both the heat and the light until it felt as if she was walking into a huge furnace.

Amelia picked her way down the rocky path. Behind her the villa was a shuttered, brooding entity lodged on its high plateau.

For a moment she wondered if anyone was watching her from the windows. Then she told herself she didn't care if they were and turned her back square to it, as if scorning the villa and its occupants.

Again the conviction came to her that she was somehow out of step with the rest of the world.

To say the whole world's against me smacks of paranoia, she thought. *But ever since the accident it feels as if I've become an outsider. And the harder I try to fit back in again, the worse it seems to get.*

She remembered being a child at school concerts. When the audience were invited to clap along with the music, there'd been a stodgy-looking girl who could never clap in time with the band. Now she knew what it felt like. The world clapped to one rhythm, she to another.

When she'd first arrived on Voros she'd thought, 'I'm home.' She'd especially liked Lucy. Now she felt betrayed; as if companionship had been hung tantalizingly in front of her, only to be twitched away again.

A lizard darted away in front of her with a flick of its green tail.

Amelia noticed more of the creatures standing on rocks at either side of her, their tongues flicking out of their mouths as they tasted the morning air. *Lucky lizards*, she thought; they could lie in the sun all day. No one judged them.

She walked on. The path was hard going. At times she had to climb up near-vertical sections of rock before picking up the track again. Then there would be sections where she had to crouch until she was nearly sitting in the dust before shuffling down a particularly steep slope.

All around her were the Judas trees. With the tallest being

no more than shoulder height she again wondered how Judas Iscariot had managed to hang himself from the slender branches. Perhaps it was a mad thought but, like some Christmas-cracker novelty puzzle, the conundrum intrigued her, and she found her mind returning to it again and again; imagining the remorseful man searching through the trees for a branch high and strong enough to support his weight when he tied the noose to it.

And the Judas trees themselves, despite the sunshine, were stubbornly refusing to blossom. They remained a mass of black branches. At times whole areas of the island looked as if they were covered with prickly porcupine-like spines because of the leafless trees.

At some points the path took her to a cliff edge. Mostly Amelia saw sea surging around rocks when she looked down. But every now and then she spied a villa resting on a flat platform. White boxes topped with red tile, they looked like toy houses from this height.

She'd still seen no people that morning. When she did see figures standing in what she took to be a cornfield on a flat stretch of low-lying land she stared at them in surprise. They looked as if they were the congregation of some weird open-air church. And they were waiting for the service to begin, or for a miracle to take place in the skies above their heads; or for something, anyway.

It took a moment or so for the penny to drop. Then she realized: they were scarecrows. Their large yellow heads made them look like sunflowers, and each scarecrow body was clad in brightly coloured clothes.

After a while she found a deep ravine in the rock. Cube-shaped boulders had broken away from the side. The appearance was of big grey cushions scattered on a dried-up river bed.

Although they were far from comfortable Amelia chose one to sit on. There she read her book, nibbled grapes and occasionally sipped her water for most of the morning.

If anything it was the solitude that appealed to her. She could see no one; no one could see her. Her only companions were the lizards – and they didn't judge her.

*   *   *

During the morning Amelia could move between shade and sun. Then, as the sun rose in the sky, the shadows shrank to nothing. As there were no trees, with the exception of a pair of stunted Judas trees, she decided to head off down to the sea where there was a good chance it would be cooler.

As she followed the twisting path again over rocks and boulders, down through narrow ravines, she found she could smell Voros. The heat was intense enough to force the herbs and pine trees to express their aromas. So the air was soon heavy with exotic scents.

As she walked, she noticed lines of bees threading their way at around knee height across the ground. They didn't fly just anywhere. Instead they followed very narrow flight paths.

Bee highways, she mused. Those knee-high aerial tracks were very clearly delineated, very purposeful, as if the bees were prohibited from straying from them by their queen. Consequently, she could see surreal patterns of these miniature flight paths right across the island, the thousands of flying bees forming what looked like shimmering purple veins across the landscape. It was all very bizarre.

Also Amelia couldn't help but wonder whether, if she broke through one of these bee highways with her legs, the insects would fall on her in a buzzing hoard and sting her savagely.

With that in mind she avoided the airborne streams of bees and headed down hill. After five minutes' near-vertical descent she found herself on a rocky ledge just a foot or so above the sea. It was far cooler there.

In a moment she'd unpacked her beach bag again, laid out the towel on the flat stone and taken out her book, what remained of the grapes, the bottle of water, and her swimsuit which she laid out over a boulder behind her.

The sea made a sizzling sound as it slid over partly submerged stones.

What were Lucy, Rachel and Catherine doing now? Stirring pots and muttering curses? Or sitting on the sofas and rocking

SIMON CLARK

back and forth, racked by scornful laughter? Wishing simply
that their guest would take up her passport and go?

But where would she go, now the welcome mat had been
pulled from beneath her feet? Not back to that drab northern
town as a tenant-cum-prisoner of her uncle and aunt?

Could she take the ferry to one of the neighbouring islands
and find a summer job in a bar?

Or should she just walk into the water at this very moment
and let the currents carry her out to sea where she'd swim and
she'd swim until she couldn't swim another stroke, and then
the undertow would exert its deadly force, drawing her—

'Lady! Lady! Here! Come here!'

Startled, she looked up.

A man of around thirty was glaring down at her from the
rocks above. He held both hands down towards her.

There was something manic about the eyes. She found
herself staring up in shock.

'Lady!'

He gestured for her to reach up and take his hands.

She looked at him searchingly for a moment.

It's Bill, she thought, startled. *Only it's Bill transformed
somehow.* His hair had been shaved; his eyes bulged in what
she could only describe as a kind of enraged passion; the
forehead was wrinkled – impossibly wrinkled into corrugations
of hard skin. Now there was something monstrously apelike
about him.

And he wanted her to come to him.

'Here!'

She shrank back against the rock as his voice echoed
shockingly from the rocks.

'HERE! HERE! HERE!'

Her head throbbed, the ache firing up above her left eye.

And suddenly she realized the truth.

'You're not real,' she told the apparition, remembering her
doctor's advice. 'You're not real, you're not real.'

But the apparition didn't dissolve into thin air. It stayed
concretely there: muscular arms; skin darkly tanned; forehead

146

wrinkling: apelike: angry; the animal passion twisting its face into something ugly.

She wanted to cry out.

The apparition bellowed. *'HERE . . . HERE!'*

'Go away!'

'Here!'

'Best do as he says.' The third voice was gentler.

'Bill?'

'At your service, Miss Thomas.'

From behind the apelike man came another one very much like him. Only there was nothing exaggerated about this one's features. Nothing coarse or distorted. The hair was curly and the forehead smooth; a pair of black eyebrows formed heavy arches above good-natured eyes.

Even so, he looked concerned and held out his hand.

'Quickly, Miss Thomas.' He nodded behind her and added inexplicably, 'The water's turned white.'

'White?' She looked back, not knowing what on earth he meant. 'The water's white?'

'Yes. Please gather up your towel and book and pass them to Gregoriou. *Quickly.*'

The urgency in his voice was enough to put her in gear. Quickly she stuffed her towel and book into the bag, then handed it to the apelike man whom Bill had referred to as Gregoriou.

So that must be the mysterious Simotas brother? Understanding clicked at last. Hence the strong, albeit distorted family resemblance.

As Amelia handed the bag to the man, Bill grabbed her by the wrists. His ferryman arms were powerful and in a second he'd lifted her from the low-lying stone platform and drawn her up towards him.

'Now back here,' he told her. 'No, not to the right – up, up, up.' He pushed her up the rocky slope for another good five or six feet before saying, 'OK, OK, this should do it.'

'But what's wrong with—'

'Look, *look*. Here it comes!'

She looked back into the rocky cove. The cliffs formed an enclosure, with only the narrowest of gaps between the rock walls opening out to the sea. At that moment she still didn't know what she was supposed to be seeing. And yet she did notice that the sea had indeed turned white, whereas before it had been a greeny-blue.

The water grew even whiter – if such a thing was possible: it was the whiteness of milk fresh from the fridge.

She guessed the change in colour had to be caused by particles suspended in the sea water. Or maybe it was literally fizzing with tiny bubbles.

Captivated, she watched as the entire body of water within the cove appeared to rise in the centre. Soon a bulge had formed in the surface, perhaps thirty yards from where they stood. In turn, this began to move towards them.

Was it a whale? Moving at a terrific speed under the water, the bow wave thrown up by its torpedo-like forward motion surging ahead of it?

'My God . . .' Amelia breathed.

A moment later the bulge transformed itself into a great curling wave that slammed against the slab of rock on which she'd been lying.

Foaming water cascaded over the slab with a roaring sound. The grapes and bottle of water, which she hadn't had time to save, were swept from sight.

Seconds later the deluge slid back from the rock, retreating down natural stone channels to pour noisily into the sea. Soon the noise dwindled, leaving nothing more than a dripping sound.

'Wow,' was all that Amelia could manage.

Bill wiped his forehead as if a major disaster had been averted. 'Phew . . . you're too near the caves. When the water goes white here you must get away from the shore quickly.'

'The caves? My mother told me about them.'

'Then I'm surprised she didn't warn you about this place. It's dangerous; very, very dangerous . . . we nearly lost you then.'

Amelia cast a glance back down at the stone slab on which

she'd been lying. And she was reminded of what her mother had said about Greek male bravado. The water pouring over the slab might have been a little more than two feet deep. Certainly she'd have got wet; the book might have been ruined; but she was sure that would have been the extent of the tragedy.

Bill's brother held out the canvas bag to her. His forehead still wrinkled furiously, while his brown eyes fastened themselves on her, fascinated.

'Thank you,' she said, taking the bag.

'This is my brother, Gregoriou Simotas.' He didn't introduce Amelia to him.

'I'm pleased to meet you, Gregoriou.' She held out her hand.

'Oh, he won't shake hands or talk to you,' Bill spoke in a suddenly carefree way. 'In fact, just now was the most I've heard him say in months.' Bill smiled, showing his white teeth. 'You must have had quite an effect on him.'

A little nervously now, Amelia smiled at the brother. The man's brown apelike eyes looked fully into hers. Then he looked away, suddenly shy.

'You certainly had a close shave there.' Bill sounded as if he wished to make the most of the rescue. 'Did you save everything?'

'Yes . . . well, everything but a few grapes.'

'Well, that's a small price to pay the gods of the sea, eh?' His brown eyes twinkled. 'But, of course, the grapes will be underground by now.'

'Underground? How?'

He looked back out to sea. 'Can you see between the two cliffs out there at the entrance of the cove?'

She nodded.

'There is a lip of rock underwater there before it drops sheer, perhaps a thousand feet to the bottom. In that underwater rock face there are many caves. Some of them open up into the cove itself, just out there beyond the boulders. Every so often the ocean piles itself up against the underwater ledge – you know, tide, currents? Then she comes surging up through passageways in the rock and erupts into this cove.' He made a kind of exploding-depth-charge gesture with his strong brown hands. Amelia noticed Gregoriou echoing the gesture, his brown eyes dramatic. 'Then the sea boils, and the force of the surge builds into a big wave which it throws against the shore . . . you were very lucky, Miss Thomas.'

Amelia smiled. 'Thanks again, I'm very grateful. But please drop the "Miss Thomas". I'm Amelia.'

'Amelia,' Bill said, pleased.

During the brief exchange Gregoriou had quickly returned to the stone slab near the sea and collected her swimsuit from the boulder she'd left it on. Holding it in front of him by the strap, as if it was a fragile vase rather than fabric, he climbed back up the slope towards them.

'Give the lady her swimsuit, Gregoriou,' Bill said and smiled at Amelia as if to say 'He means no harm, he can't help it.'

She took it, thanked him, and quickly pushed it into her bag.

Bill glanced at his watch. 'Mother will be wanting the firewood,' he said to Gregoriou. 'You'd best be getting back.'

With a reluctant look back at Amelia with his expressive brown eyes the man turned and moved quickly up the cliff and out of sight.

'Well,' Bill said smiling. 'How are you finding Voros?'

'Dramatic. Beautiful. But difficult to get around.'

'Ah, there are easier pathways if you know them. Have you seen all the sights yet?'

'Some, I guess, but I keep losing my way.'

His face brightened. 'Why don't I give you a short tour of the island. If you're not doing anything else, that is?'

She smiled at the mixture of enthusiasm and boyish eagerness in his bright eyes.

'Why not?' she said, smiling.

He held out his arm for her to take. 'Then we will fearlessly explore together. Amelia, I have some wonders for you to behold.'

Chapter Eighteen

For the next hour or so they walked along the spine of the tiny island. Bill enthusiastically pointed out features for Amelia to admire. She soon realized that Bill loved Voros. He showed her rocks that reminded him of film stars or animals. Mostly she didn't see any resemblance at all and she guessed the similarities were mainly in the eye of the beholder, like with people who could see clouds in the shapes of horses or dolphins.

Perhaps the only rock that did look like any kind of animal was a lion-shaped boulder at the far end of the island. As large as a truck, it reminded her of the Great Sphinx in Egypt. Only this gazed across ocean, not desert.

'There are no villages on the island?' she asked as they clambered down a near-vertical rock slab.

He laughed, amused. 'No, Voros is tiny. There are as many households as our Lord had disciples.'

'Twelve?' she hazarded.

He nodded. 'All belong to foreigners. Except ours – the Simotas farm.'

'But, if you don't mind me saying so, you don't have a Greek accent.'

'That's because I've lived always among you foreigners.'

'Surely you went to school?'

He held out his hand to help her over a narrow ravine which, although she could step easily across, disappeared into darkness underground.

'Bottomless,' he said, smiling as he noticed her look apprehensively down into it. 'Now we go down here . . . no, don't follow the path; use those rocks as steps. Much quicker . . . ah, school,' he said, taking up the thread of the conversation again. 'I went to an English-language school on Lesbos. I find it easier to speak English than Greek.'

'Did all your family go to school there?'

'No. My parents never went to school and as for my brother, well, you saw him. He didn't go to school either. Ah, Amelia. Keep away from where the thyme grows thickly . . . snakes. They lie under the thyme.'

Quickly she sidestepped to where there was no vegetation and continued down the natural formation of steps.

Now the two of them made body contact as if it was second nature. Bill would reach out to take her hand or arm to guide her down a tricky section of ground. Or Amelia would reach out to him to be helped over one of the many narrow crevasses that ran across the island like cracks in an old plate.

'This is our farmland,' he told her as they reached a low-lying and comparatively flat stretch of the island. He nodded towards groves of trees. 'Pistachio and olive,' he told her. 'Across there are mastic trees; once the resin from them was used to flavour chewing gum, now it's used for medicine.' He coughed and pointed at his throat to indicate it was used in cough mixture.

Soon they passed through neatly hoed fields. The soil was stony but looked fertile enough to support the small dark-leafed plants growing in lines.

'Tobacco,' he said proudly. 'Best tobacco in Greece. We sell to Switzerland for . . .' Although his English was perfect, and hardly accented at all, he had a habit of not completing sentences verbally but finishing with a mime. When he'd told her they sold the tobacco to Switzerland he suddenly adopted the pose of an aristocrat smoking what must have been a connoisseurs' cigarette or cigar. Perhaps that came with living with his all but mute brother. She could imagine them communicating by gestures and mime rather than speech.

In the tobacco fields she saw the scarecrows again with their

extravagantly large yellow heads. They were the best-dressed
scarecrows she'd ever seen. One wore a dinner jacket, another
a bright crimson cocktail dress.

Isolation breeds eccentricity, Amelia told herself.

But she found herself warming to Bill Simotas. His face was
open, boyish, his enthusiasm for his beloved Voros infectious.
She was already summing him up as a Jack the lad; someone
without a serious bone in his body.

Moments later they came upon what she took to be a fish
tank at the intersection of two paths.

Again she was prepared to be amused by the island eccentricity. A glass fish tank on a timber stand in the middle of a
field? How deliciously peculiar.

Then she realized it was a wayside shrine. One of the
thousands of little shrines that dotted Greece from the mainland
to the remotest island. Usually little larger than a TV set, and
made entirely of glass, they contained portraits of the Madonna
and Child or of saints, usually with a gilded Greek Orthodox
cross that glittered like gold. They also contained an oil lamp
that, although not noticeable by day, filled the glass box with
an amber light when darkness fell.

Without a doubt, she told herself, there was something
both romantic and deeply mystical about coming across one
of these illuminated cases after dark; a box of golden light with
their icons and crosses glittering like some kind of beacon for
lost spirits.

Suddenly Bill's flippant persona vanished. Alarmed, he hurried towards the tank, muttering under his breath. She couldn't
tell if he was swearing or praying.

She watched him open a hinged glass panel, then reach in
where a box of matches had been tucked away. His lips moving
as he murmured quickly, he relit the oil lamp. Perhaps it had
blown out in the night. Then he replaced the matches, closed
the glass door and crossed himself.

Amelia found herself touched by the man's religious devo-
tion. It had been a side of him hidden to her. Seeing his concern
that the shrine wasn't as it should be was oddly moving, like

watching someone's unexpected kindness to an animal or to a lost child.

She moved a little closer to the shrine so she could see into it. Bill by this time had taken a clean handkerchief from his pocket and was tenderly wiping the glass free of dust.

Inside, there were the gilded Orthodox cross and the lamp, its oil held in a rose-coloured glass container. Unusually, in this shrine there was no picture of Mary with the Infant Jesus. There was, however, a single large icon that portrayed a fierce-looking man who had the bearing of a priest. Certainly he had the stern beard and side-whiskers of an Orthodox patriarch.

Bill noticed her looking at the painting.

Seriously, he said, 'Saint Demetrius. Born on the island; died on the island. When the Turks attacked us he sank their fleet with his prayers. The only survivor was the Sultan Pasha. He was condemned to sieve stones from our fields until the day he died.' After crossing himself again he smiled at her. 'Now . . . it is too hot to walk much further.' Taking her by the arm, he said in a low voice. 'Can you keep a secret?'

'It depends what kind of secret.'

'I think you can.' He studied her face for a moment. 'After all, you are one of us now.'

She smiled. 'Are you sure? I'm only a tourist, after all.'

'No, you're not, Amelia. You are a resident of Voros.'

'I might not be here for long.'

'People who come to Voros either go immediately or they never leave. I believe you will stay here forever.'

'I don't know . . . I thought I might be here a month at the most.'

'OK. Let Saint Demetrius show you the way.'

'Pardon?'

She saw now he wasn't smiling; that serious side had reasserted itself. 'See?' He bent down and picked up a rock. 'Throw this at the shrine.'

She was shocked. 'No, I can't do that.'

'Yes, you can.'

'I couldn't.'

'Try and break the glass with the rock.'

'No, Bill, that's not funny.'

'I'm not joking. Throw the rock.'

'But why?'

'If you throw the rock and smash the glass it means Saint Demetrius knows you are not meant to be here; that you are an intruder and will bring only discord and unhappiness; and you will leave the island soon. If you miss, then his spirit has deflected the stone . . .'

'No, wait a minute, Bill, I—'

'You do not believe in the divinity of our saint?'

'Bill, I don't think this is fair. I don't want to risk breaking the glass.'

'And if his spirit deflects the stone then he is embracing you, Amelia. And once embraced by his spirit you will stay on the island: for ever and ever, amen.'

It's a childish initiation ceremony, she told herself. *He knows I don't want to hurt his feelings. But equally I wouldn't dream of throwing a stone at his treasured shrine. He knows that instead I'd deliberately aim to miss. And when the stone misses the shrine then I'm saying I've accepted the Voros way of life. That I'm here to stay.*

When all was said and done, it was nothing more than a crude way of manipulating someone's emotions.

He held out the stone. 'So?'

OK, she told herself, *humour him. You can't be so choosy about your friends these days. You broke your noodle, remember.*

She took the stone. He nodded seriously, as if this were a sacred ceremony and he'd just handed her some holy object.

'Wish me luck.' Her voice was tight and she asked herself, *My God, why am I playing along with him? I'll be mortified if I break the bloody thing!*

He nodded again, then stood there, feet apart, his arms folded, waiting.

Again this seemed as much a ritual to her as a christening or – or even a funeral, come to that. Bill's expression was one of grave sympathy as much as anything. As if her next action was in the lap of the gods. And nothing less than momentous.

Now this is simple, she told herself. *All you have to do is throw the stone wide.* She could (or at least she could before the accident) throw hard and accurately; now all she had to do was fake a weak, girlie kind of throw. Then they could go and do something else.

Like sit on a swing while he sings you love songs . . .

Quelling the flippant train of thought, Amelia eyed the glass box containing the bearded saint and the Cross. It was about thirty paces away. If anything it would take some skill to hit the thing. Missing by a mile was the easy part.

She hefted the stone again, judging its weight. She'd throw to the left – a long, long way to the left. That way it wouldn't look to Bill, from his angle, to be a deliberately lousy throw. Then his brand of trial by divine judgment would be satisfied.

She pulled back her arm. Then she threw the stone. Even as her arm whipped forward a kind of spasm snapped through her biceps.

She even twisted her head to look at her arm in surprise as it gave an exaggerated twitch. If anything it launched the stone far harder than she'd intended. What was more, she saw the ball of grey rock fly out in the air, not in a straight line, but in a curve that took it to the right.

Oh, God . . . Oh, my dear God, what have I done?

The words flashed through her head at least three times while the stone sliced through the air as if it had been fired from a catapult. At her side she heard Bill draw breath in shock.

Oh, God, no . . .

Chapter Nineteen

Amelia willed the rock to fall short.

But it flew like a swift, grey missile along the sunlit path. Its trajectory would take it directly into the saint's glass shrine.

At the last moment she shut her eyes.

A split second later she heard a loud cracking sound.

Beside her, Bill Simotas whispered, 'My God.'

She opened her eyes, blinked against the glare of sunlight and steeled herself for the sight of the glass box lying shattered on the ground, with the saint's icon and the cross spilled in the dirt.

Dear God. Amelia blinked, looked again. The glass was intact. She sighed with relief.

Bill walked forward on the balls of his feet, staring at an object lying on the ground.

'Amelia,' he said loudly. *'Come here: there's something you should see.'*

Slowly, she went towards the case with a sense of trepidation. She imagined that when she was close enough she'd see a crack in the glass after all.

'Look.' He reached down and, between finger and thumb, picked up an object from the ground. It was as long as a bootlace and as thick as her finger.

'See the yellow tail?' He looked at her. 'It's a viper.'

'You're not telling me I killed it with the stone?'

He nodded soberly. 'Killed it stone dead. It must have been

climbing up the leg of the shrine. The rock you threw struck it here.' With his free hand he touched the back of his head.

'Lucky shot, I guess.'

'Perhaps someone else was guiding your hand when you threw the rock, no?'

After looking into the face of the snake as if to make sure it was dead he threw it contemptuously into a ditch at the side of the track. 'The ants will make a good supper of him,' Bill said smiling back at Amelia.

'Was it poisonous?'

'Very. And we have no serum. But Saint Demetrius was standing by your shoulder when you threw. That is a powerful omen.'

She smiled weakly. The stone had hit the leg of the shrine; of that she could be sure. But whether it had actually struck the snake was another matter. The reptile might have been lying there dead on the ground all along.

For a moment she was going to suggest her suspicion to Bill. But he looked so pleased with what appeared to be the rock's divine death stroke that she decided to let the matter lie.

For a moment Bill busied himself happily with the shrine, affectionately wiping it once more with his handkerchief, trimming the oil lamp so it burned a little brighter, brushing a dead mosquito from the saint's icon itself.

The fierce-looking saint with the thunderous eyes had worked another miracle. Now Bill Simotas was going to lavish extra care on the shrine, making sure it was so clean that it gleamed.

When he was satisfied, he closed the glass door. 'I asked you if you could keep a secret, Amelia. I know the answer now.' He looked at her. 'You will, there's no doubt about it.' He nodded at the rock she'd thrown. 'We have a sign.'

'Well, I don't know—'

'You will keep it because you have a special place in Voros's heart.'

He's BS-ing me, she thought; *along with the snake and this business about some kind of divine acceptance by that sinister-looking saint in the glass shrine. All pure BS. It's all part of the game. Now came the next part. Being entrusted with the GREAT BIG SECRET. All part of the initiation ceremony Simotas-style.*

Perhaps she was going to be shown some hidden valley where the Simotases grew marijuana plants.

'This way,' he said.

For a moment Amelia thought about saying, 'No, I'm tired. I'm going home now.'

But she understood that all Bill wanted was to make her feel as if she belonged to the island and, by association, to him.

Perhaps he's lonely, she thought, as she watched his bronzed legs easily negotiate a stony slope. An all but mute brother and elderly parents were hardly stimulating company for a young man.

'Wait for me,' she called after him and knew she was consenting to whatever secret he showed her. And, what was more, consenting to whatever strings were attached to it.

They walked for little more than five minutes. Soon the ground reared up again into natural formations of rock towers.

After skirting round the bottom of one of these Bill pointed to a rock face. She followed.

There was no path now. She crossed a boulder scree to the cliff. There, Bill pointed to the fold in a rock.

She realized it was the entrance to a cave, a narrow one at that, little more than a slit in the rock and completely invisible from the path.

The sun burned down directly on her now; it felt as if a cap of hot steel rested on her head. A bird screeched somewhere. The harsh sound echoed from the stone towers.

'My secret,' he told her with a hesitant smile. 'Follow me.'

He turned sideways so he could squeeze through the slit. A second later he disappeared from view.

Amelia felt a muted sense of reluctance. But she had come this far . . .

Slipping her beach bag from her shoulder and placing it on the ground at the entrance she followed.

Instead of pitch dark inside there was a soft, yellowish light.

Once her eyes had made the transition from the brilliant sunshine to this soft glow she saw that a shaft of sunlight was falling through a hole in the cave's roof. It was little wider than a torch beam, throwing a small disc of illumination onto the cave floor, but it was bright enough to reveal her surroundings.

Bill stood a little way in front of her; he held out his hand.

She took it and together they walked deeper into the cave.

She knew she should have felt some trepidation at entering the cave with him. But he no longer seemed to be the stranger he'd been just an hour ago. *I can trust him*, she thought. *Who knows? I might even grow to . . .*

Then Amelia closed off the thought as a flush of heat rose to her face.

Don't run before you can walk, girl . . .

Bill led her deeper into the cave. They passed beneath the hole in the ceiling through which the sun poured its rays.

Then they were moving into gloom again.

He nodded ahead. 'What do you think of those?'

Covering the walls and ceiling of the cave were vines. The stems and branches were all as white as bean-sprout shoots, while the leaves were such a pale shade of green that there was barely any colour in them at all.

'What do you think of my secret vine garden?'

'You actually grow grapes in here?'

'No, not grapes.' He smiled. 'They are potatoes.'

'*Potatoes* . . . now you really are making fun of me.'

'No. They are potatoes. Can't you see them? Sure, they're little, little potatoes, no bigger than chickpeas, but they are potatoes.'

'But how do you get them to grow down here?'

'I don't.' He smiled at her, his teeth near-luminous in the reflected light. 'Potatoes were stored here during the war. They sprouted; grew; and they're still growing. Look . . . they've covered the walls and ceiling. So, we're in a room full of potato vines, see?'

She looked at the plants climbing the walls with the potatoes themselves looking more like perfectly white pearls than root vegetables.

'Water seeps through the stone,' he told her. 'The plants climb the walls, the roots work into tiny cracks searching for moisture. Another miracle of Voros, don't you think?'

'It's amazing . . . you'd make the newspapers with this.'

'What, and have people tramping into my . . . *our* private paradise?' He shook his head. 'No, Voros has everyone it needs. It's content with us.'

'Don't worry,' she told him. 'I'll keep your secret.'

'Oh, this isn't the secret. We have to go on further yet.' He looked back at her, his teeth luminous again. 'Frightened?'

Amelia gave a shake of her head.

They pressed on into the shadowed void of the cave.

It grew darker and darker; soon they had left the potato vines behind. The floor began to slope, taking them downhill. She noticed the cave had become much dryer here; beneath her feet was a dust as soft as a carpet of feathers.

Ahead the cave narrowed. And from a tiny hole in the roof another beam of brilliant sunlight shone down. This one was so slender it was little thicker than the barrel of a pencil.

'Now,' Bill announced. 'Here lies my secret.' In the gloom she could see him indicating a large boulder. Moving closer she could see it blocked another section of cave, and yet there was still a small gap between it and the cave roof.

'This is trickier to see, Amelia. You must come close to me. Closer. Put your head alongside mine.'

She did as he asked. His curly hair was crisp against her cheek, his breathing loud in her ear. Ever so loud in the confines of the cave. She heard its rasping echo. It grew louder and louder. For the first time she felt a watery sensation in her legs. The memory of the man's breathing in her ear as he held her above the railway track came pungently back to her. At that moment she wanted to return outside. Her lungs tightened. She needed to breathe fresh air.

'I'm going to show you something that might frighten you at first.' He spoke in a soothing voice. 'But don't be alarmed. Sticks and paper now. Think of them as that. Sticks and paper, yes?'

'I can't see anything.'

'Wait until I catch the light.'

He'd produced a tin lid, either from his pocket or from the rocky ledge nearby. With this he reflected the pencil-thin beam of sunlight into the passageway beyond.

'Think of them as sticks and paper, Amelia . . . just sticks and paper.'

The light reflected by the silvery lid into the void beyond the boulder revealed a hidden chamber.

She looked hard.

Those are teeth, she thought with mild surprise. *And lips.* But what strange lips. They were lips made from paper.

In a rush her eyes adjusted to seeing by the twitchy rays of reflected light. And all at once she realized she was looking at four figures lying side by side on the floor. Each wore a field-grey uniform; a rifle lay lengthways on each of their chests, its muzzle resting just below the chin and its stock between their legs. One figure wore a pair of silver-rimmed glasses; one of the lenses were missing.

Each of the soldiers – for that was what they were – had been desiccated in the dry air until they resembled Egyptian mummies. Their skin ranged in colour from differing shades of browns and yellows to an unearthly metallic green. Their faces were shrivelled but still intact. That shrinkage had pulled back the paper-dry lips, revealing still-white teeth. The same went for their eyes. They, too, were partly open, exposing slivers of dusty white that looked up with a dead gaze at the ceiling.

'I used to think of them as smiling,' Bill said in a whisper. 'That was when I found them as a boy. And I thought one day they would wake up again to protect us if we were invaded by the Turk. What fearsome warriors they'd make, hey, Amelia?' His whispers passed into the chamber beyond, echoed from the wall and came back until it was difficult to tell whether the words came from the man at her side or those mummified corpses in the chamber.

'Who are they?'

'German soldiers. They were stationed here as part of the occupation forces during the war. When they were ordered to surrender by the Allies they knew they'd never see Voros again. So . . .' He glanced at her, his eyes glittering silver in the gloom. 'They chose to stay.'

'You mean they committed suicide?'

Bill nodded. 'They manned one of the big guns on the high ground. Not that there was ever any fighting here. My father said they had a peaceful war. Sometimes I come here and think about their lives and try and guess their names.'

At that moment Amelia felt a tingle run from the bottom of her back to the top of her head.

Before she could stop herself, she said: 'Joe, Erich, Albert and Gunther.'

'My God, Amelia. How can you know their names? You've never been here before.'

With a sense of confidence she repeated the names: 'Joe, Erich, Albert, Gunther.'

As she recited the words that had all the resonance of a black-magic spell she thought about the four names written in concrete above The Palms. And about the four young men who'd come here from a colder climate. And how they'd stayed here so long they knew they could never leave.

Perhaps, she realized, they were a lot like her. And, for some reason, the realization suddenly frightened her.

Chapter Twenty

'Will you come swimming with me tomorrow morning?' Bill Simotas asked Amelia as they walked away from the cave.

She smiled. 'Yes. I'd like that.'

'Right.' He looked pleased. 'I'll come to The Palms for you at ten.'

'OK.'

Grinning, he left her after telling her the quickest way back to the villa.

After the adventures of the day Amelia threaded her way back through the rocks content to face the three other women. She still wondered if they had been talking about her disparagingly the night before, but she couldn't be certain. That uncertainty and spending a day with the likeable Bill Simotas had taken the sting out of the memory somewhat.

The sun continued to burn down. If this was March, what would July be like? You'd be able to fry eggs on the rocks.

A lizard or two scuttled away in front of her. A bluish line of bees threaded itself like some airborne vein across a hillside. She smelt the aroma of sun-hot oregano. Judas trees were perfectly motionless. No breeze stirred their branches.

Are they holding their breaths expectantly? Are they wondering what will happen between Bill and me next?

Smiling, she began the climb to The Palms, which lay on the bedrock like a dozing reptile itself.

*   *   *

Amelia stole into the villa like a thief. Silence filled it. Inside, cool air lay motionless in the rooms. Statues slumbered on their gloomy plinths.

She climbed the stairs. Peeping into the bedrooms, she saw that the three women were all fast asleep.

Not knowing whether to be relieved or disappointed at not being able to speak to them, she went back down to the kitchen. Haricot beans were soaking in a glass bowl, while someone had stuffed a chicken with sliced lemon and surrounded it with a nest of garlic cloves.

She found baked ham in the fridge and cut two thick, pink slices that she laid on a plate. Then she opened up a bread roll down the middle and rubbed it with an unpeeled clove of garlic. Into this she stuffed roughly chopped tomato, cucumber and feta cheese, then dribbled onto it a little olive oil. A jug in the fridge contained iced Nescafé. This had to be one of Rachel Stone's austere creations. She sipped it. Although cold coffee was foul, iced coffee had an aromatic mystique all of its own. She filled a glass with the black liquid.

Amelia ate the frugal meal at the kitchen table, sensing the sleeping presence of the three women in the house. A house that seemed to brood on ideas all of its own.

As she ate, she allowed memories to flow in their own loose association – whether God-given or from some other quarter whatsoever she did not know. Nor did she particularly care. She thought about the surge of white water in the cove. She pictured the ape face of Gregoriou Simotas with his forehead wrinkled into those striking corrugations. And there was Bill, of course: the handsome portrait on the other side of the Simotas family coin. The shrine; the dead viper . . . Mentally, she returned to the cave full of potato vines with light shafting down through the holes in the ceiling. From there her mind's eye smoothly moved further into the cave – deeper, deeper and deeper – to where the four young men lay dry as paper in their self-made tomb. How had they discussed their fate? Who was it that first made the suggestion? 'Let us stay here . . . let us kill ourselves in the cave . . .'

The one who fiddled with his glasses?

The one who ate the melon and spat the seeds over the cliff?

Of course, they must have loved life, mustn't they?

But they'd loved the island more.

Maybe it had loved them, too.

And some who love can never let go.

After lunch Amelia looked in on the three sleeping women again. They were still deeply unconscious. Lucy lay clutching a single leather glove. Catherine lay under a sheet that reached up to her eyebrows. Rachel's sharp nose pointed at the ceiling.

Outside, the sun blazed down onto the patio. The waters of the swimming pool were glassy.

Amelia noticed the blue-handled corkscrew lying on the patio table.

She'd decided to continue her exploration of the island. The urge came upon her to keep walking until some part of her dissolved into it, so she'd leave traces of herself in the trees, grass and rocks. Perhaps then, at last, she would stop feeling so restless.

When the island stops testing me and at last accepts me . . .

Until then she wanted to walk. Crossing and criss-crossing Voros until its landscape no longer held any mystery for her; until it was as familiar to her as the palm of her hand.

When she reached the table she paused, looked at the blue-handled corkscrew, then picked it up. It felt surprisingly light in her hand. Calmly, she drew back her arm and threw it high in the air as hard as she could.

It moved like a spark of silver through the sky. Seconds later she heard a rustle as it vanished into the clump of Judas trees beyond the wall.

The entire island appeared to be sleeping. Amelia visited its villas in turn and, from a distance, spent a moment or so studying each one. Most were greyish in colour, looking as if they'd been extruded from the living rock of the island. Red clay tiles formed the roofs. Most had swimming pools. Most were tidy, with the exception of one that crouched on a horseshoe-shaped plateau that had no view of the sea. This one's walls bore geometric painted shapes. As well as giving the impression of being tiled on the outside it lent the house an overall air of oddness. Perhaps even the villas, along with their owners, eventually surrendered to Voros's power. A power to infuse its inhabitants, whether animate or inanimate, with a certain degree of eccentricity.

Time and time again Amelia lost herself in thickets of Judas trees. Then she had to move slowly through the masses of twig-like branches or risk scratching herself to ribbons. She didn't mind being lost. If anything, there was a certain sense in surrendering control of her life to the island. If the island wished it she'd stay lost forever; if not, it would provide a path for her out of the Judas forest.

Late that afternoon Amelia returned to The Palms. She felt relaxed; the exertion had left her with a 'pumped-dry' feeling.

The sun's intensity had given way to a softer light. Cicadas chirped in the trees. The island was waking from its siesta. The villas that were as much its features as were the eyes and nose and lips of a face were coming to life too. In the garden of the untidy villa with the painted walls, a man in a straw hat sat on a tractor, while piglets rooted through nearby bushes.

At another villa on the edge of the sea a man she recognized as Julius King sat beneath a canvas canopy. He was moving his hands and she heard the sounds of a piano. A sweet melody threaded its way up the hillside to her. She looked again at him. He must have had an electric piano resting on the table but it was too far away to be sure. Then again, perhaps he was playing a recording and simply miming the keyboard actions on the table.

Nevertheless, the music did have a haunting quality. The notes shimmered across a carpet of wild herbs and echoed from rocks before washing down over her. The effect was magical. She lingered for a while before moving reluctantly on.

Ten minutes later she passed between the funeral cypresses and entered the patio of The Palms.

Lucy was there. She shrieked happily when she saw Amelia and rushed towards her. She said that she'd missed her. How was her day? What had she seen? Did she go for a swim? Firing questions at her, Lucy followed her into the lounge. On the table there was a bottle of chilled white wine. Beside it lay the blue-handled corkscrew.

Amelia gazed at it for a moment. She remembered how, still in the − albeit childish − mood for revenge, she'd simply hurled the corkscrew. She recalled how it had twinkled like a star as it hung in the sky before falling into the trees.

Now the corkscrew was back.

Strangely, she felt no surprise. The island made people odd, if not downright eccentric. She was beginning to believe that it had the same power over the laws of physics, too. If there had been any rivers on the island, she wouldn't have put it past them to flow uphill.

Rachel and Catherine came into the room. Politely, they asked Amelia what kind of day she'd had. She never mentioned the mummified soldiers in the cave. And no one referred at all to the blue-handled corkscrew that lay on the table.

Presently, Amelia picked up the implement and opened the bottle of wine. She wondered when someone would mention the corkscrew. No one did. And they talked about nothing in particular until the sun went down.

Chapter Twenty-one

'Did the corkscrew disappear again?' Amelia asked Lucy after dinner.

'Oooh, no, it didn't, as a matter of fact. It was in the drawer in the kitchen, just where it should have been.'

'We must be getting him house-trained. How does this coffee grinder work?'

'Are you plugged in, Amelia?'

'Yes.'

'Hold down the plastic lid while pressing in the button on the side.'

'Got it . . . noisy devil, isn't it?'

'Did you have a lovely time with Bill today? He's a little smasher, isn't he?'

'Very nice, Lucy. He gave me a tour of the island.'

'Oooh . . . you'll tell me everything, won't you?'

Amelia smiled and said, 'We'll see.'

'Ooh, I'll be on tenterhooks now. Boy meets girl. My heart's thumping already. Chocolate mints are in the fridge, dear. Top shelf.'

'I met the brother as well.'

'Uhm, Gregoriou . . . sad, isn't it?'

'Has he always been . . . you know?'

'I believe so, love. I hear he can be a bit of a handful at times but I think he's a good boy in his own way.'

'I can't see the mints, Lucy.'

'Come to think of it, we were running low. I'll put them on the shopping list for Bill.' She beamed. 'See, we'd all starve here if it wasn't for Bill and his little boat. One day a ship would come and find all our bones picked clean.'

Amelia tipped the freshly ground coffee into the paper filter, then switched on the coffee maker. Soon it was gurgling and hissing as it drizzled boiling water onto the coffee.

Lucy looked thoughtful for a moment. 'Amelia, what I'm going to say now isn't intended to alarm you, but if Gregoriou were ever to ask you to go . . . well . . .' She pursed her lips. You know, go for a walk with him, I'd decline politely if I were you. It wouldn't be wise to be in a situation where you're alone with him, hmm?'

'I understand.'

'Like I say, it's not his fault; not his fault at all. And he's better here with his family than locked away in an institution on the mainland. And there's Mrs Oxford, of course.'

'Mrs Oxford?'

'Yes . . . oh, hasn't anyone mentioned her?'

Amelia shook her head.

'She lives with her husband in a villa on the other side of the island. She's completely cuckoo, if you ask me.'

'Oh?'

'Yes, in fact we were just talking about her last night. You know, your mother found a wasps' nest and inside were these wasps that hadn't completed their metamorphosis . . . *metamorphosis,* goodness what a word! Anyway, your mother said how they were stunted, part-formed things, and that summed up Mrs Oxford perfectly. On a mental level, that is: mentally stunted. Certainly not all there; now . . . where did I put the milk jug?'

Amelia didn't show it outwardly, but inwardly she heaved a sigh of relief. *See,* she told herself, *they weren't talking about you after all, were they?* As they'd sat playing cards last night they'd ben talking about poor Mrs Oxford – whoever she was.

Amelia sensed a rush of gratitude towards Lucy who'd inadvertently set the record straight. A smile played on Amelia's lips.

'Thinking about Bill, are we?'

'No.' Amelia laughed; it was a light, happy sound.

Lucy gave her a knowing look. 'Mmm . . . you can't kid your Auntie Lucy.'

'Aunt Lucy my foot, you're not old enough to be my aunt. More like my big sister.'

'My big sister used to pull my hair, so I shan't be that.' Lucy shot Amelia one of her big sunny smiles. 'We'll be best buddies, OK?'

'OK.'

'So, what would you say if Bill asked you for a date?'

'A date? There's nowhere to go.'

'Oh, I don't know, Amelia . . . a romantic moonlit trip on his boat. Bottle of champagne on ice. The moon up above. His charming smile. What would you say to that?'

'Oh, I don't know . . .'

'You *can* date foreign nationals, you know. There's nothing in the Geneva Convention to forbid it.'

Amelia pushed her hair back from her face. 'Maybe I'm not ready to start *seeing* someone just yet.'

'Ouch. Sorry, I'm treading on toes, aren't I, love?'

'Well . . .'

'Oh, me and my big mouth again. You've just broken up with someone and it's still . . .' Lucy dipped her head sympathetically. 'Still hurting.'

Amelia looked at Lucy for a moment. The trust she'd experienced with her before had been restored. She decided to leap in and tell her the truth.

'Lucy. I told you about my fall.'

'Yes. It must have been terrible.'

'It was.' Amelia's voice tightened. 'But there's one thing I never told anyone.'

'Oh?'

'I'd been seeing someone for three months before the attack. At first he was pleasant, considerate and always made me feel the centre of attention; he never forgot anything I told him. I interpreted that as him just being very interested in me.'

'But there was a problem?'

'There was. It soon became clear that he was just too possessive. He became jealous if I went anywhere without him. He'd wait outside work and drive me home. If we weren't seeing each other on a particular evening he'd telephone late at night.'

'Hmm . . . to check if you were still there?'

'Yes.'

'Sounds a bit of a creep.'

'It got that way.'

'And you told him the whole thing was off?'

'Yes. Just a couple of weeks before Christmas.'

'I see.'

Amelia guessed that Lucy did see and knew where the conversation was leading.

'Well . . . he just didn't believe I'd ended the relationship. He said I was joking, or that this was some kind of test of his love; that he didn't care what I said or did, he'd always be there for me.'

'He pestered you?'

'Yes.'

'You told the police?'

'No, I thought they'd label me as some kind of drama queen or something.'

'But he didn't give up?'

'No. There'd be a dozen or so telephone calls a week. Love letters and bunches of flowers left on my doorstep.'

'Sounds ardent.'

'Very. Then, on Christmas Eve, he telephoned me at the office and said that whatever happened he wasn't going to let me go. He sounded as if he'd been drinking. There was a nasty edge to his voice, too, as if he was close to threatening me.'

'But he never did?'

'No, and that was the last I heard of him.'

'Until?'

'No, literally I never heard from him again. But, of course, just over a week later I walked across that damn' railway bridge and . . .' She made a clicking sound with her tongue and tapped her forehead. 'Goodnight, Vienna.'

'So you think your attacker was this man?'

'I think it . . . well . . . I don't know . . . but I have a feeling it was.'

'Mmm . . .' Lucy folded her arms, thinking. 'Did you hear anything about him after the assault?'

'No.'

'But you told the police about your suspicions?'

'No.'

'Oh, Amelia, why not? You might have let him get away scot-free to do it all over again to someone else.'

'Well, the police asked enough questions for them to draw their own conclusions?'

'And?'

'He'd gone.'

'Gone? Gone where?'

'Just vanished.'

'Nobody just vanishes.'

'*He* did. He'd been working as a contractor, installing computer systems, so he lived out of suitcases in hotels. His parents hadn't seen him in years. The police found he'd checked out of his hotel the day before New Year's Eve.'

'Good heavens.'

'So it doesn't need a Sherlock Holmes to deduce who threw Amelia Thomas from the bridge.'

Lucy patted Amelia's arm. 'You're here now, love. And you're safe . . . *safe* . . . remember that.'

'So you see that I'm a bit . . . well, tentative about the idea of rushing into a relationship just yet. I'm certainly not a man-hater by any stretch of the imagination. But I think I just need a bit more of a breathing space. Maybe if—'

'Lucy. Amelia. What are you two gossiping about? Rachel and I are craving a caffeine fix out there.' Catherine breezed through the kitchen. 'We're already on our second cigarette.'

Lucy smiled at Amelia, then said to Catherine, 'Just coming, dear.'

Catherine held the door open for them. 'You might like to bring the coffee out onto the patio. Rachel says there's a wonderful view of the comet.'

'Oh, signs and portents,' Lucy said under her breath. 'Let it be a good omen.'

With that they went out into the cold night air.

Chapter Twenty-two

Scarecrows in the tobacco fields stir in the breeze. A lemon dress sways from the bones of a bamboo skeleton. Above the scarecrow heads the sky is full of stars. Gregoriou Simotas is kneeling before the glass shrine of Saint Demetrius. In the darkness it is a cube filled with a soft, golden light that twinkles on the gilt cross and catches the scowl of the painted saint. Although there is a halo above the saint's head he has the face of a demon. Gregoriou Simotas prays. Both his knees rest on the dirt. The skin of his forehead wrinkles into hard corrugations. A fire in his stomach burns mercilessly. He is afraid of it. He can not put a name to it. But most would recognize that flame as desire.

After working on the ferry boat's engine Bill Simotas has gone to bed early. The engine is slowly but surely shaking itself to pieces. He swore at it, then viciously kicked one of the spark plugs into the sea. Now he sleeps with one hand bunched into a fist.

On the patio at The Palms the four women shiver. Amelia looks up at the comet and says it reminds her of a silver comma hanging there, motionless, in the sky. Lucy comments, 'It's not very big, is it?'
    Dryly Rachel prophesies, 'It'll get bigger.'
    Catherine adds in that characteristic cool voice, 'Comets? They're omens of doom, aren't they?'

Judas trees mutter secretively amongst themselves in the breeze.

And inside the house the statues stand in darkness, each one alone. The stillness is absolute. As if they have sensed momentous events drawing near.

Down at the Rocket House Julius King plays the piano. He's seen the comet, too, suspended there in the constellation of Orion. He too knows that comets are harbingers of destruction and tragedy. The melody he plays is slow, gentle, yet shimmers with a dark melancholy. Although he tries very hard not to weep, tears swell then roll out in silvery streams from his eyes . . . one of which is brown, the other blue.

For the cravings that he felt in times past – the cravings that he thought had gone forever – are back.

Voros lies beneath a new comet. It's seen the heavens change above it; it's seen when no ocean surrounded it, only flat grasslands populated by tusked mastodons that have been extinct for a hundred thousand years. It's seen flood and inundation. It saw when mothers threw their babies into the sea rather than allow them to be carried away to the slave markets by the pirate Barbarossa. It saw when later generations, great-grandparents of the Simotases, evaded reality, then ultimately reinvented it. At bedtime they told their children how babies cast into the water were raised from the deeps on the backs of dolphins. And how St Demetrius hurled his staff into the sea where it became a serpent that devoured the pirates and how it later disgorged pirate gold into a secret cave beneath the island. The children believed the story to be true. And that's all that matters.

On this gin-clear March night Voros, remote from its sister islands, shrouded by Judas trees and blasted by starlight, slumbers on. Some people claim nothing ever happens there. They are wrong. Sometimes an event strikes with no warning whatsoever. An event that will turn lives upside down. Or extinguish them for ever.

* * *

Amelia didn't make it to bed until midnight. She and the others had been standing out on the patio, talking and watching the comet, for longer than they'd intended. The night had turned so chill that the cold had reached the marrow of their bones. So even when she went to bed she felt like a frozen chicken lying there.

Come on, warm up, warm up, she told her icy legs as she rubbed them under the blankets.

Rachel, as always, had been frank. 'The sun during the day is deceptive,' she'd told Amelia. 'During March the temperature can still drop to freezing here on the high parts of the island. I've even found ice on the swimming pool first thing in the morning.'

'And penguins,' Lucy quipped impishly.

Catherine had blown a perfect smoke ring. 'Just a few more days then it will be summer, glorious summer.'

'I can't wait.' Lucy had hugged herself. 'I'm going to toast myself all day long.'

Rachel continued in her courtroom manner, presenting evidence, as it were. 'Winter isn't finished yet. Most islands in the Mediterranean have their own winds, like the sirocco or the meltemi. Sometimes, when they blow for days on end, they drive people mad – literally. Courts here will accept a sirocco blowing as a mitigating circumstance if a man murders his neighbour, for example. Here on Voros we have the Gregale winds.'

'Gregale?'

'Yes. Hard to believe, but they come all the way from the North Atlantic. They turn the sky black as night and when they blow hard nothing but the largest ships can put to sea. The storms have to be seen to be believed.'

Amelia had asked when the winds blew.

'Not long now,' Rachel stated unequivocally. 'Before the end of the month.'

Now Amelia lay in bed experiencing, perhaps, that first vanguard of cold Atlantic air. Certainly she wasn't feeling any warmer.

SIMON CLARK

When her teeth began to chatter she realized she'd never get to sleep like that. She sat up and looked at the bedside clock.

12.33.

It's no use lying here wide awake; you might as well have a hot bath and thaw yourself out.

She climbed out of bed. The marble floor was icy beneath her feet, too. The white muslin curtains around the bed and those across the windows made her think of snow. *Maybe Lucy was right about those penguins. There's probably polar bear out there, too. And Eskimos cutting circular fishing holes in the ice.*

Skin goosing beneath her T-shirt, she approached the window.

I wonder if it's cold enough to see my breath, she thought, slipping the catch.

Opening the door to the balcony admitted the night air. It was sharp as a knife.

She caught her breath and folded her arms high across her chest.

Rachel wasn't wrong. These Voros nights were cutting in March.

What's that?

Startled, Amelia tilted her head to one side, listening.

Was that a man's voice?

A man crying out, frightened, somewhere on the island?

No, surely not. It might have been a dog, its bark distorted by distance and the rocky crags.

Starlight was bright enough to reveal the rock outcrop in front of her, and the pale diagonal scar across its face that were the steps that led to the top. There, illuminated by the stars, would be the concrete platform bearing four names: Joe, Erich, Albert, Gunther, and the palm prints.

What would it be like to go up there by starlight? Perhaps she could suggest that to Bill Simotas one night. *Come climb the steps with me in the dark and we can—*

It is. It's a man crying out. Images flicked before her mind's eye of a man being chased across the stones, crying out in terror . . .

180

She reined in her imagination before listening again.

Silence now.

Even so, she turned to look in towards the heart of the island from where the sound appeared to come.

In the meagre silvery light of the stars she could just make out the jumble of colossal stone cubes that littered the landscape. More points of stone rose into pinnacles. There, lower, were the shadowed places where the ravines formed voids in the rock. In the distance lay the sea. By starlight it looked like molten silver.

As Amelia stood there, her hands resting on the balcony rail, the tiles cold beneath her feet, she saw the sea darken. Then the darkening spread to the land. It was as if its texture had altered. Smoother somehow, something like the hair on a dog's coat becoming flattened.

Puzzled, yet entranced, she watched the metamorphosis of the island before her. Judas trees that had been a froth of sticks and twigs suddenly shrank back against the earth. Clusters of individual branches became a solid mass.

What's happening? she wondered.

Why was the whole landscape changing before her eyes?

Was this the start of the hallucinations again? Was the dream mechanism becoming activated before she was even asleep?

At the edge of the garden the funeral cypress trees bent their pole-like forms towards her — as if they were bowing.

Or, perhaps, were they pointing their tips accusingly at her?

All this is your fault, Amelia, came a voice inside her head. *All your fault. You shouldn't have come. You shouldn't have been the catalyst that will change everything on the island.*

You shouldn't have seen the figure on the patio. The one with something dreadfully wrong with its face.

Darkness gathered over the rocks. In a blue-black cloud that spoke of great density. As if the darkness gathered in on itself so it could—

The fist hit her.

At least, that was what it felt like.

She jerked back. Only her tight grip on the iron rail stopped her from being thrown back through the glass door.

A second later that was swept open.

Behind her the muslin curtains became alive, streaming back into the room like pennants.

It's the storm, she thought, stunned by its ferocity. *The Gregale.*

It streamed up from the sea, flattening Judas trees, whipping the cypresses back and forth, rushing and whooping until it slammed into her again, tearing her long hair back in a scalp-stinging rush. Then it was through the balcony door, stripping the bedding from the mattress, snatching the muslin curtains. Throughout the house she heard the pounding of doors slamming. One after another. It was the sound of a dozen cannon firing in quick succession.

Then—

Silence.

A sudden silence that left Amelia's head spinning and her ears humming.

It's over, she thought.

It's over.

The Judas trees were still. The cypresses straightened.

But it wasn't over.

The wind came back. But this time from the other direction.

All through the house came the concussion of door upon door crashing into frame after frame. Now the wind rushed *through* the house towards her.

In her mind's eye she saw the torrent of air come roaring through the living room downstairs, into the hall, darting at the statues, sweeping across the stone torsos, spiralling round the marble heads, then up the stairs, to the balustrade, to the landing – smashing shut all the bedroom doors.

It would be a wild beast of a thing, leaping, snarling, shaking windows, battering doors.

And if the doors were shut it blasted them open; if open it

swung them shut with enough force to crack the plaster around the frames and shower the floor with flakes of paint.

The wind beast is looking for you, Amelia . . .

No, it isn't; no, it isn't.

Drawing a breath, her eyes wide, she turned to face it. For a second – that seemed like an hour, a week – she stood there, spine pressed to the balcony rail, facing the open doorway to her bedroom.

The bedroom door directly opposite her was closed; a barrier between herself and the raging elemental beast that tore across the landing towards her . . .

—Slip the line around your wrist, Amelia, my love. Let the weight pull you down through the water. Just take it off when you want to return to the surface.

The line cut deep into her skin. She plunged downward. Green water turning black. The pressure in her ears became knife points. Her lungs crushed by the pressure could take no more. I need to breathe, I need to breathe . . .

'Why can't I breathe!' Without knowing why, she cried out the words as her bedroom door burst open.

The torrent of air rushed at her, roaring.

White muslin curtains, after being sucked inward, were now blown outward to whip into her astonished eyes.

A split second later the balcony door swung shut against the jamb. Amelia watched as the glass became a mass of white that billowed out at her. Shattered glass struck her face. And then the air beast threw itself onto her breast.

Chapter Twenty-three

'There . . . does it sting?'

'No.'

'Well, I'll put this antiseptic cream on, anyway. It contains a local anaesthetic so if the feeling comes back it shouldn't keep you awake.'

Catherine smoothed the cream onto the scratch on Amelia's cheek. 'And we've plenty of painkillers of all shapes and sizes and colours.'

'I think I should be OK now.'

'The blind man's lost a hand.' Lucy came into the kitchen holding up a chunk of butter-coloured marble.

'Good.' Catherine dabbed more cream onto Amelia's chin. 'It'll come in handy as a paperweight.'

'Gosh, that's heavy.' Lucy laid the marble fist on a shelf.

Amelia was mortified. 'I'm sorry about the damage . . . the window and the statue. I had no idea that—'

'That the wind could be so strong? Catches us by surprise, too. We lose something every year.'

Lucy walked across, clapping the dust from her hands. 'Last time it was that patio table, remember? A great big timber thing. The wind caught it and . . . whoosh. We never saw it again.'

'That was the year before last, Lucy dear.'

'Oh, was it?'

'Last year the wind blew the door back into the little shepherd boy.'

'Ooh yes, and he lost his you–know–what.'

'And some paperweight *that* makes, I can tell you.'

'Now.' Lucy shimmied across the floor, dressing gown flowing. 'How are you feeling, Amelia?'

'Foolish.'

'Ooh, nonsense, dear.'

'I just stood and watched the storm come up over the island. I should have realized what was happening.'

'You weren't to know, dear.'

'And what's important now . . .' Catherine stopped dabbing the cream and stood back to view the result. 'Is that you're in one piece.'

'I feel all right. A bit bruised on my back where the wind knocked me against the railing.'

'At least the glass didn't go in your eye.'

'I've got the perfect medicine,' Lucy remembered. 'Some brandy that's thirty years old. I found it in the cellar when I first came to live here.'

As Lucy fetched the brandy and Catherine tidied away blood–spotted tissues and the first–aid box, Amelia experimentally stretched her arms and legs. They all ached where she'd been flung down like a doll. But everything worked OK. If anything, she was still stunned by the experience. The blast of air had been so savage it felt as if she'd been hit by a truck. And yet, strangely, it had gone as quickly as it came. Now the winds outside had subsided to a light breeze that did nothing more than set the Judas trees whispering again.

A moment later Rachel appeared with a brush and bucket. 'That's all of it. You were lucky it was safety glass, it shattered into tiny crystals. They couldn't hurt you much.'

Dear God, Amelia thought, *you sound almost disappointed, don't you?*

After tipping the glass into a bin Rachel scrutinized Amelia's face with that clinical gaze of hers. 'No harm done. You were lucky.'

Lucky? All she needed to do was repeat the word a third

time and it would assume all the dark prophecy of a gypsy curse.

Lucy must have overheard as she came back into the kitchen. 'Oh, but she's suffered a humdinger of a shock. She was fortunate not to have gone right over the balcony rail. Do you remember the timber patio table? It took five men to lift it up those steps.'

'Yes, I remember.'

'It just took off in the gales and we never saw it again.'

'I've nailed a board over the opening. But I'd keep the door shut if I were you. The Gregale winds are on their way.'

Amelia gave a nervous smile. 'I thought they were already here.'

'That was just the light starter.' Catherine closed the cupboard. 'The main course comes at the end of March. Then we really do have to batten down the hatches.' She looked at Amelia gravely for a moment, then said, 'Bill is taking the boat in for a refit the day after tomorrow. I can book a hotel room for you on Limnos.'

She's wanting me to go, Amelia told herself. *It's as if I'm some earthbound version of that damned comet. I'm bringing bad luck and disharmony to the island. Now she's waiting for me to make up my mind whether I stay or go.*

Yet, suddenly, she pictured herself on the Limnos beaches. Close by would be tavernas with tourists happily tucking into beer and pizzas; nearby would be the carefree sounds of children playing. The image tantalized . . .

'Righty-oh,' Lucy sang. 'Who's for knockout drops?' She waved the bottle of brandy.

'Let me know what you decide, dear. After all, we will be cut off from the outside world for a good week or so.' Catherine accepted a glass of brandy from Lucy. 'Only don't leave it too late, will you, now?'

The brandy was mightily potent. Fifteen minutes later, Amelia *sans* aches and pains folded herself into bed with a grateful sigh. Catherine and Lucy stayed to check the door was secure and to tidy the wind-battered room.

She heard Lucy ask, 'Amelia? Can I get you anything, love? Amelia?' Only she was too far gone to reply.

Later, much later, she opened her eyes to see Rachel Stone standing over her with a hammer in her hand.

Chapter Twenty-four

The next morning the sting had gone but the aches had started. Amelia's neck was stiff, while her shoulders were so sore anything near to a shrug would have been excruciating. If anything now, she was suffering from whiplash. That tidal wave of air had yanked her backwards with such savagery her ligaments had been stretched beyond the extent of their normal elasticity.

Lucy sailed into the kitchen with a *coo-ee!* 'How are you this morning, love?'

'Fine, thanks.' Amelia smiled, determined never to return to the role of invalid. 'I'm just so sorry I made such a terrible mess.'

'Oh, don't worry about that. Love your shorts, by the way: very sexy. Oooh, is there any tea in the pot?'

'Plenty. And I've made toast and there're a couple of eggs on the boil . . .' She broke off, realizing she was hamming up the I'm-as-right-as-ninepence act. In fact, she wasn't a hundred per cent. The ache in her neck was enough to make her wince every time she turned her head. What was more, the old pain above her left eyebrow was making damn' sure it wouldn't be overtaken by any Johnnie-come-lately aches. Already it had resumed its characteristic drilling sensation in her skull.

'Have you seen any sign of Rachel or Catherine this morning?'

'I think they're in the library.'

'Oh, gosh, yes, it's commodities day. They'll be locked into wheeling and dealing over the Internet, so I don't suppose we'll see them until this afternoon.'

'They actually run a business from here?'

'Yes. Now don't ask me the whys and wherefores . . . mmm, that tea hits the spot, *lovely* . . . as I say, stock-market dealings and whatnot are pure hieroglyphics to me. All I know is they buy low and sell high.' She giggled. 'Give me the spirit world over the commercial world any day. Now that I do understand. Ooh, I think I will try one of those eggs.'

'That storm last night . . . I thought at first it was a big bad ghost coming to tear me to ribbons.'

Lucy suddenly shot Amelia an intense look. 'And did you see anything, you know, *odd?*'

'No, not at all. It was nothing more than a common or garden gale that had blown up.'

'You won't go dismissing it all, will you?'

'What?' Amelia asked innocently.

'You know as well as I do you're psychic.'

'I don't think—'

'Now, now.' Lucy smiled disarmingly. 'It's nothing to be afraid of. And wouldn't you like another string to your bow?'

'Well, I hadn't thought of it like that.'

'You don't have to treat it as if it's a big, mysterious quest for the Holy Grail or anything like that. And, no, I'm not asking you to join me on a religious crusade. Consider being psychic as just another talent to add to your repertoire, like being able to ride a bike or use a computer or speak another language.'

Amelia, smiling, gave a little shake of her head. 'I don't think I've got it.'

'Nonsense, dear. Oooh, the honey's delicious today, isn't it? Mmm . . . cherry blossom, I'm sure of it. Now, where was I? Oh yes, as I was saying, there's no big mystique to being psychic. Everyone's psychic to a certain extent.'

'I can't imagine that I am.'

'Haven't you ever suddenly thought about an old friend for

no apparent reason? Then half an hour later the phone rings and it's them, telephoning you out of the blue?'

'Telepathy?'

'If you like. I'll see to the eggs.'

'Lucy, I'll—'

'No, really. I'm nearest. You butter the soldiers.' Lucy scooped the eggs from the boiling water, then, using her fingers, popped them into the stainless steel eggcups. 'Ooh, ouchie, ouchie – *hot.*'

'I've got them.' Amelia took the eggcups from Lucy so she could blow on her scalded fingertips.

'I'll tell you what's nice . . . sprinkle a tiny, tiny bit of nutmeg onto the soldiers. Really brings out the flavour of the egg . . . Rachel has a word for it: piquant. I don't know where she gets all those highfalutin words from, do you? She must have eaten a dictionary.'

Often Lucy's conversations were difficult to follow. She was apt to flit from subject to subject and back again, like a butterfly sampling nectar from a whole field full of flowers.

'To be psychic you have to practise at it – like learning how to be a good tennis player or mastering the guitar – practice makes perfect. Now, to practise psychometry – you know, where you "read" an object? The best way is to wear someone else's jacket or coat. Just slip it on for a few minutes, then relax, don't think of anything in particular. It won't be long before thoughts and images start slipping into your mind.' She scalped the top off the egg. 'Believe me, thoughts will pop into your head as if someone's just taken your lid off,' she tapped the top of her head, 'and dropped mental snapshots right in.'

'*Lucy* . . . Amelia. Good morning to you both.' Catherine looked in a hurry. And Amelia had the feeling that the greeting directed at Lucy was almost a warning to change the subject. 'How're the scratches, Amelia?'

'They're no trouble at all now. That cream worked perfectly.'

'Good, I'm delighted . . . now, I must love you and leave you. Zinc's tumbling and nickel's soaring, so we want to pounce at just the right time . . . Lucy, could you be a dear and slice some bread? I'm just going to brew up a jug of coffee for us caffeine junkies.'

'I'll get the bread,' Amelia said quickly, again not wanting to be seen as lazy. 'Butter?'

'No, but if you can stick the jar of marmalade on the tray that would be a life-saver. Now, who's left the corkscrew in the fridge?' Catherine glared at it in mock anger. 'Errant thing, you. There . . . if you get out of that we'll call you Houdini.' She popped the corkscrew into a wall cupboard and turned the key.

Lucy sipped her tea. 'Do you have anything exciting on the agenda today, Amelia?'

'I'm going swimming with Bill later this morning.'

'Ooh, lovely.'

'The sun's out, so it looks as if it'll stay fine for you,' Catherine added. 'Best take the cream; salt water could make the scratches sting again. Did you sleep well?'

'Like a log.' At that moment Amelia remembered waking and seeing Rachel standing by the bed, gazing down at her. There'd been a hammer in the woman's hand. 'I feel right as rain now.' She was driving the point home that she was well . . . and hinting heftily enough that they should stop fussing over her.

Catherine picked up the tray with the breakfast things. 'Oh. Don't forget we've got the barbecue at Julius King's place this afternoon at five.'

'Oooh, lovely; he's a devil with a cocktail shaker.'

'And he sings like an angel . . . if he can be chivvied to the piano.'

'I haven't really that much to wear.' Amelia pictured her meagre collection of clothes hanging there forlornly among a forest of empty hangers.

'Don't worry,' Catherine breezed. 'Smart but casual only. Besides . . .' She appraised Amelia's figure. 'We're about the same size. You could wear something of mine if you like.'

'Well, that's a full day for you, love,' Lucy said after

Catherine had gone back to surf the world's stock markets. 'Swimming with the handsome Mr Simotas, and then one of Julius's legendary barbecues.'

Amelia paused for a moment, wondering if Lucy would pick up the strand of the earlier conversation and start talking again about psychometry. (*What an ungainly word,* Amelia thought: *psychometry – it sounds like a test they give you in a mental hospital.*) But perhaps the woman's train of thought had been diverted. Or she'd remembered some promise to Catherine about avoiding the subject.

They drank their tea in silence, while Lucy stared into space, maybe seeing things that others couldn't.

'Does it hurt?'

'No.'

'Not even a little?'

'I'm more resilient than I look.'

Of course it hadn't been long before Bill Simotas had broached the subject of the scratches on Amelia's face. She'd lightly glossed over the incident, merely saying her balcony door had slammed shut in a gust of wind and that the glass had broken.

'It only winged me,' she said, smiling as if it were nothing.

'The one on your cheek is sore?' Then, as they'd sat side by side on the boulder, he'd touched her face. It was a light touch. Gentle. Sympathetic.

Her face tingled at his caress and she thought, *My God . . . can it be over fifteen months since I was touched by a man?* The tingling increased to a kind of fizz that spread through her scalp and down her neck into her spine.

'It doesn't hurt at all,' she reassured him. 'Besides, I've got some cream.'

'You need someone to take care of you, don't you, Amelia?'

She didn't know what to say. But Bill didn't wait for a reply and launched himself from a sitting position into the sea.

She watched him swim under water. He was nothing more

than a shadow slipping over a mosaic of blacks and greens and splashes of turquoise that formed the seabed.

With the question hanging there, somehow filled with so much promise, she watched him, not knowing what to say when he swam back to her.

Sunlight filled the tiny horseshoe bay. The passageway between the cliffs out to the open sea was so narrow she could have stood between it and still touched the two sides with her fingertips; it formed, she saw, a natural swimming pool.

On all sides of her the cliffs rose up sheer. She could have been sitting at the bottom of an upended cylinder.

'Very secluded; very private,' Bill had told her, his brown eyes sparkling beneath the archways of his eyebrows. 'You could swim nude and no one would see you.'

Now Bill trod water and grinned at her.

'Warm?' she asked.

'Refreshing. Very refreshing.'

'Any sharks?'

'Dozens, but I killed them dead . . . all for you.'

'Liar.'

'Me?'

'Yes, you.'

He laughed, exposing his dazzling teeth. The sound rushed around the cylinder of rock in a dizzying echo. Sea birds pitched in with their own calls and soon a symphony of echoes, bird calls and laughter went spinning round and round Amelia's head.

'Now . . .' he called. 'Throw the bread at me.'

'At you?'

'Yes, break it into pieces, then throw it at my head.'

'It'll be my pleasure.'

He trod water, grinning. She sensed his pleasure at being with her. *Perhaps this is as much a tonic for him as it is for me*, she thought, pleased. *Begone, Northern town.* And the brief image of slush-locked streets vanished from her head.

'Throw the bread, Amelia.'

'I will. Just wait until I break it into pieces.'

She tore the stale loaf he'd brought into plum-sized lumps.

'Throw it at my head.'

'Won't stones do instead of bread?'

'My God! A sense of humour as well as beauty.' He laughed. 'And you throw a stone well. You're a killer of evil serpents.'

'Why do you want the bread?'

'I'm to construct a jacuzzi.'

'In the sea?'

'Yes, in the sea.'

'Here goes.' She hurled handfuls of bread.

'Ouch . . . my eye! My eye!'

She stopped, but then saw he was teasing.

Now she aimed for his head; satisfyingly, a hunk of the loaf bounced from his skull.

'Now, come and join me here, Amelia . . . *quick*.'

The water started to bubble around Bill's shoulders. She saw that hundreds of fish had launched themselves at the bread. The effect was certainly like a jacuzzi.

Bill laughed again. 'They tickle like crazy . . . hah! *Like crazy*.'

Amelia slipped off her sweatshirt, adjusted the strap of her swimsuit and jumped in.

The fish momentarily deserted the bread at her explosive entry into the water. But seconds later, as she joined Bill in the centre of the natural pool, they returned to feed frenziedly at the now soggy bread. The biggest of the fish, she saw, were probably no larger than the palm of her hand. Thankfully there was nothing with sharp teeth or poisonous spines.

She trod water, gasping with delight as much as with the cold. The water effervesced like freshly poured champagne around her. Constantly there was the flick of a hundred fish tails against the bare skin of her arms, legs and back.

'Now tell me if you've felt anything like this before?'

She laughed happily. 'Nothing. My God! They get every-where, don't they?'

'As Francis of Assisi was to the birds so we will be to the fish.' Bill scooped a piece of bread from the water and put it in his mouth with most of it jutting out between his lips. Holding the morsel at surface level he waited a second.

With a delicious distaste that bordered on the salacious, Amelia watched as fish nibbled the bread from between his lips. Their cold, glassy eyes appeared to peer into his.

'Try it.' He threw a lump of wet bread at her.

Feeling a giddy excitement, she nipped the soggy mass between her lips and lowered her face into the water.

Fish launched themselves at her. Soon their mouths were against hers as they tugged at the shreds of bread.

A moment later Amelia let the fish finish the bread by themselves. '*God* . . . it's like they're kissing you.'

'You enjoy being kissed by fish?'

'A little too cold-blooded for me.'

'So – fishes' kisses aren't for you?'

'No, not really.'

'Here. Try something warmer.'

Bill surged through the water towards her and put his lips against hers.

He's shy, Amelia thought later. *He kissed me. He held me tight. So tight that we sank through the sea and I thought for a second we'd drown. Now he's almost pretending it hasn't happened.*

Now Bill dived to the seabed and brought pulpy lumps the size of tennis balls to the surface. 'Sponges,' he announced. 'Like the ones you have in the bath.'

'All ours are synthetic.' She smiled as she floated on her back. 'Unless that brown lump turns bright pink when it dries out.'

'Cold?'

'Not now I've got used to the water. Anyway, it's a sun trap down here. Can you feel that heat?'

'In June it will be unbearable down here. But then we can swim in the other bays. There's some good swimming on the north side of the island.'

'Isn't that coastline dangerous?' She was pleased that he'd said *we*; as if he saw them swimming the summer months away together, forever side by side.

'Dangerous? Not really, providing you're careful.' Then, smiling, he added, 'Providing you're with me. Now, I think I'll eat some of the good bread. I've brought olives, too. Hungry?'

She nodded. They swam back to the concrete platform and hoisted themselves out. The concrete was hot to the touch now. Cicadas had begun their chirping in the trees at the top of the cliff; the noise swirled around and around the cylinder of rock until it became a sizzling sound like a TV tuned to a dead channel.

For a moment Amelia watched Bill as he lay there on the platform, the sea water glistening in pearly beads on his chest.

'We'll have to come here again,' she said conversationally.

'Definitely. I'll bring the masks and we can dive.'

'How about the day after tomorrow?'

'Why the day after tomorrow?'

'You're taking the boat into Limnos tomorrow, aren't you?'

Sitting up, Bill grinned. 'Greeks don't like being handcuffed to timetables. Life serves us, we don't serve life. Tomorrow I'll be working on the farm. I've postponed taking in the boat for its refit for another two days . . . besides, my cousin telephoned to say the new engine hasn't arrived yet. He has the second-biggest boat yard in Limnos,' he added by way of explanation. 'He has the contract for the hydrofoils.'

'And he'll bring you back once you've delivered the boat?'

'Oh no. I'll be staying to work on it.'

'I thought you were coming straight back to Voros?'

'Normally, yes. But with the start of the summer season . . .' He gave a regretful shrug. 'My cousin will be busy with the hydrofoils so I need to fit the new engine myself. Then I'll strip the boat of paint, re-caulk the planking and paint her again. What do you think to bright orange? I'll make her look like a boat straight from a Van Gogh painting, yes?'

'Sounds nice,' she said, hiding her disappointment. 'You'll be gone long?'

'Ten days if all goes to plan.'

Amelia remembered what he'd just said about Greeks not being a slave to timetables. Ten days might easily become a fortnight. She experienced an ache of disappointment at him going for so long. The sensation was as sudden as it was unexpected.

Are my feelings running that deep for him already? she asked herself. *I hardly know him, do I? And already I'm pining. And what was that you promised yourself about not rushing into any new relationship? After all, didn't your last lover fling you from a bridge?*

She sat on a sun-warmed boulder and watched Bill break the bread. He passed one half to her and began to eat the other. As he did so he watched the sea, perhaps reading something she could not from the waves gently swelling through the corridor of rock into the bay.

The cicadas chirped on above her. A sweet, high sound that had to be as old as those grey hills themselves.

And, even though she tried to suppress the suspicion, she thought of the groups of single women migrating to the tourist resorts. And she thought of Bill Simotas spending a carefree fortnight away from home. What would he fill his nights with?

Annoyed that she'd had those jealous thoughts, Amelia chewed the bread harder than she needed to. *That's it with your emotions, they gang up and beat the cool sensible part of you to a silly pulp.* She shouldn't be harbouring these jealous feelings, she scolded herself. But she did. And the emotions they aroused weren't pleasant.

She thought of her mother's offer to book her into a hotel on Limnos for a while. What would Bill Simotas's reaction be if she said she would be riding with him on that last ferry out of Voros?

Once more her life was starting to become that bit more complicated.

That afternoon Amelia laid the ground by talking to her mother. Conversationally, she asked about hotels on Limnos, although she didn't add that Bill Simotas would be there at the same time.

Her mother took it as read that Amelia had decided to take a trip to Voros's bigger, livelier neighbour.

'Why not, dear? A fortnight among young people would do you good. And after all, Voros will still be here when you want to come back to it, won't it?'

Rachel Stone chose that moment to appear with the news that the zinc market had started to yo-yo. 'All hands to the helm,' Catherine sighed. 'It looks as if we might be delayed here for an hour or so yet. Would you be a dear and go to Julius's place without us? Offer our excuses, and say we'll be along about six.'

'No problem. I'll go with Lucy.'

Catherine gave that regal look over the top of her sunglasses. 'Lucy's taking a siesta. I think all the excitement last night – and the nightcaps with that rocket fuel she calls brandy – has left her whacked. She's sleeping like a baby.'

'Oh.'

'Don't worry, I'm sure Lucy will be ready to come down with us. Besides, don't worry about Julius: he's an absolute pussy cat. By the by, I nearly forgot to pass on a message from Rachel . . .'

'Catherine . . .' Rachel's voice stalked along the corridor as coldly as a ghost. 'Zinc's falling.'

'Speak of the devil. She said she's sorry if she disturbed you last night but she tacked a couple of longer nails into the board when you were asleep.'

'I didn't hear her.'

'She was concerned the thing might fly off and hit you if the wind sprang up again. Right . . . duty calls.' Catherine sounded brisk. 'Don't forget. Help yourself to whatever you want from my wardrobe. Best avoid anything too flowy, though; it catches on all those thorn bushes that run amok down there. Ciao.'

Chapter Twenty-five

＝━◆━＝

Amelia arrived at the Rocket House in a white dress borrowed from her mother. It was a minute before five and the sun still burned strongly on the rocky crags above Julius King's villa.

Judas trees crouched in the ravines like dark, primordial creatures that, for the time being, slumbered. Waiting.

Every so often a breath of air would touch the spiky branches and their black, humped shapes would stir with the sound of claws scratching on stone.

Amelia carried a bag into which she'd slipped her sandals, along with a torch (essential for the walk back, her mother had said; it would be dark by the time they left). On her feet she wore a pair of trainers for the ten-minute walk along the rocky path.

The Rocket House was as large as The Palms, although it was built at a much lower altitude and much nearer the sea. Amelia glimpsed the water through the surrounding lemon trees, glinting silvery in the clear afternoon light. This villa was much less regal than her mother's and hinted at the bohemian lifestyle of its occupant (or occupants; she didn't know if Julius King lived alone or not). It comprised two storeys beneath a red roof of baked tiles. Black-painted shutters had blistered under the relentless heat of past summers and showed layers of different-coloured paints beneath. Bougainvillaea and a host of other climbing plants snaked up over the walls as far as the eaves. The eaves, in turn, were encrusted with swallows' nests.

Complementing the climbing plants was a profusion of plant pots hanging from iron brackets. Although nothing was much in flower now (with the exception of some tiny yellow crocuses) the place would be riotous with colour in the summer.

All in all, the impression given by the mass of climbing plants and birds' nests covering the upper walls was of nature absorbing the villa; as if Voros was ever so slowly digesting this thing made by man back into itself.

As Amelia walked onto the tiled patio that surrounded a figure eight-shaped swimming pool, Julius King stepped out of the shadows of the house.

'Amelia Thomas.' He sounded delighted to see her. 'I'm so pleased you could come.'

Amelia thanked him for the invitation, adding that her mother and her two housemates would be delayed. She noticed that Julius was as striking as ever. He wore an Indian-style sarong that hid his artificial legs. Complementing that was a collarless shirt with a square neck and iridescent colours that positively hollered *Jazz*.

He moved at a slow, almost, it could be said, stately pace, but in spite of the artificial limbs there was no trace of a limp.

His dark head, so smoothly hairless, caught the reflected light of the pool. His handsome eyes, one blue, one brown, were as brightly intelligent as ever.

Laughing eyes, she thought.

'Welcome to the Rocket House,' Julius said in his refined, accentless voice. 'I've set out easy chairs under the canopy. The sun's surprisingly fierce for March. My . . . what on earth happened to your cheek?'

She repeated the story of the broken glass door again; she kept it low-key.

'Gracious, yes,' he said. 'The Gregale is a wicked piece of work. In times gone by they thought the ground opened up and the storm winds came directly from hell. Of course, that was in pre-Christian times; in those days they thought of hell as being very cold, not very hot as we do today. Forgive me, I'm lecturing. Can I offer you a drink?'

'Lucy says your cocktails are out of this world, but I'd best settle for an orange juice for the moment.'

'Very wise. The night is but young. Ice and lemon?'

'Please.'

They chatted about the island and the villa in general for a while. Julius pointed out an igloo-shaped structure in the garden that had served as a projection house when the eccentric film director Zakarov had lived on the island years before. And a row of little headstones where her pet birds were buried.

When no one else appeared, Amelia figured nobody else lived in the villa. A little while later Julius glanced at his watch.

'Oh. Excuse me for a moment, will you? I must just go and check the oven. It tends to misbehave if it's not watched over. I don't want my pastries to burn.'

Alone on the patio, she strolled round, sipping the juice, looking into the pool where the figure of a trident-bearing man was picked out in mosaic. To one side of the patio a stone balustrade guarded against a sharp drop to the sea, perhaps thirty feet below.

She looked over.

Directly under the villa lay one of the ubiquitous concrete platforms that dotted the coastline. Resting on the sea itself was a dinghy. Strolling back towards the villa again, she glanced through one of the large windows, noticing that the room inside was painted a deep burgundy. Books lined one wall, while an antique gramophone with a brass horn stood on a table. The Edwardian effect was definitely incongruous, contrasting with the Greek setting.

Beneath a canvas awning was yet another table. On this stood an electronic keyboard, and beneath a coral paperweight were pages of printed sheet music. She saw the title of the top one: 'I'll Follow My Secret Heart' by Noel Coward. Carefully, she curled the top of the sheet forward. Below that one was a song entitled 'Voodoo Eyes' by Julius King. And below that another by Julius: 'Ships In The Heat Of The Night'. They were titles that oozed the sultry, smoke-filled atmospheres of long-vanished cabaret bars, where women with white-painted faces smoked their seductive cheroots in the company of Sicilian businessmen.

Suddenly conscious of the fact that if she happened to be glimpsed by her host from window she might appear nosy, Amelia returned to the end of the patio that overlooked the ocean.

There she stood, sipping her iced drink. Strangely, she was very much conscious of her mother's dress that she wore. Although the ice cream-white cotton had been washed that morning, it still retained ghostly traces of her mother's perfume. With every movement Amelia caught the scent of it. Also there was a sense that her mother's tall, elegant figure had shaped the garment.

That should be a ridiculous idea, she told herself; *now, if you wear someone else's shoes you can immediately tell they've moulded to another's feet; people's soles and heels wear the leather in their own idiosyncratic fashion. But of course flexible fabrics like cotton don't mould in such a permanent way.*

Nevertheless, she couldn't escape the sensation that the dress *did* form a cotton cast around her. A cast she didn't quite fit.

Amelia didn't try to shrug off the odd sensation; instead, she allowed her gaze to rest on the sea, enjoying the shades of blue and the way the sea and the sky merged into one with no discernible horizon. In the distance a boat appeared to hover in the sky, until she at last made out that the horizon was much higher than she had first thought.

The air was so still – as if the whole world was holding its breath. If you were to apply a one-word description to it all, she thought, feeling deliciously relaxed, that word would be *serenity*.

The villa behind her was serene. The sea was serene. Even the warship she could see in the distance was serene.

With the glass in her right hand, Amelia absently allowed the fingers of her left to toy with the crisp cotton flaring out from her leg.

At that moment she had the feeling of an object expanding

inside her head. It came with abrupt suddenness. Something firm that grew quickly. It brought back memories of a couple of nights ago when she'd dreamt her bed had somehow lodged itself inside her head and was growing larger and larger . . .

And now it was the ship on the horizon that had dropped anchor inside her. Now it, too, was growing . . . growing . . . pressing against the inner surface of her skull . . . threatening to burst out . . .

No, that's ridiculous. She breathed deeply. Then she made a deliberate effort to fix her gaze on the piece of ice floating in her glass. As soon as she did so, and shifted her concentration, the sensation of pressure inside her head vanished.

Briskly, as if to shake herself awake, Amelia brushed the material of her dress with her free hand.

As her fingers made contact with the fabric she suddenly saw herself looking out through a window into a walled garden. A man – a very old man – was chopping at the soil with a hoe. There was a shocking juxtaposition of images. The man looked nothing less than geriatric, with his bald head sloughing skin as if it had a bad case of sunburn, yet he worked with the tireless vigour of a young man. When he looked up from his work and made eye contact with her he gave something that was closer to a leer than a smile.

She tried to turn away, but that balding head was as fascinating as it was horrible. It held her attention and wouldn't let go. A brown mottling spread between the two horns of hair. Shreds of dead skin peeled from the head, and something like ulcers stood in a red line over the crown of the skull. The man leered; his two eyes locked onto hers. There was a flash of spectral fire there that burned with an unending craving.

Those eyes had been the last thing his victims saw.

Amelia blinked slowly.

The image of the gardener and the walled garden stayed. She saw a door in the wall beyond a rose bed. *'I'm going to walk through that door soon. And I'm never coming back.'*

It came as clear as a real memory.

But I don't know the house, do I? Or the garden? Or the old man?

Yet there was a pungent sense of familiarity to it. As if she'd seen the house, its secret garden and the old man before. Only a long, long time ago.

Now she found herself pinching the cloth near her thigh. She looked down. Her fingernail had turned white with the pressure.

Now the old man's in a room with me. I'm alone with him. It's dark.

There's something like a monkey's paw . . .

Suddenly Amelia had the sensation of cold water rushing around her thighs. Bill Simotas was saying, 'When you've had enough, just slip the loop over your hand; let go of the weight. Then you'll come shooting back to the surface like a rocket . . .'

As if she was in the sea she turned, feeling like she was swimming in slow motion.

A figure had come onto the patio. There was a darkness around him. There was something awful about his face.

She wanted to run into the sea and swim away and never come back . . .

'Oh, careful, my sweet honey-child, you'll have orange juice all down that beautiful dress.'

'Ooops.' She recovered the balance of the glass. She smiled at Julius as he walked in that steady gait of his towards her. 'And I've not even touched a drop of alcohol yet.'

'Amelia, would you like to sit down for a while?' He was smiling but she sensed he was concerned for her. Had she been in the grip of some kind of fit? she thought, suddenly embarrassed. For a moment or so she'd really not been herself.

But Julius didn't indicate that anything overly melodramatic had happened. With a nod he invited her to sit on a stone bench that overlooked the sea. She followed him to it as he chatted.

'I'll light the charcoal in a moment,' he told her. 'That'll allow time for the barbecue to get good and hot before I put on the steaks.' He gave a little chuckle as he sat down. 'Steaks.

That comes from living in America for ten years. I think of steak as being the Rolls-Royce of food. Something essential to serve guests. Oh, you're not vegetarian, are you?'

'No. Steak will be fine.'

Making himself comfortable on the bench, Julius reached beneath the knees of his artificial legs. Amelia heard a click. Then, using his hands, he lifted the legs just above the knee so they folded into a natural position for sitting.

'Rather than just barbecuing slabs of raw meat I have left some overnight in my own marinade; I went mad with the cayenne and chillis so it's guaranteed to make your hair curl.'

'You sound like a man who enjoys good food.'

'Ah, I must confess, my dear, I've reached that age when happiness for me at bedtime is something eggy on a little plate.'

'You don't look old enough.' She laughed, amused by the man's friendly charm.

'Oh, but I am. As old as the hills, I am, I am.' He smiled. 'There I go, heading off into one of my old songs again.'

'You were a cabaret singer?'

'For ten whole years, yes. Out in the desert at Las Vegas.'

'What brought you here to Voros?'

'Ah, that funny thing called fate. Your life is bubbling along just fine. It seems as if it will never alter and what you are doing today you will be doing tomorrow and the next year, and the one after that. But – whooooosh – fate pops along. Then your life changes – just like that.' He snapped his fingers.

'I know the feeling.'

'So, I gave up my life in cabaret and came here to write a book. That will be fifteen years ago this fall.'

'What's it called?'

'The book?' He sipped his drink and considered. 'I don't know. I never did find a title.'

'You've not finished it?'

'Not even chapter one. As I said when I first met you, when you were all Aphrodite-like in the sea, Voros steals your wits.'

She laughed politely.

He smiled wisely. 'It's a kind of happy madness. You don't know you're mad . . . and here you can revel in your eccentricities all day long with no one to tell you to do otherwise.'

'I don't think there's that much to be said for being sane.'

'Precisely, my dear. It is those who are perfectly sane who are driven the maddest by an insane world. More orange juice?'

'Not for the moment, thank you.'

'As you wish. Anyway . . . here I can practise my unbridled eccentricity far from the world's great prying eye.' He sipped his drink. 'I compose opera now. Of course, it's a dirty great conceit. I'm not qualified or talented enough to do so, but I fill my days quite happily. And, even more happily, no one will ever see − nor hear − the finished result.'

'But they might be good. Don't you let anyone hear them?'

'Oh, I suppose those Judas trees over there listen to my efforts.'

'If only trees had ears.'

'I'm sure *those* trees hear and see in their own mysterious way.' Julius smiled. 'There I go again, airing my peculiar notions. But once you've been on Voros long enough, you become convinced that the Judas trees watch your every move, and listen to your every word.'

'While biding their time to betray you?'

'Indeed.' His eyes turned to the trees. 'That comes with naming a tree after Judas Iscariot, the man who betrayed Jesus Christ. Then hanged himself from the selfsame tree. Perhaps some essence of the monster has passed into the tree itself. Now, isn't that enough to plant the seeds of paranoia in anyone's head? Oh, enough of those blasted Judas trees. They know we're talking about them. Just look at the way they're twitching their branches; they're like a wasp's antennae.'

Amelia laughed politely again, as if appreciating his whimsical humour. But she did wonder if thoughts of ever-watchful, ever-listening Judas trees did prey on the man's mind during the dark watches of the night. When the only company he had was the slow beat of his own heart.

And did she sense that, despite Julius's cheeriness, there was a splinter of sadness embedded deep inside him?

She did find herself liking him, and if there was nothing else she could do, at least she could be good company for the evening. Brightly she asked, 'And you've written songs in the past?'

'Yes, my dear, in the long, long ago past.' He looked suddenly wistful. 'Rather more than a hundred, I believe. Sentimental songs, comic songs, quite a few melancholy numbers, too . . . something to pluck the heartstrings.'

'I wouldn't even know how to begin composing music.'

'And I also fancied myself as a jack of all arts in my arrogant youth. I wrote scripts for the stage and movies, too. Now, Amelia, that empty glass is mocking my claims to being a host. Let me get you something.'

'A white wine if you have one.'

'Mmm . . . can I tempt you to something a little different?'

'Well . . .'

'I have some black wine; you must try it.'

'*Black* wine? Is there such a thing?'

'It's only produced on one island in Greece. On Thassos, across there to the north.' He pressed the switch on the back of the artificial legs to lock the knee joints, then pulled himself upright using the balustrade. 'Do you remember the myth of Odysseus?'

She nodded.

'Well, Odysseus, after he was captured by the Cyclops, plied the one-eyed monster with black wine. Then, as it slept off its bender, Odysseus and his comrades sneaked away into the night.'

'But not before blinding the Cyclops with a pointed tree trunk first, if I remember.'

'Spot on.' Julius smiled cheerfully. 'Well, considering the black wine's mythic potency, I'll just give you a small drop at first.'

As he poured the ink-dark wine into a glass he sang softly to himself. Amelia stood with her back to the balustrade to face the villa. Meanwhile the Judas trees muttered amongst themselves.

'Here you are, Amelia dear . . . let me know if you'd like more, but some find it an acquired taste. Ah!' He exclaimed with pleasure. 'Here are the other three ladies . . . love the suit, Catherine . . . silk? Oh yes . . . exquisite, exquisite. And Rachel, delighted to see you, it must be simply ages since you were last here. What a splendid hat! Lucy, dear. Lovely to see you . . . wine? Oh, you shouldn't have, but it looks lovely. By heaven, what delicious-looking sandals, Lucy. You'll have all the sailors positively swooning, my dear.'

Lucy gave one of her characteristic delighted shrieks. 'Goodness, isn't he wicked? Oooh, is that black wine! Gosh, you girls will be carrying me back tonight!'

That more or less set the tone for the barbecue. Julius and Lucy formed a double act, pitching jokes at each other. Although, whereas Julius was charming, urbane and understated, Lucy repeatedly exploded in hysterics of laughter. But it was definitely fun. Amelia found herself joining in the banter. Catherine was her regal self; she smiled often, however, and added dry asides. Rachel, in a cool, long-sleeved blouse, was the most stand-offish of them all. Occasionally, she retreated into herself as if there was some internal question she was still seeking an answer for. Her laser eyes would rest on the patio tiles: she stared at them as unblinking as a snake until Lucy brought her back into the conversation.

As dusk fell, Julius carried out the food. Soon steaks sizzled on the grill above a golden mattress of glowing embers. Seductive aromas of cooking meat filled the air. Every so often he would add a splash of brandy to the steaks, and a great blue and orange fireball would soar into the sky. 'A speciality of the Rocket House,' he murmured. 'Steak a' l'Incendium . . . food of the gods. More black wine, Lucy, sweetheart?'

'Just a touch.'

'Here, darling. Fill your boots, there's plenty more where that came from.'

'Are you trying to get me drunk, Mr King?'

'Most assuredly, Miss Morell. Most assuredly.'

'You rascal. Isn't he a rascal, Catherine!' Then Lucy's great whoop of laughter rang out across the hillside.

Amelia laughed along, too. She'd volunteered to man the barbecue.

So, now armed with a set of tongs, she turned chicken drumsticks, steak, cuts of swordfish and corn cobs; her fingers tingled from the heat of the orange embers.

Every so often Julius would glide into the villa and return with more trays of food. Cucumber, peppers, olives, creamy yogurt dips, bread, black-eyed beans. And tomatoes that must have been giants of their species: they rested in the bowl like enormous red globes.

Julius adopted the persona of a conjuror as he unveiled each successive dish. 'And there's popcorn if anyone wants it – that's my own personal weakness; perverse, I know. I've sprinkled it with sea salt so it's guaranteed to give you a devil of a thirst.'

Above the patio the sky darkened. Stars appeared. At first just in ones and twos. But the next time Amelia happened to glance upwards it looked as if the sky had been sprayed with diamonds. Stars brighter and bigger than she'd ever seen before crammed the heavens. Bats skimmed through the air like swift, dark angels.

And across the darkening face of the island Judas trees whispered. Just for a moment, she saw the humped growths of branches as Julius King had described them. As if they were mysterious, other-worldly beings that had invaded this remote block of stone in the middle of an otherwise empty sea.

And in a second or so of mental displacement, her own mind strangely sidestepped outside herself: in a shift of perspective she saw herself and her companions as if she was looking through whatever weird eyes the Judas trees might bud, should they undergo a freakish twist of evolution. She saw the five creatures cooking meat around their campfire. They babbled in their own coarse tongue and moved to their own inexplicable agenda, the male with the iron legs, the four females devouring the flesh of animals: interlopers, all of them. Trespassers that must be assimilated or destroyed.

My God, it's starting to happen again, she warned herself. Her imagination was as slippery as a greased snake; it didn't take it long to slither free of her grip. Gripping the tongs firmly, she marshalled hunks of sizzling meat into neat lines on the grill.

'Who's for steak?' she asked in a deliberately bright voice. 'I've got two . . . no . . . three ready. One quite well done.'

'Oooh, I'll have that one, if I may,' sang Lucy. 'And is there a very rare one for Rachel?'

Catherine looked up from nibbling on a sliver of carrot. 'Rachel prefers her meat cooked to the point where, on a good day, a vet might just revive it.'

'Not for me,' Lucy laughed. 'I like the edges burnt crispy. There, shall I hold the plate, love? Got it. Ooh, this tzatsiki is delicious, Julius.'

'The secret's in the mint. I crush it just moments before serving, so the sap's as fresh as it could possibly be. Right, who's for more grog? Lucy?'

'He *is* trying to get us drunk,' Lucy giggled girlishly.

'Of course, it's the only way to get you to sing along with me at the piano.'

'No! I'll do nothing of the sort. You could take the rust off railings with my voice.'

'How absurd, my dear. You have a perfectly wonderful voice. Say when.'

'When.'

Julius stopped pouring within a millimetre of the glass's brim. 'You should have been on the stage, Lucy dear.'

'Yes, to sweep up the orange peel afterwards.'

'Of course, in all seriousness, I don't recommend the stage as a career to anyone. Frightfully precarious business, the stage.'

This led Julius and Lucy to duet a verse or two from 'Don't Put Your Daughter On The Stage, Mrs Worthington.'

As the song ended, Lucy dissolved into that bubbling laughter again. 'Didn't you know Noel Coward, Julius?'

'Oh, yes. Extremely well. I swam naked in his swimming pool once. Only to discover he'd invited the Queen Mother and one of her daughters, I forget which one, to tea. Of course, they had tea by the swimming pool and I had to smile, make polite conversation as they nibbled Dundee cake. While *I* trod water in the pool for two hours. No mean feat when one has no legs. You see, for the life of me I couldn't figure out how to extricate myself from the pool while stark, staring naked. And then, when the Queen Mother, the dear lady, finishes tea with Noel she stands and says to me, "How charming to meet you, Mr King, we always love your shows." And then to Noel Coward she says, in a voice as sweet as silver bells, "Thank you for the invitation, Mr Coward. We will remember with fond affection the freshness of your tea. And the clarity of your swimming pool."'

Even Rachel laughed at this one – albeit it quietly.

'Golly, doesn't he tell 'em well.' Lucy was enjoying herself hugely. 'Tell Amelia about the wedding party in Cuba with Fidel Castro.'

'Oh, you know I will, Lucy. I air my anecdotes like people air their bath towels. But first, I'm just going to unearth a bottle of port I've been saving for a special occasion such as this.'

Lucy shimmied across the patio towards Amelia. 'I think I'll try a bit of the swordfish,' she bubbled. 'Isn't it a lovely barbecue?'

'Yes,' Amelia said truthfully. 'I haven't laughed so much in ages.'

'Isn't Julius priceless?'

'Has he really met all these people?'

'Gosh, yes! Arab princes, pop stars, movie stars – you name them. Ooh, those lamb chops look wonderful, too. Can you pop one onto my plate, dear?'

They chatted for a while. Rachel and Catherine had moved across to the other end of the patio to look at the lights of a distant ship.

The air was smoky, wonderfully aromatic. Amelia felt intoxicated as much by the atmosphere as by the exotic-looking black wine.

'Did Julius tell you about the wine?' Lucy asked.

'That it was what Ulysses used to get the Cyclops drunk?'

'It must be good stuff if it makes you sleep through getting your eye poked out.'

Amelia smiled. 'At least he has his corkscrews under control. Not like our little runaway.'

Lucy suddenly looked serious. She gazed at Amelia gravely for a moment before saying, 'I meant to talk to you about that.'

'The corkscrew . . . why?'

'What's happening isn't all that unusual, you know.'

'You mean it's always disappearing and turning up in odd places?'

'Yes.'

'But wasn't Catherine blaming Bill Simotas for that?'

'Well, he's the convenient rational explanation.' Lucy glanced across at Catherine and Rachel to make sure they couldn't overhear. 'But these *things* do happen. No one knows why, but when there is a psychic in a house, even an unwitting psychic, all kinds of inexplicable *things* can start happening.'

'You mean the corkscrew was sort of . . .' Amelia gave a little puzzled shake of her head. '. . . sort of spirited away?'

'If you like, yes. Look, Amelia, take this with a pinch of salt if you like. But I think you should be forewarned. There are two psychic people living in The Palms now – and they are you and I—'

'*Lucy.*' Amelia injected humour into the way she spoke the name in the hope she could turn the whole conversation into a piece of whimsy.

But Lucy remained serious. 'Bear with me, Amelia,' she whispered in a still-friendly way. 'We have two phychics living under one roof. Sometimes it unbalances the equilibrium, then peculiar things happen. We might find the fuses begin to blow for no reason; toilets might flush in the middle of the night when no one's pulled the handle. One day we might get up and find certain kinds of food taste strange, as if they might be going "off" for no real reason. Why, when I was in my teens my mother would go into the kitchen to find the milk bottles upside down on the worktops. When she moved them all the milk rushed out.'

Lucy shook her head, puzzled.

'No one knew how it was done,' Lucy continued earnestly. 'But someone – or something – had somehow managed to turn the bottles full of milk upside down, then removed the foil tops. When they were upside down the rims formed a watertight seal with the worktops. But the second someone moved them, *fff-tt* . . . milk all over the place.'

'You don't really think something like that will happen here?'

'I don't see why not. It's not even that unusual. Happens all the time.' She smiled. 'I sometimes think it's those on t'other side putting on a little show. So we don't forget them.'

'I've not noticed anything that much out of the ordinary. Except for the corkscrew, of course.'

'Perhaps nothing much will happen. You never know. But sometimes it can get a bit noisy. And if you aren't ready for it, it can be alarming.'

'Have you ever been frightened?'

'What, me? Never. But remember when I mentioned my ex? Things started happening around the house that drove him to distraction. He was always complaining that when he was alone in the house he could hear feet running up and down the stairs. And that the cans of beer he bought would taste like vinegar after a day or so. When the hairdryer exploded in his hand that was the final straw: he ran for the hills.' She smiled. 'Forewarned is forearmed, Amelia. If anything does happen it will be short-lived. The equilibrium soon finds its own balance again and everything goes on as before.' She patted Amelia's arm. 'Watch the steak, dear. It's a little bit overdone.'

'Oh, damn.' One steak had burst into flame. Amelia pulled it to one side of the grill, then doused it with wine from her glass.

Lucy gave one of her little secret smiles. 'Any worries and you see your Auntie Lucy, right? Mm . . . I think I'll try that well-done steak with your black-wine dressing.'

At that moment Julius returned. 'Ladies,' he said with that polite charm of his. 'Ladies, can I tempt anyone to sweet?'

'Gosh, we'll all burst, won't we?' Lucy beamed. 'After coffee can we persuade you to play some of your songs for us?'

He smiled. 'Oh, if you insist.'

'We do.'

'Well, I might be able to recall a medley or two,' he allowed.

And that was how the evening wore on. Julius served them a syrup-laden baklava, then coffee and brandy. After that he sat at the piano and played. His shaved head dipped gently to the rhythm of the music; his eyes were closed; and the expression on his face suggested he'd found some link to paradise. Lucy and Rachel sat on chairs facing the piano while Catherine and Amelia leant back against the balustrade with the sea below them.

Moths flitted in and out of the lamplight. Starlight lent a touch of silver here and there to the ocean. Amelia listened with such a sense of well-being. The meal had been wonderful; the black wine of Thassos nothing less than magical. A gentle glow warmed her from head to foot.

If anything, the wash of the waves complemented the sounds of the piano. Between them they wove a seamless melody that rose across the hillside to haunt the silent ravines of the island. There the notes echoed through the dark mass of Judas trees where they finally died.

The sense of presence Amelia had experienced on the balcony of her bedroom a couple of nights ago came smoothly to her. And then as smoothly went. It was something vast and quietly powerful. Perhaps it was the spirit of Voros, calling on its tenants.

No doubt Lucy would have agreed, with a twinkle in her eye.

Amelia smiled to herself. If only the essence of perfect evenings like this could be bottled.

After a while the new comet showed itself in the sky. It hung there like a silver comma among the constellations. She knew a comet was supposed to be an omen of ill fortune. But tonight the serenity was indestructible.

Still smiling to herself, she listened as the music played on.

Chapter Twenty-six

The sun broke like an egg onto the island.

One moment it was a white sphere sitting just above the rock crags in the early-morning mist; then it cracked wide open, spilling a light of pale runny egg-yolk yellow all over the boulders, ravines and cliff faces.

Amelia had lain luxuriously in bed after waking. At last she'd eased herself out of bed. Now she stood on the balcony, watching the sunrise. The dark patches that were the Judas trees at last took on some of the sun's glow; their leafless branches dully reflected the light. And as the light filtered through the branches to wake the cicadas the insects began to sing one by one.

It was a little after seven. Amelia and the others had only got back to the villa at midnight by the light of their torches.

Normally she'd have stayed in bed another hour or so yet. But she was meeting Bill Simotas later that morning, once he'd finished some chores around the farm. And despite her continuing drowsiness she found she couldn't sleep any more. His smile seemed to have screwed its way deep into some corner of her brain.

Smiling to herself, she showered, pulled faces in the mirror until she giggled, then went downstairs to the kitchen, slapping the marble bottoms of the statues as she went.

Everyone should feel this good sometimes, she thought. A sense of anticipation had gripped her. *Something extraordinary's going to happen today,* she realized. *Something special.*

On the kitchen table sat a whole watermelon. Into its dark green skin someone had driven the corkscrew.

She paused to look at it for only a second.

Then, singing to herself, she drew it out.

(*Like King Arthur drawing the sword from the stone*, she declared happily.)

And then, still singing, she made herself breakfast.

There were still another two hours to go before Amelia was due to meet up with Bill at the shrine of St Demetrius. Only now a restlessness had set in.

Leaving the villa, the canvas beach bag over her shoulder, she headed along the high spine of the island. Above her the sky had become an intense blue. There was no breeze. The sun soon made itself felt, the pressure of its heat loosening the scent of the oregano and thyme from the herbs that grew wild there.

She passed through thickets of Judas trees. There it felt like wading through the sea. Even the spiky uppermost branches only reached her shoulders, while below there was a deep liquid shadow through which lacewing flies passed, their wings glinting green like shavings of emerald.

Already the bees were commuting to work along their bee highways. The lines of flying insects formed what looked like an intricate network of blue-black arteries across the landscape.

As Amelia crested a hill she paused to wipe a trickle of perspiration from her eye. Heavens above, she would certainly be ready for that plunge into the sea. Already she imagined the tingle of morning-cool water against her skin.

Why not shock Bill, she thought wickedly; *why don't you suggest we swim naked today?*

Grinning at the mental picture of his surprised expression, she walked on.

On impulse, she took the right-hand fork in the path. It ran down steeply into a gully and for a moment she thought she'd followed a dried-up stream bed by mistake. Beneath her feet were pebbles that rolled, threatening to spill her onto her bottom. Soon, however, it levelled to become a little more path-like.

She stepped over one of the streams of bees, as if she were stepping over a strand of barbed wire; their buzzing sounded like the hum of tiny electric motors.

Ahead of her was a grove of olive trees. The ancient trunks were gnarled, the branches twisted, reminding her of old men being frozen into the same position by a warlock's spell.

She walked through them, passing from shade to sunlight.

Don't stop there, Amelia, you'll be frozen just like them; you'll become a beautiful, long-haired statue, locked there for all eternity.

The flight of fancy amused her. Perhaps this place would inspire her to become a writer. Then she could sit by the pool with a laptop computer and compose stories. At the end of the day Bill would return from working the fields, carrying with him a basket of freshly picked peaches; then they'd eat a simple meal of cheese and salad (not forgetting a glass or two of chilled white wine) by the light of the moon.

Now that was an altogether more appealing flight of fancy.

She stepped over an ant army marching across the path.

Never in a million years would she have thought of spending her life with a farmer. Especially a Greek one. Most of the men she'd dated had come from the slick suit-and-tie world of PR where men drove fast cars, not tractors. And, in turn, those men were driven by ego not sustained by faith. They pursued rewards that were transitory. Here on Voros, people enjoyed lives that were somehow eternal; they were in touch with what was 'real'. Now those men from her PR past suddenly seemed shallow and self-absorbed.

Amelia remembered the way Bill Simotas had so earnestly tended the glass shrine of the saint. The idea of a man of strong morals appealed to her in a way she found surprising. Perhaps in a city a man of Bill's uncomplicated character might seem out of place, but here it synchronized itself perfectly with the eternal rhythms of island life.

Still daydreaming, she found herself in a villa's backyard.

'Hello, there!'

A tall man stood beside a tractor with a cloth in his hand. He'd been wiping the headlights. The tractor itself stood beside the villa wall.

'Good morning,' she said. 'Sorry. I was looking for a way down into the cove.'

'Oh, not to worry,' the man said, giving the headlight glass one last polish. 'Just cut down by the side of the villa. If you follow the flight of steps to the right it'll take you down to the sea. Not that it's wonderful swimming down there . . . too many sharp rocks. *There!* Clean as a new pin.'

The man stood back to admire the tractor's paintwork that shone like a ripe, red apple. 'Beautiful, isn't she?'

'It's a lovely-looking machine,' she said, unsure how to compliment a man on his beloved tractor. 'Is it new?'

'No, seven years this spring, and not a mark on her. *Not one.*' He wiped a dust speck from the mudguard with his fingernail. 'Lovely day, isn't it? You can feel the ozone going in there.' He slapped his chest with a hand. 'Wonderful, wonderful.'

For a moment or so Amelia made polite conversation about the weather.

She'd seen the man before from the top of the hill. His was the villa with the untidy backyard and the walls painted in charcoal squares to resemble tiles. As she talked she heard a rustling in the undergrowth. That had to be the piglets she'd seen a few days ago. Now they nosed unseen under the bushes.

The man was thirty-ish, tall, fair-haired and wore a straw hat with a striped band. His voice suggested he could be, or perhaps might have once been, an army officer. It was very how-now-brown-cow and belonged to a man who sipped whisky and soda in some oak-panelled officers' club.

'Of course, now we're waiting for that blasted Gregale,' he told her, nodding at the sky. 'No point in doing anything much until that's been and blown itself out because it leaves such a blasted mess.'

'I've heard about it; it's supposed to be pretty ferocious, isn't it?'

'Blasted ferocious. Never seen it?'

'Only what someone called a light starter the other night, though it was fierce enough for me. I'm new here.'

'Oh, a newcomer? Jolly good. We don't get many of those. Must get you to meet the wife. She loves a good gossip about the outside world.'

'Of course.'

'Just a thought, why don't you have a cup of tea with us?'

'Well . . .'

'I was just about to brew up, anyway. Grab a pew.'

He nodded toward a rickety bench.

'Thank you.'

Amelia didn't really want to stay, but to make an excuse now to go would seem downright antisocial. After all, if she was to fit into this tiny microcosm of society on the island she must make the effort.

Gingerly she sat on the bench. It rocked back. She found she had to lean forward to stop it from tipping backwards.

'There . . . made that myself. Good piece of timber, that.' He gave the bench a sharp nod as if acknowledging sterling work from one of his infantrymen. 'Good show. Now, I'll rustle up some tea.' He went to one of the villa windows and spoke to someone inside. 'Got a visitor. Newcomer to the island. Could you run to a pot of tea?'

Then he returned to stare at the tractor for a moment.

As he admired the machine Amelia suddenly realized something strange. *What on earth does he do with the tractor? There aren't any fields near by.* The villa lay at the bottom of a rocky slope beyond perhaps two dozen olive trees. And where was there a lane or even a track leading away from the villa that the tractor could use?

For a moment she puzzled over the mystery as the man looked over his tractor. At last he gave the big back tyre an approving, even loving pat. 'Damn good machine, this. But then, I like to see a good tractor. Best one I've seen recently is a Massey-Ferguson, on Samos. It belongs to the monastery there. Big, beautiful brute it is. You could have hitched this villa to the tow bar and dragged it across to the other side of the island.' He gave a satisfied nod. 'I love to see a good tractor. Nothing like watching a tractor cut a field of prime-quality hay.' He had a habit of talking in a way that made it seem he was talking to himself.

Amelia found herself nodding politely but unsure whether she should make a comment.

And should I introduce myself? I don't even know his name.

He sniffed. 'I said to Simotas the other day: "Mr Simotas, you could take a crop of hay off that top field; waste of good hay ploughing it in like that. I'd cut it myself for a couple of gallons of diesel. Of course, he's got no way of baling it. But I told him he could use that shack of his in the vineyard as a hayloft.' The man sniffed the air again. 'But if he doesn't ask me soon the Gregale will come and it'll pluck every blade of grass out of the field and scatter it somewhere over Turkey. In fact, if he got himself a good tractor – something like this,' he patted a fat tyre, 'he could plough that soil much deeper. Then he could plant spuds. Now, you can't go wrong with spuds. Not like his tobacco: that can be eaten down to the stalks by any old insect that comes along. If you get a wind from the south-east it can bring the locusts in and they'll eat everything that's green.'

Without interrupting his talk the man suddenly made a lunge for the bushes. He drew something out that gave a thin squeal and kicked its legs. Why the man had suddenly chosen that moment to snatch a piglet from the shrubbery God alone knew. She watched baffled, as the pink shape struggled in his arms.

The man continued blandly, 'Now, potatoes can lose a lot of their foliage, can take a hell of a lot of punishment . . . sit there, Tyrone . . . but the spuds underground are unaffected. There's a lot to be said for a good crop of spuds.'

What she'd taken to be a piglet was actually a child. It looked about four years old, but it was the most thickset child she'd ever seen. Although it wouldn't be fair to describe the boy as fat, he reminded her of a section of log. The arms and legs were short but the torso seemed unusually long and thick.

As the man continued talking about seed potatoes the little boy seemed suddenly resigned to sitting there on the bench beside her. The boy said nothing now and didn't even move. He just stared woodenly into space.

Amelia found herself wanting to stare at him but forced herself instead to make eye contact with the man while nodding politely.

Even so, she could see that the little boy beside her had coarse hair that had been so roughly cut it stuck out at different lengths from his head. Sprinkled throughout the hair was what looked to be an equal mixture of cornflakes and blades of grass. If anything, he resembled a very cheap and very badly made doll. Even his nose and ears were only rough-and-ready bud shapes.

As the man talked, she found her eyes travelling back to the bushes where she thought more piglets had been rooting in the grass. There, in the shadows, she glimpsed another child of around three; again, it had hair that looked as if it had been trimmed with a bread knife. It shuffled on all fours with a breadcrust in its mouth.

'Oh, tea. Delicious.' The man nodded in the direction of a frizzy-haired woman in a long skirt. She carried a tray that she set down on the top of a tree stump.

'Isabella's ready for a gossip about what's happening in the outside world. Milk?'

'Please,' Amelia said, although now she was foraging for an excuse to go.

'Milk, Isabella,' the man said. 'Isabella loves it here as much as I do, but I imagine she'd like to visit the shops again.'

Isabella didn't say anything during tea. In a dim light she could have passed for a school teacher. There was the suggestion about her of a university education. Yet she never made eye contact with Amelia and stared into space. And despite what the man said about her being hungry for gossip she never uttered a single word.

Amelia shivered and asked herself: *Why has the light gone from your eye?*

Once the little boy made a snuffling noise. As if in a daze, the woman reached out and stroked his knee.

The man climbed up to sit in the tractor seat where he sipped his tea while staring forward into thin air. 'I was telling our new neighbour here about the tractor. I do love a good tractor, you know . . .'

Amelia experienced a delicious sense of relief when she at last left the villa. The woman remained on the unstable bench; the man still sat high on the tractor.

As Amelia climbed the hill she glanced back, ready to give a neighbourly wave as she gratefully escaped from the place. She noticed the children 'playing' in the bushes. They'd reverted to piglets again. At least, that was what they resembled from this distance.

The man and his wife, however, didn't look up at her so she didn't wave.

Turning away from the family scene below that was, no two ways about it, depressing, she headed for the Simotas farm.

She reached the shrine at ten to twelve. Five minutes later Bill came striding through the olive groves, calling half a dozen 'Good mornings,' a wide smile lighting his face.

As they headed for the cove she told him about her visit.

'Oh.' He raised his dark eyebrows in sympathy. 'Mr and Mrs Oxford and family?'

'Oh, so they're the Oxfords,' she said, remembering over-hearing her mother talking about Mrs Oxford.

'At least now you've met them.'

'Yes. But have you seen the children?'

'Mr Oxford used to own a farm in his own country.' Bill shook his head. 'He was fined by the authorities for spraying with chemicals that are banned.'

'You mean his—'

'Amelia, Amelia. It's a beautiful sunny day. We won't dwell on the Oxfords, yes?'

'Yes.' She smiled. 'I mean, no.'

As he walked, he twisted sideways to show her a mesh bag that contained snorkels and face masks. 'We'll dive today. I have a special place where the sea is as clear as unwatered ouzo. Can you hold your breath?'

'A bit, not that I practise much.'

'You hyperventilate first.' He breathed rapidly in and out. 'Like that. You'll hold your breath for three, four, five minutes; no problem.'

'I don't know if I can manage that long.'

'Nonsense.' He laughed. 'Now we'll do something you'll remember all your life.'

'Sounds adventurous?'

'Why not? We only can die once, yes?'

'Well, if you put it like that, how can I refuse?'

'Good. You'll love it. You'll want more and more.'

By now they'd reached the narrowest part of the island. From the high rock spine they could see the ocean lying far below them, to both their left and right, as if they were crossing a bridge. Gulls glided on the airstreams coming up over the cliffs. In the distance a pair of warships moved, sleek as grey panthers.

Bill saw her looking at them. 'One Turk, one Greek. They like to have their little dances. Now, cut down to the left here, Amelia. Watch the path, it's very steep.'

'Left? But that will take us onto the north side of the island, won't it?'

'Yes.'

'We're going to swim down there?'

'Of course.'

'But I was told it wasn't safe to swim from the north shore.'

He made a *fffft* sound and smiled as if she'd said something cute but babyish. 'Of course it is safe.'

She gazed down uncertainly. The coastline looked as jagged as a serrated knife. 'If you're sure?'

'Of course I'm sure, Amelia.' He flashed her a smile. 'Trust me. You *do* trust me, don't you?'

She nodded and smiled back.

Then she followed him down to the sea.

Chapter Twenty-seven

Amelia thought: *I'm going to die.*

The path to the edge of the sea was nothing less than treacherous. At times she found herself descending near-vertical sections of rock. Yet even here the whip-thin branches of the Judas tree grew out from cracks in the cliff.

Far below the sea frothed white around rocks. Heart thumping, a sheen of fear-induced perspiration slicked her face.

Dear God. This climb was suicidal. And, once more, she thought: *I can't make it. I'm going to die.*

'Nearly there, Amelia.' Bill Simotas brimmed with good-natured confidence. 'Like I said, you'll remember this forever.'

'I will if I break my neck.'

He laughed as if she'd cracked a joke. 'Yes, I suppose you will . . . look, see the lizards?' He nodded at a slab of rock where a dozen or more green lizards basked. 'They're sun worshippers, too . . . just like you foreigners. Now, watch this last section.' He shifted the bag on his shoulder so it wouldn't slip. 'It's a little trickier than the rest.'

'I'll never get down there.'

'Of course you will.'

'How? It's sheer.'

'Amelia, Amelia . . .' He laughed again as if she'd said something amusingly childlike. 'Turn around. Face the rock as you go down. It's like descending a ladder.'

Descending? It's more like a death-defying climb down Mount

Everest, she thought grimly. And, of course, after the swim would come the ascent . . .

'It'll be much better when they install a lift,' she muttered.

'A lift? Yes, much better.' Bill laughed again, the sound echoing up the rock face.

Gingerly, Amelia climbed down the last section of cliff. At one point she grasped hold of the leafless branches of a Judas tree; slender as those of a weeping willow.

'Amelia! No!' Bill shouted so loudly she nearly fell.

'What's wrong?'

'Hold on to the rock, not the branches; otherwise you'll fall.'

'They seem strong enough.'

'Amelia, they don't call it the Judas tree for nothing. It will betray your trust in it, believe me.'

She shot a weak-as-water smile down at him. 'I believe you.' Releasing the thin branch, she found a handhold in the solid rock. By now her legs had begun to shake, while an itch had begun its irritating work between her shoulder blades. But there was no way she could reach to scratch it as she clung to the rock face.

'There must be an easier way, Bill Simotas.'

'There is, Amelia Thomas. We could have just jumped.'

'Very funny. Maybe I'll stick to this way after all.'

A few moments later, to her enormous relief, she was standing on a slab of rock at the edge of the sea.

Now it didn't seem that bad. The sun shone gloriously. The sea, a deep, deep blue, appeared to have the consistency of cooking oil. A thick, viscous liquid that hardly moved.

'Calm as a bell,' Bill announced.

'Clear as a bell, you mean.'

'That too.'

Singing to himself, he began unpacking the bag. There were masks, snorkels and fins. He strapped a plastic-sheathed diver's knife to his calf. Also there in the bottom of the bag was a ball of orange string. It was the tough nylon sort that she imagined could be used to bale hay or repair fishing nets.

For a while he busied himself, laying out diving gear, taking off his T-shirt and shorts to reveal his brilliant red swimming trunks. A gold chain twinkled against the tan of his neck.

Amelia took the opportunity to sit down on the slab of rock, heave off her trainers, then dangle her feet in the sea, relishing the coldness around her toes.

This had to be one of the remotest parts of the island. There were no villas or landing stages anywhere nearby. The coastline of sheer cliffs simply stretched out to her left and right with no sign of any sheltering coves.

While, in front of her, just a couple of feet under the surface of the water, a tongue of pale rock ran straight out to sea like a submerged pier.

Soon she found herself beginning to relax again after the climb. The sun warmed her skin. The gentle lapping of the water soothed her. She was already wearing her swimsuit under her clothes so she slipped off her top and shorts and laid them on a nearby boulder.

High above her a seagull wheeled in the sky. From the top of the cliffs came the distant chirp of the cicada. Could this be anything else but heaven on Earth?

'Now we'll work up an appetite for lunch,' Bill told her. 'Here. Take your gear and follow me.'

She saw that he'd cut a couple of lengths of the orange string that he carried in one hand. In the other he held his mask, snorkel and flippers.

Smiling an affirmative, Amelia picked up the diving gear and followed him. After a few paces he stepped off the slab of rock and into the sea. Then, with the water coming up just over his knees, he began to walk, following the tongue of submerged rock that jutted out from the cliff.

'Don't worry,' he said. 'There are no sea urchins . . . and the stone here is smooth.'

'Where are we going?'

'Trust me. You'll see.'

The tongue of rock was as straight as a road and almost as

wide. At either side of it the water turned suddenly dark. That darkness, she realized, suggested great depths.

'You've been swimming here before?'

'Of course. Since that high.' Implausibly he indicated the height of a three-year-old. 'I could swim as soon as I could walk.'

'It looks deep.'

'It is. That's why we're here.'

'What's the string for?'

'Ah, ha.' Smiling, he tapped the side of his nose.

You silly thing, Amelia, you know the string is so he can tie your hands together behind your back . . .

Stop it, she told her runaway imagination. *Bill's just being playful. There's a perfectly rational explanation for the string.*

Of course there is. He's going to wrap it round your bloody neck and pull like crazy . . .

She bent down and splashed water onto her stomach. Perhaps the shock of the cold would distract her ridiculous imagination as it tried to unnerve her.

I'm nervous because of the deep water. Deep water always makes me nervous. But there's no reason to be nervous, I can swim like a fish. Besides, I trust Bill, don't I?

She remembered the kiss during their first swim together. Was there anything to that? Or, for Bill, was it simply a spontaneous gesture of affection like a slap on the back?

She paused. It seemed an awfully long walk from the shore.

Glancing back, she saw the pale tongue of rock running beneath the water.

To her left and right now there was only the viscous-looking sea surface. She thought: *Any thicker and I'll be able to climb onto it and walk on water.*

What was that?

Just behind her something had splashed. She saw concentric ripples spreading outwards. But only for an instant; it was as if the water was thickening by the moment.

Bill didn't notice – or appeared not to notice, anyway.

He hummed to himself. But this melody didn't sound at all cheerful.

It's probably some hymn of praise to that sinister-looking saint in his glass box, she thought with a shiver. *All praise to you, the priest with the menacing eyes; you sinker of ships; you stifler of babies' cries . . .*

Amelia bit her lip. Her imagination had found a weak spot now; it was boring away there, trying to break her self-control.

A splash came from behind her again.

She turned.

There was nothing there. Only the sea like oil.

'We're here,' he announced with what seemed startling suddenness. 'Ready for our big adventure?'

'Yes.' Her own voice sounded brittle somehow. She smiled and said 'Yes' again, making it sound softer, calmer.

'Good.' He pulled his face mask onto the top of his head. 'We've reached the end of the rock. Down there.' He pointed to an area of water just a step or so away from his feet. 'The ocean bed lies a thousand feet below us.'

Amelia stepped back as if a block of ice had been pressed against her chest. 'The sea's a thousand feet deep? We're going to go diving there?'

'Yes.'

'You're joking, surely?'

'No, that's why we're here.'

'But *that* deep?'

'Of course, that's the general idea, my little pomegranate. Put on your mask.'

'I think I'll watch you first.'

He grinned boyishly. 'You'll do no such thing.'

'But—'

'Amelia, you promised.'

'But I didn't think we'd be diving here on the north side of the island. Especially not into a thousand feet of water.' She'd started talking in a friendly, almost jokey way. But now she felt the colour drain from her face, and the words were coming out through her lips with more force. 'Really, Bill. I don't think I can.'

'Amelia, you said you trusted me.'

'I do. But—'

'Ah, but nothing, my little pomegranate.' Still smiling, he looked at her levelly. 'Believe me . . . trust me, too . . . you'll love it. Now, what do you say?'

She didn't reply.

'Look,' he said gently. 'Now for a geography lesson. Here, in the eastern Mediterranean there is more salt in the sea than in nearly any other ocean. This is because more water is lost through evaporation than is gained through the inflow of rivers. So, if the sea is very salty then it makes you very buoyant. Yes? You couldn't drown here if you tried.' He grinned. 'See . . . taste it.' He cupped his hand and scooped sea water to his lips. 'Ah. Very salty.'

Amelia felt her friendship with Bill now hung in the balance. She didn't want to lose it.

Steeling herself, she said, 'What do I have to do?'

'Good girl. Brave girl!' His grin was so infectious she smiled back. 'Now, here's the clever bit.' Reaching down into the water he pulled out a concrete building block. 'I brought dozens of these by boat and dropped them into a hollow in the rock. It saves me carrying them down that rotten cliff, yes? Hold out your hand.'

She obeyed.

He'd knotted one of the lengths of string so it formed a loop at one end. This loop he slipped over her hand as far as her wrist. The other end he threaded through one of the hollow sections of the block and tied it back firmly to the main length of string.

'There. You're now wedded to your diving weight. Heavy?'

'Yes. Very.'

'Good, this is your express lift to take you down deep. Very deep.'

'Bill—'

'Pull down your face mask, Amelia. Now make sure the weight line is around your wrist.'

'Bill, why can't we just swim? Why do we have to use these concrete weights?'

'We need to sink fast.'

'Why?'

'Think of the exhilaration.'

'I don't think I can hold my breath long enough.'

'You'll manage.'

'Bill—'

'Start taking deep breaths now. Hyperventilate.'

A shadow skimmed across the ocean towards her.

Feeling suddenly cold, she looked up. A dark cloud had slipped across the sky to cover the sun. She glanced back at the island. It seemed far away. A ridiculous distance at that. As if they'd walked miles along some phantom road out to sea.

But they couldn't have. *Not that far, surely?*

'Don't worry,' he was saying. 'I've tied a big loop around your wrist. See. It's very loose. When you've had enough, just slip the loop over your hand; let go of the weight. Then you'll come shooting back to the surface like a rocket. Do you follow?'

A throbbing pain sprang up above her left eyebrow.

God, this is all I need, she thought bleakly. First the pain. Then reality would give way to the rogue images that forever prowled some nether region of her brain . . .

'That's it, Amelia!' Bill yelled in her ear. 'Now take a deep breath. Do it. Yes. That's it. *Now go!*' He might have been helping her . . . If anything, though, it seemed as if he pushed her over the edge; held her for a second (so she could hear the sound of his breathing in her ear); then let her go.

The tongue of rock was gone now.

Cold ocean stabbed like ice. The surface slapped her face mask. Then she was below it. Beneath her was only water. Dark and endless. Without a breath of air to breathe.

The weight line around her wrist dug deep into her skin. She looked at the puckered skin in wonder. The sensation of the string circling her wrist was astonishingly sharp. Like cheesewire.

Any tighter and she could imagine it cutting through her skin, slicing arteries and tendons.

Three feet below her she saw the block of concrete to which she was tethered by the orange line. The block swayed, spun.

Oddly, it could have been a grey balloon, dipping and spinning on a breezy day, tethered to her wrist. Only the downward force it exerted was immense.

She held on desperately to the lungful of air as she rushed downward vertically as if falling from a – a . . .

—*a bridge.*

A bridge that was a thousand feet high.

Water streamed past, tugging at her hair, vibrating the snorkel mouthpiece against her teeth.

Above her she could hear callous laughter. Laughter that was impossible because of the distance to the surface. But laughter nonetheless. Laughter that cackled endlessly, mocking her stupidity.

Below her she could see only a gulf. One that was vast and dark. And deadly . . .

Chapter Twenty-eight

Down she plunged. The speed of the fall towards the sea bed dizzied her.

By this time Amelia was diving head first through the water with her feet trailing somewhere above her.

Every now and then she caught a glimpse of the undersea cliff face that must have lain beneath the tongue of rock. Grey. Pitted with holes that might have been the openings to tunnels. It blurred by her.

Shoals of fish, tiny as teardrops and just as silvery, parted for her to fall through them.

Nothing's going to stop me now, she thought . . . *nothing. I'm going all the way to the bottom. I'm going to fall a thousand feet. I'm going to hit rock bottom. I'm going . . .*

A dark shape moved like a torpedo to her right. Whether it lunged at her or away from her she could not tell.

Hitherto the water had been clear. She'd seen fish; sea horses; there'd been a blood-crimson jellyfish suspended in the water like a polythene bag.

But now visibility closed in. The deeper she plunged, the darker it became. She might as well have been diving into outer space; only this was starless – darker than heart-blood.

Her lungs burnt now with the need for air. Although she tried hard not to, little spurts of breath burst from her lips to bubble by her ears, before running like the hard teeth of a comb back through her streaming hair.

Fish moved aside with flicks of their tails. In front of her the orange line stretched out to the grey concrete block.

Stabbing pains punched through her ears. The water pressure must have been colossal.

It squeezed the air space inside her face mask smaller. It wasn't long before the glass pressed in against the tip of her nose.

How much deeper before the glass implodes?

The need to breathe became a screaming pain inside her chest. Her throat spasmed.

God, I need air, I need air, I need to breathe.

And above this chanted mantra Amelia told herself: *He's tricked me. He lured me out here to make this dive. His only aim was to weigh me down with concrete. Send me on a one-way journey to the ocean floor.*

—need to breathe, I need to breathe, I need to breathe . . .

He's murdered me. He's succeeded where Luke failed.

Another voice struggled from her memory. It was Bill in the sunlight, saying: *'Don't worry. I've tied a big loop around your wrist. See. It's very loose When you've had enough, just slip the loop over your hand; let go of the weight. Then you'll come shooting back to the surface like a rocket . . .'*

Her eyes wide, staring into darkness that rushed at her, engulfing her like some aquatic version of hell, she suddenly knew what she had to do.

She reached out to her right wrist, around which the loop of orange string was tied.

Trying hard to concentrate – trying hard to remain calm – she attempted to slip the string from her wrist.

The string gripped her tightly, digging into her flesh.

She worked at it. The fingers of her left hand, distorted by the water, looked way too big and pulpy. They could have been as thick as bananas as she tried again to slip the string away from her wrist. Once that was gone the block would fall away into darkness and leave her free to soar back to the surface.

Then she was plunged into the middle of a shoal of fish.

These creatures were big, ugly things with downturned mouths and green scales that were dull with moss.

The kind of moss that grows over dead faces in tombs in a post-mortem caul.

The pain in her ears rose to a whistling scream.

Damn that string. He said he'd tied a loose loop. This was nothing of the sort. It had pulled as tight as a hangman's noose.

She looked down beyond the swaying lump of concrete. Whereas before there had only been the fogged darkness of deep water, now a shape had begun to emerge.

A dark oblong that tapered to a point at one end.

Surely she couldn't be a thousand feet deep? Even a diver with their own air supply couldn't reach this depth.

The shape was too regular, too straight-edged to be natural.

—*I need to breathe, I need to breathe, I need to breathe . . .*

The chant inside her head made her renew her attack on the string looped around her wrist. With a huge effort she drove the thumb of her left hand in between the twine and her skin. Gripping the cord she tugged, trying to pull it free.

It stayed there. She might as well have been handcuffed to the concrete block.

Please, I need to breathe . . . I need to BREATHE!

Her lungs were balls of fire inside her chest.

She levered at the string again with her thumb.

Suddenly the loop scraped over her wrist bone, swished over her knuckles. And then it was gone.

Instantly she felt herself stop, turn, then begin to float upwards.

Joy burst through her. She was free of the concrete weight. *I'm going up*, she thought. *I'm going back to the surface.*

But all that way? How deep did I go? If I'm hundreds of feet deep there's no way I'll make it back.

Already whole mouthfuls of air were spurting through her lips.

If only I could hitch a ride on those bubbles, she thought wonderingly as they went spinning and turning to the pale ceiling above her that formed the surface of the sea.

Swim! She knew she must swim if she was to have any chance.

She kicked her legs and pulled at the water in a desperate swimming stroke. It was as if she now climbed through the sea.

If only I could grab hold of the bubbles and let them carry me upwards. If only . . .

Her head oozed with vertigo. What little oxygen remained in her bloodstream was all but gone.

Consciousness was leaving her.

Please, please, I need to breathe . . . I must breathe . . .

An explosion sounded in her ears.

It was the last of the air, erupting out through her mouth and nose. She could hold on to it no longer.

For a second everything fell silent. It was as if in that long-drawn-out moment her existence hung in the balance.

Perhaps God is deciding whether I live or die, she thought distantly. *He's making up His mind now. Perhaps if I'd only made an offering to the saint in his glass box . . . if only I'd promised to give him something of myself . . . anything.*

A brilliant light filled Amelia's world. It seared her eyes. It roared through her skull like a Pentecostal flame.

That was the moment when the underside of the ocean's surface split around her head.

Thunder filled her ears.

Seconds later she realized that the thunder was *her*. She was drawing in huge quantities of air as she trod water, her mask and snorkel torn off in her hand.

A hand seemed to swim out of nowhere to grab her arm, then pull her out onto the tongue of rock. Dizzily she sat there, the water coming up to her elbows. Her breath stuttered through her throat in huge, ragged gasps. Her heart thundered massively.

'Hey, Amelia. Great dive! I watched you go down and down . . . You must have gone down a hundred metres. Maybe more.'

She erupted to her feet, water cascading from her hair and skin to splash back down into the sea. *'You bastard.'* Fury poured through her and she hurled the face mask at him. 'You bastard! You nearly killed me!'

Bill Simotas was all wide-eyed innocence. 'Kill you? Are you crazy?'

'No, I'm not crazy. I nearly drowned . . . you'd tied a bloody slip-knot round my wrist. I couldn't get it off. The damned thing nearly pulled me all the way down to the bottom.'

'Amelia—'

'Don't you "Amelia" me.'

'I tied a slip-knot?'

'Yes. It pulled tight around my wrist.' She showed him the black mark where the noose had tightened. *'See?'*

Bill gestured imploringly. 'No, no, no. You're mistaken. I tied it *slack*. All you needed to do was straighten your hand and . . . *pfft!* the loop would just come away.'

'I'm telling you. It drew tight!'

She began to walk towards the shore, her legs churning water to foam.

'Amelia, my love . . . that's not possible. You must have panicked.'

She ignored him and walked on.

'Amelia. I wouldn't hurt you for the world.'

Still she walked on, surging through the sea, creating a bow wave that moved away in a 'V' from her.

'How about we go out in my boat, yes? We'll go to Limnos. There, I have a cousin with the best restaurant in Greece.'

'No, thank you.' Her voice was ice.

'Why won't you believe me? I wouldn't try to kill you. That would be madness.'

'Everyone on Voros is mad.' She shot him a savage glance. 'That's what Julius King says and, boy oh boy, do I believe him.'

'*Ack!* What does he know? He doesn't know what it's like to be with a woman! He knows nothing!'

She had by this time reached the shore. Dripping, she

climbed out onto the rock and swung her hair fiercely, spattering the boulders.

Grim-faced, Bill climbed out too. He stood with his hands on his hips, watching her as she pulled her clothes on over her wet swimsuit.

His eyebrows formed black arches over his eyes that now narrowed as they regarded her. 'You should dry yourself,' he told her. 'You're wet.'

'Thank you. I know that,' she said with an icy politeness. 'And now I'm going home.'

'Did you really think I would kill you?'

'The line pulled tight around my wrist. I couldn't move it. I thought I was going to drown.' She stuffed the towel back into her bag. 'Can you understand that? What it's like not to be able to breathe?'

'I saw you below me. I was admiring you.'

'Admiring me,' she repeated grimly. 'There's nothing admirable about choking to death.'

'You didn't.'

'No, and no thanks to you.'

Bill still looked at her with all the innocence of a little boy wrongly accused of pilfering from the biscuit tin.

He sat down on a boulder, his legs folded, and stared out to sea. 'I'll stay here.'

'Stay there.'

'I will stay here until I am like those German boys in the cave. Until I'm bones and skin.'

'Stay there until your eyes dry up and fall out for all I care.'

He nodded, solemn. 'I will.'

She pulled on her shoes. No mean feat, considering her feet were still wet.

'Did you see the ship?'

She didn't answer and began to pick at the laces.

'You must have been deep enough,' he prompted.

For the first time since surfacing she noticed that a blanket of cloud now covered the sky from horizon to horizon.

'Amelia, did you see it?'

'Yes, I saw the bloody ship.' She found she couldn't stop a smile reaching her face at the look of hurt and innocence on his face. 'I saw it. I wish I hadn't – but I did.'

'You did well. I myself have only dived that deep a few times before.'

'I didn't feel as if I did well.' She held up her arm with the painful crush mark ringing her wrist.

'Ouch, ouch.' He spoke with consideration. 'You panicked . . .'

'Panicked, my foot.'

'. . . Or I was . . .' He gave a shrug and an apologetic smile. 'Or I was careless.'

Suddenly Amelia felt it impossible to be angry at him.

It's hardly likely that he's taken it into his head to kill me, is it now? she found herself reasoning furiously. *After all, he could have done it just by shoving me off the cliff as we came down here. He wouldn't do something as unnecessarily elaborate as tying the weighted line to my wrist!*

You've been an idiot, Amelia, she scolded herself. *You've become paranoid.*

That comes from breaking your noodle.

She found herself smiling constantly now; she could even almost feel her own eyes twinkling – twinkling outrageously, at that – as she looked at him sitting pixie-like on the boulder. A dark-skinned Greek pixie. With black eyebrows like the overhanging eaves of a house.

He stood up to face her, the sea water beaded on his face and chest. 'Let me see your wrist, you lady foreigner.'

She smiled, feeling a sudden wicked purr inside her chest. 'What? Allow myself to be scrutinized by a rough Greek sailor boy like you? My, what are you thinking of?'

He took her wrist in one hand and ran his fingers over the bruising with the fingers of his left. His touch was gentle and, without a shadow of a doubt, soothing.

'Mmm,' he murmured. 'Better in a day or two. I could crush some strawberries and massage in the juice.'

'That will help?'

'I haven't a clue, but it would be nice to try, mmm?'

She *mmm*-ed back and smiled. It was a warm smile now.

He spoke softly. 'I'm forgiven?'

'I wouldn't go that far.'

'And how far would you go?'

'Well, if you're very nice and contrite I think I—'

'What's wrong?'

'Mmm? There's someone up on that rock across there.'

'Are you sure?'

'Yes. Can't you see them? They're standing next to that piece shaped like a chair. See them?'

'No.'

Amelia tilted her head to one side.

'Perhaps it is my brother,' Bill said carelessly. 'I have work to do. Perhaps my mother sent him here to remind me.'

'No, they weren't . . . they were a different build.'

'You can still see him?'

'No. He's gone.'

Bill looked at her. 'Tricky climb, that; up to that rock.'

'It doesn't matter.' She smiled. 'Now, what was that you were saying about taking me to the best restaurant in Greece?'

'We could go this evening.'

'But could you bring the boat back here in the dark?'

'No need. We can stay at my uncle's.'

Bill grinned.

She found herself grinning back. 'My uncle's . . . my foot.'

He picked a strand of hair from her cheek and pushed it gently back over one shoulder. 'Well,' he asked. 'What is your answer?'

Chapter Twenty-nine

'I said we'd better batten down the hatches, Lucy dear.'

'Ooh, don't you love all this bluff sailor talk, Amelia? Nothing so romantic as a good storm.'

'Romantic, my eye.' Rachel Stone sniffed. 'When the Gregale blows it's a pain in the neck. It turns us into prisoners in our own home.'

'Anyone for coffee?'

Rachel persisted gloomily, 'The phone lines will come down, too. Mark my words.'

Amelia set down the coffee on the living-room table as the three women busied themselves. First they'd taken in the patio furniture, then they'd fastened the upstairs window shutters.

'Best bring in the hanging baskets, too,' Catherine ordered.

'I've already done that.' Lucy beamed.

'Well done, that woman. Rachel, did you get the closing prices on naphtha?'

'It's down two.'

'Good. If the phone lines are still up in the morning we'll move some of the money into it from zinc.'

'If they're still up,' Rachel reiterated gloomily. 'I dread this time of year.'

'Oh, it won't be as bad as that. Who's for my shortbread?'

'Please,' Amelia said and Lucy headed for the kitchen.

Amelia had returned to the villa that afternoon, intending to pack for an overnight stay on Limnos. Bill had arranged to pick her up from the landing stage at five in his boat. He'd gone on to explain that he'd be staying on in Limnos while the boat had its refit, but that his cousin could bring her back to the island the following day.

Amelia had decided to see what the coming hours would bring before reaching a decision about returning to Voros immediately.

Only she hadn't counted on the change in the weather. There was no sign of the gales yet the spiky mass of Judas trees were still. They resembled a plague of hedgehogs, clinging there to the rocks. The cloud, however, hadn't blown over. And even though it was still mid-afternoon the island lay in shadowed gloom.

There's something morbid about the place now, she thought. The gloom lent the rocks and ravines a sinister air. And the swimming pool had become a mirror that reflected the cloud, turning it dark and inky, as if it had been filled with liquid darkness rather than water.

Amelia felt an uneasy stirring in her stomach. *I hope the gales don't come today*, she thought. *If it holds off I'll be on the ferry by five. An hour after that we'll be stepping off the boat onto the harbour at Limnos.*

She allowed herself to imagine the bright lights and even brighter laughter in the taverna. Chickens rotating on spits over a fire; people dancing happily; the wild, twisting melody of a bouzouki. All in all, it would make an energizing start to whatever the night would bring.

Lucy returned with a plateful of golden shortbread. 'The sea's still calm, Amelia.' She scrunched her shoulders up around her ears in delight. 'I'll keep my fingers crossed that it stays fine for you.'

'Can you tell when the Gregale is coming?' Amelia asked.

'Don't worry,' Rachel said. 'I'm sure Bill Simotas won't blow away in the breeze.'

Catherine poured coffee into the cups. 'The early indications are that it's on its way. The cloud's always one sign. But it might be like this for a day or two yet before the winds start to blow in earnest. Milk?'

'But it'll come.' Rachel uttered the words with the profundity of an Old Testament prophecy. 'And when it does it's murder.'

They sat in silence for a moment, drinking coffee. Amelia found her gaze roaming from statue to statue. The broken heads gazed back at her. In the distance a clock ticked away the dead seconds with irritating slowness. Dear God, the next couple of hours were going to be long ones.

Amelia spent the afternoon packing. There was no hurry about it (and she didn't have that much to pack); nevertheless, she spun out the folding of her dress, wiping her sandals with damp tissue paper, checking again her brushes, perfume and toiletries.

After she'd showered, she returned to the bathroom to examine her teeth. They looked strong and white. Nevertheless, she felt an urge to floss them. Come to think of it, her nails, too, needed attention.

Suddenly she realized she was taking pride in her appearance.

That's the first time in fifteen months, she realized wonderingly. It was fifteen long months since she'd painted her nails or applied mascara or chosen a shade of lipstick. And that had been the night of the New Year's Eve party at Andy's where people either crowded into the kitchen to giggle over joints of marijuana or into the living room to watch a TV comedian cheer in the New Year. After that she'd left alone in the dark. She'd taken the short cut across the railway bridge. She'd heard a dog howling. She'd felt hands grab her from behind. She'd—

No. Don't do this to yourself. She looked at the pair of glittering eyes in the mirror. *You don't need to remember all that now. You don't have to think about the hospital. Nor those miserable months in your Aunt Mae's house, with the witch twins and cousin John who was always so eager to destroy your peace of mind. You don't have to remember what you saw mounting the stairs night after terrible night . . . no* – she corrected herself – *what you thought you saw . . .*

Her heart was bumping against her ribs. A throb had begun in the bone above her eye. It was like a tiny motor lodged there; she could feel the beat of its tiny piston.

With a deep breath she snatched at the dental floss and began to clean between her teeth until her gums bled.

Catherine and Lucy saw her off at the front door. Rachel skulked in the kitchen.

'Have a lovely time,' Lucy cried gleefully. 'Paint the town red for me!'

'Don't worry, I will.' Amelia smiled.

Catherine looked over the top of her glasses. 'If you decide to stay on, give us a ring, won't you?'

Amelia said that she would. Fussy as a mother hen, Lucy kissed her on the cheek and squeezed her hands. 'My goodness! My heart's going so fast it could be me going instead of you. Take care now!'

After another round of goodbyes Amelia walked away from the villa with the bag containing her best clothes over her shoulder. For the ferry crossing she'd simply chosen a shirt and jeans.

She headed down the path that took her from the front door of The Palms, now left broodingly alone in the afternoon gloom, to the top of the steps. Cut into solid rock, they zig-zagged down out of sight to the landing stage.

She could have walked down to the Simotas farm and met Bill there. After all, he kept the ferry boat moored at the Simotas landing stage, but it would have meant a longer walk carrying her holdall. At least here it was all downhill.

The grey cleft in the cliff face swallowed her as she went down, concentrating on the steps in front of her.

Now I wouldn't like to come down here in the dark, she told herself. *Put one foot wrong and you'd go tumbling down all the way to the bottom. Besides, you don't know who stands quard on the steps at midnight, do you?*

Why, Amelia, you know it will be the man with the ruined face.

She chased the errant thought out of her head by picturing Bill's grinning face as he rounded the bay, his hand on the tiller of the boat, its motor beating steadily.

And you look good, do you hear, Amelia Thomas? she told herself firmly. *You look the best you've done in months.*

Adrenalin powered her descent. Soon she was standing on the concrete landing stage. The urge to pace up and down was irresistible. She surrendered to it, walking backwards and forwards like a sentry; while all the time her stomach fluttered with excitement.

My God, I'm like a schoolgirl on a first date. Will he come? Won't he come? If he does, will I make a fool of myself? Will I sound crass? Will he like my clothes? Will he notice the spot on my chin? I'm sure there's one coming there; it feels tender. Oh, my God, and here I am rabbiting away nervously. It's the excitement; that's what it is; sheer knee-trembling, butterfly-stomached, heart-in-your-mouth excitement. She smiled, amused by her own thoughts that were nothing less than intoxicating.

As she paced, she let her gaze range up over the grey cliffs. Here and there was the spiky bristle of a Judas tree. Above the battlements of living rock the sky had become dreary and rock-like itself, only its colour was nearer black than grey.

The cicadas had become mute. She saw no birds.

There was still no breeze. The sea retained its cooking-oil appearance, the surface staying smoothly viscous.

Amelia listened for the *putt-putt* of Bill's boat. There was only silence.

A glance at her watch told her it was a little after ten to five. There was plenty of time yet. The adrenalin had made her almost skip down all those steps in record time.

She checked her purse, then looked at her reflection in her pocket mirror. Her eyes were near-luminous, the pupils enormous. Excitement had lit a flame inside her.

She glanced at her watch again. Eight minutes to five.

God, time was dragging itself out.

For the next couple of minutes she imagined what she'd order from the menu in the taverna tonight. *Stuffed vine leaves.*

Mousaka, perhaps? No, keep it light. And don't touch the fish. In fact, avoid all seafood, come to that. She liked octopus deep-fried in breadcrumbs but it didn't like her. Galloping indigestion was the last thing she needed tonight. *Come to that, avoid anything with too much garlic. My God,* she thought, amused, *at this rate you'll be settling for a lettuce salad and hold the dressing.*

At five to five she heard a rustling sound above and behind her.

She turned. The Judas trees that grew from the rock face were twitching their branches. The rustling sound, something like loose papers being rifled through, grew louder and the Judas trees shrank back against the rocks.

'Great, just great,' she murmured.

A body of air was moving across the face of Voros. It rustled through the branches of the trees, and made the carpets of wild herbs ripple like the surface of a green pond.

At that moment she heard the steady beat of the ferry motor. That same familiar sound – like a pan being struck by a large spoon.

As her eyes locked onto the wishbone rock through which the boat had to come she noticed a swell. Waves rose out at sea, squeezed through the twin halves of the rocks, then rolled across the cove toward her. Seconds later they slapped against the concrete platform beneath her feet.

They weren't large. Nevertheless, some were crowned with a curl of foam.

'Great, just great,' she repeated, frustration rising.

Amelia found herself standing on tiptoe, trying to see over a wall of boulders in the hope Bill's boat would be just beyond.

She glanced at her watch. Three minutes to five. Still she could hear the ghost sound of a boat. But there was neither hide nor hair of the thing itself.

Then, at one minute to five, the boat hove into view. Bill swung it so the prow was facing the gap between the wishbone rocks. He was by himself and she felt a sudden glee at the thought of them being alone together.

She watched it chugging towards her.

Hallelujah! So miracles do happen.

Standing higher on tiptoe, she waved. Bill raised his arm to wave enthusiastically back.

In a moment the boat would glide through the wishbone rocks into the cove. Then he'd be standing to help her aboard.

Even at that moment, with the boat still a good hundred yards from her, she was opening her hand in anticipation of clasping Bill's.

She watched the vessel. The engine chugged solidly. Bill worked the tiller. But the wretched thing was getting no nearer.

Damn it. If the boat went any slower it would be going backwards.

Water curled along the craft's flanks. Bill stared ahead of him, his concentration fixed at some point in the cove.

This went on for thirty seconds — a frustrating, irritating thirty seconds at that.

Then she saw Bill shake his head. It was a sudden shake, signifying defeat.

What now?

She watched, bewildered. Why had he turned the boat?

This time when he waved to her it wasn't an exuberant hello, it was a signal.

He'd turned the boat to the left and was waving for her to follow.

Deeply puzzled, she walked quickly along the platform and off it onto a narrow ledge of rock that ran on between the cliff and the sea.

Bill eased the boat along slowly, so it was easy enough to keep pace with him.

But what's he want me to do? she wondered.

Maybe he'd pick her up from the rocks further along the coast?

She followed the rocky ledge just feet above the now-rolling ocean for a good five minutes.

By this time the boat had disappeared behind a series of

rocks rising out of the sea, but just moments later she saw it again. He turned it towards the shore and came within about fifty feet of the rocky ledge.

'Amelia!' He had to shout above the hiss of surf and the sound of the boat's motor. 'Amelia . . . hello?'

'Hello. What's wrong? Why couldn't you come into the bay?'

He gave an expressive shrug. 'The water was against me. It wouldn't let me through . . .' He shrugged again and jerked his head up at the sky. 'The Gregale's coming. It does crazy things to the sea.'

'Bill . . . Bill!' She had to shout above the noise. Also Bill was having trouble controlling the boat. He repeatedly had to wrestle the tiller back and forth while revving the boat's motor.

'See,' he called. 'She's being pulled onto the rocks.'

'Can you pick me up from here?'

'No. See the reef?' He pointed into the sea between the boat and the ledge on which she stood. 'I'm sorry, Amelia. I must go now before the storm hits.'

'Which landing stage shall I go to?'

'Sorry?' He cupped a hand behind his ear.

'Which landing stage? Where will you pick me up?'

Again the apologetic shrug. 'I can't bring the boat back to the island now. Look at the sea . . . she's in a temper.'

'You mean you have to go on without me?'

'I'm sorry, Amelia.'

'Oh . . . *damn.*'

'I'm as annoyed as you are . . . but we'll have to postpone our dinner together tonight. OK?'

Amelia was far from happy, but she didn't show it. She nodded and allowed an understanding smile to come to her face.

'Damned bad luck, eh?' Bill called. 'But don't worry. I'll borrow my cousin's boat and come for you in a couple of days. How's that?'

'That's fine.' She kept the stoic smile on her face.

Then a larger wave tugged at the boat, spinning it on its

axis. 'In a couple of days, then.' He grinned and waved. Then, not risking the proximity of the submerged rocks any longer, he opened up the throttle and the boat surged away from the island.

Amelia waved before retracing her steps along the rock ledge to the platform.

In a few moments the boat had dwindled to a speck. Seconds after that she lost sight of it amongst the waves. The sea wasn't too rough. At least he should make it to Limnos safely. But why oh why couldn't the gales have arrived a few minutes after Bill had? She would have been with him on the boat now. Damn.

Double damn.

She gave the cliff face a slap. 'That's for you and nature conspiring against me,' she told the island.

By the time she reached the concrete platform the waves were sending splashes of foam across it to wet the steps.

She looked up at them before climbing and sighed. 'Well, Voros, you've got me all to yourself for the next couple of days.'

With that, and a frown on her face, Amelia began the long climb back up to The Palms.

Chapter Thirty

'Force majeure.' Catherine made the announcement as they sat down to sandwiches that evening.

'Oh? And what's that?'

Rachel sniffed stonily. '"Force majeure", Lucy. It means "superior force".'

'Oh? Meaning?'

'It means when the forces of nature conspire against one and take away either (a) your capacity to shape events or (b) your ability to prevent certain events happening. Would you pass me the olives, please, Amelia?'

'Well, that's happened to me a few times in the past.' Lucy gave a trill of laughter. 'But most of my forces majeures were man-sized and man-shaped. Ooh, I thought we'd run out of the pickled walnuts. Fancy one, Amelia?'

'We have now,' Rachel stated coolly. 'We'll have to wait until Bill Simotas has the ferry running again before we get any more supplies.'

'We're marooned.' Lucy clapped her hands together, pleased. 'Fancy that. Who's going to be Man Friday?'

Amelia still felt disappointment weighing in her stomach like a stone. 'Doesn't anyone else have a boat?'

'Well, nothing big enough to safely make a sea crossing to another island.'

'Ours is just for hopping round the little coves,' Lucy said, popping the last walnut into her mouth. 'Mmm . . . scrumptious.'

'Bill said he'd be able to borrow his cousin's boat and collect me in a day or two.'

'I wouldn't hold your breath,' Catherine said dryly.

'Once the Gregale gets up nothing can get near Voros.' Rachel carved herself a piece of ham. 'We have waves twenty feet high. Even large ships have been driven onto the rocks when the winds get up.' She looked down her long nose. 'And once they do come they blow for days on end. There's nothing you can do. One might as well go to bed and stay there until it blows itself out.'

Lucy reached across and patted Amelia's knee sympathetically. 'I'm sorry you had your night out spoilt. We three will do our best to put a smile on your face.'

Amelia believed in Lucy's ability to be the life and soul of any party. Rachel, however, was a different kettle of fish. Once more she'd withdrawn, brooding, into her own world, only emerging every now and again to utter a bleak warning about the impending storms.

Catherine was her usual brisk self. 'Do you play cards at all, Amelia?'

'Not much.'

'I'm sure you could pick up blackjack quickly enough. Twenty-one or bust and all that.'

'Yes, I remember that one.'

Her mother looked over the top of her glasses at her. 'I told you Voros would be about as lively as the grave, didn't I?'

'I like it here.' Amelia was determined not to sound self-pitying. OK, yes, she *was* disappointed by the postponement of her dinner date with Bill, but it wasn't the end of the world, was it? 'I'm sure it is a different place once this Gregale has gone and blown itself out.'

'It is. Then it's as quiet as a sunlit grave.' Again her mother gave the dry smile. 'Now, who's for a glass of wine?'

'Of course, we should ration ourselves.' Rachel's doom-laden voice again. 'It might be a fortnight before we have any more supplies.'

Lucy laughed as if to deliberately dispel the sense of impending doom that Rachel appeared to be suggesting. 'Rachel, love, you know we stocked up on everything over the last couple of weeks. We've got simply loads of food, and how many bottles of wine?'

'Three hundred of the little beauties,' Catherine answered. 'And enough brandy to float a wee boat.'

'There,' Lucy said, beaming. 'It won't be so bad, will it?'

Rachel shrugged as if not convinced. 'We'll run out of something . . . we always do. Cigarettes?'

'Plenty.'

'I'll get the wine.' Catherine headed for the door. 'The sun might not yet be over the yard arm, but in this murk who can tell?'

Outside, the slab of cloud had settled lower over the island. The top of the pinnacle of rock where the palm prints lay pressed into concrete was hidden by mist. For the first time the island looked truly wintry.

Catherine returned from the kitchen; she was empty-handed. 'Wine's off.'

'Off?' Rachel wrinkled her forehead. 'It can't be.'

'The corkscrew has vanished again.'

'Oooh, the little rascal.' Lucy pressed her lips together.

'Three hundred bottles and we can't even get into one.'

'Force majeure,' Lucy said, pleased to use the unfamiliar phrase. 'Forces beyond our control.'

Rachel sniffed. 'Told you something would happen.'

'I know.' Lucy clapped her hands together. 'Why don't we hold our first evening class?'

'Pardon?'

'Why not show Amelia how to make your perfectly wonderful dry martini?'

Catherine nodded her approval. 'Anything if it's alcoholic and comes with a screw top. Rachel, will you be teacher?'

Rachel let out a little sigh as if it was an imposition. Nevertheless, she said that she would. Amelia joined in and brought the bottles from the kitchen. If anything, the air of a prison was settling on the villa. Its sudden and unwilling inmates realized they would have to make the best of things until the weather improved.

Outside, the island lay in near-darkness. Behind the cloud the sun must have been setting. Amelia thought about Bill and hoped he'd made it to Limnos. But then, there was no reason to think that he hadn't. Even so, her imagination did deal her the sudden image of an upturned boat in heaving seas, with Bill lying face down in the water, as cold as one of those marble statues that even now frowned down on her.

'Did you get plenty of ice?' Rachel asked.

'Yes.'

'And a sharp knife for the lemon?'

'I've brought the paring knife.'

'That will do.'

'Oooh, goodie.' Lucy looked pleased. 'I love dry martini. I'll sleep like a top. Ooh! Did you hear that?'

They paused for a heartbeat or so. For, all of a sudden, air rushed over the villa, raising a fluting sound. It blew again and the flute-like notes rose and fell.

'Oh, doesn't it sound *so* melancholy?' Lucy said.

'A sad song for lost love.' Rachel abruptly clamped her mouth shut after this, as if she'd let slip some secret.

'Uh-oh, ghostly music to take us up to the witching hour.' Lucy sounded deliberately light-hearted. Perhaps, like Amelia, she sensed a melancholic mood slipping over the villa. As if someone had died – or was about to. And that they were only biding their time until the inevitable showed its face.

And what face (or whose face) is that? Amelia asked herself, shivering from head to toe.

'Someone had best switch on the lights,' Catherine said.

'I'll do it.' Amelia quickly brushed the light switches with her hand. The room grew brighter – an oasis of light surrounded by the growing darkness outside.

The wind blew harder; the ghostly flute-like notes sounded louder. Although this time they were more discordant.

As if deliberately aiming to drown that lost-soul music, Rachel began to talk. She spoke louder than she usually did and, tellingly, she didn't leave a space between the words that the mournful fluting might fill.

'Amelia. Come round to this side of the table with me,' Rachel said. 'Have you made dry martinis before?'

Amelia shook her head.

'Take a glass for everyone — that is, if everyone's on for a drink?'

'God, yes,' Catherine said.

Lucy held up her finger as if in class.

'Then put a chunk of ice in each glass to chill it.' Rachel moved deftly, her long fingers like spider legs. 'Take the cocktail shaker. Add plenty of ice. Then a good slug of gin . . . enough for each person. There.'

The wind blew harder. Beyond the window, Amelia saw the Judas trees shiver, then flatten towards the ground before the force of the air that had rushed in from the faraway North Atlantic. She shivered, too. The cold air had found every chink in the door and window frames to spill inside. A door began to bang somewhere in the house. A mocking sound, as if made by some spiteful ghost.

'I'll get it.' Catherine stood up and regally smoothed her clothes. 'You fix those drinks good and strong, Rachel. We're in for a bumpy ride.'

Rachel continued with the cool gravitas of someone listing points of evidence in court. 'Once you have a good measure of gin and the ice in the shaker, add the dry martini. But only a drop. A tiny drop, at that.'

Lucy added brightly, 'In fact, don't they say the secret of a good dry martini is to simply show the shaker the ver- mouth bottle?'

'Absolutely . . . but . . . there . . . I've added around a teaspoonful. Now take the lemon, cut away the skin to reveal the zest. Peel off some of the zest; now tip the ice from the glass and rub the zest on the inside of the glass and around the rim. See? It'll actually look quite unattractive, as if something unwholesome's been smeared there. A kind of oily residue. Now . . . stir the cocktail shaker.'

'Shouldn't it be shaken not stirred – as Mr Bond would have it?'

'No, Lucy, dear. Stir, don't shake . . . and there you have it. One dry martini.' Rachel poured the clear spirit into glasses. 'Try that, Amelia.'

Amelia sipped hers. It was pure gin. And it seemed about as palatable as neat bleach. 'It's lovely,' she said gamely. 'Very refreshing.' If they were going to be trapped in the villa together for days on end, she decided she'd make a superhuman effort to fit in. Why, in twenty-four hours she'd probably be calling everyone 'dear' and quoting Shakespeare.

That is, if we haven't slaughtered each other by then, she thought darkly.

At that moment her mother returned.

'What is it, Catherine?' Lucy asked, standing. 'What's wrong?'

Catherine, taking a deep breath, looked from one to the other. 'Perhaps you should all come and take a look at what I've found.'

The wind blew harder.

And the eaves played their own lunatic fluting revel.

Chapter Thirty-one

Catherine breezed regally from the lounge to the entrance hall. 'Just look where our corkscrew has managed to hide itself now!'

They all followed her. As always, the statues waited with their characteristic ghostly expectancy.

Rachel, arms folded, coldly looked up. 'How did it get up there?'

'Not by itself, that's for sure.'

Amelia and Lucy looked up, too.

'Someone's got a terrifically long pair of arms,' Rachel observed. 'It must be twenty feet above the floor.'

Lucy looked up with an expression of excitement. 'Unless it's Twizzel.'

'Who on earth's Twizzel?'

'The boy with elastic arms. Don't you remember?'

Amelia smiled. 'No, who was he?'

Rachel sniffed, dismissive. 'Probably one of Lucy's clients.'

Amelia sensed a sudden prickliness between Lucy and Rachel.

'No, dear,' Lucy said. 'A character from a children's story book. Surely you remember Twizzel?'

'I'm probably not old enough.'

'But how on earth did the corkscrew get up there?' Amelia asked the question to distract the two women from what might become an argument.

'Another one of Voros's colourful mysteries,' Catherine said.

Amelia looked up. Twenty feet above her a timber beam ran across the ceiling. Screwed into that was the blue-handled corkscrew. To reach the beam would require a good ladder – or an equally good set of wings.

Catherine sighed, then said dryly, 'Does anyone interpret this as God telling us to cut down on our drinking?'

'Or perhaps it's that Simotas brother.' Rachel's laser eyes glared at the corkscrew. 'You know, the peculiar one?'

'Gregoriou?' Lucy raised her eyebrows. 'What makes you say that?'

'The last time the Gregale blew up he began behaving strangely, didn't he?'

'Come to that, we all get a bit tetchy,' Catherine said. 'Four or five days of storm-force winds is enough to make anyone irritable.'

Rachel glared. 'I tell you I *did* see him standing on my balcony, looking in at me.'

'It was dark. You couldn't be sure.'

'Oh, I'm sure, Lucy. Thank heaven I'd locked the balcony door.'

'That was never Gregoriou in a month of Sundays.'

'Who was it, then? One of your spirits?'

'Rachel, really—'

'One of those from the "other side", coming to haunt me for my past crimes committed when—'

'Ladies.' Catherine clapped her hands like a teacher restoring order to her class. 'Ladies. This isn't helping to retrieve our mischievous corkscrew.' She smiled. 'Besides, I think the Gregale is already starting to rub us all up the wrong way.' She glanced up at the ceiling. 'First we'll retrieve that. Then we'll all have a good stiff drink.'

Rachel sniffed. 'I'll fetch the ladder.'

'You'll need a hand, dear. It's buried under all those old velvet curtains.' Catherine looked at Lucy, then rolled her eyes up at the corkscrew. 'Keep an eye on it to make sure it doesn't skedaddle before we get back.'

Catherine and Rachel headed for the kitchen where the entrance to the basement lay.

Amelia stood beneath the corkscrew and looked up at it again. For a moment she thought she saw the handle turn as if it had begun to unscrew itself. But then she noticed one of the spotlights that lit a fragment of statue head was swinging in the draught. She was seeing nothing more than a moving shadow cast by the corkscrew.

From the eaves came the discordant flute-like notes as the wind blew. And below that was an ever-present rushing sound that could have been the surf or, equally, the sound of the rising breeze blowing through the Judas trees.

She glanced round at the smooth walls that ended in a profusion of moulded vines, grapes and tiny satyr heads in the corners of the entrance hall. The statues stared impassively at her. The Medusa, still lacking her spotlight, glowered darkly from the shadows.

Lucy looked at her, raised her eyebrows and said, 'Blimey.'

Amelia stepped from beneath the corkscrew. At that moment the image of it suddenly unscrewing itself from the timber and plunging down into the top of her head shone crystal clear in her mind's eye. 'Bloody thing,' she said in a low voice to Lucy. 'How do you think it got up there?'

Lucy gave a knowing smile. 'Really, Amelia. You know as well as I do.'

As they talked, their voices dropped to whispers as if they'd entered a church.

'Come on, honestly, Lucy. You really think that some kind of . . . supernatural force put it there?'

'Don't you?'

'It's not likely, is it?'

'How else do you explain how it got up there?'

'Someone could have done it by standing on a ladder.'

'But that *someone* would have had to be one of us, wouldn't it?'

Amelia shook her head, unsure how to reply to that one.

'That would mean,' Lucy continued, 'either that one of us is a practical joker, or . . .'

'Or?'

'Downright insane.'

I did it. It's me. I bought loads of blue-handled corkscrews. I plant them here, there and everywhere. I'm doing it to drive my mother mad. Revenge for how she deserted me as a child . . . These thoughts positively spewed through Amelia's head. In a way it would be easier to confess, thereby supplying a rational explanation. Even if it was confessing to something she had not done. She'd not even touched the corkscrew in the last twenty-four hours; that was the God-honest truth. After all, what Lucy was suggesting was beyond the pale, wasn't it? That 'spirit hands' or ghosts or some force they didn't understand had planted the corkscrew there, twenty feet above the marble floor. And for what reason? To tease them? To set one woman against another? To drive them insane?

Lucy gave a reassuring smile. 'I told you what would happen. You get two psychic people together in a house and all kinds of barmy stuff goes on. I've seen things like this happen before, remember?'

'But why the corkscrew? What does it mean?'

'I don't know . . . I suppose some might try and interpret this in a Freudian kind of way. You know, the penetrating shaft of the screw; or . . . or how the corkscrew is an implement that removes the cork blockage and liberates the liquid inside . . . that liquid being symbolic of emotion.'

'So you could interpret it that way? That this whole phenomenon is connected with repressed emotion?'

Lucy patted Amelia's arm, smiling. 'Of course you could, and lots of psychics do; they think their talent empowers them to interpret what happens as if they're astrologers or psychiatrists or something.'

'But you don't think of it in those terms?'

'I think that perhaps those on t'other side are just being playful.'

'So these . . . these "forces" you talk about don't have some kind of agenda?'

'If it is I hope it's a benign one. Look, Amelia, I don't think they simply leap out uninvited and say "Hey, listen, mortals,

there's a whole psychic world out there you don't know about."
They drop hints and clues to arouse our curiosity. Then when
our curiosity is aroused *they* give a little more so we'll meet
them half way.'

'Something like a courtship?'

'Something like that.'

'If only they'd leave the corkscrew alone. It's getting on
people's nerves the way— *oh.*'

'What?' Lucy looked round as if someone had walked in.

'Uh, I thought I saw something out of the corner of my
eye.' Amelia looked round the empty hallway. 'It must be an
insect or something.'

'Are you sure it was an insect?'

'It was nothing, really.' She cleared her throat. 'Lucy?'

'Yes?'

'Remember when you told me about a method of practising
psychometry? You know, the art, I suppose you'd call it, of
reading objects.'

'Yes, I remember. Why?'

'Well, the other evening I wore my mother's dress. And for
a moment I had the strangest sensations here.' She touched the
side of the head. 'As if whenever I saw an object, whether it
was a table or . . . or even a ship out at sea . . . I imagined it
was somehow inside my head and growing bigger. I know it's
ridiculous.'

'Oh . . .' That was all that Lucy said. And suddenly she
looked serious.

'Can that be an effect of psychometry?'

Lucy looked uneasy. 'Anything else?'

'Just images . . . like random snapshots of people and events.
As if I was remembering things I'd never actually experienced
in the first place.'

'Yes, it could be that.'

Amelia realized that the tone of Lucy's voice had changed.
As if she'd taken a step back to partly disengage herself from
the conversation.

Lucy continued uneasily, 'Of course, the only way to

confirm the images are based on real events is to talk it through with the subject.' She rubbed the side of her head as if sensing something there herself. What was more, Amelia noticed the woman's eyes had taken on a distant look, as if she was recalling some pungent memory of her own.

'I remember a walled garden,' Amelia continued. 'With a large vegetable plot and there was a man who— Lucy?'

'Hmm?'

'Lucy, what's wrong?'

'I think something has got in, Amelia.'

'Got in?'

'Into the villa.' Lucy looked round. 'I saw something above the stairs. It just sort of flitted . . .' She licked her lips; they were dry and pale.

From the corner of her eye Amelia saw a dark shape. She turned sharply in an attempt to see it properly but it had gone again.

She saw Lucy do the same. First she was staring up the stairs, then she suddenly turned to look in the direction of the living room.

Again Amelia glimpsed something; it was dark and moved fast, very fast.

'It might be a bat,' Amelia ventured.

'Or a bird.'

Amelia crossed her arms, rubbing them as she did so.

Lucy's head twisted sharply again as if she'd seen something fly just on the peripheral edge of her vision.

'Poor thing.' Her voice sounded oddly flat. 'It'll hurt itself if we can't get it out of the villa.'

For a whole thirty seconds this continued. The pair of them would stare in the direction they thought they'd seen the flitting ghost of a shape. Only there would be nothing there. A second later, they'd glimpse – or sense – something behind them.

The wind drummed on the front door. Cold air flooded through the gap beneath it to freeze their ankles.

'God, it's cold.' Lucy rubbed her arms. Then repeated in a whisper, 'Oh, God it's cold . . . cold, cold, cold . . .'

'Mind the door, Rachel . . . lift your end over the table.'

Catherine and Rachel came through the kitchen door, carrying the ladder.

'Got it, Rachel.' Catherine looked across the hallway at them, raising the ladder a little as she did so. 'Lucy, I'm afraid your plate of shortbread ended up on the floor. This thing isn't so much heavy as unwieldy.'

Amelia said quickly, 'Let me help.'

She'd no sooner got the word 'help' through her lips than something clattered at her feet.

'Oh? We won't need the ladder after all.' Bending down, she picked up the fallen corkscrew. *'Ouch.'*

She didn't so much drop the corkscrew as throw it to the floor as if it had burnt her.

'Amelia? What's wrong?'

Frowning, Amelia looked at her fingertips.

'Amelia?'

'The corkscrew.' Amelia shook her head, as if faced with a puzzle she couldn't solve. 'It was cold. Freezing cold.'

Outside, the cold winds blew through the branches of a Judas tree. To Amelia's ears it sounded like dry limbs stirring in the depths of a pit.

Chapter Thirty-two

The winds scour Voros. They slice through its ravines; tear through its olive groves; rip at thickets of Judas trees like a titanic garden rake. Invisible jets of air that are the rake's tines claw away anything that's not rooted deeply into the island soil. Grass, branches, fistfuls of thyme, whole bushes are caught up, swept over the clifftops to go whirling away through the night sky into oblivion.

'It was a dark and stormy night.'

'At least all within was bright and warm and cheerful.'

'Isn't that taking poetic licence too far?'

'Cheer up, Rachel. It might never happen. More wine?'

'Please. Cigarette?'

'Why not?'

Catherine gave a dry smile. 'See? We've got everything but the boy.'

'Lucy? Are the telephone lines down yet?'

'No, Rachel. At least they weren't an hour ago . . . oh, are those pistachio nuts?'

'What's left of our meagre ration.'

'Oooh, lovely. Can I pinch one?'

'Be my guest.'

Amelia had settled down by the fireplace with a book. The rest had spread themselves out across the lounge to thumb through magazines or, in the case of Rachel Stone, to stare

269

into space with those laser eyes, as if watching shapes no one else could see.

The wind sounded, as Lucy put it, like a barrelful of monkeys.

By now, the time was nudging midnight but Amelia sensed no one was ready for bed yet. The endless rushing noise of the wind set everyone on edge; it was hard to relax. The corkscrew, placed on the table where everyone could keep an eye on it, was getting plenty of exercise and the third bottle of wine of the night was now half-empty. But still everyone remained alert. Amelia felt as if she'd drunk nothing stronger than water.

'God,' Rachel breathed. 'Will you listen to hell's own music?'

The fluting notes had suddenly soared into a mad crescendo. At that moment an object cannoned against the closed shutters.

'There goes one of my potted garlic plants,' Catherine murmured and lit another cigarette.

Lucy smiled. 'It'll probably crash through some poor Turk's roof in a couple of hours from now.'

'It wouldn't surprise me in the least, dear.'

Rachel scrutinized her wine as if it had taken on an unpleasant flavour. She sniffed it, then set the glass down. 'It's hardly the time for it, but I think I'll go and soak in a hot bath. My neck's starting again.' She turned her head from side to side, the muscles stiff. 'I'll be down in half an hour for a nightcap if anyone's up.'

'We will be, dear,' Catherine said. 'I don't think anyone's going to sleep through this.'

Amelia cocked her head to one side, listening. 'Don't the gales ease off at night?'

'The Gregale's not your usual storm. It'll probably quieten down a little around one-ish.'

'Then it comes back with a vengeance just after dawn.' Catherine stood up. 'Well, it's not going to do me any good just sitting here and pouring wine down my throat all night. I'm going to pour wine down my throat and sort the larder out. Half of that packet stuff's out of date.' She must have noticed Amelia's look of surprise. 'Don't worry, dear. I'm not barmy yet. Once you've lived with the Gregale for a couple of days you'll end up doing your ironing at three in the morning. We've all done it.'

With that, she refilled her glass and walked out of the room.

'And that just leaves us two.' Smiling, Lucy reached for another pistachio nut. 'Mmm. Lovely. But if you see me picking up another one stop me. Otherwise I'll have a raging thirst.'

'Don't worry. I'll wrestle you to the ground.'

Lucy laughed. 'That's the stuff. Swing me round the room by the hair, then pin me to the fireplace.' She grinned. 'The truth is, I can resist everything but temptation.'

'More wine?'

'Oooh, go on then. *Minx, you.*'

The wind, as much for a change as anything, now opted for a deep humming rather than the previous fluting. It *thrummed* through the house. Windows vibrated in mad harmony.

Lucy waited until Amelia had refilled her glass with the white wine. 'You mustn't worry about what happened earlier to the corkscrew.'

'But you have to admit it's . . . well . . . disconcerting.'

'Only because you're not used to it.'

'I don't know if I care to be.'

'Oh, nonsense. Don't you find your brush with the super-natural exhilarating?'

Amelia thought about the dive with Bill Simotas that morning and decided she'd had enough exhilaration to last the rest of the summer.

Lucy steamed on enthusiastically, her eyes shining. 'But this kind of phenomenon is so commonplace.'

'You mean things going bump in the night?'

'More or less.' She nodded, then took a hefty sip of wine. 'You've heard of John Wesley?'

'I think so. Didn't he found the Methodist Church?'

'That's the one. Well, his family lived in a rectory in a

little place called Epworth in England. Now, in the seventeen hundreds the whole family experienced supernatural activity just like we have.'

'But not runaway corkscrews?'

'No, nothing to do with corkscrews. But the father, the Reverend Samuel Wesley, even published a pamphlet, called, I think, *An Account of Sounds and Disturbances* – no, let me get this right: *An Account of Noises and Disturbances on My House at Epworth in December and January 1716.*'

'Snappy title.'

'Rather long-winded, isn't it? But in it Wesley described all kinds of uncanny goings-on: incessant banging at night; footsteps; the sound of coins being poured onto the floor; bottles being smashed. All inexplicable.'

'It's a wonder it didn't drive them mad.'

'On the contrary, the children were amused. They even gave the poltergeist a name: Old Jeffrey. At least they had a sense of humour, didn't they?'

'As long as we don't get our version of Old Jeffrey I'll be perfectly happy.'

Lucy regarded Amelia for a moment.

Amelia met her gaze and smiled. *She thinks this whole business is getting to me. She thinks I'm frightened.*

'Amelia. You said that when you wore your mother's dress you had a sensation here, inside your head?'

'Yes.'

'Like something expanding?'

'Why? Is that common with psychometry?'

'Well, it seems to affect people in different ways. I had a colleague, a lady in her seventies, who always described the experience as erotic. But I've never felt that way.'

'Still, I *was* in physical contact with my mother's dress. And you said that to make a reading you must touch something that belongs to someone else.'

'Oh yes, absolutely. And I've no doubt you have the gift, too.'

'But, just for the sake of argument, let's say this works,

this psychometry. I don't see how touching another person's watch or shoe can tell you all about that person, even down to who their grandparents were, what they did for a living, or whether they liked kippers for breakfast. Even if the watch or shoe, or whatever, captured images like a videotape it could only ever show you a fraction of what the owner experienced, couldn't it?'

'Ah, now there's the great mystery. How can performing a reading by, for example, holding someone's watch that they might have only owned for three or four years reveal information about when the individual was a baby, or if their father fought in a war, or even if the subject will one day give birth to a daughter who will go into politics?' Lucy took a sip of her wine. 'No one knows the answer, of course. We can only hazard educated guesses.'

'Guesses? It all sounds pretty murky to me.'

'Well, the easy way to understand it is this: simply imagine that the answer to every question you could possibly ask is contained in some enormous data bank. And I mean *every* answer, whether to a question about the past, present or future.'

'And that data bank is contained in the every shoe, watch, or lock of hair or whatever?'

'It might be. But it's easier to think that the object you hold in your hand contains an access code to the data bank. You could even think of that bracelet you're wearing as the address of the Amelia Thomas website. And that website, wherever it is, whatever it is, contains everything about Amelia Thomas: such as your personality profile, if you like Chinese food, if you're likely to suffer from chilblains in the future; if you're grandmother's hair was long or short. Everything.'

'You could even tell me what my father was like?'

'Yes.' Lucy spoke quickly, then looked uneasy, as if she'd said too much.

Amelia continued. 'Did you know I've never met my father?'

'Well . . .' Lucy gave a sympathetic shrug. 'I do know your

mother never mentions him so . . .' She shrugged again. 'So, Rachel and I took it that the subject was out of bounds.'

'But if I gave you this bracelet to hold you could describe my father?' Amelia's heart was beating hard as she slipped the bracelet over her still-sore wrist where the weight line had snapped tight.

'Well, dear . . .' Lucy hesitated.

'But you can?'

'Oh, yes. Yes, I can.'

I'm opening a can of worms here. The realization came to Amelia in a dizzy rush. *If my father was a handsome film star or Danish prince my mother wouldn't have hidden his identity from me, would she now? But my father is a guilty secret. I don't know his name. I don't know whether he's alive or dead. But it's his blood as much as my mother's that's running through my veins. For Godsakes, I might even look like him.*

Feeling a sudden surge of recklessness she held out the bracelet. Lucy looked at it as if it might be swarming with bacteria.

Afraid of opening that can of worms, Lucy?

There was something wormy about dear old dad, wasn't there? And there certainly will be now . . . down there in his narrow box.

Amelia didn't know where those thoughts came from but for all their strangeness they seemed grotesquely apt.

Lucy leant back in her chair. 'I don't want to do the reading, dear.'

'Why not – *dear?*'

'You know why. You saw something the other night at Julius's party.'

'I saw – or at least pictured – an old house with a walled garden. The house was big; the kind that would have had servants once. And all the time there was this sensation here. I still get a queasy feeling when I think of it. I saw the ship and imagined it had somehow got into my head, and that it was growing, bigger and bigger. I can't describe the sensation but it was really quite awful. I—'

'Amelia. *Amelia.* I'm not the one to tell you this but . . .'

The wind blew harder. A drumming began on the walls. Like something monstrous wanted to get in.

And in the depths of the house a door crashed shut; the sound rolled like thunder through passageways and rooms. Cool air slithered up Amelia's legs.

'No, I shouldn't have to be the one to tell you,' Lucy was saying. 'But you shouldn't be kept in the dark. After all, it's not some evil secret, is it?'

'What's not an evil secret?' Amelia looked at Lucy's shining eyes in bewilderment.

'Two years ago your mother had an operation. She had to go to Athens for it.'

A cold sensation oozed through Amelia's stomach.

Lucy gave a little nod as if to encourage herself she was doing the right thing. 'It was a brain tumour.'

'A brain tumour.' The room with its shattered statues seemed to rush in on Amelia. Stone faces thrust at her own. Staring at her. Searching her face for a reaction. '*A brain tumour?* She never mentioned anything . . . I didn't know . . . I thought she was just busy . . . and when I had my accident . . . oh, my God.'

'Oh, I'm sorry, love.' Lucy leant across and squeezed Amelia's knee. 'It must be a terrible shock. And the news shouldn't have come from me . . . and perhaps you shouldn't mention it to Catherine. She doesn't want anyone to treat her like an invalid. After all, she's not.'

'You mean she's all right now?'

'Oh, yes, love. The operation was a success. A complete success. And they only gave her one set of chemo. My God, how she used to joke about what would happen if her hair fell out. "I'm going to get myself a long red wig and become a femme fatale" she'd tell us. But she never lost so much as a hair. Except where they'd shaved her for the operation, of course.' Lucy touched the side of her own head, then rubbed her fingers as if they'd come into contact with something ever so slightly sticky. She shook her head and beamed. 'She's as well as you or I now.'

Amelia still felt herself mentally lagging behind. Lucy had assured her that her mother was healthy now, but even so she found herself repeating in a whisper, 'A brain tumour?'

'It just came out of the blue. She hid the symptoms at first, but then grudgingly – you can imagine the way it is with your mother – grudgingly she admitted to vertigo, double vision and—'

'And a pressure inside her head.'

Lucy's lips tightened, then she nodded. 'Yes . . . awful pressure.'

Amelia touched her own head, remembering the sensation there the other night. Something expanding remorselessly, cruelly.

Lucy filled Amelia's glass. 'But your mother is better now. Remember that.'

There the conversation petered out. A moment later Lucy helped herself to another pistachio nut and said, 'I told you to fight me if I had another one of these.'

Amelia gave a wan smile. And then a little later she made a comment about an actor in a magazine looking older despite the cosmetic surgery he was championing. It fell silent again. The statues stared coldly at the two women.

And, as sometimes happens, the engine that had driven conversation between two people had broken down. They tried to get the thing going again. But all that came out were oral telegrams. Disjointed statements. Questions that were answered with a nod or shake of the head. Passing remarks that needed no elaboration.

Amelia knew full well: *I've opened that can of worms. And do you see? Do you see? There's no way of closing the lid.*

From across the night-time ocean the storm winds blasted Voros. Julius King sat in his living room and listened to the sound of his own breathing.

In the bedroom that was decorated with coloured foil Gregoriou Simotas lay, his forehead ridged with corrugations even in his sleep. The prominent lines echoed the gullies and ravines that deeply etched the island. He muttered fitfully as if some animal was sinking sharp teeth into his finger as he slept. But still he couldn't wake.

Out across the island the branches of the Judas trees whipped back and forth. Then were pressed brutally to the ground before leaping to shake their twigs at the sky like so many tiny fists.

Flecks of foam hurled from surf rode high on the breeze to burst against pinnacles of rock many hundreds of yards from the sea.

Torrents of air sang through the holes in the cave of potato vines. They squeezed through apertures to find the mummified bodies of the soldiers within. Draughts ebbed and flowed through cracks in dried skin. They ruffled the remaining tufts of the dead men's hair, then ever so slightly inflated their shirts. The draught subsided and the shirts of the mummies deflated. The draught returned; the shirts reflated. For all the world it looked as if those four dead men had begun to breathe again.

At the junction of the pathways in the olive grove, those cold currents of air at last found a way into the shrine of Demetrius. Rushing at the burning oil lamp, they plucked at the wick.

Guttering, the lamp flickered, then went out. With the death of the light something else in the saint's glass-box shrine seemed to die a little, too. Now a colder body of air stole onto the island. And not so far away, in the villa known as The Palms, Amelia Thomas shivered down to the very marrow of her spine.

Chapter Thirty-three

High in The Palms midnight came and went. Gales buffeting the villa left the occupants too restless to go to bed just yet.

After a while, Amelia moved through into the kitchen where her mother had bagged out-of-date food and was now taking a chicken out of the freezer to defrost.

'Nearly forgot to do this earlier,' Catherine said as she placed the chicken on a plate. 'And I hate trying to defrost food in the microwave; it always comes out part-cooked and part-frozen still. Oh, will you pass me the scissors, please?'

Amelia watched her mother cut packaging away from the chicken.

Her mother looked healthy enough; there were no signs of any operation scars from when the surgeon removed the brain tumour. But then again, her hair would have grown over any marks on the scalp.

Snap, Mother, she thought; *now we've both ended up with holes in our skulls.*

'Can I get you a drink of anything, moth—' She corrected herself with an apologetic smile. 'Catherine?'

'No, I'm fine for the moment, thank you, Amelia. But I'll join you all for one of Lucy's rocket-fuel brandies before bed. Goodness, do you hear that storm getting up?'

'It's surprising anyone sleeps through this.'

'You tend not to at first. Then it catches up with you all at once and you sleep like death itself. Will you be a dear and just snip the rubber bands around the legs while I hold the chicken up? There, excellent.' As she went to wash her hands at the sink Catherine said, 'I did warn you that you might feel isolated on Voros.'

'No, I like it here. Really I do.'

'I'm afraid now you might have to grow to like being marooned for a while.'

'What would happen if there was an accident or someone fell sick?'

'In a word: tough. When the Gregale blows no one can get away from the island for days. And no one can come to us.'

'Not even in a large boat?'

'Oh, they can get within half a mile or so, but then they need to transfer people to smaller boats to ferry them in. The problem is that once the sea gets whipped up around the bottom of the cliffs it would be suicidal to try and even get close in a small boat.'

'Surely a helicopter could reach the island?'

'Not when the winds are blowing. Besides, as Lucy pointed out, aircraft are forbidden to fly over the island. We have to face facts. We're well and truly marooned for the next week or so.'

Amelia thought about Bill's plan to return in a couple of days in his cousin's boat. Had he been serious? Or was that just to let her down gently? In fact, wouldn't that make the perfect excuse not to come back for her? And all the time hordes of single girls would be heading for Limnos, determined to have a good time come what might.

Catherine turned from the sink to face Amelia. Shrewdly, she looked over the top of her glasses at her. 'Amelia, you're not having second thoughts about staying here after all, are you?'

Why does she keep asking if I'm happy here? It's as if she wants me to leave.

Catherine didn't wait for a reply; instead she said suddenly, 'Amelia, I had a telephone call from your Aunt Mae a couple of days ago.'

'Oh?'

'She explained how you'd left.'

Amelia pressed her lips together and nodded. *Here it comes . . .*

Catherine said, 'What did your doctor have to say about you travelling?'

'He didn't recommend it. Not yet, anyway.'

'You took a bit of risk, then, coming here alone?'

'I suppose so.' Suddenly Amelia felt herself slipping into the role of sullen little girl being reprimanded by mother.

'You might have been taken ill on the plane.'

'I know, but I was desperate to get away, Catherine. That . . . that bloody family were driving me mad.'

Catherine regarded her over the top of her glasses. 'Hmm. They would have driven me mad, too.' Her face relaxed into a warm smile. 'And I think I would have done exactly the same as you. Got the hell out of there as fast as I could.'

Amelia returned the smile, pleased and relieved. The little girl inside her had been let off the hook. She said, 'I suppose I could phone Aunt Mae and apologize, and thank her for her . . .' she gave a little shrug. '. . . hospitality.'

'That won't be possible, unfortunately.'

'Oh?'

'The phones are down. Happens with every Gregale. They'll be kaput for days.' Her mother smiled warmly again. 'Come on, it's time we asked Lucy for a tot each of her rocket fuel.'

An hour later Amelia slipped into bed. She lay looking up at the ceiling. Even though the windows were shut the white muslin curtains still rippled in fifty or more different draughts. The curtains that enclosed the bed moved gently, too.

Perhaps tonight in the kitchen she'd come close to making a connection with her mother. Some of that 'distance' that had always existed between them had lessened . . . well, a little, anyway.

Amelia did want to talk in a more intimate way with her mother. She wanted to ask about her mother's illness. And one day she wanted to find out about her father. She had, of course, a mental image of him, just as children have a secret 'internal' portrait of what God looks like. In her childhood she had always imagined her father as some dashing figure with film-star looks. Who always wore a warm smile on his face. She'd even woven fantasies about why he'd not stayed with her mother or why he hadn't visited his daughter. These ranged from him being an explorer or a soldier, and even to him being a spy who'd been captured by a foreign power. This one had stemmed from watching a James Bond movie one bank holiday afternoon on television. In this particular fantasy she'd discovered where her father was imprisoned. She'd lie awake at night, imagining how she'd tame some wild moorland pony and how together they'd trek over exotic mountains and deserts until at last they found the fortress where her father was held. Then she'd heroically rescue him; he'd recognize her instantly and hug her and tell her how he'd thought about her every single day . . .

Of course, that had been a long, long time ago.

But as she lay there, listening to the *thrum* of the wind against the walls, she wondered again about her motive for coming to the island.

Deep down, did I believe that my biological father lived here secretly with my mother? An exiled prince in hiding, is he? Or a rock singer in retreat from the pressures of stardom?

No, those were childish fancies. Her father, if he was still alive, probably didn't even know she existed. Despite children's distaste at the idea of their parents making love, the truth of the matter was that they did. And there was no reason to suppose that her cool, aristocratic-looking mother had never enjoyed a one-night stand or two.

With these thoughts going around inside her head, Amelia at last, despite the sound of the rising storm, fell asleep.

An hour later she was awake again. In the distance she heard the *slam-slam-slam!* of what she took to be a door or shutter banging in the gale. The wind had taken to making its mad flute notes round the eaves again. Amelia sat up in bed. The white muslin curtains moved in ghostly rolling waves in the draught.

A light came on at the top of the stairs, enough of it spilling under the bottom of the door to show her the shapes of the furniture in her room.

The slamming suddenly stopped. Amelia heard Catherine's voice telling either Lucy or Rachel that she'd managed to close the offending shutter.

'If this keeps up,' Amelia heard her say, 'we'll have to draw up a rota for who gets up to see to what.'

With that, the light went out.

If this was going to be the nightly pattern during the life of the Gregale then Catherine had been right about them being in for a bumpy ride. Mixed with the rushing of the wind, the discordant fluting notes around the eves, the sound of the *thrumming*, were a hundred or more other sounds. From the light sighing of the draughts through the doors and the rustle of the curtains to the sound of sticks and other airborne debris battering the outside walls of the villa.

In her mind's eye Amelia could see surf pounding the island, the Judas trees being bent and sometimes broken before the torrent of cold air. In fact, even as she listened, she heard a distant crackling as if branches were being snapped one after another.

Oh, my God, what have I let myself in for . . .

The prospect of day after day of endless gales was maddening.

She lay staring up into darkness. Five minutes passed. Then ten.

At last sleep took her. Only now the driving winds raced through her dreams . . .

Chapter Thirty-four

'John! Keep the noise down!'

Amelia shouted furiously at her cousin from her bed. One of his Internet parties was running its usual rowdy course.

'John! I'm trying to sleep!'

Her voice echoed from the stone walls; loud enough to shock her properly awake.

The deep pounding continued.

Bang . . . bang . . . bang . . . bang . . .

Slow, rhythmic, startling. Frightening, even.

It spoke of some great, dark force. An indefatigable beat. Driving. Muscular. The beat of a ghost drum that calls to dark legions.

She switched on the light. Instantly it flickered and dimmed before slowly brightening again.

Of course there is no John, she told herself as she rubbed her eye. Cousin John was thousands of miles away, sleeping above that grotty hardware store.

She was on Voros. And that wind – that *damned wind* – was blowing harder than ever.

The deep crashing beat continued somewhere deep beneath her. As if the heart of the house, beating louder and louder, was approaching some crisis point.

With an effort Amelia dispelled such eerie thoughts. No. It was only fair it should be her turn to lock whatever shutter or door had broken free in the gale.

Yawning, she climbed out of bed, slipped on her dressing gown and sandals and headed for her bedroom door.

Damn . . .

She didn't even have to pull it open; the moment she turned the handle and disengaged the catch the door burst inward. As if trying to sock her one on the jaw. She flinched back. The edge of the door missed her by a hair. Immediately, an icy blast rushed by her, as if eager to take possession of her bedroom.

She shivered. The draught swirled over her bare legs, raising gooseflesh. Fastening her dressing gown, she moved out onto the landing where she switched on the light.

Here the crash of the unfastened door was so loud as to be painful. At this rate it would be torn from its hinges if it wasn't secured soon.

She leaned over the balustrade at the top of the stairs. Straight away she saw that it was one of the pair of big front doors that had been forced open in the storm.

Through the gap she glimpsed the outside world. A stream of twigs, leaves, grass, along with a whole conglomeration of other debris, sped by. Now, with the opening of the door, some of it was being diverted inside. Dry leaves swirled in circles. A paper bag fluttered onto the head of a statue.

Amelia went quickly down the stairs.

The lights flickered again.

Don't fail on me now, she thought, *the last thing I want to do is walk to that open doorway in the dark.*

She reached the bottom of the stairs and had begun to cross the hallway when she heard a voice from above. 'Careful, Amelia. Don't let the door swing back at you, it weighs a ton.'

She turned to see Catherine looking down at her. Lucy came to the top of the stairs too, yawning and tying her dressing-gown belt.

The noise was too great to reply properly. Instead Amelia gave a wave to say she'd heard Catherine's warning, then grabbed the door as it swung away from her. Throwing her own body weight behind it, she slammed it shut and slipped the bolts across.

Instantly the sound of the wind dropped to a muted roar.

Leaves and grass stalks began to settle on the marble floor.

'Who on earth left the door open?' Lucy asked as she came down stairs.

'Strange.' Catherine shook her head. 'I could have sworn I locked and bolted it before I went to bed.'

Amelia pushed back her tousled hair. 'It's lucky it didn't come off its hinges. I don't think there's any damage, anyway.'

'The bolts were drawn back?'

'Yes, and the door was unlocked, too.'

'How peculiar.'

'Might Rachel have been out for some reason?'

Catherine shook her head. 'I hardly think so; not in that filth; you can hardly stand up in it.'

'It's not going to let us have a peaceful night, is it?'

'Get used to it if you can, Amelia.'

'Yes, love, console yourself with thoughts of all those hot summer days ahead.' Lucy smiled. 'You'll be fed up to the back teeth with barbecues by the time we've finished.'

'Try me.' Amelia smiled as she pulled a grass stalk from her hair. 'What time is it now?'

'Just gone five.'

'Marvellous, only another three hours until breakfast.'

Amelia started back up the stairs; the lights flickered, seemingly in harmony with every step she took.

She was almost at the top when Rachel appeared. Her eyes were sharp as if she was on an urgent errand. 'Did anyone hear that noise?' she asked quickly.

'*Did we?*' Lucy laughed. 'The door nearly broke itself off its hinges.'

'No, not that. Something else from outside?'

'No, dear. I haven't heard anything but those dratted winds. Has anyone else?'

The other two women shook their heads.

Rachel, however, hurried downstairs, still fastening her dressing gown. 'Something's wrong.' Her brow furrowed. 'I could hear something above the storm.'

'Like what, dear?'

'I'm not sure. Amelia, would you give me a hand to open the front door?'

'Careful – I've only just got the thing shut.'

'I'll only be a moment. I want to hear if it comes again.'

'Just wait a second,' Catherine said briskly. 'We'll all give you a hand: that door turns into a monster when there's a wind blowing. The last thing we want is anyone breaking their wrists if it bursts open again.'

Once more Amelia returned to the door. She slid back the bolts and turned the key. It felt as if a dozen fists were drumming on the timbers on the other side, wanting to get in.

Out there were men with blighted faces. Ghosts. Who had ruined faces slashed with wounds that were like a dozen new maws: open-mouthed, full-lipped. Bleeding.

The men wanted to come inside.

No! Amelia pressed her lips together hard. *There's no such thing.* Why did her imagination run away like that? It was like she had a malign spirit inside her head; ready to torment her the moment she let her guard slip.

She took a deep breath. 'Ready. Best grab the handle. I'll steady the back of the door.'

The wind pushed hard. So, rather than opening it, the women allowed the currents of air to push the door open, with them acting as brakes to prevent it crashing back into the doorstop.

'We can't stand in the doorway!' Rachel shouted as the freezing air blasted through it, driving grit into their faces. 'Come outside! Quickly! Now close the door!'

A moment later the four women stood outside.

In front of them the island was a dark writhing shape. It was never still, not for a moment, as the gale passed back and forth over it like some monstrous garden rake.

'Hell's teeth.' Lucy pulled a dry leaf from her mouth. 'This is horrendous.'

We certainly make a dramatic spectacle, Amelia told herself wonderingly. *Four women in white dressing gowns that flutter spectacularly in the gale that roars at them.* Admittedly the other three looked more exotic in their white silks and satins, while Amelia's towelling gown with a hood appeared a little more humdrum.

And yet, despite all the sound and fury, it was such a dry storm. There hadn't been a drop of rain.

'Do you hear it now?' Catherine asked above the noise.

Rachel shook her head; her long hair rippled straight out like a pennant.

'Perhaps we should go in,' Lucy suggested. 'We'll not gain anything standing out here.' She stamped her numbed feet. 'Apart from pneumonia.'

Rachel appeared reluctant. She looked upwards. But all that lay above them was streaming cloud. In the near-dark it was nothing more than a boiling mass of shadows. Not so much as a solitary star showed through.

Amelia looked round. Great blocks of stone, pinnacles of rock, swathes of shaking Judas trees. Ravines that were a glistening black now, like rivers of liquid darkness. It all struck her as being somehow unearthly. As if by chance she'd found herself on a ghost world.

What was more, the storm no longer appeared to attack the island. If anything, Voros seemed to suck the air into itself. As if it had become a vortex – or a whirlpool that dragged the elements inward to imprison them somewhere deep inside its stony heart.

Voros is pulling everything into itself, she thought.

It is a hungry mouth. It is devouring the world. It wants – no, it needs *to suck the outside world dry. It needs to consume. To possess. People who are brought its way are kept here. Like those four German soldiers in the cave. Or that sunken hospital ship with its hundreds of doomed passengers. Like Lucy, Rachel and my mother. They came but now they will never ever leave.*

And me. It wants . . . it wants . . .

As Amelia stood there in the gale her thoughts didn't seem like idle fancy. It was more a realization of fact. Of how things really were.

She shivered. The wind fluted beneath the eaves . . .

'*There.*' Rachel turned her head slightly. 'There: did you hear it?'

'No, dear.' Lucy looked puzzled. 'What was it?'

Suddenly Amelia did hear something. They all did.

A tremendous cracking sound. As if a peal of thunder had sounded directly above them.

At that same moment the landscape was lit by brilliant flashes. Amelia looked up. Through the cloud came a light. It was as if a fragment of the sun was falling to Earth.

'What is it?' Lucy's voice was a cry. 'Is it the comet?'

Rachel reacted angrily. 'Of course it isn't, you bloody fool! It's a plane!'

Amelia had time to register the sheer nastiness in Rachel's voice before the fireball came. She watched, stunned, as a mass of flame punched through the bottom of the cloud; it carried on coming, passing low over the roof of the villa, shrieking like fury. Spitting out fire. Howling. Shaking the earth beneath them.

Then it plunged out of sight beyond the cliff.

'Oh, my God,' Catherine breathed. 'It's come down into the sea.'

Rachel was thinking the fastest. 'Wait here, I'll get the flashlights.'

'What can we do?' Lucy sounded anguished.

'We can see if there are any survivors. Lucy, get on the phone to the police.'

'But the phone's not working; it went down yesterday.'

'Well, keep trying. If you do get through, tell them a jet has crashed into the sea just north of the island.'

Lucy nodded and with Amelia's help opened the door to allow Rachel to enter.

Moments later Rachel returned with the three flashlights.

'Did anyone see any parachutes?'

'I didn't even see a plane as such,' Catherine told her. 'Only a fireball.'

'The plane is what I must have heard.' Rachel checked the

torch. 'I could hear the sound of jet engines. The pilot must have been circling the island in the hope of finding somewhere to make an emergency landing. Everyone got something on their feet? *Good.*'

With that, she led the way.

Chapter Thirty-five

'Careful how you go,' Catherine told them. 'Those steps are going to be treacherous down there in the dark.'

An icy draught raced across Amelia's bare legs; the dressing gown flapped uncomfortably. She wished there had been time to change into jeans and a sweater. But if there were people in the water every second would count.

Even though the ocean was out of sight from up here, she could see it in her mind's eye. A boiling cauldron of foam, cataracts rushing through the clefts in the rocks, the sea transformed into a monstrous thing.

Glancing back at the villa, she saw the electric lights through the shutter slats dip once more as the electricity supply faltered.

That figures, Amelia thought with a sense of resignation to the inevitable. *Voros is now sucking the electricity out of the cables. Just as it sucked the air from the sky. And like it sucked the sense out of people's heads.*

Deep down, Amelia recognized these as a bizarre association of ideas. But this insane, madcap weather did that to you. The wind blew so hard it seemed to scatter all logic before it.

And now it gusted with enough power to take the breath from her lungs. Even before she reached the end of the gently sloping path that led to the steps she was panting hard.

'Everyone OK?' Rachel flashed the torch back at them. 'Catherine? Remember to use your flashlight.'

Catherine looked blankly at her.

'Switch on your flashlight, Catherine.'

Catherine appeared to shake herself out of some reverie and switched on her torch. Now, in the combined light of the three torches, they illuminated a whole swathe of the garden.

Amelia saw the funeral cypresses being snatched backwards and forwards by the wind. Grass, leaves, shreds of wild thyme and oregano flew past them. Constantly grit flew with a stinging power into their faces. Amelia felt as if her hair was being dragged out by the roots.

She angled her torch so she could see the concrete path in front of her. Just ahead were the steps that lead down to the water's edge and the landing platform.

'Could you tell where the plane came down?' Catherine shouted over the noise of the storm.

'To the north,' Rachel replied; immediately a grass stalk flew into her mouth; pulling it out, she continued: 'But it didn't look far away. And I'm sure it came down in the sea, otherwise there'd be flames . . . careful now, we've reached the steps.'

In the random flash of reflected torchlight Amelia saw the worried expressions of the two women. They weren't prepared for any kind of emergency whatsoever. Never mind a plane crash. What if a passenger plane had gone down . . .

Amelia closed off the unwelcome images the idea brought. Instead she concentrated on climbing down the steps in the dark.

Although the storm was fierce, still there was no rain; the grey rock beneath their feet was dry as age-old bones.

As they descended they passed clumps of Judas trees that lashed out at them with their whip-like branches. Amelia flinched as a branch tip caught her cheek with astonishing ferocity. Gritting her teeth against the pain, she carried on.

Once or twice on the long climb down she glanced at the sky. Dark. Totally dark. No sign of dawn yet. *If it ever comes,* she thought bleakly; *especially with this cloud.*

'Oh.'

Turning, Amelia saw her mother had stopped and then sat

down heavily on the step. The woman put the torch down beside her and pressed her fingertips to her temples.

'Catherine?' What's the matter?'

'Uh . . . nothing, dear. I'll be all right.'

Rachel paused and fixed her sharp eyes on her. 'Catherine?'

'Sorry . . . I feel such an idiot. It's one of my blasted migraines.'

For a second Amelia looked at her mother's chalk-white face. The sudden onset of pain seemed to have aged the woman in the space of a few moments. Amelia was shocked to see how old and fragile she'd become.

'Mother,' she said, forgetting to use Catherine's name. 'You can't come down here with us.'

'If I sit for a moment or two . . .'

'No. I'll help you back to the villa.'

Rachel cast a despairing look down the steps. In her mind's eye she was seeing drowning men and women. In fact, they were so close to the water Amelia could feel a fine spray on her face from the still-invisible ocean.

Amelia met Rachel's eye. 'I must help my mother back to the villa.'

Rachel nodded.

But, as Amelia helped her mother to her feet, she heard Catherine say fiercely: 'No. Amelia. I'll be all right. You go on down with Rachel.'

'But you look—'

'*I'll be fine.*' Catherine seemed to regain some of her strength. 'Believe me, I can make it back myself. I'm not a geriatric yet. OK?'

'OK.'

'It's just this stupid . . . inconvenient migraine.'

Migraine be damned, Amelia told herself firmly. Then two more words came into her head, words that were somehow dark and unutterably frightening. *Brain tumour.*

Quickly now, Catherine climbed to her feet and started to ascend the steps. 'Go on down,' she said without looking back. 'I'll see if Lucy's managed to get through on the telephone.'

With that she became a white, almost elemental shape gliding up into darkness.

Rachel didn't actually say, 'Come on, we've wasted enough time already,' but she did touch Amelia on the elbow and nodded downward, encouraging her to continue down the steps.

Amelia angled her torch downwards and resumed the descent, Rachel at her side.

The wind roared up the cliff at them, literally standing their hair on end. Grit stung Amelia's face. She found herself narrowing her eyes to slits to try and avoid being blinded by it.

Now she could hear the rushing sounds of the sea. When she licked her lips they tasted salty.

'Nearly there,' Rachel shouted.

Amelia thought grimly: *But in God's name what do we do when we get there?*

When Amelia and Rachel reached the bottom of the steps they found themselves in a world crammed with movement and sound. Waves broke over the concrete landing platform. Spray moved in vast white curtains through the darkness. Ghost shapes on the march. And all the time the noise of the sea and the storm was deafening.

Amelia gasped as freezing spray struck her face.

For a moment the pair stood two steps up from the platform. They stared out to sea, playing their torch beams on the surf.

God, what a sight we are, Amelia thought with that sense of detachment that often comes with even the direst emergencies. *We could be a pair of she-spirits. Here we are at the edge of the sea, clad in billowing white, our long hair streaming out, our eyes luminous and ghostly in the reflected torch beams.*

'God Almighty,' Amelia heard Rachel say, awed.

'See anything?'

'Nothing yet. You?'

'Nothing.'

'Can you work your way along the rock ledge?'

'I'll try.'

'*Here.*' Rachel's laser glare fixed on Amelia's face. 'Take my hand. And for God's sake hold on.'

Rachel's grip was as strong as a man's. Together they walked sideways, backs to the cliff face. Moments later they'd left the concrete platform behind. Just at arm's length below them the sea surged and sucked at the rocks with a power that seemed to Amelia nothing less then colossal.

Every so often they'd pause to shine the torches out to sea. Amelia for one couldn't believe that anyone would survive out there for more than a few moments. The waves were mountainous. Constantly there were explosive concussions, as if depth charges were exploding all around the island, turning the water a ghostly white.

'There!' Rachel shouted and pointed down almost at their feet.

Something flat and dark turned over in the surf.

'It looks like part of a seat,' Amelia said.

'An ejector seat?' Rachel hazarded.

'Maybe . . . Are those wires coming out of the back of it?'

'Dear God, it is, isn't it?' Rachel's troubled gaze focused on the water, searching for survivors. 'It's part of the wreckage.'

'At least it can't be a passenger plane . . . it must be a jet fighter . . . a small military jet, anyway.'

'But if that's the seat the pilot can't be far away.'

Holding Amelia's hand with a numbing grip Rachel moved on, half crouching, as she shone the light out to sea, the yellow beam turning white surf to the colour of rust.

Suddenly the grip became positively crushing. 'There! Over there! *Is that a parachute?*'

Chapter Thirty-six

There was no doubting what Rachel had seen. A billowing white form lay on the surface of the water. It rippled and snapped in the gale just like a sheet on a washing line.

Running out from it, a tangle of cord.

'Can you reach it?' Amelia asked.

'No.' Rachel wiped the sea spray from her eyes. 'But the sea's driving it this way. Wait a moment.'

By now the waves had reached the rocky ledge. Foam swirled over it and soaked their feet. The cold was shocking.

'Take this.' Rachel handed Amelia the torch. 'Now keep a good, tight hold of my hand. Got it?'

'Yes.'

'You won't let go, will you?'

Amelia shook her head. Anyone falling into that seething ocean wouldn't last two minutes.

Rachel crouched, then leaned out, her hand extended towards the billowing canopy of the parachute. Her eyes also searched the surf beyond it. Amelia knew she was looking for survivors.

'Got it!'

Rachel pulled hard on Amelia's hand; so hard, in fact, that Amelia thought both of them would tumble forward into the water.

Quickly she shifted her balance and braced her feet against the rock. Her feet were wet inside her sandals and slipped against the inner soles. She leaned even further back to compensate.

At last Rachel straightened. She had a grip on the sopping wet mass of parachute material.

Amelia rested the torches in a hollow in the rock and helped as best she could. She grabbed the parachute canopy as Rachel began hauling it, dripping, from the water. They could have been manhandling some gigantic sheet from a washing machine. Hugely heavy because the material was saturated with water, it still caught the wind and partially inflated, almost crushing them back against the cliff face.

Dear God, it's like fighting some sea monster. Amelia struggled to wrap the parachute into a more manageable bundle as they pulled it from the sea. And at that moment the sodden material was at the core of their purpose in being there. They *had* to land the thing, dripping and water-laden and heavy as concrete though it was.

At that instant she didn't think about the real reason why they were hauling it in.

'Keep pulling!' Rachel yelled. 'Harder, girl!'

'I am!'

'Pull harder! The sea's taking it back.'

Amelia's wet feet slipped on the inner sole of her sandals. Furiously she kicked them off. Now, standing barefoot on the rock, her grip was better. She pulled hard. The parachute billowed up into her face, blinding her, half suffocating her too as the wet material pasted itself over her mouth and nose.

She lifted her head and gasped in a lungful of air. More sea sprayed into her face. Her hair stuck to her face like a caul across the face of a newborn child.

'Nearly there,' Rachel shouted. Then she added something that made Amelia stop dead. 'Can you feel how heavy it is? There's someone still attached to it.'

Amelia had never entertained the idea that the pilot might still be buckled to the chute. She'd been looking for someone bobbing freely in the sea, still wearing a bright orange life-jacket.

'Get the rhythm!' Rachel shouted obliquely. 'Hand over hand together . . . like it's a fishing net.'

Suddenly Amelia understood. She nodded. Then, both pulling together, they hauled the material in towards them, just as if they were fishermen pulling in the catch at the end of the day.

Seconds later the material ended and they were pulling on the canopy lines. These were thin and slippery with sea water. Every moment or so the water, rolling back from the rocks, would tug the lines and whatever lay at the end of them back, as if to draw the parachute and its load down into the depths. Then the two women had to brace themselves and pull fiercely to avoid being dragged off the ledge and into the sea. Both panted and sweated and swore under their breaths.

Rachel called, 'Almost there, almost there . . . pull! *Pull!'* They continued drawing in the lines, tugging at that unseen dead weight. It seemed like a labour that would never end.

At last Amelia heard Rachel catch her breath in surprise. 'Stop. Stop pulling!' Then she added what suddenly seemed a dreadful sentence: *'I can see a head.'*

From that angle, with the billowing canopy loosely gathered in front of her, Amelia could see nothing. But suddenly she felt very cold; even the storm seemed to shift into the distance; she could hear her own heartbeat. Surprisingly, however, her voice sounded calm when she asked the question. 'Is he alive?'

Rachel's grey-eyed gaze shifted to Amelia's spray-streaked face. 'I can't tell. Keep pulling. We need to get him clear of the water.'

The battle resumed. They carried on hauling in the lines hand over hand. Now taking the weight of a man half out of the water, those lines became as taut as guitar strings.

All Amelia could see in that near-dark was a still darker form in the sea at her feet. But when she pulled again she saw a helmet that was bone white in colour. The figure hung by the parachute straps.

'Amelia. Grab his arms.'

Amelia did so. Her back muscles ached like fury at the

weight of the man, but together they managed to free him from the water and laid him on the ledge.

'Back,' Rachel said sharply. 'Stand back. Pass me the flash-light.'

Amelia passed it to her, then stood with her back to the cliff. Rachel bent over the man. She must have unbuckled the harness and then removed the helmet, but Amelia could see none of this activity. The sea spray formed a mist between herself and the two figures. Also, the parachute canopy still flapped freely at one side; sometimes the wind caught it and folded it over the man and Rachel as if trying to enclose them both in the white fabric.

Amelia shone the torch down at the prone figure. This was more to help illuminate the scene for Rachel than for her to see anything herself. The wind-blown spray concealed the details from her. And she found herself thankful for that.

She looked downward. The only part of the man she could see in detail were his feet. Again in a detached way she saw his boots: they laced high up his shins, were highly polished, and drops of water stood in hard, round beads. Black leather contrasted with bright yellow laces.

'Amelia . . .'

Rachel held up her torch for Amelia to take. She then turned back as if she was looking at the man's face. A moment later she knelt up and twisted so she could make eye contact with Amelia.

Amelia knew. 'He's dead, isn't he?'

'I'm afraid so.' Rachel showed no shock; she sounded quite self-controlled. 'Just give me a moment.'

Amelia, shining the torch, angled her own body so she could look down at the man. Rachel moved so that she deliberately blocked Amelia's view. 'No,' she said. 'Best not.' Her mouth tightened. 'I don't recommend it . . . he must have hurt his face when he fell into the sea.'

'What are you going to do now?'

'I'm going to fasten the helmet buckle . . . then I'll pull the visor back down.' Rachel swallowed, looking suddenly queasy. 'So we can't see his face, OK?'

'You're sure he's dead?'

'I've seen his face . . . I'm sure. Believe me, I'm sure.'

The emphasis was enough for Amelia to be glad that she hadn't seen the man's injured face for herself.

A moment later Rachel said, 'There. Done.' She climbed to her feet, her sopping silk dressing gown now transparent.

Amelia shone the torch on the body of the pilot. The black flying suit was unmarked. As were the hands that protruded from beneath the suit's elasticated cuffs. Although Amelia did notice the skin had turned a pale blue. The helmet was firmly buckled in place. If anything, there in the dark, it resembled a skull. Gleaming with that same bone whiteness. Rachel had pulled the visor down so it covered all of the man's face.

'We'd best get a move on,' Rachel said. 'If the storm gets any worse we might get waves breaking right up over the ledge. Take his right arm . . . I'll take his left.'

It wasn't pleasant. But then, Amelia felt no fear as she thought she might have. In fact she was filled with a kind of emotional neutrality. This was a grim job, but it was one that had to be done.

'Got him?' Rachel sounded in control, too. 'I'll get his left arm. *No!* Don't get too close to the edge of the ledge.'

'What about the parachute?'

'Leave it. It's soaked; it'll weigh a ton.'

'Shouldn't we look for anyone else?'

'We will – as soon as we've got him somewhere safe.'

Safe?

'Safe' seemed an odd choice of word, somehow.

But Amelia realized they had a moral duty, if not a legal one, to store the body until it could be collected by the authorities.

Between them, gripping an arm each, they half carried, half dragged the body along the rocky ledge. Amelia's back and thigh muscles ached mercilessly. Every so often the helmeted head would roll limply and clump painfully against the side of her own head.

After what seemed an age they made it to the mooring

platform. This was now covered with a sheet of water a couple of inches deep.

Rachel looked down and said, 'You can't see the edge of the platform . . . whatever you do, don't step off the end.'

Amelia shook her head and realized she was too exhausted to give a verbal reply.

'Up there.' Rachel panted. 'To the boathouse. He'll be safe there.'

Supporting the dead – the utterly dead – weight between them, they inched their way up the concrete ramp to the twin doors of the boathouse. One-handed, Rachel managed to open one of the doors. Then, buffeted by winds and spray, they made it inside.

Amelia shone her torch down onto an open area of concrete at the side of the boat. 'Here?' she managed to pant.

Rachel nodded.

Grateful to be relieved of the weight, they lowered the corpse onto the ground. Rachel quickly straightened the man's legs then, after a pause, folded his arms over his chest.

'OK.' She breathed deeply, then looked at Amelia. 'Ready to see if there's anyone else out there?'

Amelia nodded gravely.

Once more they went out into the storm.

Chapter Thirty-seven

'Here, Amelia, get this down you.'

'How's—'

'Shh . . . it's hot tea. I've put plenty of sugar in, so don't complain.'

'But how's my mother, Lucy?'

'She's fine now.'

'But she looked like death on the steps an hour ago.'

'It's just one of her migraines, Amelia dear . . . they come on just like that. Now, drink your tea.'

Rachel sipped hers. 'Is Catherine in bed?'

'Yes.'

'Has she taken anything for it?'

'Yes, I saw to that. Now, would anyone like whisky in their tea?'

'No, thank you.'

Lucy's expression was deeply sympathetic. 'Here, let me dry that hair of yours, Amelia.' She began to rub the girl's head with the towel. 'My goodness, the two of you have had an ordeal tonight. I wouldn't wish what you've been through on anyone.'

Rachel sniffed. 'It had to be done. The pilot's body will need to be returned to his family for burial.'

'But is he Greek or Turkish?'

'I can't say.'

'If he's Turkish then he's probably a Moslem. Shouldn't the funeral take place before sunset on the day of death?'

305

'That's not possible.' Rachel, cool, composed, sounded matter-of-fact. To Amelia it seemed as though she discussed the man as dispassionately as if she were talking about the weather. 'The sea's still too rough to bring a boat in yet.' She sipped her tea. 'In fact, it might be like that for days. The body will be perfectly safe in the boathouse.'

Safe. She was using that word again, Amelia thought, chilled. *Is the corpse of the drowned man safe . . . or are we safe from the drowned man?* After all, Rachel had padlocked the boathouse doors shut as they'd left.

Oh, Mr Drowned Man, you can shout and shout as much as you like – but you're not coming out of there . . .

Why did I think that? What a stupid idea. Amelia massaged her temples.

Tired, that's all. Bone tired. She tuned back in to Rachel's and Lucy's conversation.

'So there was sign of only one person?' Lucy was asking.

Rachel nodded. 'With luck, it was a single-seater aircraft. Anyway, Amelia and I searched as much of the cliff bottom as we could and we saw nothing else.'

'No wreckage or anything?'

'Nothing much to speak of. I dare say, though, that more will be washed up in the next day or so. No chance of the phone working, I suppose?'

'Still completely dead, I'm afraid.'

'That figures, with this damn storm blowing.'

'Poor things, you must be frozen.'

Rachel stood up. 'We are. And I, for one, am going to have a hot bath. Then I'm going back to bed.' She glanced at the kitchen clock. 'For what's left of the night, anyway.'

A period of calm now followed the storm. The winds still blew but they'd dropped to a sighing sound. Outside it was still dark. Although dawn couldn't be that far away.

Rachel left her cup in the sink and headed for her room. Amelia told Lucy she was doing the same. If anything, she now had an urge to scrub her fingertips where they'd come into contact with the drowned man.

Does Rachel have that same sticky sensation on her fingertips? Amelia asked herself. *As if she's crushed a big fat bluebottle between her fingers.* Amelia doubted Rachel felt the same way.

'Did Rachel tell you that the pilot's face was injured?'

Lucy shook her head. 'In what way?'

'I don't know. She wouldn't let me see.'

'Amelia, are you all right?'

'She wouldn't let me see the man's face. She pulled the visor down to hide it. But I can't help but remember when we saw – or imagined we saw – the figure on the patio by the pool. There was something wrong with its face, too. And I wondered if the same—'

'Amelia. *Amelia.* Come on, love. This must have come as a nasty shock for you.'

'Yes . . .' She took a steadying breath. 'I suppose it has. Right, I'll go and have a shower, then grab some sleep.'

'I can come up and sit with you.'

'No, honestly, I'll be fine.'

'OK, but if you need me just shout. All right?'

'Thanks.' Amelia shot Lucy a grateful smile. 'And don't worry. I'll be fine.'

The hot water was stinging. But Amelia endured it. As well as taking the chill from her bones it also scalded away anything that might have clung to her fingertips.

She made a point of singing to herself as she towelled herself dry. The sudden silence after she'd turned off the shower seemed just that bit quieter than normal.

Which is a daft thing to say, she scolded herself as she rubbed her hair. *You can't have a quiet silence any more than you can have a dark black. Silence is silence and black is black; they are both absolutes.* She realized the thoughts running through her head were largely nonsense, but she allowed them to run on anyway. If she thought about something – anything – her mind wouldn't return to the drowned man lying there in the boathouse with his ruined face . . .

She steered herself away from the image and thought

about Bill Simotas instead. He'd be asleep in his cousin's villa now.

Alone in his bed, he might be thinking about her.

Briskly she left the bathroom. A moment later she was in bed.

Damn. I forgot to switch off the light.

And as it was the main bedroom light, not the bedside lamp, she'd have to climb out of bed again.

Thoughts of those cold tiles beneath her bare feet provoked a shudder.

Stuff it, she thought with rock-solid conviction. *I'll sleep with the light on tonight.* No one could complain about that. *I'd sleep with the radio on, too, if I had one. After all, it's not every night you pull your dead father from the sea . . .*

Amelia sat up in bed, her scalp prickling.

Dead father?

What absurd impulse made her think the man was her father?

She wondered about returning to the kitchen for that tot of whisky – a bloody big tot of whisky, at that. But working hard to gain entry to her head was the idea that there was nothing wrong with the dead man's face; that Rachel had deliberately kept his identity secret; that the man was, in fact, Amelia's father. He'd been trying to reach the island when the plane had developed a fault; he'd been forced to parachute out into the sea. What was more, he wasn't really dead. Rachel had hidden that from her, too. Now he was probably recovering consciousness in the boathouse. He was pulling himself up groggily to sit with his back to the boat, a pool of sea water spreading all around—

No, no. No. This was a crazy line of thought. It harked back to her childhood fantasies that her unknown father was a spy.

She gripped the sheets in her fists. *That man isn't your father. That man is a stranger. He's dead. Now stop being childish; get him out of your head – and go to sleep.*

Amelia lay for half an hour or more. Exhaustion waged a silent war with her imagination. Her body needed sleep; her imagination explored what had happened as a tongue explores a newly chipped tooth.

Time and time again her imagination took her out through the front door of the villa, then down the path to the steps. It took her down, step by step, to the sea. There the waves still surged over the concrete platform. And there was the boathouse.

In her mind's eye she glided through the darkness towards it.

Breezes sighed over the cliffs. Judas trees whispered at her, telling her who she'd find lying there in the boathouse.

Effortlessly her imagination carried her to the doors of the boathouse; she slipped through the timbers as easily as a ghost. There on the floor between the wall and the boat lay the drowned man.

My father . . .

Here he is. His black flying suit is slick with sea water. More pools round the body. There are the boots with the bright yellow laces. The laces which he tied into double bows with his own two hands. His white helmet gleams like a skull. The visor is no longer pulled down. Now you can see his face.

Is it the face of the father you've never even seen?

Or is the face terribly disfigured? Perhaps torn in two when he ejected from the crashing plane? Or perhaps it is the face that—

No. I've had enough of this. Amelia climbed back out of bed and went to the bathroom where she brushed her teeth so fiercely that the gums bled. Then, once more, she returned to bed.

Again, she realized she'd not switched out the light.

But she didn't care. She pulled the sheet over her face. Determinedly, she closed her eyes.

Now all she could hear was the sigh of the breeze running through the Judas trees. The sounds it made were the sounds of someone breathing. She centred on that. The rhythm of it was relaxing. She relaxed with it. Presently her muscles softened, a warmth spread out from her stomach, and she knew she was falling at last into a much-needed sleep.

★ ★ ★

Some time later. It seemed a long, long time after that Amelia awoke. Darkness thickly filled the bedroom. A complete darkness that did not allow her to see so much as a fingertip in front of her eyes.

But I didn't switch off the bedroom light.

Who switched off the light?

And who is touching my face?

Laying flat on her back, she didn't move a muscle. Someone was stroking her forehead. Their fingers were cool, almost cold. But their movements were unhurried and very, very gentle.

Mother . . .

Amelia realized she was still half asleep. She might have said the word or, then again, she might merely have thought it.

She tried again. 'Mother?'

The fingers traced a line from her right eyebrow, arching up across her forehead to make a circular motion – really quite fondly – above her left eyebrow where she'd injured her skull. Perhaps her mother could feel the nub of bone that would begin to ache so mercilessly when Amelia was tired or distressed.

The caress was soothing. Her head didn't hurt now. She looked up into darkness. It was too dark to see her mother. But she imagined her concerned, even gently caring expression.

'Mother . . .' She'd dropped the 'Catherine' in favour of the word she'd hardly ever used in her life before. 'Mother? Was I dreaming? . . . I'm sorry if I woke you.'

The cold fingers traced a line down the side of her face to her jaw. The touch was pleasant.

Amelia allowed her body to relax. 'Mother . . . I used to have such terrible nightmares. Aunt Mae probably told you. It's stupid . . . but I must have yelled the house down when I first left the hospital. I think I scared my cousins half to death. Did I make a lot of noise just now, mother?'

The stroking continued. Amelia felt the very tips of the cold fingers moving slowly up to her forehead. It was the action of a parent soothing a child who had been woken by a bad dream.

It was pleasant to lie there, allowing her mother to stroke her forehead. But she knew that would be selfish; her mother wasn't well; that migraine attack had been crucifying. Her mother had looked so fragile, down there on the steps.

'Mother? How are you feeling now?'

Amelia turned her eyes to where she imagined her mother must be standing.

Darkness still hid everything within the room. She could, however, see the dim grey blocks that were the curtained windows. Morning light must be spilling over Voros now.

Her eyesight suddenly sharpened.

Beyond the balcony door she saw the silhouette of a man. The moment she registered the fact, she saw the shadow hand reach out to twist the handle of the balcony door from outside. The handle on the inside squeaked slightly as it was depressed.

'Mother! Someone's trying to get in!'

Shouting, Amelia flung herself out of bed.

Instantly, a strong pair of arms encircled her to stop her running any further. Reaching down, she grasped material and realized she'd become entangled in the muslin curtain that surrounded the bed. There were no restraining arms after all.

'Mother. Switch on the light. It'll frighten him away!'

She disentangled herself by spinning out of the curtain. 'Mother?'

Why didn't she turn on the light?

The intruder had opened the door by this time. Instantly the breeze caught the curtains there and they rippled out towards her like spectral arms.

Bare feet slapping against the tiles, she raced to the wall and turned on the light.

'Mother—'

Amelia stared at the side of the bed where her mother had been standing to stroke her face. She blinked.

Apart from herself, the bedroom was empty.

She darted a look at the door that led outside to the balcony. It stood part-way open. Heart thumping, she raced to it, switched on the balcony light. The balcony was deserted.

In the dawn gloom beyond, Judas trees danced madly on the grey rocks.

Amelia turned back to fix the empty, the coldly empty room with an accusing stare.

It was then she noticed what lay on her bedside table. The object had been just inches from her sleeping head; almost touching it.

'Oh, my God,' she whispered. Then she shivered right down to the root of her spine.

There on the table stood the drowned man's helmet.

She took three paces towards it. She saw the words printed on it in an incomprehensible script. The black visor was down as if to hide what might lay within. The pilot's helmet was bone white.

It possessed all the fleshless horror of a skull.

Chapter Thirty-eight

Lucy was shocked. 'The helmet, you say?'

'Yes.'

'Where is it?'

'On the bedside table. Right next to my pillow.'

Both women paused outside Amelia's bedroom door.

Lucy gave a weak smile. 'Why don't the lights ever seem bright enough at a time like this?'

'Lucy, we can wait if—'

'No. No.' She took a steadying breath. 'We're brave souls, aren't we? Remember, I said this kind of thing would happen. You get two psychics under the same roof and things begin to fizz. Now don't you worry. We'll just look through the doorway. If—'

'Lucy—'

'If . . . if we don't look like the look of what we see, we'll just step back out again and wait until daylight.'

'Lucy. Amelia. What's the matter?' Rachel emerged from her bedroom, belting her dressing gown.

'As we say where we come from: something's up.' Lucy gave her weak grin again; an almost apologetic smile, Amelia thought.

'Something's up? What do you mean?'

'Amelia woke to find the pilot's helmet on her bedside table.'

Rachel's nostrils flared. 'The helmet? Don't be ridiculous.' With that, she swept past them into Amelia's bedroom.

Although from that angle Amelia couldn't see her bed, nor her bedside table, she saw Rachel's sharp eyes locked on to them.

A moment later Rachel stood back as if to invite the two women to enter.

Coldly she asked, 'Where exactly is the helmet, Amelia?'

'It *was* there,' Amelia told Rachel later as they went downstairs.

'But it's not there now?'

'I *saw* it.'

'And the intruder on the balcony?'

'Yes.'

'But he's not there now. Nor is the helmet.'

Rachel opened the front door. The breeze, not nearly as strong as it had been earlier, still gusted in, carrying with it dry leaves. 'I'll go and check outside. You two wait here.'

'No.' Amelia made herself sound level-headed. She didn't want to be written off as hysterical by this laser-eyed woman. 'I'm coming with you.'

'I don't think that's a good idea, Amelia. Do you, Lucy?'

'Well . . .'

Amelia strode toward the door. 'I'm coming.'

'Suit yourself. Lucy, dear?'

'Yes, Rachel?'

'Will you stay here in case Catherine's been woken by all this . . . *upset?*'

Without waiting for a reply Rachel walked out through the doorway. Amelia almost had to run as Rachel marched around the side of the villa. Absurdly, Amelia felt as if she was running to keep up with an angry parent.

The cypress trees still swayed in the breeze. Above the pinnacles of rock, layer upon layer of cloud of differing shades of grey slid across the sky. Whip-like branches of Judas trees swung back and forth. The air was cold. The atmosphere in and around the villa was, if anything, colder.

Amelia pulled her hair from her eyes. 'You do believe the helmet was there?'

She was rewarded with a snort from Rachel. 'I do not.'

'But—'

'You know as well as I do, you silly girl, that the helmet is on the dead man's head in the boathouse.'

'It wasn't. It was on the bedside table.'

'So who put it there?'

'I don't know.'

'The intruder?'

'Yes . . . maybe.'

'Maybe?'

'It was dark.'

'Why should anyone do that?'

'I don't know.' Amelia was rattled. Rachel was like the counsel for the prosecution once more, intent on demolishing a witness's testimony – an unreliable if not downright flaky witness, at that.

Lips pressed together as if she'd been forced to sort out a stranger's dirty laundry, Rachel did her duty. She looked for signs of the intruder on the patio; she glanced in the pool, now frothed by the action of the wind and soup-like with debris. There was no one there. And no sign that anyone had been there.

Then she worked her way round to the back of the villa where Amelia's bedroom overlooked rocky crags and copses of Judas trees.

'I don't see anyone,' Rachel announced after her sharp eyes had scoured the ground. 'And I certainly can't see any signs anyone's been here.'

'It's hardly surprising.'

'Why?'

'There's no soft earth where they could leave prints. Anyone could have walked across those boulders, then—'

'Shinned up the drainpipe? Climbed onto your balcony?'

'Yes.'

'But why, Amelia?' Rachel stared hard at her. 'Why should a

man go to the trouble of climbing onto *your* balcony and looking in at *you*?'

'I don't know . . . perhaps . . . perhaps because . . .'

'Because you felt you needed some extra attention?'

'No.'

'So you invented an intruder?'

'Don't be ridiculous. Why would I—'

'Like you invented the silly story about the pilot's helmet magically appearing on your bedside table?'

'It was there. I *did* see it.'

'Amelia. "It was there" and "I did see it" are two completely different statements. You might have *thought* you saw it. But did you touch the helmet? Did you handle it?'

'No.'

'Is the helmet in your room now?'

'No, of course not.'

'Isn't it?'

'Well, you didn't see it, did you?'

'No.' Rachel folded her arms. 'But it might have been hidden out of sight.'

'But who would do anything so . . .' Amelia stopped dead. 'Wait a minute . . . *now wait one minute*. Are you saying that I went down, took the helmet off a dead body and brought it up here?'

Again that unwavering gaze of Rachel's. A moment's pause, then: 'So if you and I go down to the boathouse now we will see the helmet still on the body?'

'Of course we will!'

'So the helmet didn't appear on your bedside table?'

'No . . . wait a minute here, Rachel. I didn't say . . . I didn't mean that.'

'What did you mean?'

'You're firing questions at me like I'm a murder suspect or something. You confused me.'

'Do you find yourself getting confused easily?'

A cold fury began to fill Amelia. 'Listen to me, you *bitch*. Stop treating me as if I'm on trial. I have not touched that helmet. When I woke up I saw an intruder. A moment later I saw the helmet on the table. I don't know who put it there. I don't know why they put it there. Got that?'

Rachel considered. Again she was cool, unflustered. 'Amelia. Ever since you arrived here objects have been inexplicably moved. Or disappeared.'

'No, wait a minute . . .'

'The corkscrew was a running joke. But I know Lucy found her hand mirror smashed in her bath. And I had some money in my jewellery box—'

'I don't believe this, Rachel! You're saying I smashed a mirror and stole the money?'

'I'm saying—'

'It's the first time I've heard about this.'

'Calm down, Amelia.'

'I *am* calm, Rachel.'

'You don't want to disturb your mother any more than you have done, do you?'

'That's sly, isn't it? Making me out to have upset my mother? So I brought on the migraine, did I?'

'I didn't say that. But she's been under more stress ever since you arrived here.'

'No. Don't you dare pin that on me, Rachel.'

'But why have our possessions suddenly started disappearing or being moved?'

'I don't know.'

'Amelia, I don't know much about you. Only that you're Catherine's daughter and that you've not been well.'

'I—'

'And that's why you've come here. To recuperate.'

Amelia stared at Rachel in shock.

'From the look of you: how pale and thin you are. I can guess, however, what you are recuperating from.'

'Wait, just wait; are you—'

'I don't want to hear any sordid confessions about how no one ever loved you or—'

'You think I was taking drugs?'

'That doesn't matter. But ever since you came here your behaviour has been childish. Don't think I've not noticed your sulky expressions, or the way you allow your mother to wait on you hand and foot—'

'That's not fair.'

'Like she's your personal slave—'

'I haven't. I've done my best to help out.'

'Or the way you always need to be the centre of attention.'

'I don't believe it.'

'Keep your voice down, Amelia. The whole island doesn't need to know, especially your mother.'

'I am not shouting. Why must you think the helmet and the . . . the intruder are nothing more than me drawing attention to myself?'

'I've said my piece, Amelia. Just think about it. Now we don't have to mention it again, do we?'

Cow . . . the cow . . . the jealous cow. If anything, it was Rachel who'd had her nose put out. That's why she had seemed so frosty right from the start. It was as if a child had seen its parents bringing a newborn baby into the house.

'And,' Rachel was saying coldly, 'if you stop interfering with our personal possessions we can let this distressing matter drop once and for all.'

Amelia shook her head. 'I have not touched anything. Lucy says . . .' She trailed off.

'Lucy says what?'

Amelia sighed, reluctant to continue.

'Come on, Amelia, Lucy says what?'

'Lucy says that the household objects being moved might result from a psychic disturbance.'

Rachel fixed her with her glare. 'Psychic disturbance. *Psychic disturbance?*' She breathed out through her flared nostrils. 'My God, have you got a nerve! You nasty little thing.'

'It's true. I didn't believe in this kind of thing – the supernatural. But I've seen things I just can't explain.'

'No, I don't suppose you can, can you?'

'How can you explain the corkscrew burying itself into the hallway ceiling?'

'Hasn't man invented something called a ladder?'

'You bitch . . . you miserable, jealous bitch. You're accusing me of everything, aren't you? You're nothing . . . nothing but . . .'

Amelia was so angry she couldn't speak. She glared at Rachel and Rachel glared back. At that moment Amelia wanted to grab that stick-like woman by her stringy hair, then rub her nose in the dirt. Thoughts of the woman's expression of shocked surprise as she looked up through a mud-smeared face made Amelia burn inside with something that felt very much like lust.

But what happened next took her by surprise.

Rachel's long body whipped forward, her arm swung and the palm of her hand connected with the side of Amelia's face. Her head seemed to ring like a bell at the ferocity of the blow.

'Enough is enough,' Rachel hissed, holding up her hand as if it was a weapon she wouldn't be afraid to use again. 'I want no more of this babble about the supernatural or psychic forces. Do you hear? *No more.*'

With that, she turned and walked back towards the door.

Amelia looked up at the windows, suddenly embarrassed that somebody might have witnessed the blow. By now her face was burning as if it had been scorched by fire.

Gingerly she touched her cheek. At the same moment a lump came in her throat, her stomach muscles twitched.

The she felt her cheeks and realized tears had started to pour from her eyes.

I don't believe this, I just don't believe this, she thought over and over again. She was stunned by the injustice of it. This was like being convincted of a crime she hadn't committed. The sense of outrage tightened her insides into knots.

Now she couldn't stop herself at all. Folding her arms so she was hugging herself, she sat on a stone beneath her bedroom window and sobbed.

Chapter Thirty-nine

The morning after they had pulled the drowned man out of the sea was quiet. Relatively quiet, that was.

The telephone was still down. Lucy tried every hour on the hour without any joy. The earpiece only gave up a ghostly sigh or two at best.

Amelia had retired to her bedroom for a couple of hours. She'd examined the bedside table. She'd half hoped there would be some tell-tale drops of sea water left by the helmet. At least that might provide a little evidence of what she had seen. There was nothing.

Then she'd gone to the bathroom and examined her cheek where Rachel had slapped it. The pink mark had almost vanished. It still burnt, however. But by now this was probably more the result of her own anger rather than the force of the original blow.

For a while she contemplated venturing downstairs to grab some coffee and a slice of toast, but she found herself reluctant to face anyone. Especially not that vicious little cow Rachel.

And did Lucy know? And her mother?

Why hadn't she, Amelia, slapped Rachel back? Or bent down, seized a handful of stones and flung them into her staring eyes? *That would teach her. Little cow, little bitch . . .*

Amelia felt the anger and the shame – and the injustice – working inside her again. How dare Rachel suggest she'd been the one to hide other people's possessions? Hadn't she had enough of that at Aunt Mae's? Her cousins, she knew for a fact, had pilfered money, pens, perfume and anything else they could get their hands on.

She took a deep breath and lay back on her bed, her hands clasped behind her head. This was getting her nowhere. Maybe the Gregale was at the root of all this. It blew hour after hour. It made them all edgy. The Gregale had downed the plane. The man had parachuted into the sea where he'd floundered for a while in the waves, the parachute dragging him down. When he could no longer keep his head above the surface it had drowned him. Now her mother was sick with a migraine; and she and Rachel were cranky with each other. Yes, the more she thought about it, the more it seemed that the Gregale was to blame for everything.

Outside the day was grey. Cloud lumbered over the island. Every now and again the winds would blow the Judas trees until their branches rippled in a dark mass of whipping twigs.

When would the damn' things blossom or grow leaves? Why did they look like bunches of dead twigs?

It was an irrational thought and Amelia knew it. She could hardly stand on the balcony and harangue the weather, or implore the leaves to appear on the trees.

She returned to the bathroom and dabbed her hot cheek with cold water.

The wind blew outside. It brought the fluting notes back. She listened for a moment as they rose and fell. As she did so, she turned her head to one side and examined her cheek, pulling her hair back over one ear.

The pink had almost gone.

Did she really look gaunt?

She could see her cheekbones, true. But she had never considered that she'd become actually gaunt after that hilarious fall from the bridge that had cracked her skull like an egg.

The wind took the eaves by storm. A dizzying swirl of flute sounds echoed from the tiled walls of the bathroom.

She couldn't become a recluse here. She couldn't allow Rachel to intimidate her so much that she never left her bedroom, could she? That would be like a return to that miserable house of Aunt Mae's. A prisoner in her own bedroom. Fed on scraps thrown through the door. So miserable the only way out was to make a noose from a belt. To tie it to the bed post. To slip the noose over her—

No.

Don't think that.

Already ridiculous ideas were insinuating themselves into her head. And why, in heaven's name, had she thought of her fall from the bridge as being *hilarious?*

'There was nothing hilarious about that, buster,' she told her reflection. 'And nothing hilarious about staying in hospital . . . or all those drugs; or running up credit cards buying clothes for babies that don't exist . . .'

Thrummm . . . Those cold Atlantic air currents drummed against the windows. The flute-like notes joined in. Sometimes they were high as a whistle, sometimes they were deep as a man's voice.

'Well, Amelia Thomas, you can stay here and look at your reflection all day, or . . .'

She baked a batch of cakes. Once Rachel's white face appeared at the door; then as quickly as a ghost it had gone.

Amelia made a jugful of coffee and, leaving it in the living room, called Lucy and Rachel, inviting them to help themselves.

Half an hour later she went into the living room to find that the coffee hadn't been touched. She poured it away.

After checking that the cakes were browning nicely she looked in on her mother. Catherine was sleeping soundly. Her aristocratic features looked so delicate. Her hair, loose now, formed a fan on the pillow.

On impulse Amelia looked in on Lucy.

Lucy was sleeping soundly, too, curled kitten-like beneath the blanket.

Outside Rachel's door she paused, then put her ear to it. She could hear the sound of rhythmic breathing and guessed that Rachel slept, too.

After that, she went back downstairs, by the watchful statues that never slept, and into the kitchen. Although it was chilly in there, despite the oven being on for the last hour, the baking smells helped make it at least a tolerably comfortable place to be.

In a little while she turned out the cakes onto baskets to cool.

Through the windows Amelia could see the Judas trees on the rocky landscape. The wind running through them made them appear to move, as if they were swarming up the slopes towards the villa like an invading army.

On the steps that led up to the old artillery platform where the soldiers' palm prints were impressed in the concrete she thought she saw a figure.

She returned to the task in hand. The washing-up held her attention for the next fifteen minutes. Humming to herself, she wished there was a radio. With the little money she had left she could buy one, and then hand it over gift-wrapped and tied up with a bow of ribbon to the three other women as a present from her to all of them.

Would that be a peace-offering?

Or an apology for all that she'd done?

But then, she had done nothing.

What Rachel had said just wasn't true; it was as simple as that.

Amelia mopped the floor with hot water and bleach until her eyes smarted.

After that she swept away the leaves that had drifted into the entrance hall in the wind. Two of the dozen or so spotlight bulbs that illuminated the statues had blown but she couldn't find the spares, so that was one job left undone.

For a time she sat in the living room. After a while, however, the hostile stares of the statues were enough to drive her back out again.

She found the front door had somehow managed to open itself. More leaves had blown in. She swept them back out.

To drive the bleach odours from her clothes she took a walk outside. On the patio she gazed at the sea. It was as grey as the cloud above it and she couldn't tell where water ended and sky began. Fantastically, a Woolworth's carrier bag floated in the swimming pool. Could it have been blown here a hundred miles or so to land in the water?

But then, hadn't they told her that anything was possible once the Gregale began to blow?

After all, her mother had joked darkly once that 'When the gales have been blowing for a day or two you feel like cutting your throat — just for something to do.'

From the villa's eaves came piping sounds as the air currents played over them. The Judas trees started a concerted whispering. Their branches felt at the air like a million insect antennae. Did they sense the approach of another storm? Or the approach, perhaps, of something else?

For a second Amelia thought of the cold form of the drowned man lying in the boathouse. The bright yellow laces would be dry now. Would the body swell? What was the face really like behind that great white skull of a helmet?

And then she thought about Bill. Perhaps he was sitting in a taverna, drinking coffee from a tiny china mug. That black-tar coffee which he'd wash down with a glass of water. She pictured him for a moment, his Adam's apple bobbing as he swallowed a mouthful before rejoining a conversation with his cousins about . . . about what? Football? Boats? Women?

She smiled a secret smile to herself.

When she checked to see that the cakes were cool she sniffed one; then another. They smelt sour. She checked the butter, expecting it to be rancid. No, that was OK. She sniffed the cakes again. But they smelt funny . . . funny peculiar, that was.

She threw them into the bin.

Lucy had been testing the telephone at regular intervals to see if the connection had been restored. But with her asleep in bed Amelia suspected that it hadn't been checked for a time.

Switching on the hallway spotlights, she went to one of the downstairs phones. It was housed in a niche beside a statue with a shattered face.

There was no dialling tone. Not so much as a crackle of static, in fact.

As she replaced the receiver another spotlight bulb blew.

Instantly the hallway grew gloomier; the shadows deeper; and, somehow, the expressions on the statues' faces a little more sombre.

Amelia made her way back to the kitchen. She'd almost reached the door when another bulb blew. The shadows darkened.

The winds blew hard. Voros had taken everything the weather could throw at it for the last ten thousand years. It could take more, much more. And it would probably still be there in another ten thousand years: a tiny stage of rock in the sea where life-and-death dramas would be played out. Mourned. Forgotten. Then played out all over again. Whether it was when the hospital ship *Atlas* foundered on the shore and its four hundred bedridden troops plunged to the ocean bottom where their ribcages even now formed nests for eels. Or just a few hours ago when the pilot, entangled in the lines of his parachute, drowned within a few feet of the shore.

The wind blew hard across Voros. Amelia watched from the kitchen window. The effect on the Judas trees was always different with every gust. Moments ago their slender branches had looked like insect antennae sensing the air. Now there was something sinuous about their movement. The branches rippled in the breeze; it combed them all in the same direction, so it seemed to Amelia that threads of energy flowed through the dozens of trees.

'Oooh, have you got any butter there? Pardon me.' Lucy

yawned as she bustled into the kitchen. 'Goodness, I've slept like someone screwed the lid on.'

'Butter?'

'Yes. My hair was in such a mess I thought I'd use my curling tongs . . .' She held up her arm. 'The silly things popped in my hand. There were sparks all over the place.'

'You're burned. I'll get the first-aid box.'

'No.' Lucy pronounced it as a long-drawn-out *Nooooo*. 'A bit of butter will do the trick. It's just the top of my finger there that got scorched.'

'Are you sure you're all right?'

'Thank you, Amelia, you're a love for caring.' She beamed. 'But I'll be fine. My fault, of course; those tongs were so old they were probably used by Joan of Arc. Oh! Have I said something blasphemous? She was a saint, wasn't she? The one who was burnt at the stake?'

'For witchcraft.'

'Goodness,' Lucy said happily. 'We'll have to be careful, won't we?'

After the argument with Rachel that morning Amelia wasn't keen to allow the conversation to turn to anything about psychic matters or supernatural activity.

She especially didn't want to be reminded of seeing the drowned man's helmet on her bedside table.

'Ooh, that feels better.' Lucy rubbed a glob of butter onto her finger. 'I thought you might have had an hour in bed after all last night's drama?'

'I feel wide awake. I planned to do some baking but the cakes . . .' Smiling, Amelia shrugged. '. . . They all turned out wrong.'

'Funny-tasting?'

Amelia nodded.

'I thought this might happen.'

At that moment the kitchen door shut with a crash.

Amelia looked round, startled.

Lucy didn't look fazed. 'Draughts,' she said quietly. 'Or perhaps it's the *other thing*.'

'Any more butter?'

'No, thank you. I'm fine.'

'Coffee?'

Lucy yawned again. 'Uh, no, thanks all the same. I might turn in again. Once the Gregale gets up you find yourself grabbing what sleep you can.' She looked at Amelia, concerned. 'Are you sure you're all right, dear? You look a little jittery.'

'I imagine it's after last night. It's unsettled me, that's all.'

'Well, don't do without your shut-eye, dear. I've known people who've been so deprived of sleep because of these silly storms that—'

'They go off their heads?'

'Well, they behave out of character, let's say.'

They talked for a few more moments, then Lucy left the kitchen, saying she was going to try and sleep a little more.

Amelia returned to staring out of the window. Once she thought she saw a figure on the steps again. Mainly, however, she gazed at the Judas trees; at their ever-changing shapes as the currents of cold air moulded, then remoulded them. Now it looked as if a great pulse of power ran through them.

Instantly the fluting sound began again. It sounded madder than ever.

That afternoon Amelia went up to her mother's bedroom. Gently knocking, she opened the door. 'Catherine? Catherine?'

'Yes.' The voice was faint.

'I didn't wake you, did I?'

'No . . . I've been awake a little while.'

Amelia stepped inside. Her mother had sat up in bed, but in the gloom of the curtained room all Amelia could make out was a pair of silvery eyes.

'Can I bring you anything, Catherine?'

'I was just about to take another painkiller.'

'Isn't it any better?'

'Don't worry, dear. I think I'm on the mend. It's just that these bloody migraines come like a bolt out of the blue. More than anything I'm annoyed with myself for letting you down last night.'

'Don't worry about that.' Amelia's eyes were growing accustomed to the gloom now. She saw Catherine sitting there, tired and drawn. Her face looked so extraordinarily delicate. As if its bones had been replaced with those of a bird.

'Oh . . . pardon me.' Catherine yawned. 'What time is it?'

'Just after two.'

'Have you eaten?'

'Yes, don't worry about me. Can I get you anything?'

'Not yet, thanks. These migraines leave me feeling sickly as much as anything. I think it's the double vision that does it. God, it makes me feel so old and useless . . . uh . . .' She touched her temples. 'Would you be a dear and pass me that packet of capsules . . . they're on the table by the book.'

Amelia did so and watched her mother crack a couple of capsules from the blister pack, then swallow them. There was a bottle of water on the bedside table. Amelia refilled the glass.

'Mm . . . thank you, Amelia. How are you feeling now?'

Had Rachel spilled the beans about what happened this morning? Suddenly a ferocious torrent of images gushed through her head. Of Rachel prancing in to sit on the end of her mother's bed, then rocking backwards and forwards as she gleefully relived the argument that morning; then miming the stinging slap; while all the time her eyes blazed with nothing less than exultation.

Amelia carefully told her mother that she was fine, that she planned to try and get some sleep.

Her mother, resting her head back onto the pillow, talked drowsily. She gave no indication of knowing anything about Amelia's row with Rachel; or the accusations that had been volleyed at her.

'It must have been trying last night. I'm sorry for you . . . and of course it was a tragedy for the young man and his family. You wouldn't have thought his commander would allow him to fly in weather conditions like this.'

'The phones aren't working yet so we haven't been able to notify anyone.'

'Damn' weather. It always happens.'

'Has anyone got a mobile?'

'Lucy brought one with her, but they don't work out here. Something to do with magnetic ore lying under the island. That's why there's no point owning a television . . . everything gets scrambled to damnation . . . Uh, you must be bored out of your mind, Amelia.'

'I'm OK, honest.'

'All the better when Bill gets back, eh?'

Amelia smiled. 'And when the sun starts to shine again.'

'Yes, that, too.' Catherine yawned. 'That too . . .'

'Catherine?'

'Yes?'

'Have you mislaid anything recently?'

Catherine smiled, sleepy. 'You name it . . . everything seems to sprout legs in this place . . . everything . . .'

'You don't . . .' Amelia, pausing, nearly didn't ask the question. But she knew it must be broached. 'You don't think I've taken anything that doesn't belong to me?'

The wind sighed round the eaves. A deep flute sound surged, then dipped.

'Catherine?'

Amelia leaned forward to look down at her mother. Her eyes were closed. 'Mother?'

The sound of her breathing was steady. She'd probably not even been awake to hear the question. Quietly, Amelia padded out of the bedroom and into her own.

Amelia crept into bed.

Will I ever sleep through this? she asked herself. *The wind sounds like someone sobbing.*

Other questions crowded in on her, too.

Will I be able to stay on here, now that Rachel's said what she has? The cat's well and truly out of the bag now. The woman hates me, doesn't she? She must have resented my presence here from the beginning. And there's something shrewd and scheming about her. No doubt Rachel could turn the other two women against her. Especially if she could persuade them that Amelia was a petty thief.

The wind blew harder. It *thrummed* against the windows. The draughts played silly games with the curtains. Raising them like spectral arms. They seemed to reach out graspingly to Amelia. As if they could seize her and drag her into their folds, where the soft fabric could slowly smother her . . .

There she would melt. Voros would absorb her into itself. Just as it had done with the young German soldiers in the cave; like it was doing even now with the drowned pilot.

In a detached way Amelia realized she was falling asleep after all. Her strange fancies about curtains that had become spectres and her *self* being sucked away by the island were obviously some blend of waking thought and impending dream.

Hadn't the doctors told her that the mechanism inside her brain that generated the dreams had been damaged by her head injury? That she could easily begin dreaming even when she was wide awake?

The on–off switch was broken. It was as simple as that.

Even now, as she hung poised between wakefulness and sleep, she could see that the drowned man lay on the floor beside her bed.

Why? Aren't I so close to him that I could just roll over and reach out and touch him with my fingertips?

I can see his black rubber suit. I can see the yellow laces in his boots. I can see the helmet that's the colour of bone.

And it would be no trouble to just reach down, take hold of the visor, flick it open.

Then I would be able to see his face, wouldn't I? I could see the injury. The one that Rachel thought so shocking that she hid it from me.

Or is it my father lying there in the flying suit? And is that the sound of his breathing?

She lifted herself up onto one elbow and looked down.

Beneath the visor was the cleanly shaven chin. There were the alien-looking words written in black on the helmet; they were as mysterious as hieroglyphics. One was probably the pilot's name.

Which one?

She tilted her head to one side to see better.

No, they meant nothing to her.

She lay back in bed once more, secure in the knowledge that this was a dream. Nothing but a dream. A flight of unconscious fancy.

So, the drowned man lay on the floor beside her. The dead body had invaded the security and privacy of her bedroom.

Aren't dreams funny things?

Wouldn't monkeys dressed as bandsmen soon come marching through the door, playing musical instruments?

Or would she dream she was swimming through the oceans with dolphins?

This dream would change soon enough . . . she was sure of it.

She lifted herself back onto one elbow again and gazed down on the drowned man.

This is a dream, she thought, *and you will disappear soon*. But the body did not vanish.

And the dream didn't change.

Chapter Forty

Voros stirs. Judas trees raise themselves to their full height. Like dead men readying themselves to walk once more.

A thousand feet below the waves conger eels in the SS *Atlas* sprang out from their ribcage nests. Snapped their jaws at the water as if an unseen predator threatened them.

In the villa known as The Palms the telephones were reconnected. Only no one was awake to use them. For ten minutes or so the lines hummed with electricity, ready for human speech to flash along them at the speed of light with news of the drowned man. But then a tiny component in the automatic exchange melted and the telephones lines died again.

As they did so another spotlight that had diligently illuminated a grim-faced statue with no nose exploded.

The faraway *pop!* woke Amelia.

Her first thought was: *The drowned man is lying next to me.* She twisted her head to look down at the floor beside her bed.

Tiles, a woven rug, a dropped earring. But no body.

Not that there ever had been, she told herself firmly.

Then she bravely stepped out of bed.

As she began to pull on her sweatshirt and jeans she noticed the time was a little after six. Despite the gales rattling around the villa she'd slept soundly for almost three hours.

Sleep was the best medicine of all. Now she felt rested. In control. Memories of the row with Rachel were less vivid.

If no one had started already she would make the evening meal for everyone. Something simple. This wintry weather made her hungry for steaming platefuls of hot northern cooking. As she fastened her sandals she thought about making heaps of mashed potato. What would go nicely with that? A stew of some sort? It might seem lazy but she was sure there were cans of stewed beef in the pantry.

Humming to herself, Amelia went downstairs.

Now perhaps only six or seven of the little spotlights still worked. Most of the statues stood broodingly in deep shadow.

Outside, the evening was already drawing in because of the cloud. It would be easy to suspend disbelief and imagine that someone had spent the last few hours steadily concreting over the sky.

The wind blew with a droning sound. There was going to be no early let-up of that.

Amelia opened the front door and looked out. Fingers of cold probed at her; her hair fluttered; she had to screw her eyes nearly shut to avoid the wind-borne grit. Voros now looked bleak, inhospitable. *A prison island*, she thought. *A grey rock in a grey ocean where people are sent to die.*

The only weather they hadn't had was rain. But even that might be a relief — or at least a contrast to the endless rush of air across the grey crags.

Resolutely she closed the door, determined to shut the unpleasant weather out.

She switched on all the lights in the kitchen. At least it would be bright in there. Finding the potatoes, she began peeling, singing to herself as she did so, and moving purposefully fast to stimulate the blood flow in her veins.

There were cans of beef stew. She opened two, spooned them into a pan, then added a tin of baby carrots.

Rachel appeared. If anything, her face was even whiter and her hair somehow darker. It was a mess, too, Amelia noted.

As if she'd slept badly. Maybe nightmares had her in their clutches, too.

Rachel moved around the kitchen as if she was alone in the room. She made herself a hot drink, then glided out as silently as a ghost.

Neither woman had acknowledged the existence of the other.

You're as thin as a stick and miserable as sin. The observation ran through Amelia's head as Rachel walked out through the kitchen door. *Have you ever been loved? Have you? Pity the poor man who woke to see those laser eyes boring into his.*

Amelia scraped potatoes. Then she opened a bottle of beer. When she took a sip it tasted as sour as the cakes she had made earlier. Still singing lightly to herself, she tipped it down the sink.

The brightness inside the kitchen accentuated the gloom outside. It was only when she heard the front door blow open with a bang and went to close it again that she noticed the level of grey light was no dimmer than before. It hung somewhere between daylight and dusk. Deep down, she wondered if Voros had slipped into limbo – a twilight world between the one she'd always known and some dark hereafter where the souls of the dead roamed.

An Isle of the Dead.

A place nearer to hell than heaven.

A little after six-thirty she made herself a cup of tea into which she dropped a slice of lemon. Normally the idea of tea with lemon instead of milk didn't appeal in the remotest but right then she didn't trust the milk to taste anything like milk.

Amelia took tiny sips of the scalding brew, not really getting any pleasure from it but pleased that she'd somehow outwitted whatever malign force had been making food and drink taste unpleasant to her.

A moment later Lucy came in. 'Heavens, I feel better for that. Slept like a top! Oooh, do I smell supper? Stew and mashed potato, oh lovely – I haven't had that in *years*.'

'You look bright.'

'I feel it. I think I've managed to catch up on the old beauty sleep in instalments. Is there any more tea in the pot?'

'I've just made it so it should be fresh.'

'I think I'll help myself to a cup. I came down ready for a drop of something stronger but I'll pace myself.' Lucy laughed. 'I'll be sloshed by nine if I start now. Can I do anything for you, love?'

'You can find the corkscrew for me, if you will.'

'Goodness. It's not vanished again, has it?' She turned, looking. 'No. It's there on the knick-knack stand where it should be.' She beamed. 'By gum, I'd best not call it the knick-knack stand in Rachel's presence or she'll scowl at me. Like *this*.' After making a pantomime scowl Lucy paused and adopted a fixed stare. '"That, Lucy dear, is known as the utensil rack. And don't you forget it."' It was a passable impression of Rachel. Amelia laughed, genuinely amused.

They chatted amiably for the next twenty minutes. Amelia felt what tension remained in her neck begin to ease. As always, Lucy was button-bright and full of smiles. She suggested red wine with the stew and selected a couple of bottles which she opened. 'We'll let them breathe a little, shall we?' She sniffed one of the corks. 'Mmm, this one's from Kefalonia. It always reminds me of sherry, but it's not nearly so sweet. Oh, watch your potatoes, they're boiling over . . . Did I tell you I've just tried the phone again?'

'And?'

'Dead as a doornail, I'm afraid.'

Steam billowed from the pan as Amelia put the lid to one side. 'So we're stuck with our guest for a little while longer.'

'Yes. It is tragic though, isn't it?' She sipped her tea thoughtfully, then added, 'I wonder who he is . . . *was*.'

'I expect we'll find out in a day or so.'

'Yes. I expect we will. We must send flowers to the funeral . . . uh, I wondered when that would start.'

The lights dipped from their usual brilliance to a sudden glow; they grew so dim that Amelia could comfortably see the individual filaments in the bulbs without being dazzled.

'Does this happen often?' she asked.

'When the Gregale blows, very often. And it's not that uncommon at the best of times. Oh dear, it's such a bind, though, when there's a power cut and it's as dismal as this outside.'

'I'll get the candles.'

'Good idea, love.'

Amelia had remembered seeing candles in the cupboard by the window. When she went to get them she happened to look out. There stood the grey tower of rock against a grey sky. From here she had a clear view of the steps that ran up around the outside of it.

A figure stood on the steps, gazing fixedly down at the villa.

In fact, whoever it was seemed to be watching Amelia as she stood in the window.

Although they were too far away to identify, she saw the figure was dressed in black. And there was something about the head . . .

'What is it, Amelia? Not started raining, has it? As soon as the downpour comes at least it means the end of the Gregale for another year.'

Amelia shook her head.

'Not visitors, surely?'

'No.' She shook her head again quickly. 'No, it's nothing.'

'It certainly seems an interesting *nothing*.'

'No, I thought I saw someone, that's all.' Amelia smiled with a dismissive shrug to show it was nothing of importance.

Lucy moved towards her, tilting her head to one side so she could see through the window.

Amelia smiled at her before returning to stirring the pan of stew. 'They've gone now, anyway.'

'No, they haven't. They're still up there on the steps.'

Deliberately keeping her tone light, Amelia asked, 'Recognize them?'

'No, they're too far away . . . they're dressed in something black, though, aren't they?'

'I think so.'

For a moment both women stared out at the distant figure that somehow stood as still, and as forbidding, as the statues in the hall.

It was Lucy who broke the spell. Without explaining why she did it, she abruptly drew the blind, blocking the view of the figure. Then, with a deliberate brightness, she said, 'Awful weather. I'll make some Yorkshire puddings to go with the stew. Now, what did I do with my apron?'

Chapter Forty-one

The atmosphere at dinner was tight with expectation.

Of what exactly Amelia wasn't sure. But she was certain — *positive*, in fact — that words would be said or actions would be taken later. And there would be something cataclysmic about them. Lives would change. Personal histories would be altered.

Perhaps I will kill someone, she thought and then spooned more tomato soup into the bowl. That was the mood that gripped her: that she could do anything, even if it was out of character, outrageous, even criminal. *I could laugh in my mother's face . . . or demand to see a photograph of my father.*

Because you've got one somewhere, haven't you, mother dear? Somewhere in a place that's so secret you think no one will ever find it. But there is a photograph of him. Smiling, handsome, sharing the same wide expressive eyes as Amelia Thomas. He'd have the same sensual lips. The same broad forehead.

Then there's Rachel, nipping tiny pieces of bread from the roll, and then taking equally tiny sips of soup from her spoon.

Does she think I've put something horrible in the soup? With that great bony nose of hers is she trying to filter the odours; separate out the tomato and the basil to find a disgusting stench underneath? Or perhaps she imagines I've sprinkled in a little rat poison that I found in the basement?

Then there's Lucy. Lucy is sweet, innocent somehow. And, as they say, she has no side. She believes in the world of the supernatural. She's

339

tried hard to learn about it. She's attempted to cultivate her psychic side and made herself 'see' ghostly images of people long dead. Amelia sensed the woman's longing to learn. Lucy ached to know about the world of spirits. *But if she was to die tonight she'd know in an instant. She would be one of them. So, if she, Lucy Morell, is convinced of the reality of the spirit world why doesn't she do something about it? All it would take would be a step from the edge of the clifftop, or a little nick with the carving knife—*

Aren't you the ridiculous one, Amelia? she told herself. She lifted another spoonful of tomato soup to her mouth. *Why are you letting these ridiculous thoughts into your head? Why don't you make the effort to think lucidly about sensible matters? After all, you'll have to consider earning a living in the not too distant future. And when you're with Bill Simotas again how will you act with him? If he offers to take you wreck-diving again will you go? Now . . . these are the things you should be considering. You shouldn't be simply allowing your imagination to wash round in its own stupid little world.*

She ground a little pepper onto the surface of the soup. Not that she wanted it, but it was a perfectly rational thing to do. Unlike laughing in her mother's face, and unlike driving the bread knife into Rachel's long white neck.

'What a day.' Catherine announced. 'Won't we be glad when all this is behind us?'

'How are you feeling now?'

Catherine waved Lucy's question away as if it wasn't worth asking. 'Oh, perfectly fine, dear. Silly migraines, they come and go like . . .' She clicked her fingers. 'Mmm . . . what lovely soup.'

'That was Amelia's creation. I don't know what she put into it but just smell it . . . it's *lovely*.'

'Lovely,' Rachel echoed dully.

Lucy beamed. 'My contribution was the croutons. And you know something? For the first time I've actually got them to stay crunchy in the soup! Gosh, listen to that.'

They listened.

Rachel sniffed. 'I don't hear anything.'

'No, exactly. The gales have dropped.'

'It won't last.'

Catherine smiled.

Amelia noticed how pale her lips were, her eyelids too; they were all but transparent. 'It isn't over until the fat lady sings.'

'Or, to be precise, until the rains come.' Rachel put her spoon down on the plate beside her half-consumed soup. 'The rain is the Gregale's final act.'

Lucy smiled. 'I imagine it's the rain that somehow acts as a trigger for the Judas trees. Within hours of the rain falling they blossom. Ooh, you should see it, Amelia. Pink, pink – *pink!*' She tore at a piece of bread and ate hungrily. 'The whole island becomes this riot of pink blossom. Why we don't get landscape painters here I'll never know.' Then she added wistfully: 'And later, when the blossom begins to fall, it looks just like wedding confetti.'

'It's a mess.' Again, Rachel sounded as if she was setting the record straight for the benefit of a courtroom. 'The blossom fills the pool. It takes hours to get it clean again. We should cover the pool with a net.'

'Everyone finished?' Amelia slid back her chair. 'I'll bring in the next course.' She was trying hard to be useful – not the freeloader that Rachel had accused her of being.

Rachel looked down her nose at the bowl of soup.

Filled it with poison, didn't I, dear?

Amelia stifled a smile as she took the soup plate from beneath the woman's long nose.

Right now, Rachel is remembering all those urban myths she's heard about what embittered bakers do in the dough, Amelia told herself. *When they're wanting to exact a little revenge upon their employer, or when they're displeased with life in general.*

'Anyone tried the phone recently?' Catherine regally dabbed her lips on a napkin.

'I did,' Lucy said. 'No joy, I'm afraid.'

'Poor man.' Everyone knew what Catherine referred to. 'He was probably no more than a boy. Oh? Red wine . . . yes, exactly the right food and right weather for it. Do you need a hand, Amelia?'

'No, you stay there, moth— . . . Catherine.'

'Tut, I'm no invalid, dear.'

'I know, but I can manage . . . oh, damn, is that the front door again?'

'Keep it locked.'

'I do, Rachel. It must be faulty.'

'It isn't.'

'That may be so, but the damned thing keeps blowing open every ten minutes.'

The exchange certainly wasn't heated. In fact, it was lower in volume than the rest of the conversations and perfectly polite. But Amelia noticed Rachel's expression: she heard undercurrents there.

'The lock's probably sticking,' Lucy said diplomatically, if not entirely logically. 'I'll go and see to it. Goodness, I hadn't noticed how dark it's become. Wait a mo, Amelia, I'll bring the bowl through with me.'

They went through into the hallway together. Amelia, with the soup plates in her hand, watched Lucy hurry to the open door, then push it quickly shut as if she were afraid a tiger would rush through from outside.

Gripping the bolt handles, she slid them across one by one.

'There . . .'

'It wasn't the wind that blew it open,' Amelia said matter-of-factly.

'No, it wasn't. Come on, let's get that meal served up. Brrr.' Lucy shivered and hurried away from the door, looking back over her shoulder at it as she did so.

They ate in silence for a while. As with the living room there were statues in the dining room. The stone figures stood with their backs to the walls, staring coldly at the four women at the table.

Amelia noticed that, like every other statue in the villa, there wasn't a whole one among them. All were missing a piece; either a hand, a leg, a piece of torso, a fragment of head.

The fat one by the window leered at her.

'I made plenty of mashed potato, so help yourself to as much as you like.'

'And lovely it is too, Amelia,' Lucy enthused. 'Gosh, and you've added crushed walnuts, too.'

Rachel said nothing, but put her fingers to her lips as if removing a tiny piece of walnut shell. 'Really delicious . . . the carrots melt in your mouth.'

Catherine said, 'We must cook for Julius one day soon. Of course, we have to take the food to him, he can't negotiate all our steps in his condition. Would you pass the salt, dear?'

Lucy picked up the bottle. 'Any more wine for anyone?'

'Just a drop for me,' Catherine said.

Rachel shook her head, her eyes cool as ever.

'Please.' Amelia held out her glass. 'I was ready for this tonight.'

'And don't think all your hard work has gone unnoticed.' Catherine patted Amelia's hand. 'And it's very much appreciated. But make sure you get plenty of sleep. You have to snatch it when you can when this silly storm blows up.' She touched her temple, then disguised the action by stroking back her hair. 'I remember a couple of years ago we didn't get a wink of sleep for forty-eight hours.'

Lucy laughed. 'We were seeing pink elephants coming out of the walls by the end of that.'

'It can be trying,' Rachel conceded.

'Very trying.'

'Oooh, there go the lights again.' Lucy looked at the lamps. 'Best keep those candles handy.'

The lights had dimmed so much that only a red glow filtered through the shades. Once more Amelia could look at the filament in the bulbs without being dazzled.

Voros is sucking the power from the cables, she told herself. *It's a greedy, greedy island. It gives us a quiet place to live in the sun.*

But it wants so much in return. Julius King said it was a place that stole your wits.

But as well as people's sanity it wants souls. She thought about the wreck of the hospital ship lying at the bottom of the sea; it was so close that the hull touched the island. And then there were the mummified soldiers in the cave; and now there was the drowned man in the boathouse. If he was still there.

For a while the lamps remained a dim red, casting hardly any light. The statues, glowering man-shapes in marble, seemed to grow in size in the near-dark.

Lucy and Catherine weren't fazed. They chatted about a proposed trip to a neighbouring island when Bill returned with the ferry boat.

Then, as if Voros had decided it had taken what it considered sufficient dues for the moment, the electricity returned to full voltage; the lights brightened.

'There.' Lucy breathed deeply. 'Back to normal at last.'

But even as she said the words Amelia saw her turn her face away from the window.

As if she'd looked out and seen something that had frightened her there.

Chapter Forty-two

Immediately after dinner Catherine announced that she was tired and would go straight to bed. It was approaching ten. For the moment the wind wasn't blowing nearly as hard as it had been. Instead, a mantle of silence and complete darkness had settled on the island.

To Amelia's relief Rachel retired to her bedroom, too.

So she and Lucy made coffee for two and took it, with cups, cream and a bottle of brandy, into the living room where they set everything on the coffee table.

They made a point of switching on all the lights before drawing the curtains tightly.

'There. Safe and sound,' Lucy said, pleased. 'Best to make sure the candles and matches are to hand, just in case. I don't trust those generators on the Simotas farm as far as I can blooming well throw them. Now . . . brandy?'

'Please. A large one.'

Lucy smiled. 'Me, too. We've earned it.'

Amelia poured brandy into large balloon glasses while Lucy poured the coffee.

'Cheers, Amelia – cheers, all.' Lucy raised the glass to the statues, then stuck her tongue out at the one with the dour face and piercing eyes. 'Well, all except you, Mr Misery Guts.'

Amelia thought Lucy's flippancy was a bit like whistling in the dark.

'What now?' Amelia asked, curling snugly into a sofa.

'A sing-song round the piano? Or hide-and-seek outside in the dark?'

'Ooh, not on your nelly . . . are you trying to make my hair stand on end or what?'

'Or what.' Amelia smiled. Perhaps if the two of them could be pleasant and kind to each other it might form a protective shell around the villa. Something to keep out the ghouls and ghosties.

She sipped the brandy. It was the one referred to as 'Lucy's rocket fuel'. A trail of fire blazed its way inside her. She shuddered. It was awful, really. But she took an even bigger swallow. *Alcohol keeps away the bogeymen, too.*

'Does that hit the spot?'

'It does, Lucy; it does. Shortbread?'

'Go on, then, just one piece.'

'Do you ever miss not seeing much of the outside world?'

'No. Not at all, really.'

'But don't you ever wonder what's happening?'

'You mean wars, famines and terrorists blowing up innocent people?'

'Something like that.'

'If you read the newspapers or watch the television you only seem to see bad news. That can't be good for you, can it?'

'I can see your point. Here, let me top you up.'

'Thanks. Oops, I'm dripping onto the table. Can you pass me the coaster? Thanking you. The truth is, Amelia, I haven't seen a newspaper in more than five years.'

'Really?'

'Believe me, after the first couple of weeks you begin to wonder what you saw in them that was so interesting.'

'And you don't even own a radio?'

'Radios have terrible reception here. Again, it's to do with the magnetic ore down there.' She pointed at the floor. 'Plays havoc with all kinds of electrical equipment.'

'But Catherine and Rachel use computers?'

'True, but they have a habit of crashing every couple of months; oh, the songs and dances we've gone through when

346

they've gone kaput. That same interference probably messed up the poor pilot's instruments, too.'

'So civilization's hi-tech comforts don't suit Voros?'

'The more old-fashioned and unsophisticated electrical equipment is, the better it works here. Like that old gramophone of Julius King's'.' Lucy sipped her coffee.

'And you never hanker for fast cars and television?'

Lucy shook her head. 'Never. Civilization is like an addiction: you miss it like crazy when it's first taken away from you. But once you've gone through the cold turkey process you don't give a damn . . .' She dropped her voice into an imitation of a man's. '"Civilization? Frankly, my dear, I don't give a damn."' She chuckled.

'But you continue your work here, your psychic work, that is?'

'Yes. I find I can "read" objects more deeply in a more relaxed state. One day I hope to write a book about it. It will be an instruction manual for people who don't think they are psychic.'

'So that they'll be able to walk into an old house and see those images from hundreds of years ago?'

'Oh, yes.' Lucy spoke matter-of-factly. 'It's all a question of practice.'

'Like riding a bike?'

'Absolutely.' Lucy beamed. 'More brandy?'

Amelia smiled. 'Absa-bloody-lutely.'

'A woman after my own heart. Say "when."'

'Three, two . . . when.' The atmosphere was relaxed for the first time in days. Amelia sensed the time was ripe.

'Lucy?'

'Yes, love?'

'Remember how I told you that I never knew my father?'

Lucy hesitated slightly. 'Yes, I remember.'

'I've never heard anything about who he was, or what he did. I've never even seen a photograph of him.'

Lucy nodded, a look of quiet sympathy on her face.

Amelia continued, 'I don't even know if he's still alive.'

'I see.'

'Would you be able to tell me something about him? If I gave you my gold chain to hold?'

'We–ell . . . psychometry isn't an exact science, you know.'

'But it's possible you could?'

'It *is* possible, if I were to do a reading.'

'Would you do one now?' Amelia reached up to unfasten the clasp at the back of her neck.

Lucy reached out a hand to stop her; the action was gentle and almost apologetic. 'Normally, I'd be happy to.' She gave a weak smile. 'But these aren't normal times. For the best results we both need to be relaxed and in a good frame of mind. You see, it's not only the weather that's been stirred up over the last couple of days.'

'You mean the spirit world?'

'You're teasing me now.'

'No, I'm not.'

Amelia saw Lucy give her a searching look, obviously wondering if she was being mocked.

'"Spirit world" is an old-fashioned term. But ask any scientist. There *are* universes other than the ones we know.'

'And each one contains the knowledge of all things in all the universes.'

'That's my belief, yes.'

'Lucy, I want to know something about my father. And I want to know now.'

Lucy had stiffened; her voice had taken on a polite but distant edge as if she didn't want to be drawn down the path where Amelia was leading her. She shook her head. 'Why don't you ask your mother when she's feeling better?'

'Why can't you tell me now? This business of not knowing about my father has been burning away like an ulcer in here . . .' she pressed both hands into her stomach '. . . for longer than I can remember.'

'Amelia—'

'You don't know what it's like.'

'Amelia, please, love. I would like to help you: really I would . . .'

'But?'

'But now isn't the time.'

'You think it might be dangerous for us to go . . . to go delving into the world of the supernatural right now?'

'Imagine the supernatural is like the sea. On a calm day, fine, go swim in it. But all this upset, the storm getting people all edgy, you and Rachel finding that poor drowned man; well, everything's got stirred up. Turbulent, if you like. We might see things that would distress us.'

'You've experienced this before?'

'Yes, but not as intense as this. Can't you feel that sense of foreboding all around us . . . like *something* is going to happen?'

'Will I see it if it does?'

'Perhaps.'

'Because I'm psychic, too?'

'Don't mock me, dear.'

'I'm not. But you believe I *am* psychic?'

'Yes.'

'Here, give me your hand.'

'Amelia?'

Amelia reached forward and gripped Lucy's wrist in her right hand while she held the woman's lucky-charm bracelet between the finger and thumb of her left.

'Amelia, I don't think this is the time . . . listen, it's not safe. Not now.'

Amelia ignored her. 'Then I close my eyes like this.'

'No, Amelia . . . stop – *please*.'

Neither of them were shouting; in fact, the exchange was closer to whispers. But Amelia's patience had evaporated. Enough was enough. All her life she had felt as if she'd been kept in the dark; that there were truths she should have known by right, only they were kept secret. Now, she reasoned, if there was some supernatural mechanism that would reveal those hidden truths about her and about her father, she would use it for herself.

That reckless impulse surged through her once more. If she could pressurize Lucy into showing her how to use this gift, so much the better.

As she gripped Lucy's wrist and charm bracelet she said, 'I'm doing this right, aren't I? Eyes closed? I'm touching an intimate possession of the subject?'

'Amelia, please . . . this isn't right. You're risking—'

'I'm picturing a blank television screen inside my head. Nothing . . . nothing . . . *wait.*'

'Amelia . . .'

'Lucy, wait, something's happening.'

'No, Amelia, not like this; you should—'

'I can see something. It's like a big bright picture in my head.'

Lucy groaned in protest.

Faster now, Amelia whispered, 'A girl working in a super-market. She's thinking there's more to life than this.'

'Amelia, you're making fun of me.'

'No, I'm not. I'm serious. I'm deadly serious. I see . . . wait, I see an old lady at a stove. She's boiling beetroot, and . . . and for some reason she's ladling them out into a big bowl full of cold water . . . and there's salt in an old shoe, no, that doesn't make sense, does it? It can't be. But I see salt in a shoe and she's tipping it—'

'Amelia, please, this— ouch . . .'

'Then there's a house with roses in the front garden.'

'Ouch, please, love, you're holding my wrist too tightly.'

'Pink.' Amelia smiled in triumph. 'Pink roses. And standing at the door is a man. He's young, in his thirties. With short hair. It's black. Receding. Back at the temples here. He's wearing a brightly coloured shirt, denim shorts and—'

'*Amelia?*'

'And in his arms he's—'

'No—'

'He's holding a grey cat with black ears.'

Lucy suddenly stiffened and looked at Amelia with huge glistening eyes. 'What did you say?'

Amelia saw the other woman shiver deeply.

'Amelia . . . what made you say that? How do you know about Tarka? What else have you seen?' Now she sounded frightened. More frightened than she'd ever sounded before.

'The cat also has a black tail and wears a blue collar.'

Amelia released the woman's arm at the sound of Rachel's ice-cold voice suddenly cutting across the room. Both she and Lucy turned to see Rachel step through the doorway.

Rachel continued dispassionately: 'The cat wears a blue collar with a bell – and the name of the house is Faraway.'

A look of even greater terror raced across Lucy's face. *'Faraway?'* she said, rising. 'How do you both know about that?'

Rachel nodded, as if reaching a conclusion. 'You recognize the description of all three? The cat, the house, the man?'

'Yes, of course. I used to live in a house called Faraway. The cat is Tarka. The man is Martin Welles. I was going to marry him, only . . .' She looked accusingly at Amelia then Rachel. 'But how do you *both* know?'

Amelia said gently. 'Lucy, I saw it here.' She touched her temple and smiled. 'Just as you said I would.'

Lucy's eyes fixed on hers. They were round, silvery; shot through with fear and wonder.

'So you're psychic, too, Amelia?' Rachel walked across the room towards them. 'You can hold an object in your hand, and see a person's life history appear in your head?'

Lucy raised her arm, awed. 'She held my charm bracelet.'

'Lucy, are you sure she didn't hold this first?'

Amelia looked at what Rachel held up in her hand. 'What is that?'

'Probably nothing of significance. Just a photograph of a man who's standing holding a cat in front of a house. Oh, look, ladies. You can even see the name of the house engraved on a piece of wood by the door. *Faraway.*'

Amelia shook her head, puzzled. 'I've never seen that photograph before. Lucy . . .'

Trembling from head to toe, Lucy took the photograph from Rachel. 'Where did you find this?'

'Just out in the hallway. Right under the nose of Hermes, of all places. Someone must have dropped it.' She looked at Amelia. 'A bit careless of them, wasn't it?'

'I don't understand . . .' Lucy frowned. 'This was in an album in my wardrobe. How did it get down here?'

Rachel made a pretence of bemusement. 'It's a mystery. Like it's a complete and utter mystery that a bundle of my private letters have been taken from a cash box in my room. Oh, there's about twenty thousand drachma missing as well, but that's not nearly so important as the letters.'

Amelia's blood ran cold. Rachel had assumed the role of arch prosecutor again.

'Amelia,' Rachel said in that voice of ice. 'Can you figure out how Lucy's photograph wound up on the hallway floor?'

Amelia shook her head.

'Or how my letters and an envelope containing banknotes vanished from my room?'

'Lucy,' Amelia appealed. 'Believe me, I've never seen that photograph before.'

'But you described it to me. You described my ex-fiancé. The rose garden.'

'I did. But I saw it inside my head, just as you told me I would.'

Lucy shook her head. She looked ashen. 'No . . . no.'

Rachel folded her arms. 'Lucy, you'd better go and check your room. If anything's missing make a written list. It'll be useful later.'

Amelia made as if to hold Lucy's hand but she backed away round the sofa. 'Please,' Amelia said. 'You believe me, don't you? I've never seen the photograph. I've never touched anything in Rachel's room.'

Lucy avoided eye contact with Amelia now. Turning, she hurried from the room.

'Oh, you are a silly girl, Amelia.' Rachel adopted a deliberately sympathetic tone, as if addressing someone who couldn't control their own actions. 'What have you done? *What have you done?*'

'I've done nothing.'

'No?'

'No.'

'It sounded a pretty convincing display. Pretending to be psychic to impress Lucy. But you did need someone on your side, didn't you, dear?'

'Rachel, I don't—'

'Come on, Amelia. Did you think you could get away with this petty thieving?'

'I've not stolen anything.'

'Do you know where my letters are?'

'No.'

'My money?'

'Of course not. I haven't touched it, have I?'

'Yes, Amelia, I believe you have.'

'I haven't . . . Dust your room for my fingerprints if you want to.'

'You think you're a clever little thing, don't you? Butter wouldn't melt, hmm?'

'I'm sorry about your money and your letters but—'

'Well, if you haven't got them, who has?'

'You're not going to believe me, but Lucy's been say-ing—'

'Oh? So we're back to supernatural forces, are we? Ghosts stole my letters? Hands from beyond the grave purloined Lucy's photograph? Is that it?'

'I don't know. I can't explain it, but I've been seeing things that aren't − or should not be − there.'

'Convenient.'

Amelia took a deep breath. 'Tonight, I thought I saw the drowned man out there on the steps.'

'Good God, you're so desperate to avoid responsibility for your actions you're even trying to blame the poor devil we pulled from the water. Hell, that really does take the biscuit . . .'

'I didn't say it was him who took your possessions. I said that something's not *right* here on the island. Something strange is happening.'

'My God, I agree with you there, Amelia Thomas. It *is* strange. Very strange. And wicked, too.'

'But I'm sure I saw the pilot.'

'Which is impossible, isn't it?'

'I don't know.' Amelia shook her head in confusion. 'Unless . . . unless he isn't really dead.'

'Of course he's dead.' Rachel snorted. 'If you'd seen the state of the poor devil's face you'd know.'

'But if he isn't? If he's wandering out there somewhere?'

'Don't be so stupid.'

'You're not a doctor; you don't *know* he's dead for sure.'

'He had massive injuries to his face, Amelia. No one could have survived that!' Rachel raised her chin so that she looked down her nose at Amelia like it was a gunsight. 'Now I'm going to conduct a thorough audit of my room. If anything else is missing it will be added to my list.'

With that, she swept out, leaving Amelia miserable and alone with the silent, watchful statues.

Chapter Forty-three

Amelia managed to remain alone in the room full of statues for no more than three minutes. Their stone eyes, that seemed so cold and malignant, bored into her. Whichever way she turned, the figures would still be there. The huge statue of the bearded man was especially forbidding. With the dimming of the lights his expression had grown even more evil; shadows gathered darker and darker around his ferocious eyebrows.

It took no stretch of Amelia's imagination to picture the statues climbing down from their plinths, then advancing on her, their joints grating stone upon stone, their arms held out, ready to crush the life from her fragile bones.

The brutal ferocity of the image frightened her so much that her heart lurched inside her chest. Now, probably more than at any other time in her life, she needed companionship, a friend to talk to. But now – certainly more than any other time in her life – she'd never been so alone, or friendless, or so isolated. It was as if she'd been made prisoner in some nightmare castle beyond the ends of the earth.

Heart thudding, her breath coming in frightened gasps, her gaze flew from one statue to another, her eyes locking on to each pair of stone eyes. And, it seemed to her, those eyes burned back with menace and hatred.

That was when it became too much. As she felt her heart surge up into her throat with a force that was nothing less than choking, she fled the room.

It was no better in the hallway. There were yet more of the statues. From shattered faces eyes burned coldly at her, the stares accusing.

This is all your fault, Amelia.

All your fault.

For a moment she thought of begging Lucy to let her into her room. But Lucy would be no friend now. She believed that Amelia had rifled her private possessions.

The other two women would be out of bounds, too. Rachel would be conducting an 'audit' of her possessions (as the stick-thin woman would so coldly put it). While Catherine would be too ill to disturb.

The sense of isolation surged at Amelia in icy waves.

The truth is, she told herself, *I'm not welcome here any more. I'm no better than a trespasser, or a burglar. All three women want me to be gone from here as quickly as possible.*

And, as if the three personalities could somehow invoke the spirit of the house itself, she felt the very fabric of the building beginning to hate her, to reject her. It worked most powerfully through the statues. They stared at her with undisguised hatred.

Frightened, she looked round that dark vault of a hallway. It could have been some subterranean tomb now that most of the spotlight bulbs had blown. What few working bulbs remained lit the statues from bizarre angles. Now the stone figures appeared enlarged, swollen somehow. Once perfectly proportioned torsos and elegant legs and slender arms had become bloated. Deformed monsters that haunted the chaos of half-light and shadows.

I want out, Amelia thought, with a sudden concrete conviction. *I want out. I want to go away. I want to go before I die here. Because that's what will happen if I stay. I'm not welcome here. I'm a trespasser. I shouldn't be here.*

With a dark dread spreading up through her stomach to fill her chest she turned and lunged for the door.

After a struggle with the bolts she swung it open.

Outside the darkness was near-total. The wind had dropped

to almost nothing. Yet, even so, a ghost of a breeze had set the Judas trees murmuring again, as if they were discussing dark conspiracies among themselves.

She took a step forward, away from the house. If only she could put some distance between herself and its malign presence.

Far away she heard the rumble of the surf; it reminded her of the ominous growl in the pit of a dog's throat before it attacked.

To her left were the funeral cypresses. In the little light spilled by the house they stood as dark as Gothic columns.

In the back of her mind there'd been some dim, half-crystal-lized notion of running away. But where? The other residents of the island were strangers. Even Julius King would probably recoil from her throwing herself on his mercy. There was no boat that could take her away from the island.

Face it, Amelia told herself. *You're trapped here. A prisoner.*

Even as she thought the word *prisoner* the breeze rose a little. In the near-darkness Judas trees moved their branches; for a moment it looked as if the whole island was seething, as if some evil growth pulsated on its face.

And, at that instant, the sound of air currents through the branches rose from a murmur to a clattering of stick upon stick, branch upon branch, until the trees themselves shouted at her.

The wind rose, grabbed a handful of her hair and tugged it painfully. Wind-borne dirt blew into her face; grit fiercely stung her eyes. Shouting Judas trees bellowed their disapproval of her; it was as if she faced an angry mob. A mob who wanted her dead.

At that moment she knew the whole of Voros had turned against her.

When she had first arrived on the island she'd sensed it had welcomed her. It had wanted her to live there. But there were conditions attached; a price she had to pay; favours she had to return. She recalled Julius King's comment that Voros stole your sanity. That to live here you had to surrender part of your mind and self-control to its will.

Amelia had smiled at the comment, considering it whimsical.

But beneath the joke there was a truth there. A truth that was hard, dark and incontrovertible.

You *could* live on Voros. But only if you were prepared to pay the rent with your very soul.

A sudden shriek of wind sent the Judas trees into a mad clattering that sounded like laughter – cruel, mocking laughter – to Amelia's ears.

Flute sounds played a vicious cacophony around the eaves of the house. *God, yes,* she thought, *this is music for the damned, all right. A requiem for lost souls.*

The island spat more dirt into her eyes. Blinking from the stinging assault she knew there was nowhere to run.

And, bit by bit, step by step, the wind drove her back to the house. Seconds later she was closing the doors behind her. Immediately the gale dropped. A throbbing silence filled the hallway. A kind of phantom heartbeat. Pulsing darkly. She looked round. If anything, it was gloomier. The electric light was dying by inches. And all the time the statues' eyes burned coldly with an even deeper hatred.

She took a deep breath to steady her thudding heart.

Then she whispered to herself, 'Oh, God help me.'

For a few minutes Amelia forced herself to perform mundane tasks, in the hope that the activity of washing dinner plates and pans would in itself impose some kind of normality on her environment. The clink of plates, slipped steaming and dripping onto the drainer racks, would help counteract the unearthly sounds coming from outside. And her focusing on the suds in the sink would take her eyes away from the accusing, hating stares of the statues in the hallway beyond the kitchen door.

She'd begun wiping the dishes with a towel when Rachel appeared, wearing a long coat and boots.

Amelia waited until Rachel was halfway across the kitchen

floor. She sensed the woman standing and staring at her word-lessly for a full ten seconds. Clearly, Rachel wasn't going to be the first of the pair of them to speak.

At last, Amelia turned to face the forbidding woman with the hawk-like nose and piercing eyes.

'Rachel?'

'This isn't something I'd choose to do,' began Rachel in that formal courtroom voice of hers. 'But, in the light of what you said earlier about seeing the pilot and the helmet, I think it incumbent on me to go down to the boathouse and check that nothing's been disturbed.'

In a spirit of reconciliation, Amelia said, 'I'll come with you.'

'You'll do no such thing.'

'But you can't go down there by yourself.'

'I, Amelia, am not prone to an over-active imagination.'

'But you don't—'

'*Amelia.* I don't require your company. Understand that.'

'Rachel, I'm sorry, I only wanted—'

'I don't care what you want. You've caused enough trouble. I suggest that once you've finished here you go to bed.'

With that, Rachel turned on her heel and swept coldly out of the kitchen.

Why has my life gone so wrong so quickly? Amelia asked herself as she returned to the dishes. *This is nothing less than a gypsy curse.* Everything that could go wrong had gone wrong.

At that moment she knew to the depths of her bones that, even if she went to bed now and stayed there, trouble would still come looking for her.

Chapter Forty-four

After Rachel had left for the boathouse, Amelia prowled the kitchen, searching for a chore, the more mundane the better, to take her mind off the situation.

The lights flickered with every surge of wind outside. Periodically they would dim, and with the gloom, shadows would creep like bloodstains across the tiled floor.

At one point she decided to simply drink herself into oblivion.

To wake up with a stinking hangover instead of this restless prowling was certainly a fair exchange to her mind. Only when she took a mouthful of brandy from the glass it tasted like stale vinegar. She spat it out into the sink. Even when she rinsed her mouth with plain water from the bottle in the fridge, that, too, possessed a stagnant flavour.

The island's driving me out, she told herself bleakly, with a rock-solid conviction. *It's driving me out; it wants rid of me. But where can I go? I can't leave at this moment. Bill won't be back with the ferry boat for days yet. Maybe that's it. Maybe it simply wants me to leap into the sea. Then swim and swim until I can't swim any more.*

God . . . This sense of loneliness, of exclusion, was driving her to distraction. She wondered if all suicides felt like this before they—

She squeezed out the incoming thought before it could shape itself.

With all the edginess of a cat walking on hot metal she went to the living room and remained there for a few moments until the relentless pressure of the statues' glares drove her out again.

For a while Amelia retreated to her bedroom, but if anything it was worse there. The muslin curtains moved restlessly in a hundred different draughts, conjuring up into her mind corpse-forms wrapped in sheets. While the light of the bedside lamp cast shadows of the bedposts onto the wall in the shape of an executioner's gallows.

Right now, she knew, her mind was ripe for seeing things that were not there. Just as she had after her fall. When those monstrous ghost-forms with leering faces and eyes like axe wounds would climb the stairs to her bedroom every night. Shuddering, she remembered blundering into the twins' room to scream at them to run from the ghosts. No wonder the girls had been scared half to death of their strange cousin.

And now it was threatening to start over again. The storm had made her imagination fertile; her mind would be receptive to anything now . . .

A great monstrous serpent sliding in through the open window with yellow, venomous eyes . . .

Or maybe the pilot bursting in through the door . . .

No. Stop it, she told herself. *Don't let your imagination take control.*

The curtains at the window billowed as if thick bodies pressed monstrously behind them.

Gulping, Amelia shot from the bedroom, closing the door on the phantom shapes behind her.

Once more she headed downstairs. Not that she wanted to go down there, any more than she'd want to enter a room full of open coffins.

But where else was there to go?

Back again, Amelia, dear?

The statues greeted her with their cold stares.

Go away, Amelia. Go away, go away, we don't want you . . .

They all but whispered into her heart with their stone

362

voices. Cold, cold voices that shimmered with hatred and disgust.

Go back into the sea, Amelia. Swim away from here. We don't want you.

'Shut up.' Immediately she pressed her lips shut to stop any more words coming out.

'What's wrong, cuz? Afraid people might think you're mad, talking to statues?'

Her cousin John's voice rang so clearly in her head he could have been standing just behind her.

And when she heard a door bang, she spun round with a gasp, expecting to see him standing there as large as life with that sarcastic smile on his face.

Instead she saw Rachel at the door.

The woman had paused in the doorway, one arm holding the door open. Behind her the night outside seemed to pulse like a great dark heart.

There was a sense of something vast and ghostly prowling there that for the moment – at least – remained hidden from Amelia's eyes.

Slowly, as if any sudden movement would shatter the door, Rachel pushed it shut, then turned the key in the lock. Deliberately she slid one bolt home after the other.

After that she turned, then walked purposefully for the stairs. Her face, pale enough at the best of times, was now white as raw pastry. Her eyes were fixed on the stairs ahead. Her face was expressionless.

Immediately, Amelia sensed something had happened down at the boathouse. She moved forward. 'Rachel? Is the body still there?'

The woman didn't answer; she didn't even acknowledge Amelia's existence. She merely stared ahead. Her eyes were dead-looking, as if she'd encountered something on her lonely walk down to the dead-man's resting place. And that *something* had the dark power to snatch the life-light from her eyes.

'Rachel? What's wrong? What did you see?'

The woman walked steadily, even mechanically to the stairs.

SIMON CLARK

As she began to climb them Amelia noticed an object hanging from the woman's hand. At first she couldn't identify it in the gloom, then light reflected from one of the statue's faces revealed it. There, swinging loosely in Rachel's cold, lifeless fingers like a hangman's noose, was a lace from the drowned pilot's boot.

'Rachel?' Amelia said again in a low voice. But it was clear the woman wouldn't answer.

Amelia waited for Rachel to climb the stairs and disappear into her room before she returned to the kitchen.

For a while she sat hunched on the kitchen stool, arms folded tightly. What had Rachel found down at the boathouse? Was the dead man still there?

Of course he must be. Dead men don't walk.

But anything on this Godforsaken island was possible, wasn't it? The thought had no sooner crossed her mind when dozens of images cascaded before her inner eye. Why, the corpse might be standing behind her at this very minute.

Once imagined, the image hardened into near-reality in her mind and she turned quickly on the stool to look behind her.

Of course, there's no one there, she scolded herself.

Nevertheless, her eyes scanned the deserted kitchen. Brass pans gleamed like dead faces on the wall. The wine rack formed so many silently screaming mouths. The tap dripped into the sink, a hollow heartbeat of a sound.

The dead don't walk, she told herself. *The dead don't walk.*

The dead don't . . . but she stopped herself completing the sentence. To repeat it a third time would turn it into an Old Testament curse.

No, the dead don't walk on Voros, Amelia – they run.

She went to the sink and pulled the plug. Once more she'd return to that endless treadmill of mundane chores. Anything to divert her mind from this upside-down world where she found herself prisoner.

'Oh, Amelia, you shouldn't be bothering with the dishes now. Go to bed and grab some shut-eye; I'll see to that.'

Amelia whirled round. 'Catherine?'

'Yes, dear?'

Amelia stared. 'Are you all right?'

'Of course I am, dear. It'll take more than a headache to lay me low.'

Amelia watched Catherine sweep across the kitchen in her flowing white dressing gown. There was something ethereal and heart-stopping about the sight. Amelia found herself unable to take her eyes off her mother. The woman's skin was bluey white, her eyes were wide, uncannily wide.

Why doesn't she blink? Amelia asked herself.

She stared at her mother's eyes. They were so large and white. Even egg-like in their sockets.

Why doesn't she blink? A fear, as big and as dark as it was irrational, surged up through her stomach.

Her mother turned to her. Then she did blink. It was long, slow: not so much a blink as the eyelid moving tongue-like in a slow, caressing motion over the eyeball.

And just for a moment Amelia doubted if the woman was there at all, believing that she was imagining her ghostly presence; just as she'd imagined the snake sliding through the window or the dead pilot racing along the hallway with the speed of a train.

'What's wrong, Amelia, dear?'

'Eh . . . nothing. Just tired, I suppose.'

'You do look a bit peaky.'

'It's the storm. It makes you nervy after a while.'

'I did warn you, dear, didn't I?' Catherine smiled. 'You mark my words, after this has blown itself out the local papers will be full of stories of fights and probably a murder or two. The storm does that to people: sends 'em crazy.' Her eyes widened even further into two white globes that burned with an uncanny fire.

'I can well believe it,' Amelia said uneasily.

'In fact, just listen to that.' Catherine held up her finger. The gale had surged again across the island. Pan-pipe notes fluted around the eaves, a booming sound echoed down the chimney, while even in the kitchen Amelia could hear the psychotic clattering of the Judas trees' branches.

'It's enough to make even an angel harbour dark thoughts,' confided her mother. 'Now. Let's treat ourselves to a cup of tea.'

'Good idea.'

'Earl Grey?'

'That would be nice.'

She returned to the stool to watch her mother busy herself filling the kettle and spooning tea into the pot.

On the one hand Amelia was pleased and relieved – very relieved – by the company. But there was something odd about her mother's appearance. The whiteness of her face, not to mention the glittery aura that surrounded her, was troubling. If anything, the woman could have been sleepwalking; it was as if she wasn't entirely synchronized with reality.

Amelia tried hard to rationalize. Perhaps it was the medication. If the migraine had been a bad one Catherine might have made quite free with the painkillers.

Again Amelia felt a need to prove her usefulness. At least now she could keep an eye on her mother and usher her back to bed if she became ill again.

'Now,' Catherine announced. 'I was thinking about installing a new barbecue. We do have an old cast-iron thing, but I am considering asking Bill to build me something a little more permanent. Stone, perhaps. What do you think?'

Amelia was pleased that the conversation had drifted into small talk. No doubt Rachel would tell Catherine all about what had happened that evening, the disappearance (or theft?) of the photographs, cash and letters. But perhaps, for a little while at least, they could, Amelia told herself, play mother and daughter.

After all, the future was unclear now, and most definitely smeared with ominous possibilities.

Chapter Forty-five

Despite the strangeness of the atmosphere in the kitchen, indeed the strangeness that pervaded the whole storm-torn island, Amelia concentrated on playing the role of good daughter.

Catherine made the tea. Amelia set out cups, saucers and cake on the table.

Streams of air now ran through the Judas trees with a laughing sound.

There was something mocking about it. A goading and a taunting. As if daring Amelia to run outside and confront it.

The island has turned against me, she thought calmly, laying cake on a plate. *It's rejected me because I won't play by its rules, or pay the price of staying here. I won't be like mad Mr Oxford, gloating over his tractor all day as his malformed children crawl in the dirt. Or be like Lucy who sees ghosts eating melons. Or Julius King, mentally adrift in some world of his own, devoting his days to composing operas that no one will ever hear.* She thought of the film director who had shut herself up on the island with her sons. How she made perverse home movies. How she dominated her sons so expertly that they retreated into an alcohol-soaked world and insanity to escape her power.

The sounds the breeze made in the Judas trees became louder. Mocking. Goading.

She told herself: *It's trying to lure me out there so it can destroy me. But I can beat this. If I pretend everything is normal, everything is sane, I will survive.*

'Be a dear, Amelia, and get the milk from the fridge. Or would you prefer lemon?'

'Milk will be fine.'

They sat down to the table. Catherine sipped her tea appreciatively. 'I forget how dry this storm makes you. Plays havoc with the skin, too.'

Amelia tasted her tea. She almost grimaced but forced herself to remain composed and take another drink. Insanely, the liquid in the cup tasted of blue cheese. An intense fungus taste that made her tongue burn.

It's not real, she told herself solidly. *The tea doesn't taste of mouldy cheese. It can't. Otherwise my mother would have tasted it too. It's this island. It's playing tricks on me, trying to drive me crazy, so I'll do something insane like leap from a cliff or try and swim away from it.*

'Lovely tea,' Amelia said and knew the comment sounded lame.

'Lovely.'

'Maybe we should bake a cake?'

'It's getting rather late for that, isn't it, dear?'

'Maybe. But I don't think I could sleep a wink through this.'

'Nor me, dear.'

'Cards?'

'Too hard to concentrate, with the devil piping away on the roof.' Her mother smiled. But it was one of those smiles that only involved the mouth and not the eyes. Her eyes protruded from their sockets like boiled eggs. Meanwhile, the pupils had contracted to fierce black dots, and still there seemed a touch of unearthly flame concentrated there.

Amelia forced the small talk on. 'The barbecue . . . gas or charcoal?' She was trying valiantly to say anything to keep the sound of the chattering trees at bay. 'Gas is quicker, isn't it?'

'Yes, dear. But . . .' Wincing, Catherine suddenly touched the side of her head as if a hard object had struck her, then as quickly recovered. 'But . . . it doesn't impart the same flavour, does it?'

'I suppose you're right.'

'Odd that smoke, a toxic pollutant, should turn a piece of ordinary meat into something so extraordinarily delicious.'

Amelia smiled. 'Food of the gods.'

'Absolutely, dear. Food of the gods. Where did Rachel go?'

'Rachel?' The way Catherine had spoken suggested that Rachel had been with them just a moment ago. 'Oh, she went out . . . to check everything was all right. I think she's gone to bed now.'

'Ah . . .' Her mother's eyes burned, unblinking. 'The Gregale will have blown half the garden over Asia Minor by tomorrow. Nothing is safe from it. Nothing.'

'Mother, do you feel all right?'

'Now, now, Amelia, what did I tell you? It's "Catherine", not "mother". "Mother" makes me sound so old. I'm not old, am I?'

'No . . . not at all; I just wondered if—'

'Now, where's Lucy?'

Amelia knew her mother was in no state to hear about what had happened earlier. Instead, she gave a weak smile. 'She went to bed a couple of hours ago.'

'It's a wonder she can sleep at all in this. More tea?'

'Thank you.' It still tasted of blue cheese; but Amelia wouldn't allow the island to defeat her. 'Can I get you more tea?'

'No, not for me, Amelia dear, thanks all the same. Cigarette?'

'No, thank you.'

'You don't, do you? Wise. Very wise.' Catherine lit one herself, then said suddenly, 'Lucy's a bit . . . you know.' She tapped the side of her head.

'You mean this business about seeing things?'

'Oh?' For the first time her mother registered surprise. 'Oh, we all see things on Voros, dear. Didn't you know that? It comes with the territory.' The uncanny fire flared brighter in Catherine's eyes. 'But Lucy's convinced she can write a book about it all. A big book that will make big money. I tell her, time and time again, "Don't worry about it, dear. Rachel and I make enough to keep all of us."' She broke off suddenly and fixed her eyes on Amelia. 'You see them, too, don't you?'

'See what?'

'Ghosts, dear. Ghosts.'

'I . . . no. No.'

'Oh, you will, dear, you will. The trick is to get used to them. Why, after a while you don't even notice they're there. It's like living next to a railway line. At first the sound of it all is murder, then *pfft*, suddenly you don't notice them any more. But Lucy will insist on making a song and dance about it.'

'Mother—'

'It's Catherine, dear, Catherine.'

Amelia was dumbfounded. 'You mean *you* can see things that aren't there?'

'Naturally, as I said, if you live on Voros it goes with the territory . . . uh . . .'

'Catherine. What's wrong?'

'Migraine – bloody thing.'

Catherine pressed a hand that was nearer to blue than white against the side of her head. Amelia noticed, too, how grey and lifeless her fingernails were.

'Catherine, let me get you back to bed.'

'Nonsense, dear.'

'You don't look at all well.'

'I'm fine, really.' Again, Catherine forced her mouth to smile but her eyes glittered with such a cold, other-worldly fire that it sent shivers down Amelia's spine.

'Catherine. I insist.'

'And *I* insist I'm perfectly all right.'

'Catherine, at least—'

'No, I will *not* let a silly little headache pull me down.'

The wind thrummed against the windows. Once more, mournful notes like those of pan pipes called across the island to haunt the hillsides before dying out there amid the lonely ravines.

Amelia watched her mother. The woman wasn't well. That other-worldly aura about her seemed even more marked. Her talk of seeing things that weren't there was surely anything but rational. Now Catherine looked as if her every muscle had tensed against the pain. But still she wouldn't let it beat her.

'I'll ask Bill Simotas to give me a quote for that barbecue. If this damn storm doesn't blow us all off the island in the meantime.' She suddenly fixed Amelia with those blazing eyes. 'Don't go out when it's blowing up a storm. It's too dangerous. People have died on the island during the Gregale.' She took a deep breath as if trying to control a pain spearing through her skull. 'One of Zakarov's sons was decapitated by a roof tile. Did I tell you that, Amelia?'

'No, Catherine.' Amelia was scared of the woman now.

'A brother of old Mr Simotas was simply blown off the cliff into the sea. Never seen again. Don't go outside, Amelia, don't go out whatever you do. Who's that?'

'"Who's that?"' Amelia echoed, heart thudding. 'What do you mean, mother?'

'Someone's come into the kitchen.'

Amelia looked round. It was dimly lit, for sure – the shadows leapt out darkly with every flicker of the lights – but she could see no one there.

'There's no one in the kitchen but us, mother.'

'Someone came in. Just then. I saw them come up to stand behind you. Who is it, Amelia?'

Skin crawling as if icy centipedes were running over it, Amelia looked round. 'There really is no one there. We're alone.'

Now Catherine clamped a hand like a great blue-white spider against her head. Her lips formed a circle as the pain surged in near-harmony with the shrieking wind.

Amelia froze, not sure what to do for the best. Her instinct was to get help. But who from?

Momentarily the pain seemed to ease a little. Catherine took a deep breath. 'Bloody thing,' she muttered. 'Bloody, evil thing inside my head. It won't give up. It won't.' Her eyes opened; a fierce light flared inside them as she focused on an object behind Amelia.

'Don't think you can come back and claim her,' Catherine said icily, addressing someone Amelia could not see. 'She's nothing to do with you. And you've no rights over her.'

'Mother . . .'

'Uh . . . you don't see him, do you?'

Amelia turned round. There was nothing behind her but the copper faces of pans and the vacant eyes of spice jars in the rack.

'No, I don't see anyone.' She looked back at her mother, her heart pounding, her skin like ice. 'Who is it that you see?'

Catherine gave a snort of contempt. 'Who do I see? What I see is only the man who fathered you.'

Amelia reeled as if she'd been slapped. She spun round yet again. The lights flickered, a bald shadow of monstrous size lurched across the wall, then rocked back into itself and vanished.

Amelia glanced through the kitchen door to the hallway. One of the spotlights, flickering as it failed, sent the shadow of a statue – a naked old man with puckered, demon eyes – rushing back and forth across the walls and floor.

Amelia heard her mother give a snarl of anger. She turned to see her raise herself to her feet. A look of fury stained her face darkly. 'No . . . you're not doing to her what you did to me. Leave her!' Her eyes blazed. *Leave her alone!*

Then something disintegrated behind those two shining eyes. Amelia watched her mother in horror. This was like witnessing a once-elegant building dissolve into sudden ruin.

Catherine tottered sideways, holding her head as if something solid was erupting from her skull. A second later she fell down onto the tiles.

Amelia took a step back. Then she immediately recoiled, as if she'd pressed against a block of ice. She looked around. There was nothing but empty air behind her.

And yet, just for a second, she could have sworn she'd been embraced by something cold, odious.

Shaking off the sensation, she turned to look down at Catherine. The woman was unconscious, her eyes closed.

'Catherine . . .' she began but instantly discarded the name, choosing instead what her heart told her was right and proper to use. 'Mother. Mother? Are you all right? Mother . . .'

The woman lay deeply unconscious, her breathing shallow. 'Mother, what's wrong?'

Amelia had no sooner asked the question than she supplied her own diagnosis. The words pealed through her skull, as vivid as they were ugly.

Brain tumour.

Chapter Forty-six

Right from the start Amelia knew there was no way of moving her mother; she was a dead weight. Equally, she knew she couldn't leave her unconscious on the kitchen floor. The tiles were brutally cold. A draught blew from under the cellar door.

Quickly she fetched a sheet and a blanket from the laundry basket. Within a moment she'd rolled her mother onto the folded blanket that would cushion her from the bone-hard tiles. Then she laid the sheet over her, tucking it under her and around her head like a hood to protect her face and neck from the chilling draught.

Inescapably, she felt that she was covering a corpse; her mother beneath the white sheet was a carcass shape. Her skin was cold and had a bluish colour; her face was expressionless, eerily blank, as if her unconsciousness had the morbid power to erase her features, leaving her face skull-like.

'Oh, mother,' she whispered. 'What shall I do, what shall I do?'

Once more she went to the laundry basket and returned with one of Lucy's sweatshirts which she folded into a cushion to place beneath her mother's head. Then, even though her mother must have already been protected sufficiently from the cold, she pulled a red jacket from the washing machine. The appearance of her mother was still that of a cadaver beneath a sheet on a mortician's slab. The image was too powerful an omen.

The jacket hadn't yet gone through the wash cycle and was dry, probably waiting for a day when the gales wouldn't tear it from the line and send it flapping through the sky as far as Egypt. She placed the garment over her mother's chest so the collar rested just below her chin.

Then, for a full minute, she stood with her back to the wall, her chin pinched between her finger and thumb. Her mother didn't move. The woman's breathing continued: shallow, fast, slightly throaty in a way that made Amelia want to cough to clear her own throat.

What now?

She couldn't wait here forever.

The wind outside rose to a scream that vibrated the window.

There was a hungry note shooting through the sound, a sense of anticipation, like a beast scenting food.

The light in the hallway swung loose on its flex. Once more it sent the bald, monstrous shadow of the statue eagerly into the kitchen. The shadow could have been scampering gloatingly over the still cadaver shape of her mother, pawing her, before oozing back into the hallway.

Come on, Amelia, she told herself. *Your mother might be dying. You can't just stand here and watch it happen.*

She stood tense and still against the wall for another minute before making up her mind what to do next.

Then, taking a deep breath, she moved.

Leaving the kitchen silently, she slipped through into the hallway of shifting shadows, then up the stairs to the landing.

A deep bass sound thrummed through the walls of the house. It seemed to rumble from the depths of the earth itself.

On the landing were the four shut and silent doors of the bedrooms. She stared at them. For all the world it seemed they stared back – sullen, unfriendly, willing the intruder to turn back from them.

Amelia licked her lips. *Rachel or Lucy? Which one do I choose?*

She paused for a second, doubting whether either could

help. But anything was better than leaving her mother lying cold as death on the kitchen floor.

She tapped on Rachel's door.

No reply.

She tapped louder.

Outside the wind blew louder, drowning her knock with a shrieking of high-pitched notes.

'Rachel . . . Rachel . . .' she called softly, as if afraid of waking someone. 'Rachel. Catherine's collapsed. I can't wake her.' Her voice rose in volume as she spoke into the dead wood of the door. 'Rachel. I think she's really ill this time . . .'

She tapped louder. And the wind replied with a mocking tap at the door downstairs.

'Rachel, please.'

A flurry of scratching noises clawed their way across the roof.

'Rachel. If not for my sake then for my mother's. Catherine needs you.'

She tapped harder on the door. Waited. Draughts seethed up the stairs and around her bare ankles. 'Rachel?' There was no answering voice; in fact, no sound whatsoever. The room might have been empty as a cave for all she could hear.

Amelia knew she couldn't just turn away and leave her mother to lie there on the kitchen floor. Determinedly, she took a firm hold of the door handle, then swung the door open.

Rachel, sitting on the bed, her back to the headboard, stared at her.

Amelia met the glassy stare; a feeling of defiance crept into her heart.

Rachel licked her lips. They were loose-looking, wet. 'What kept you, sweetheart?' She gave a long sigh. 'I've been expecting you for hours and hours . . .'

The woman's head nodded heavily. Just for a second there was a hint of a smile on her lips. Then her face returned to a vacant, impassive expression.

Amelia moved deeper into the room, her eyes locked onto the woman. For a second she stared at her, not understanding what was happening. Yet, almost straight away, she saw a burning candle on the bedside table; a darkly stained dessert spoon lay beside it. And, tied so tightly around Rachel's arm that the skin puckered, there was a shoe-lace. It was the bright yellow lace from the drowned man's boot. But why go to the—

Then the clues clicked into place. Quickly Amelia scanned the table for what she knew she'd find there. And there it was, lying in a nest of tissue. A hypodermic. The hollow needle gleamed pink with a little smeared blood.

Rachel nodded drowsily, her eyes reading Amelia's face. 'Go on, Amelia, sweetheart . . . feast your eyes on it, why don't you?' A ghost of a smile touched her lips again. 'Enjoy my degradation – mmm? Make the most of it.'

Amelia shot her an acute look. 'Rachel. What did you find when you went down to the boathouse?'

'Mmm?'

'Listen, Rachel. Is the body of the pilot still down there?'

'I've kept myself clean for nineteen months, one week, and four days . . . Thought I'd beaten it.' She looked up. 'Thought wrong, didn't I?'

'Rachel, did you find something that made you do this?'

'Narcotics. Cures pain. Narcotics . . . Narcotic-sss.' She turned the 's' of 'narcotics' into a snake hiss, drawing it out until there was no more air in her lungs.

'Listen. Where's the pilot?'

'Narcotic-sss . . .'

'Rachel, for God's sake why have you done this to yourself?'

'Mm? Oh . . . it wasn't for the sake of God, or for Jesus, or Marx, or Bill Gates, or – or the man in the moon.' The smile twitched again on her face. But it didn't conceal the deep-rooted sadness there. The woman noticed the bootlace tied to her arm. Swinging it drowsily back and forth, while staring at it, she said, '*He* left this behind . . .'

Rachel leaned back to stare at the lace digging into her forearm. The skin was speckled with old needle scars. 'I kept clean for nineteen months, one week, four days . . . now *he's* driven me to this . . .'

Turning on her heels, Amelia left the room, slamming the door behind her.

The time for being timid was over. She pounded on Lucy's door.

'Lucy . . . Lucy! Open the door!'

She paused, thinking she could hear someone move behind it. 'Lucy, open this door. Now!'

Hesitantly the door opened. Lucy's white frightened face hung in the shadows beyond. 'I'm going to bed, Amelia. I can't take any more tonight.'

'Lucy. Listen. My mother's ill; she's out cold.'

'Rachel can—'

'Rachel's no use to anyone. She's injected herself with something. Heroin, I think.'

'Oh, poor Rachel.' Lucy's voice sounded as tiny and as frail as an old woman's. 'Poor girl. I thought she was over it now. Where is she?'

'She's all right. It's my mother I'm concerned about. Do you think you can help me get her to bed?'

'I . . . I suppose so. Let me just get my dressing gown.'

A second later she returned, belting the white gown. 'Is she downstairs?'

'In the kitchen.'

Lucy stepped cautiously out from her room, her eyes constantly roving round the landing as if expecting to see predatory forms springing out from the walls.

'I don't like the look of her,' Amelia was saying. 'She wasn't talking rationally, and she was in pain . . . she kept holding her head here.' Amelia touched her own temple.

'Oh, dear . . . I'm sorry.' Lucy's haggard face was a picture of worry. 'Tonight of all nights. Poor thing. We won't be able to get her to a doctor just yet.'

'That's what I'm worried about. What if she's suffered a relapse and the—'

Lucy suddenly reached out and grabbed Amelia's hand as

they reached the bottom of the stairs. The force she gripped it with was painful.

'Amelia . . . have you . . . you know, *seen* anything tonight?' Her eyes roved round the hallway.

'No. Nothing.'

'It's a bad night, Amelia. A bad night. I don't like it. Don't you feel it on your skin? Like electricity?'

'Lucy, all I want to concentrate on doing is getting my mother into bed. She's lying on the floor through there.'

'Yes, yes.' Lucy still sounded distracted; her head twitched this way and that with every sound. 'I wonder what they're playing at,' she continued in a hushed voice. 'Why don't they just come out and show themselves?'

'Lucy, please. Once we've taken my mother upstairs you can go back to bed.'

Still with Lucy gripping her hand, as if afraid of being snatched away by some intruder, Amelia headed for the kitchen.

By now they were moving through the body of the hall, between the lines of statues. A snake-haired Medusa glared down at them from a great height, while the shadow of the bald monstrosity ducked and bobbed along the walls as if stalking them.

That walk through the hallway, bizarrely enough, became an absurdly long march. The statues had multiplied into armies, it seemed.

Fractured legs. Faces with chunks gouged from foreheads. Broken stone arms. Noses, jagged smashed things, that endowed the faces with a look of stone cold fury. The line of deformed statues seemed to run on forever. And, all the time, the wind cried bleakly.

'Rotten monstrosities,' Amelia heard Lucy say while staring at the statues. 'Rotten ugly monstrosities. After all this is over we should get hammers, smash them into little pieces and throw them into the sea.' Then she clammed up tight as if she'd uttered blasphemies.

They were at the mid-point between the kitchen and the front door when they sensed its approach.

Amelia heard movement outside. Just as if some huge form was coming towards them across the island. A great body that moved slowly, yet with an inevitable pace, heading for them.

She heard the funeral cypresses creak, the rustle of Judas trees being flattened before a terrible force.

Stones crunched as if beneath approaching feet. And they must have been the feet of titans at that, huge, crunching and grinding the path stones to grit.

The two women froze. They stared wide-eyed at the closed doors.

Here in the tides of blackest night they had a visitor.

The creaking and rustling and sighing and grating of stone on stone, timber on timber grew louder, louder, louder . . . then fell away to sudden silence.

There was a sense of *pause*, of the world holding its breath.

Amelia glanced at Lucy. Lucy briefly met her look, terror in her eyes. Then she turned back to look at the door. They waited for a knock on the wood. Or for the handle to simply turn.

They could not now move their gazes from the door. Its solid timbers, its iron studs and bolts, was the only barrier between them and what prowled across the face of the island.

The silence lasted another two full seconds.

Then that silence was destroyed.

Both doors burst inward with a crash.

Instantly air, like an armoured fist, hit them, knocking them back on their heels. They covered their eyes as grit stung them. Leaves, dirt, grass, even branches rode the gale as it stormed into the villa, whooping across the statues, tugging at the lights.

Then the hurricane had passed them.

As if it wanted to run wildly through the house to see what lay in every room. Amelia heard door after door bang open. Somewhere from upstairs came the crash of breaking glass as the wind found a poorly secured window and dashed it back against the wall.

A moment later the inrush of air had subsided enough

for Amelia to speak. 'Stay here,' she told Lucy. 'I'll bolt the doors shut.'

Lucy had said nothing. Eyes fixed, she stared at the open doorway and the rushing windswept nightscape beyond.

The doors hadn't, thankfully, been torn from their hinges by the storm. With an effort Amelia heaved the doors back shut, then bolted and locked them.

When she returned to Lucy she saw the woman had armed herself with one of the walking sticks from the hallway stand.

'Lucy, come on.'

But Lucy was looking up at the tops of the walls. Her head twisted, ducked, then lifted. It was as if dozens of birds had flown into the villa and she was following them with her eyes.

Amelia looked up but saw nothing except a few leaves settling in the air.

'Lucy . . .'

Lucy didn't appear to hear. She'd backed against the wall, the walking stick raised like a sword.

'Lucy, what's wrong?'

In a tiny, strangled whisper the other woman said: 'They're here. They've got into the villa.'

'Lucy, what's got into the villa? I can't see—'

Amelia had to move back quickly as Lucy slashed at something unseen above her head. Then she was hacking at something at ground level, before she backed away, raising the stick across her face as if an invisible attacker had lunged at her.

'Lucy?'

The woman didn't reply now. She didn't even appear to be aware of Amelia standing in the hallway with her. Her attention was taken entirely by swarms of things – *invisible things* – that flew at her head or circled around her.

Lucy slashed at the air with the stick continually now. Her eyes were darting after something that was small and fast.

Amelia pleaded. 'Lucy.'

But even as she spoke she knew she'd lost her. Face distorted with fear, eyes uncannily bright, Lucy slashed again and again at thin air. Then, step by step, she backed away again. A moment later she'd reached the bottom of the stairs. Then, still moving slowly backwards, she worked her way up the staircase. All the time her eyes followed invisible birds, or bats, or heaven knew what.

There was nothing Amelia could do but watch the frightened, haunted woman slowly ascend the stairs.

Lucy no longer cried out. Every scrap of her concentration was fixed on the invisible flitting things that swooped at her as if to claw out her eyes.

Dear God . . . Amelia took a deep breath. The more she watched Lucy the more she too could see (or imagined she could see) those darkly flitting shapes.

Now she fancied she heard the sound of membranous wings.

But no. That was sheer imagination.

There's nothing there, she told herself, desperately clenching her fists, *there's nothing there*.

A moment later Lucy had disappeared from sight. Almost immediately Amelia heard the sound of a door being closed. Lucy was back inside her fortress again. No doubt she'd scramble back into bed, pull the sheet over her head, and lay there wide-eyed and terrified until daybreak.

With her only ally gone Amelia returned to the kitchen. Catherine lay on the floor in her cocoon of white cotton sheet. Still unconscious, her breathing was shallow, scratchy-sounding. Amelia touched the woman's forehead. Shocked, she snatched her fingers away. Her mother's face was cold. Colder than a marble headstone.

She found herself staring at her mother's nostrils, waiting for each inhalation that would cause the sides of the long aristocratic nose to draw in a little. And as she watched she convinced herself that every breath she saw her take would be the last.

She's dying were the words that set themselves firmly in her mind. *She's dying. And all I can do is watch her slip away.* And it seemed so cruel that Catherine would have to spend her last moments on earth lying there on the hard, unfeeling tiles that still reeked of bleach.

Amelia slipped her hand beneath the sheet and found her mother's fingers. For a moment she held the cold hand in hers.

'No, mother, it's not fair. You deserve better than this. I'm going to get help . . . don't worry; I won't be long . . .' Perhaps some part of her mother could still hear her, so she repeated softly again and again, 'Don't worry. I'll soon be back . . . please hang on.'

After pulling the jacket up higher and plumping up the sweatshirt beneath her mother's head, Amelia went quickly upstairs. Then, taking a quilted jacket from her mother's wardrobe, she slipped it on and once more prepared to go out into the night.

Chapter Forty-seven

The storm had eased a little by the time Amelia left the villa. Even so, winds still whistled round the eaves of the house. For all the world it sounded like the mad pipings of a lunatic musician. Notes ran from deep bass sounds that made the inside of her ears itch to screeching high notes that made her teeth vibrate so much they hurt.

For the first time in hours she felt the purr of that insidious pain above her left eyebrow.

Determined still, she shut the villa doors behind her, switched on the torch, then worked her way round to the patio. Torchlight revealed the concrete slabs, the constant stream of grass and leaves that flowed through the air, the monstrous shapes of the Judas trees that shook and twitched and writhed with the animating power of the gale.

Focusing on the need to bring help for her mother, she crossed the patio. Now it was a bleak expanse of windswept concrete. Nothing like the pleasant sitting-out area she'd enjoyed just a couple of days before.

The beam of her torch flashed across the surface of the swimming pool. Transformed into a mass of scum and matted leaves, there was something deeply unhealthy about its appearance, as if poison had leaked from the interior of the island, tainting the once-clear water.

Amelia didn't pause; she couldn't allow the island to work that same toxic magic on her own mind. Ahead stood the pair of funeral cypresses. Beyond that was the dark void of the island itself. The torch failed miserably to penetrate that far into the darkness. At best its weak beam gleamed against the geometric cubes of stone that lay tumbled across that dark and haunted landscape like the weird houses of some goblin town.

Pushing on against the currents of air, she passed between the funeral cypresses and out into the darkness. She tried hard to stop her imagination running away with her. But there was every reason for it to do so. Out here on the naked body of the island she'd never felt so lonely. Or so threatened. The darkness was swollen with a hundred potential dangers. From catching a foot on a rock to the night hiding a man who'd stalk her, unseen, to an even more remote part of the island.

It was hard not to think of Bill's brother. Hadn't she been warned of Gregoriou's sinister behaviour when the Gregale blew? How did she know that he wasn't following her now, his heart beating with some dark passion?

She walked faster along a path which was little more than a jumble of fractured rock. The gale, by turns, blew hard into her face, trying to push her back; then, with a spiteful change of direction, it would blast against her back, sending her reeling forward, her feet slipping on the rock, her arms reaching out at either side as she tried to maintain balance.

But still Amelia pushed on. Her torch beam played over dreary cubes of stone, then over crags; suddenly it would find a cluster of snarling Judas trees that would whip and curl. Looking like the tentacles of monsters erupting from the grey bones of rock.

She knew there would be no specialist medical help on the island. But, she had told herself, if she could persuade someone strong enough to help her get her mother off that cold kitchen floor it would be a start.

The branch of a Judas tree whipped out and struck her mouth. Recoiling from the stinging blow, she stared at it in disbelief. She could have sworn the gale had been blowing in the other direction. But somehow the tree had lashed out at her *against* the current of air.

The damned things are alive, Amelia told herself morbidly. Alive in an animal sense, rather than a plant sense.

They know I'm close to them. They're trying to stop me.

The pain above Amelia's left eyebrow buzzed; from that a thin needle-sharp stinging began to work its way deeper into her head. The suddenness of it made her open her mouth. Instantly a leaf fluttered into the back of her throat. She gagged before she could spit it out.

Damn' island, damn' island . . .

Grit blasted into her face. Screwing her eyes nearly shut so she wouldn't be blinded she forced herself on, hoping she could follow the path. Even so, lurking unpleasantly in the back of her mind was the possibility that a rogue path might take her to the edge of a cliff. In the darkness, with the roar of the surf and the storm, would she even notice the edge? Try as she might, she couldn't shut out the mental image of herself simply falling over the cliff edge and into the boiling maw of the sea where she'd never be found.

Holding one hand across her eyes to shield them from the stinging machine-gun fire of grit, she angled the light down to the ground just in front of her, grimly locking her attention to the path.

The path alternated between a slippery smoothness and rock slabs pitted with holes that pulled at the muscles of her feet and ankles. Every few paces there would be a crack five or six inches across that would surely rip a ligament if she accidentally put her foot into its stone jaws.

The wind rose: Amelia sensed its beast-like force. A whole blizzard of grass and leaves filled the air.

No. I won't let you beat me, she told the island. *I won't. I'm not just another blade of grass or a stick to be blown away into nothingness. I am Amelia Thomas. I have the power to choose what to do in my life. I decide where to go. I decide what to eat, I decide what to wear. If I choose to help my dying mother then that's what—*

At that moment she found herself suddenly in a clearing by a villa. The gale was less intense here.

Blinking, she stood looking round, not even sure where

she was exactly. A fragment of swallowed leaf made her cough once more.

The blond man looked down from the tractor seat and sang out pleasantly, 'Isabella. We've another one for tea.'

Chapter Forty-eight

Dazed, Amelia looked up at him.

'Sorry, I've forgotten. Do you take sugar?'

Air currents surged around Amelia Thomas, tugging her hair until it hurt. The sight of the man on his tractor, the tractor that forever sat by the villa as uselessly as a landlocked ship, had derailed her. In fact, there was a moment she didn't believe the figure was real.

'Sugar?' the man asked again blandly.

'No.'

'No sugar, Isabella,' he called towards the villa. There, a shutter banged to and fro in the wind. Another hung crazily by a single hinge. A steel bowl rolled across the patio with a clattering sound. A single flickering light swung from the porch. Shadows surged madly.

'No, sorry. I – I mean I can't stay for tea.'

'Oh dear. Isabella does love her chats.'

'Mr Oxford, my mother's ill . . .'

He looked at her with blue eyes as bright as glass, as if to prompt her to say more.

Amelia continued, stammering. 'Catherine Thomas . . . do you know her?'

'I know her, yes, of course.'

'I'm terribly worried about her. I wonder if—'

'Catherine Thomas. Yes. Haven't seen her for a long time now. Mmm, last harvest it was. Ah, yes, I remember now, because there was a fine head of maize that year. Isabella! Are you ready with that tea? Guest's getting thirsty, dear.'

'No, really, Mr Oxford, thank you but . . .'

He wasn't listening. The man returned to gazing lovingly down at the tractor's steering wheel. He wiped away a speck of wind-blown dirt, then stroked the circumference of the wheel with his fingertips. Even in utter madness there was a deep-felt tenderness in the action.

She took a step back. The shutters clattered angrily, while high on the cliff a monstrously bleak gale howled its fury.

To ask Mr Oxford to help her would be a waste of breath. He was lost in his own tractor-filled universe. Nothing was going to lever him from that machine.

As she took another step back, instead of stone something soft yielded beneath her heel; she heard an 'uh' sound.

One of the Oxford children crawled on the ground behind her. She must have stood on its hand. Guilt for her carelessness gave way instantly to shock. The child was like the rest of the Oxford progeny: a long torso, short arms, stumpy legs. There was the same stuck-out hair that looked as coarse as any you'd find on a cheap doll. The nose and ears were rough and ready buds. Tiny eyes seemed more like babies navels than genuine eyes.

Only this child of the Oxfords was worse than all the others.

Part of its head was missing. If anything, it resembled a melon from which a slice had been cut. The V-shaped depression ran from the top of its head down as far as the ear, inscribing a deep valley in the skull.

'Uh.' It held up a bruised paw. 'Uh-nn . . .'

She looked up at Mr Oxford. 'I'm sorry, it was clumsy of me.' But he'd not noticed. Instead, he continued in a voice that was as hollow as it was matter-of-fact. 'Now if the ferry boats did stop running for ever we would run out of food. We consume more than the island can produce. At present, anyway. But if Simotas turned the tobacco field over to spuds then we'd be all right. Otherwise we'll be burying our children by Christmas. Isabella! Can you manage with that tea?'

Amelia glanced into the dead windows of the villa. Shutters still slammed. One pane of glass had shattered. Blade-like shards sparkled on the soil where the children crawled.

She glanced back down at the child with the segment of skull either surgically removed or missing congenitally from its head. The scar was bluish; the skin flaky.

By rights, the child should have been dead. Then again, anything on this lunatic island was possible.

'Isabella? Guest's getting thirsty.'

Now more figures wormed their way out of the darkness. Amelia counted five of the stunted children. Some moved on all fours, others slithered like snakes on their bellies. All had that coarse hair that looked as if it had been trimmed with a bread knife.

'Simotas lacks a really good tractor. He needs a model like this.' Mr Oxford stroked the steering wheel. 'A Case four-wheel drive with a bit more grunt below the hood.'

The naked children crawled towards her. As she watched, one raised itself onto its haunches and held up a hand. A dead snake dangled from it.

From the direction of the villa came a loud crash. Instantly a bleating cry started; for all the world it reminded Amelia of a newborn baby. She wondered, shuddering with horror, if another child had been born into the Oxford's demented world.

Mr Oxford sang out pleasantly from high on the tractor seat. 'Isabella? Currant buns with the tea would be nice. Hurry up in there, guests can't be kept waiting for ever.'

The sight of the pulpy, crawling things reaching imploringly out to Amelia was overwhelming. At last she turned and scrambled up the hillside and into darkness.

She made her way up, up and up. Through the thickets of Judas trees, between funeral cypresses, across slabs of rock that could have been tumbled headstones in some monster graveyard. The light of her torch revealed little more than a bare few yards of the terrain in front of her.

For whole minutes she scrambled forward, searching for the path.

Do I go on? she asked herself, panting. *Or back?* Thoughts of her mother lying cold and unconscious on the kitchen floor were a nagging ache inside her. But if she were to return without help what could she do? Rachel was no use. She'd still be squatting there on her bed, lost in a narcotic haze. Lucy would be no better. The woman was simply off her head with fear.

No, she'd have to press on, she thought. There must be someone who could help.

She followed the path. Gusts pushed her on. Leaves and grass filled the air like snowflakes. The light of the torch revealed swathes of grey rock and yet more of the Judas trees that swarmed across the earth like a disease. When the beam flashed on them the branches gleamed with spectral fire.

And all the time she heard their hostile voices as the air hissed among them.

She went deeper into the ravine. If anything, it amplified the monstrous roar of the storm. Even from here she could hear the thunder of surf crashing into the cliffs below with killing force.

She pressed on, her arm aching from holding the torch out in front of her. Every so often the air torrents carried branches along the ravine; they swirled out of the darkness with the speed of demons. Each time she had to hurl herself one way or the other to dodge them.

Behind her they went, clattering like the bones of dead men hurled against rock.

A moment later she emerged from the furrow of rock. Below her she recognized Julius king's villa.

She wasn't surprised for a moment to see that phantoms dressed in grey coffin shrouds danced along the walls.

Why, if the spirits of the dead can't enjoy a night like this, who can?

A dark and stormy night. A night when all of Voros comes alive to kill the intruder.

Me.

I, Amelia Thomas, am the intruder.

The thoughts oozed with all the oily smoothness of utter irrationality. Mad thoughts for a mad night.

The storm left her feeling drunk on its savage power. The night-time trek across the alien landscape had disorientated her, utterly dislocating her from reality.

So, if the dead danced at Julius King's villa so be it: what concern was it of hers . . .

Tottering unsteadily, she made her way through the gale towards the villa.

Grey phantoms danced. One played a curling serpent of a horn; his eyes were full of sparks and his mouth shrieked with a dreadful light.

You're not real.

She formed the words defiantly in her head.

You're not real.

But the phantoms continued their dance. Writhing forms entwined limbs on an altar.

Somewhere on the path, she told herself, she'd crossed the boundary from her own universe into the dark, seething, gluttonous pit of hell itself.

Lunatic images sneaked easily into her head.

A winged skull. A hand with tentacles for fingers . . .

You're not real.

The voice of reason, however, was a faint noise inside her head . . . it was dying from the onslaught of what she saw . . .

'You're not real.'

As she walked up to the dancing figures they quit the wall so they could dance over the material of her mother's jacket.

She touched the wall of the villa where a two-dimensional phantom romanced a swaying skeleton.

Then, shielding her eyes, she turned suddenly to the igloo-shaped outbuilding that contained the film projector. A flickering light dazzled her. Just behind it she could make out the projector spools turning round.

'Julius,' she called. 'Julius? Is that you?'

She glanced back at film of the phantoms cavorting on the wall behind her.

'Julius? My mother's ill . . . I'm worried about her. Do you know if your telephone is working?'

She advanced on the projection house. Now she could hear the clicking of the projector itself as it played one of Zakarov's insane films on the wall of the house.

Behind her, her own shadow was cast, massive and monstrous. It grew larger and larger as she approached the light source. On her chest phantoms, skeletons and demons cavorted. Speech titles appeared, deforming, blurring, then sharpening.

'Julius?' She tilted her head to one side as she tried to see through the dazzling outpouring of light. 'Julius. Is that you?'

'It is I, child.'

'I'm sorry to trouble you. My mother's ill. I wondered if I could use your phone?'

'She's sick?'

'Yes, she collapsed about an hour ago. I've had to leave her on the kitchen floor.'

'Oh, my poor girl, I'm so sorry.'

'Is it all right if I try your phone to—'

'My dear. I'm terribly sorry. My telephone isn't working; this wretched storm must have broken the lines . . . oh, my dear, what can I do? What can I do?'

There was genuine compassion in his voice. Still she couldn't see him properly. She saw the hairless head in silhouette. He appeared, as far as she could tell, to be sitting in a chair beside the projector.

'I wish I could help,' he said regretfully. 'But the truth of the matter is I've had more than a little to drink. And being *sans* legs is absolutely no help whatsoever.'

'I wondered if you might be able to suggest . . . *oh!*'

'Don't be alarmed by what you see, child.'

'I'm sorry . . . I didn't realize. I thought you were alone.' She found herself panting with shock.

Julius had company. Kneeling next to him, aping the pose of a devoted pilgrim before a saint, was another figure.

At that moment her eyes adjusted to the brilliant projector light. There, in the flickering glare, his great soulful brown eyes locked on hers, was Gregoriou Simotas.

Before she realized it, she was running. Phantoms burst back across the wall again. End titles scrolled upward across a burning skull as high as the house itself.

Behind her she heard Julius shout in sudden alarm. 'Gregoriou! Gregoriou! No!' Something heavy toppled with a crash. '*No! DON'T!*'

Chapter Forty-nine

Amelia felt as if she was on the run. She raced up the hillside away from Julius King's villa, the torchlight swinging this way and that, illuminating blankets of rosemary and thyme. And always the clumps of omnipresent Judas trees, their branches looking like spiky insect antennae.

She shouldn't have run from Julius. But what she'd seen had taken her by surprise. In another context she would have said that Gregoriou had been committing an evil assault on the elderly black man. But there clearly had been an intimacy there. And Julius must have submitted willingly.

But, no, she couldn't dwell on what she had witnessed; she must concentrate on finding help for her mother. There were other villas on the island. Surely someone could help.

By now she'd reached the highest of the island's paths. Immediately the storm eagerly pushed her along Voros's rocky spine.

As soon as she grew half-accustomed to the push of the winds at her back, they changed direction with savage glee and threatened to drag her back the way she'd come.

The light of the torch itself seemed to be blown by the winds, too. The beam flickered, then bent, then sprang back to illuminate a cluster of chattering Judas trees. Or the light would slash across box-shaped boulders that looked like so many goblin houses.

As she toiled along the wicked path, her hair yanked so

painfully by the storm that tears needled her eyes, she found herself believing those stone blocks possessed occupants.

She imagined that peeking from them were the faces of the Oxford children grown old. She saw their bud ears, their bud noses, their tiny, pouched, belly-button eyes.

The one with the hunk cut from its skull reached from his goblin house and invited her in.

Even at this stage the island was giving her the opportunity to submit to its authority. She only had to relent; she only had to accept that the price she had to pay would be her sanity; she only had to do the things expected of her. If she surrendered her reason and her own free will to the island, then she could step into the goblin house and stay there forever.

What's happening to me? Amelia asked herself. *Why am I thinking these things?*

She couldn't abandon herself to those strange notions. Not with her mother lying there on the kitchen floor. She might be dying. Amelia had to find help at any cost.

The pain returned to drill deep into her skull above her eye.

She pressed her hands to her temples.

She'd not slept more than a couple of hours in the last three days. Sleep deprivation had formed an unholy pact with her old fall injury.

She all but begged herself: *Hold on to what's real. Don't fall prey to the hallucinations again. On a night like this it will kill you.*

It only needed her to take a few steps away from the path. The cliff edge was no more than twenty paces away. And hundreds of feet below surf thundered with that brutal killing force. Just a few steps astray; she'd disappear as if she'd never existed at all.

Gritting her teeth, she pushed on. The path took her higher and higher along the spine of the island. The winds grew stronger.

A few minutes later she reached the highest point of the island. From here she could look down to both her left and right at the luminous ocean surf. It seethed across rocks, whiter and angrier than she'd ever seen before.

Even from here she heard its thundering roar. A monstrous sound, fierce enough to run up through the very fabric of the rock to shake her feet.

Amelia imagined the vibration of that roar ringing the island like a bell. It would pass up the cliff and into The Palms where a white-faced Lucy would be pressing her hands to her face, praying for the storm to pass.

It would touch, too, the stick figure of Rachel Stone fighting her own demons as the heroin-laden blood oozed through her brain.

The vibrations would reach up to the concrete gun platform where the palm prints were set. And the self-same vibrations would reach deep down into the heart of the island.

There, the potato vines would tremble in the cave. Dust shaken from the roof would sprinkle the dried faces of the four dead soldiers as they patiently waited for the end of time.

Even at the bottom of the sea, in the wreck of the hospital ship, conger eels would sense the vibrations and twitch in their nests of human ribcages.

She shivered.

If anything, the eastern end of the island was stonier than the other. Here there was less vegetation. Even so, a tenacious dwarf form of the Judas tree still grew from every fissure. Branches rattled with the sound of skeletons dancing. When the torchlight splashed among them, they glimmered with that same spectral fire.

The path was even more difficult to follow. Now putting a single foot wrong would send her crashing over the cliff into the sea hundreds of feet below.

Her eyes fixed on the pool of light ahead. How much further to the other villas?

I feel as if I've been walking for hours, Amelia told herself. *This is a tiny island, but now it's as if some dark magic has transformed it into a land mass the size of a continent, or even a whole world. A bleak, goblin world. One that consisted of rock and Judas trees;*

while, all the time, the roar of storm and surf fused to form a hymn for lost souls.

As her jacket ballooned open she struggled to fasten it.

The gale invaded the garment, forcing fingers of cold air deep into the sleeves. Then, as if they'd probed far enough, the storm caught hold of her, dragging her backwards. Almost losing her balance, she caught hold of the branch of a Judas tree – and thirty miles away across the sea Bill Simotas sat upright in bed with a cry. He didn't know what had woken him so suddenly, or why he was shivering as if he'd plunged his hand into Arctic waters. He found the Greek cross that he wore around his neck and held it tightly.

High on Voros's cracked stone spine Amelia held onto the branch as the wind tried to draw her down towards the cliff. Beneath her feet pebbles rolled as easily as ball-bearings.

Even as she tried to recover her balance she felt the branch break in the grip of her fist. Already the dead force of gravity pulled her downward towards the precipice. Stones loosened by her feet rolled down the slope to fall over the edge. They would have a long drop to the sea. And an even longer fall through the dark water to the ocean bed.

She lurched forward, throwing her own weight forward, as the branch snapped. By sheer luck her foot found a firm slab of stone.

Then, regaining her balance, she walked on into the jaws of the gale. The light from the torch played over the evil path. The very landscape oozed treachery. From the jagged stones that hurt the soles of her feet to the deep fissures that threatened to break her shin bones if she put a foot wrong.

Voros has a dozen villas, she told herself. *So where are they?*

Surely they couldn't blow away in the storm, could they?

Even so, she despaired of finding anyone able-bodied – or sane enough – to help.

When she thought the path would never end she suddenly saw the ruined watchtower ahead. This was the very end of Voros itself.

Of the ruin not a standing wall remained. This might have

been the last place on earth. A wind-scoured, storm-blasted slab of rock where no living thing could survive for long.

Beyond the ruin the island terminated in a cliff edge high above the sea. Beyond that there were only raging air currents that separated the island from the Turkish mainland fifty miles away. In the dark void out there she glimpsed water spouts moving with the eerie grace of swan necks.

Bewildered, she looked round for the missing villas. She'd been told they weren't far from here. But where?

Step by step, foot after foot, she forced herself through the onslaught of rushing air. When at last she reached the edge of the cliff she looked down, shining the feeble light of the torch towards its base.

There, maybe five hundred feet below, at the bottom of sheer cliffs, was a horseshoe-shaped bay. Clinging to the shore were nine villas.

Despite herself she laughed. A bubbling laugh that was dark and throaty. A laugh that didn't seem to belong to her at all. The villas were so much beyond her reach they might as well have been on the dark side of the Moon. There was no path. The only way to reach them would be by boat. In that angry sea it would be impossible.

At last Amelia faced the truth. She was alone. Certainly as good as alone. No one could help her.

She forced herself to stand against the gale. The force of it sucked the breath from her lungs. Her chest laboured to draw in air.

There was nothing she could do now but return to her mother at the villa and face the coming hours. Whatever they might bring.

Chapter Fifty

The return journey was unreal. The force of the storm and the darkness corrupted her perception of reality.

At one point Amelia looked down from a hillside at the Simotas farm. The flickering light in the glass shrine burned yellow like an evil eye among the gloom-shrouded olive groves. Scarecrows twirled and danced. Sometimes a gust of air would catch one and send it running across the fields.

A darker figure raced amongst them. At first she thought it was another scarecrow, but this shape ran with a demonic vitality against the flow of air.

It was Gregoriou. Any thought of going down there to ask for help at the farm was dispelled as savagely as if blasted away by the storm.

First, she would have to get by Gregoriou somehow. Without a shadow of a doubt, she would have to confront him somewhere down there; she imagined his fiercely wrinkling forehead, the ape-like eyes beneath the dark archways of his eyebrows. He wouldn't let her pass. He would think she was going to the farm to tell them about what he'd done to the old black man.

No. There was nothing she could do but return home alone.

She quickened her pace, sensing rather than seeing the path ahead of her.

The batteries in the torch were dying. The light it cast was now a dim, buttery yellow.

'I'm sorry, mother . . .' she found herself rehearsing the words. 'I'm sorry I couldn't help you when you needed me . . . I'm sorry.'

The pain above her eyes purred.

How it softly, softly purred . . .

Kitten-like.

Mother had a cat like that. It had grown from a kitten to a tiger in her head; now its sharp teeth snapped their way through brain tissue like a . . .

No: Amelia felt her mind slipping away from her . . . as it did, so memories that were oddly lucid came back to her. She was standing on the patio of Julius King's villa. There she was, white and crisp, in the dress she had borrowed from her mother.

When she'd worn the dress the latent power that was psychometry had whirred into life . . .

Psychometry . . . what an ugly, inelegant word . . .

When I touched the dress I felt an object growing in my head. What I was sensing was my mother's tumour. Growing there as rapidly as a cluster of mushrooms.

Whenever I touched my mother's dress I saw in my mind's eye a house within a walled garden

That's where my mother lived long ago.

There was an old man who worked in the garden. An old man with a bald head that peeled like it had horrific sunburn.

Who might he be?

If only I could ask mother when I get back.

She touched the sleeve of her mother's jacket. Instantly pain lanced right through her skull. So intense it came as a flash of light.

'Mother . . .' She knew she felt what her mother felt. She experienced a swirling rush of desperation. She could almost feel the pressure of the kitchen floor against her cheek, as cold and as dreadful as a mortuary slab.

'Mother . . . you're dying.'

404

A sudden urgency snarled through Amelia. She had to get back home now. She set off at a run.

The island would have none of it.

Its jagged surface tripped her. Amelia fell, landing on her chest and grazing her chin. She reached out to grip at the branch of a Judas tree to help herself up. It felt as flexible as a piece of rope. Instantly the treacherous branch snapped; she fell forward again, jarring her arms.

'Careful, cuz. You'll break your noodle.'

Her cousin John stood on the top of the slope, beaming down at her, his arms folded in that same self-satisfied way she'd seen dozens of times before.

'I won't,' she told him, panting. 'I won't do that again.'

'Oh? Why not? You've fallen before.'

'I didn't fall, I was—'

'Pushed, yeah, right.'

'Go away, you're not real.'

'I'm as real as you are, cuz.' Then, giving that mocking little-finger wave, he began to laugh.

As she struggled to her feet she saw the dressing gown he wore grow longer and longer until it touched the ground; it kept on flowing.

And, laughing, he grew taller and taller until he was as high as a tree.

Then, to accompany his mocking laugh, came the mean, thin sound of his two sisters singing:

> *Humpty Dumpty sat on a wall,*
> *Humpty Dumpty had a great fall,*
> *And all the king's horses and all the king's men*
> *Couldn't put Humpty together again . . .*

'Go away!' she screamed. 'You're not real!'

The laughter continued. Scornful. Malicious.

Furious, she swept the light at the figure.

There was nothing there but the pole-straight form of a cypress tree.

Above it, the mass of funeral-black cloud lumbered across the night sky, unseen; but Amelia sensed its weight that seemed to have the malevolent power to crush and stifle her.

Taking a deep breath, she pushed on along the path. Ahead, the way was thick with shadow.

As she walked as fast as she dared she felt a new sensation in her breast. One of pressure, as if a weight bore down on her heart.

She wondered if some empathy with her mother communicated what the woman was feeling as she lay on the floor.

Amelia moved faster. Judas trees swarmed thickly at this end of the island. They were closing in on her, she was sure of it; she saw them trying to block her way.

Abandoning caution, she began to run once more.

In a little while she passed Julius King's now darkened villa, then the Oxfords' home; Mr Oxford sat motionless on the tractor seat; pulpy white shapes wriggled far below in shadow-smeared gloom.

Ten minutes later, her back itching with perspiration, she saw The Palms. No lights showed in the villa. Now it looked like a forbidding mausoleum of a place; something that housed not the living but the dead. The long-dead, sucked clean of their souls.

Cold. Abandoned.

Slipping, sometimes losing her footing, she scrambled along the path, then burst through the twin funeral cypresses and onto the patio.

Home. But at that moment of knowing she was just seconds from where her mother lay in the kitchen she feared to enter. She dreaded what she might find on that icy floor. The realization that she might be too late, that her mother might be already dead resonated deep inside her bones.

Slowly now, on the balls of her feet, Amelia stepped into the house.

And at that moment the island entered the eye of the storm.

The winds dropped to nothing. A silence, a complete and total silence spread raven wings over the house.

Closing the door behind her, she made her way along the hallway of watching statues.

The house was silent. There was a sense of abandonment; as if it had been empty for years.

Slowly she walked beneath the glowering stone faces. The old man in cold marble stared down his long nose at her. The last of the lights had died. Now only the torch lit her way. Its light, too, had dimmed to a smudge of orange.

At the kitchen door she reached out to turn the handle.

And halfway round the world, in the northern town where snow still clung to the rooftops, her cousin John stared at his computer screen. He'd been eating a pizza crust, but the website he'd found on the Internet was such an education even for him that he forgot to chew. The video footage had taken forever to download; now he was determined to suck the thing dry of every drop of entertainment value before going to bed. Only, as he watched, the video cut from a crowded mattress to an image of a girl carrying a torch and entering a darkened kitchen. Puzzled, he tilted his head.

There was something familiar about the girl.

As he watched, she shone the torch at some long, white mass that lay on the floor . . .

He was about to lean towards the screen to look more closely at the girl's face but he was, at that moment, distracted.

His twin sisters were awake; they were shouting something about a man coming up the stairs. He heard one of his sisters cry out: *'His face!'*

In the kitchen on Voros Amelia shone the torch down on what lay on the floor. She recognized the jacket and the bed sheet.

She looked blankly for a moment.

Her mother was gone.

Chapter Fifty-one

Amelia stared at what the torchlight revealed. The sheet and jacket were as she'd left them on the kitchen floor. For all the world, it looked as if her mother had simply been drawn from them like a hand from a glove. Now she was gone.

Once more the storm surged. The turbulent air shook the window until it sounded like the pounding of tribal drums.

And again the winds attacked the eaves, drawing out a whole cacophony of notes. The storm music was wilder than ever. From shrieking whistles to a bass sound that boomed with all the dark force of a cathedral organ playing the requiem for a dead king.

She shone the dying torch around the kitchen. The brass pans on the wall shone as palely as the faces of corpses; jars and bottles reflected the light like so many dead eyes.

And all through the house came a roaring blast of ice-cold air that sent doors slamming shut one after another.

'Mother!'

The force of the wind caught the sheet and sent it slithering across the kitchen floor.

'Mother!'

There was no reply except for a shrilling pan-pipe note followed by the crash of more doors.

Gripping the torch hard, her heart pounding, Amelia left the kitchen. Quickly she checked the stairs, then the dining room. Statues leered stonily back at her. If anything, there was a look of smug satisfaction on their faces, as if to say: *We knew it would come to this, Amelia. We knew your life would end here.*

'Mother!'

Amelia returned to the hallway and battled through the torrent of air cascading through the open doors. Leaves, grass, even sticks were carried into the house on the storm.

A branch the size of a man's thigh bone struck her so hard in the face that she nearly fell.

With her breath coming somewhere between a sob and a cry, she forced open the door of the dining room.

Immediately a figure with outstretched arms lunged forward.

She shouted.

At the same moment she realized that the figure was a statue.

Toppled from its plinth by the force of the gale blowing through the room, it crashed to the floor, exploding into a thousand marble fragments.

She scrambled over the ruined statue towards the patio doors.

They were open. Remains of the white muslin curtains, torn to tatters by the storm, snapped furiously at her face.

Feverishly she ran through the open doorway and onto the patio. Someone had been here; someone had opened the doors.

'Mother!' she called. But the storm tore the call from her mouth and dashed it across the house in a flurry of shrieks.

The winds had reached hurricane force now.

Hanging onto the column that supported the first-floor balcony, she scanned the patio. What she did see was blurred by the relentless stream of debris. But there were only bare stone slabs, the benches, the pool whipped to foam.

She turned to see a white shape come spinning from above. Crackling like a firework, it flapped from the night sky and wrapped itself briefly round a cypress tree. Then it was torn loose and disappeared once more into the night.

Almighty God. If the storm got a good enough grip on her it would carry her away, too.

Beyond the patio wall the evil, humped shapes of Judas trees shouted their raucous approval.

The pain throbbed above Amelia's eye. And, just for a second, it seemed she saw herself as the Judas trees saw her. She imagined them budding eyes, not leaves. She imagined they saw that feeble girl clinging to the iron column, her long hair streaming out. She sensed their lust at her imminent death: a big enough windborne branch would crack her skull; a slate torn from a roof a mile away would slice off her head like a butcher's knife. She sensed their hatred and their loathing and their disgust. She'd come to Voros; she'd not played by its rules; now they, the island, and everything that grew from its soil or crawled across its rocks wanted her done with. They wanted her gone; destroyed; annihilated; her flesh and her spirit torn to less than nothing.

The pain throbbed more deeply, like a steel spike being forced deep into her brain.

She knew she was losing her grip on reality.

The column beneath her hands turned from iron to snake-skin; she felt serpent ribs beneath its skin.

No . . . she couldn't let the island destroy her like this.

'Mother!' She howled the word in anger as much as fear. *'Mother!'*

The wind tore across the swimming pool, all but splitting the water into two distinct halves.

Amelia looked into the spitting stream of grit and leaves.

Now, as well as scum and wind-borne debris in the water, there was something pulpy-looking. White as a meat worm.

Amelia lurched across the patio, willing herself against the flow of air. It might have been a sheet, but it didn't look right. It could be . . .

No . . . no. That was no sheet. She saw a shape beneath the water. A flowing white dressing gown, outstretched arms, hands with fingers splayed, a head with a cloudy halo of floating hair.

'Oh, God . . .' She whispered in pure horror, 'Oh, God no . . . God, no, no . . .'

She didn't hesitate. She launched herself forward, landing with a tremendous splash in the centre of the pool.

In a second she'd grabbed the dead weight of the woman. 'Mother . . .' Her voice was a stunned murmur. 'Oh, mother, what have you done to yourself?'

Keeping her mother's dead white face above the surface of the water, she drew her to the side.

At that moment her mother's eyes opened; she gave a shivery breath; then coughed. A weak sound with *Death* written in it through and through.

'Mother. Don't worry. I'll get you out. Don't worry, you're safe now . . . it's me, Amelia.'

Her mother looked up into her face. There was something childlike about the woman. A vulnerability, a helplessness.

'Amelia?'

'Yes, I'll get you out of here. Then we'll get you some dry clothes—'

'Amelia.' Her mother reached up and gripped her arm, her gaze locked onto hers. 'No. Listen, Amelia. They want someone to die tonight. They're going to get me instead of you.'

'Mother, I don't understand what you're saying.'

'They're getting me, Amelia.'

'Mother—'

'It's happened for longer than anyone knows. Voros demands a sacrifice. It used to be satisfied with one of the Oxford children every year. But it's greedy. Now it wants . . . *quality*. It wants you, daughter, my dear.' She drew in a lungful of air. 'But it can take me instead. Shush, dear. I've never given you much.' She gave a wry smile. 'Perhaps this will make up for all those missed birthdays . . . Christmases . . .'

'Mother, that's not possible. The island can't demand human sacrifice like—'

'Hush, dear. That's the way it is. It's as simple as that. Now, do you forgive me?'

'There's nothing to forgive.'

'I was such a lousy mother. Lousy to the core . . .'

'No, mother. I love you. Even when you weren't there you were important to me.'

'Forgive me, Amelia. Please.'

'Of course I forgive you, but—'

'Now, let me go, Amelia. I really think the time has come . . .'

Shock ran through Amelia like an electric current. 'No, I'm going to get you out of this pool and into the house.'

She'd barely finished the sentence when Amelia felt a spasm run through the woman's body. Her eyes closed.

'Mother . . . mother?'

Panting, her whole body aching, Amelia pulled herself out of the pool. Then, kneeling at the side, she hauled her mother out onto the slabs. Water pooled round Catherine's head, the dark stain accentuating the glaring whiteness of her face.

'Mother . . . mother, can you hear me?' She rubbed her mother's sodden hand, its fingertips lined and puckered. There was no response. *'Mother . . .'*

She placed her hand on the side of Catherine's neck. There was a pulse – just – but it was weak and fleeting, feeling almost like the wings of a butterfly beating frantically beneath the skin.

The storm blew on. The notes were now drawn out into a long wailing sound. They carried over the villa, across the island and into the lonesome gulf of nothingness beyond.

And yet the sound of the Judas trees had fallen to a rustling whisper. If anything, it seemed as if they were listening closely to the events being played out on the patio.

'Mother, please wake up.'

Amelia's head throbbed as though a second heartbeat had started up inside her skull.

The ground softened around her. The slabs pulsed in harmony with the beat inside her head. The pool suddenly glowed a luminous green.

She couldn't hang on any longer. The hallucinations she'd held back through sheer will-power invaded her brain. She recognized the metallic taste on her tongue that accompanied them; the rhythmic beat inside her skull. All the symptoms were there.

Amelia looked down at her mother's face. Now it, too, seemed to glow with an inner light. It highlighted those bird-fragile bones of her face. Her skin seemed more marble-like than ever. Near-transparent. She saw the veins like spiders' webs beneath the skin.

It didn't surprise her when that tracery of veins grew and spread out across the stone slabs beneath her. It was like watching time-lapse photography of a delicate root system growing through soil. Side roots branched off tap roots in an ever-growing, increasingly complex pattern – ever more intricate, ever more fine.

Nor did it surprise her when the sizzle of the air through the branches of the Judas trees became music. A strange, unearthly sound softened by distance.

And it didn't surprise her at all when she looked up to see the dark figure on the patio. Her eyes travelled from his boots, laced with strands of orange flame, up the black rubberized suit to a head encased in a helmet that gleamed as white and as hard as a skull.

The pilot stood before her, just as, deep down, she had known he would.

He didn't move. But he was staring at her as she held her mother's body in her arms.

Then, slowly, he was moving towards her, his arms reaching out.

She closed her eyes, imagining the feel of the gloved hands around her neck.

She must have blacked out for a moment because when she opened her eyes again she saw he'd picked up her mother and, holding her like a young girl in his arms, her hair spilling loose over his shoulder, he'd turned his back on the villa. Amelia watched him walk between the funeral cypress trees.

'You're not real . . . *you're not real.*'

Those had been her magic words that had destroyed many a hallucination. Only this time the image of the pilot remained.

The figure was as darkly solid as the rocks over which it walked.

And in the gloom those laces of orange fire seemed to light his way.

Amelia found she was on her feet, following. Dazed, she scrambled over the enchanted goblin landscape that was haunted Voros.

She watched the figure as it reached the steps that led up to the platform where the German soldiers' palm prints had been set in concrete long ago.

Steadily it ascended.

She saw the pale ghost-like form of her mother hanging limply in his arms, her bare feet swinging down.

Why was he taking her to the platform?

What was up there?

Her mother should be in bed.

She'd die of cold out here.

Thoughts whirling, Amelia's head thudded in time to the distant singing of the Judas trees.

Desperately she followed.

She couldn't let her mother slip away from her. Not now they'd met again after spending so many years apart.

Amelia reached the grey flight of steps and started to climb them. They took her higher and higher, twisting and turning skyward. Always the pilot with his fiery laces seemed just ahead of her; fast as she might run, she could never catch up with him as he carried her mother away.

Why was her father avoiding her?

She shook her head groggily. *Father?* Why had she thought of the pilot as her father again? *He's not my father; he's some stranger that sheer ill-luck killed; and that sheer chance brought to the island.*

Her head swirled. Veins of light snaked in forking tongues across the rock in front of her. Her mind had let go the real world. For the first time she wondered if she could even find

415

her way back to it. The thudding beat in her head grew stronger. The ancient song of the Judas tree grew louder and louder . . .

Ahead, the steps took one last sharp turn to the left before ascending to the platform where they ended.

She saw the dark form of the pilot with his white helmet and flaring orange laces pause for a second as if steeling himself for the last stage of the climb; gently, he shifted the position of Amelia's mother so her head rested on his shoulder.

My father's waiting for me . . .

Amelia tried to suppress the notion but she couldn't.

'You're not real,' she told the phantom-like figure in front of her, but there was no conviction in her voice. 'You're not real . . . you're not my father.'

The pilot turned and climbed the steps. A second later he was out of sight.

Amelia scrambled up the last section of steps herself on all fours; perspiration half-blinded her; she was panting so hard that her chest convulsed and her throat burned.

It only took a few seconds, then Amelia had reached the platform, too. Far below her was the bone-pale shape of the villa. Above her lumbered the ceiling of cloud.

And in between was her, the concrete gun platform – and nothing else.

Unsteadily she walked to the platform's centre. She turned round and round, looking for her mother and the phantom who carried her.

But now there was only the emptiness of bare concrete. A cold void that no one, or no one thing, could fill.

At long last, the Gregale played its final act.

Amelia sank to her knees. Before her were the palm prints, fingers splayed for ever out. Dazed, she stared at them. She was too exhausted to move.

She still couldn't move when the first drops of water hit the ground. At first they were just single splotches, one after another. Then, swiftly, they became a drenching downpour.

At last the rains had come.

That was where, an hour later, Julius King and Gregoriou Simotas found her.

Leaving

Greece has three thousand islands. Voros is one of the smallest.

Little more than the top of a mountain that sank beneath the sea, it is of no strategic importance. Few visit it. Those who do sense profoundly that it is a haunted place. But haunted by what or by whom no one can ever say. Only that there is a truly ghostly sense of *presence* there.

As it had done every spring for ten thousand years, Voros flushed pink.

Blossoms that had gestated through the winter in the buds of the Judas trees burst from their cases within a few hours of the falling of the first drops of rain.

Soon the island glowed a fresh, living pink. A colour so succulently vivid as to be unearthly.

And, at last, the sun began to burn through the clouds; its strength would keep them at bay for a whole summer. Now the sea was a calm blue; white birds hung on rising currents of warm air; lizards basked, luxuriating in the sunlight.

Just seven days later Amelia Thomas packed her bag.

The events of that night a week ago were dreamlike. Every few moments she ran through them, as if running her tongue over a new tooth.

After finding Amelia huddled half-conscious on the platform, Julius King had climbed laboriously down the steps on his steel legs. Ahead of him, Gregoriou had led the way, carrying Amelia in his arms. It had been a ghostly echo of Amelia following the pilot with her mother in his arms.

Perhaps it was all part of the ritualistic loop. In that cauldron of experience – her mother's death and disappearance – and her own emergence from the ordeal, Amelia sensed a rebirth of herself.

No one seemed to attach any great mystery to Amelia's mother's death; certainly the police didn't. Julius King had told them about the repeated statements in Catherine's diary that if the cancer returned she'd take her own life. Rather than 'expire in hospital like some incontinent old biddy' – as she had written in that crisp, no-nonsense way of hers. He'd also shown them empty blister packs of painkillers, the contents of which she'd downed with wine. In short, the police concluded that Catherine Thomas had taken an overdose, then simply walked into the sea.

The only body to be found was that of the drowned pilot. It was still laid out in the boathouse, arms crossed upon its breast, the two orange laces still in the boots, the visor still down to hide the face.

Amelia didn't tell the police that she'd seen the pilot walk, or that he'd carried Catherine away. It wasn't important now. Not that the police would necessarily have disbelieved her, anyway. There was many a Greek island where people believed the dead walked at night.

Quietly, the military authorities spirited the man's body away. Amelia Thomas never discovered the pilot's name, or even the name of his family, so she could not even send flowers to the funeral.

During the time before Amelia had completed her plans for departure, Rachel and Lucy had seemed as insubstantial as ghosts. If she'd told them they weren't real (so invoking her old spell) she could well have believed that they'd have vanished before her eyes.

Now, as Amelia closed the front door of the villa, shutting

off the watchful statues in the hallway, she felt no sadness at leaving Voros.

She'd done her best to say her farewells to Lucy and Rachel, but the pair of women continued to live in a twilight world of their own, spending most of the time sleeping or wandering wraith-like around the villa.

That morning, however, Julius King and Gregoriou Simotas had made the trek up to The Palms to say goodbye. They'd stood side by side on the patio, smiling kindly at her. Gregoriou's forehead still wrinkled ferociously despite the smile, while his soulful eyes shone with happiness. Julius King, black as coal, one eye blue, one brown, clasped Amelia's hand and said, 'We'll miss you, honey child.'

She'd smiled.

Julius's own smile broadened. 'Isn't there anything we can say to persuade you to stay?'

'I don't think I'm ready to live on Voros yet. Or perhaps it isn't ready for me.'

'There will always be a place for you here, Amelia, if you should change your mind.'

'. . . your mind,' echoed Gregoriou, nodding and grinning. She smiled. 'Maybe one day.'

Julius gave her hand a warm, affectionate squeeze. 'Remember, dear, Voros doesn't give up on people so easily.'

Then Julius King had left. She'd watched him make his laborious way down the steps, with a concerned Gregoriou gripping the man's arm, anxiously ensuring he made it safely to the jetty where their boat waited. There was something deeply tender about Gregoriou's solicitude. And Amelia found a bubble of happiness rise inside of her as she watched them.

Love can come in mysterious ways.

The villa door thudded shut with all the finality of a tomb entrance being closed.

Amelia shouldered her bag, then checked her watch. She had a good forty minutes to kill before Bill Simotas arrived with the ferry to take her on the one-way journey to Limnos.

With the sun shining, she followed the path towards the steps that would take her down to the bay.

A path forked away to her left, leading to a high section of cliff. It might be pleasant to walk on the clifftop for a little while, and say her goodbyes to the island, before using the steps one last time.

For the first time during her stay she'd found a path that was level, sandy and pleasantly easy to walk upon.

Perhaps Voros is giving me one last treat before I go, she mused, smiling to herself.

The path turned further to the left, then sloped gently into a thicket of unusually tall Judas trees. She entered their pink-blossomed world, savouring the fleshy tints of light as she passed beneath the branches.

It's funny, she thought, smiling; *you might think you've grown to know a place, but even the most familiar of landscapes can still spring a surprise on you.*

She'd never noticed this path before. Or the thicket of tall Judas trees it led into. Not that it mattered much now: in a moment or so the path would rise towards the clifftop, taking her out of the thicket.

A breeze played among the branches, eliciting from them a gentle but persistent whispering. Pink blossom floated down onto her like confetti. It was like leaving church after a wedding. Smiling to herself, she imagined a handsome groom striding beside her.

The path curved more to the left. Seconds later, she realized it wouldn't take her to the cliff at all; instead, it seemed to be drawing her deeper into the interior of the island.

She glanced at her watch. Not to worry. There was still plenty of time before the ferry boat arrived.

At a leisurely pace, she retraced her steps.

The path forked yet again. She was confident she'd entered the thicket by the right-hand trail.

Still unhurried, still smiling, still at peace with herself, she followed the track into the pink tunnel of Judas trees.

Amelia thought she'd accurately retraced her steps along the path beneath the trees.

But they were becoming denser on either side of her. The shadows were deeper. The light falling through the blossom was closer now to red than to pink.

Amelia glanced at her watch. Ten minutes now until the ferry arrived. But then, Bill would hardly go without her and leave her marooned here, would he?

Shifting her holdall to the other shoulder, she retraced her steps, still not hurrying; still confident of reaching the landing stage on time.

The path ran straight for a while before appearing to turn back on itself. Pink blossom again swirled down, confetti-like, alighting on her hair and arms.

The sun climbed higher. The temperature beneath the Judas trees rose. The world beneath the blossom grew yet more intensely pink. The branches whispered, 'I love you.'

Or so it seemed to her as she strolled along.

Smiling, Amelia let the holdall drop to the ground. Relieved to be liberated from its weight, she walked on, choosing a path that would surely lead her out of the trees.

And when her feet became irritated by the chafing of her shoes she slipped them off to walk barefoot. The sandy path was beautifully cool against her toes. Wonderfully soft. She loved the sensation.

Slipping off her jacket, she let that, too, fall to the ground and walked on deeper into the grove.

It was at that moment she told herself, 'I've lost my way.'

The thought echoed in her mind once more as she continued her journey into the heart of the wood: *I've lost my way* . . .

But Amelia found that she couldn't hold on to the notion. For she could only gaze in wonder at the pink splendour of the Judas trees as they slowly, but surely, closed in on her.